YOU ARE DEAD

PETER JAMES

MACMILLAN

First published 2015 by Macmillan
an imprint of Pan Macmillan, a division of Macmillan Publishers Limited
Pan Macmillan, 20 New Wharf Road, London N1 9RR
Basingstoke and Oxford
Associated companies throughout the world
www.panmacmillan.com

ISBN 978-1-4472-5574-1 HB
ISBN 978-1-4472-5577-2 TPB

1 3 5 7 9 8 6 4 2

A CIP catalogue record for this book is available from the British Library.

Typeset by Ellipsis Digital Limited, Glasgow
Printed and bound in Great Britain by CPI Group (UK) Ltd, Croydon, CR0 4YY

FOR MY BELOVED LARA

1

Logan was driving fast in the pelting rain, hurrying home, glad that her shitty day which had gone from bad to worse, and then progressively worse still, was nearly at an end. She was looking forward to a large glass of chilled white wine and a sneaky cigarette on the balcony before Jamie got home. The familiar Radio Sussex jingle played, then the female presenter announced it was 5.30 p.m. and time for the news headlines. As Logan listened, with half an ear, she was blissfully unaware that by this time tomorrow evening she would be the lead item on the local news, and the subject of one of the biggest manhunts ever launched by Sussex Police.

Her catalogue of disasters had started as she had got out of bed, late for work, with a splitting headache after a tiresome dinner with clumsy, untidy Jamie and tripped over a boot he'd left on the carpet. She'd stumbled forward, gashing her big toe open on the edge of the bathroom door. She should have gone to hospital, but she couldn't spare the time for the inevitable wait at A&E, so she'd bandaged it herself and hoped for the best.

Then to add insult to injury she had been flashed by the same damned speed camera she had driven past every working day for the past few years, at a careful 32 mph. Somehow, today, in her rush to get to work for her first appointment she had totally forgotten it was there, and had gone past it at well over 45 mph.

The gilding on the lily came when one of her partners in the chiropractic clinic – the woman who brought in the largest share of their income – announced she was pregnant with triplets, and intended if all went well to be a full-time mum. Without her income stream, the future of the place could be in doubt.

Overshadowing all of that were her concerns about Jamie. He

stubbornly refused to accept anything was wrong. But there was; there was so much wrong. His untidiness, which at first had amused her, had grown to irritate her beyond belief – especially when he'd told her crassly that it was a woman's role to keep the home tidy.

So she had tidied up. She'd scooped up all the clothes that he had left lying on the floor, and his beer cans and dirty beer glasses – left after a bunch of his friends had come round to watch the footy – and dumped them down the rubbish chute in the corridor of their flat.

She was grinning in satisfaction at the memory as she indicated right, braked, then halted her car at the entrance to the underground car park beneath their apartment block in Brighton's Kemp Town. She pressed the clicker to open the electric gates.

Then, as she drove down the ramp, she was startled by a figure lurking in the darkness. She stamped her foot hard on the brake pedal.

2

Within seconds of answering the phone to his fiancée, Jamie Ball sensed something was wrong.

The connection was bad as he drove his battered old VW Golf down the M23 towards Brighton in the heavy rush-hour traffic and pelting rain, and it was hard to hear what she was saying; but even through the crackly line, he could hear the unease in her voice.

'Are you OK, darling?' he asked.

'No,' she said. 'No, I'm not.'

'What is it?'

'There's a man down here in the car park. I just saw him. He tried to hide as I drove in.'

Neither of them liked that underground car park beneath their apartment block. Their small ninth-floor flat, close to Brighton's Royal Sussex County Hospital in Kemp Town, had views to die for, across the rooftops and far out into the English Channel, but the car park always gave them the creeps.

It was poorly lit with many totally dark areas, and there was only minimal security. Several vehicles lay beneath dust sheets and never appeared to be moved. Sometimes, when he drove down there, Jamie felt he was entering a mausoleum. If Logan arrived home on her own late at night, she preferred to park on the street and risk a ticket in the morning rather than go down there in the dark.

He had repeatedly warned Logan to make sure the electronic gates had closed behind her before driving on down the ramp. Now the scenario he had always feared seemed to be happening.

'OK, darling,' he said. 'Listen to me. Lock your doors, turn around, and drive straight back out.'

She did not reply.

'Logan, did you hear me?'
He heard her scream.
A terrible scream.
Then silence.

3

Felix is fine with the fact that I kill people. He gets it, he understands my reasons. I have a sneaking feeling he'd like to do the same himself, if he had more courage. Harrison's not so sure about the whole moral issue here. As for Marcus – well, really he's dead against it – no pun intended. He thinks I'm a bad person. But hey, it's good to have smart friends who have opinions, and aren't afraid to express them. Personally, I've always respected people who speak their mind.

They say a true friend is someone who knows everything about you, and still likes you, but I would question that *unconditional* aspect of friendship. We need friends to keep checks and balances on us, to help each of us keep our perspectives, our moral compass. But I have to say that Marcus is wrong. I'm not really a bad person, I'm just a victim. All of us in life, all of us are victims. We're all prisoners of our past, in some form. Our past defines us in ways that are not always obvious. It's only later, on occasions, when you read something that touches a nerve, or your therapist points out some connection you had never made. That's when you have the *light-bulb* moment. When suddenly it all makes sense. And you can justify everything.

I've just started my next *project*. She's a young lady in her mid-twenties, slim, pretty, with long brown hair – the way I like all my *projects* to look. I've been following her for the past three months – from a distance mostly, but also on her Facebook page and through her tweets. I like to make a thorough study of my projects, working out the best way to take them, then thinking about what I'm going to do with them. It's the anticipation that really gives me the bang. It's like going online and looking at the menu of some great restaurant I plan to eat in. My beautiful dossiers.

Logan is quite a girl. She's fit, in every sense. Runs marathons, was due to get married, though that's not going to happen now – and that's nothing to do with me. But that all helps me, navigating by my moral compass. She can't treat men the way she has.

She needs punishing.

4

In summer, Hove Lagoon, a children's park and playground with two large boating ponds, a skate park and a children's paddling pool, behind the seafront promenade lined with gaily painted beach huts, would be teeming with people. Children, under the watchful eyes of mothers, grandparents, au pairs or nannies, would be playing on the roundabouts, slides and swings, or in the little pool, or sailing their toy boats on one of the two rectangular ponds that gave the place its name, and which they shared with learner dinghy sailors, windsurfers and wakeboarders.

Many would be stuffing their faces with ice creams or sweets purchased from the Big Beach Café, its utilitarian whitewashed walls, blue windows and steeply pitched roof belying its uber-cool cocktail bar and diner interior – the inspiration of its latest owner, Big Beat musician Norman Cook, aka Fatboy Slim.

But in the gloom of this foul December Thursday afternoon, with cold rain pelting down, and a strong, gusting wind, the whole place was forlorn and cheerless. A solitary elderly lady, in a see-through sou'wester, walked a reluctant dog, the size of a large rat, on a lead attached to a harness.

A group of workmen in fluorescent jackets, hard hats and ear defenders, working overtime beneath floodlights, were drilling open the path in front of the café. One, the foreman, stood away from the group, head bowed against the weather, holding up a tablet in a waterproof case, taking measurements and tapping them in. A cluster of cars and a van were parked nearby, as well as a noisy, yellow mobile generator.

As his drill bit broke through a fresh strip, and he levered it out of the way, one workman suddenly shouted out, in a foreign accent,

7

'Oh God! Look!' He turned anxiously towards the foreman. 'Wesley! Look!'

Hearing his cry above the din of their machines, all the other workmen stopped, too. The foreman stepped forward and peered down, and saw what looked to his untrained eye like a skeletal hand.

'Is it an animal?' asked the workman.

'Dunno,' the foreman said dubiously. Nor could he tell how old it was. It could have been there decades. But he couldn't think of any animal that had a paw or claw like this. Except a monkey, possibly. It looked human, he thought. He instructed all three men with the drills to concentrate on the immediate area around the hand, and to be careful not to drill deeper than necessary.

More chunks of the black asphalt were levered away and a skeletal arm appeared, attached to the hand by black tendrils of sinew. Then part of a rib cage and what was, unmistakably, a human skull.

'OK!' the foreman said nervously. 'Everyone stop now. Go home and we start again in the morning, if we are permitted. See you all at 8 a.m.'

Wondering whether he should have stopped the men sooner, he went over to the van, opened the rear doors, then climbed in, rummaged around, and pulled out a tarpaulin. He laid it over the exposed parts of the skeleton, weighing it down with chunks of rubble. When he had finished, he unholstered his phone and dialled his boss, to ask for instructions. They came back loud and clear.

He ended the call, then, as he'd been told, immediately dialled 999. When the operator answered, he asked for the police.

5

Shaking with fear, Jamie Ball pulled his Golf over onto the hard shoulder of the motorway, halted, and dialled Logan's number again. The phone rang, six times, and then he heard her voicemail message.

'Hi, this is Logan Somerville. I can't take your call right—'

He ended the call and immediately redialled. *Answer, darling Logan, answer, please answer, please answer!* Again it rang six times and her message started up. A lorry thundered past, inches from his little car, shaking it and spattering it with spray. He closed his eyes, thinking, feeling close to tears. He could call the caretaker, Mark. Or their next-door neighbour who had a key to their flat.

But he had heard her scream.

Something had happened.

His car shook again as another juggernaut thundered by, far too close.

He ended the call and immediately dialled 999.

6

Some idiot, an hour or so ago, had mentioned the Q word. Just as in the theatre world, where there was a deep superstition about mentioning the name of the play *Macbeth* – all thespians only ever referred to it as 'the Scottish play' – so in the police world it was considered a jinx to say that a day was *quiet*. And sure enough, within minutes of the tubby, fully kitted constable breezing into the Communications Department of Sussex Police Headquarters to have a word with his wife, who was one of the radio controllers, and letting slip that Q word, it had all started kicking off, it seemed, right across the county. There was a sudden spate of three separate, serious road traffic collisions; an armed robbery in Brighton; a man threatening to jump off the notorious suicide beauty spot, Beachy Head; and a missing four-year-old boy in Crawley.

The Comms Department, which was housed in a very large, open-plan room on the first floor of a modern block on the sprawling HQ campus, handled all emergency calls made to Sussex Police throughout the county, and housed the CCTV system. It was presided over by Ops-1 – the call sign for the Duty Inspector in charge. Among the responsibilities of these inspectors was the granting of authority for use of firearms in a spontaneous incident, and running and controlling any vehicle pursuit in the county.

This afternoon and evening's Ops-1 was Andy Kille, a tall, strongly built, former British parachuting champion, in his early fifties, with a handsome face, etched cynical from almost thirty years of police service, and topped with a thin fuzz of close-cropped greying hair. Dressed in uniform dark trousers and a short-sleeved black top, with 'Police' embroidered in white on the sleeves, his inspector pips on his epaulettes and his ID card hanging from his neck on a blue lanyard, he currently sported a substantial and uncharacteristic pot belly – the result of recently having given up smoking and compensating by binge eating.

Kille sat at his desk in a cubicle-like space at the rear of the room, surrounded by an array of computer screens and monitors. One displayed a map of the county. Another constantly updated him on all the incidents currently running. A third, with a touch-screen, operated as his eyes and ears on the department he presided over.

On the wall at the far end of the room were monitors that displayed the performance statistics, whilst over his desk a separate screen showed images from four of the five hundred CCTV cameras around the county, as well as monitors displaying the current news. With the aid of his different and separate keyboards and a toggle lever, Kille could rotate and zoom any of the cameras within seconds. Thirty people worked in this section, most of them civilians, identified by the white embroidered words 'Police Support' on their sleeves, and royal blue polo shirts as opposed to the black ones of the police. Several were former police officers. At busy times there could be the best part of one hundred people working over the two levels.

At a row of desks beneath the CCTV cameras sat the radio operators; each, like almost everyone else in the room, wearing a headset. These were the people who liaised with the police officers who had been dispatched, both in vehicles and on foot. Most radio operators had a CCTV screen for the cameras on their particular area, when needed. Alongside them sat the emergency-call handlers. Emergency – 999 – calls were signalled by a low klaxon, so that in the rare instances all the call handlers were occupied, others in the room, also trained, would be alerted to answer.

Amy Wood, a placid, motherly, dark-haired woman, had twenty years of service answering emergency calls, and was one of the most experienced in the room. She loved this job, because you never knew what might happen in just ten seconds' time. And if there was one thing, above all else, she had learned, it was that whenever you thought you'd seen it all, you were always going to be in for another surprise. She never cared for Q days so she was always secretly glad when things kicked off. And how, in the past hour! She had answered calls from witnesses to two different road traffic accidents, a man whose girlfriend had been bitten by a neighbour's dog, someone in Bognor Regis who had just been dragged off his bicycle and seen it ridden away, and someone, who sounded off his face on drugs, complaining that a neighbour across the street kept photographing him.

The bane of her and her colleagues' work was the constant stream of hoax calls, and the even larger volume of calls from mentally ill people, around the clock. One particular elderly lady with dementia called fifteen times a day. It was a fact that twenty per cent of all 999 calls for immediate police response were mental health issues.

She had one on the line right now. A young man, crying.

'I'm going to kill myself.'

His hysterical voice was barely audible above the crackling roar of wind.

'Can you tell me where you are?' He was phoning from a mobile phone, and the location of the cell tower receiving and transmitting his signal showed up on her screen. It was in the town of Hastings and he could have been in any of a dozen streets.

'I don't think you can help me,' he said. 'I've got problems in my head.'

'Where are you?' she asked him calmly and pleasantly.

'Rigger Road,' he said and began blubbing. 'No one understands me, yeah?'

As she spoke she was typing out a running incident log and instructions to a radio dispatcher.

'Can you tell me your name?'

There was a long silence. She heard what sounded like *Dan*. 'Is your name Dan?'

'No, Ben.'

The whole tone of his voice was worrying her. She completed her instructions with Grade One, which meant immediate response – and to be there within a maximum of fifteen minutes.

'So what's been happening this week to make you feel like this, Ben?'

'I've just never fitted in. I can't tell my mum what's wrong. I'm from Senegal. Came when I was ten. I've just never fitted in. People treat me different. I've got a knife, I'm going to cut my throat now.'

'Please stay on the line for me, Ben, I have someone on their way to you. I'm staying on the line with you until they get to you.'

A reply flashed back on her screen with the call sign of a police response car that had been allocated. She could see on the map the pink symbol of the police car, no more than half a mile from Rigger Road. The car suddenly jumped two blocks nearer.

'Why do people treat me different?' He began crying hysterically. 'Please help me.'

'Officers are very close, Ben. I'll stay on the line until they get to you.' She could see the pink symbol entering Rigger Road. 'Can you see a police car? Can you see a police car, Ben?'

'Yrrrr.'

'Will you wave at it?'

She heard voices. Then the message she was relieved to see flashed up: *Officers at scene.*

Job done, she ended the call. It was always hard to tell whether would-be suicide calls were real or a cry for help, and neither she, nor any of the others here, would ever take a risk on a call like this one. A week ago she'd taken a call from a man who said he had a rope round his neck and was going to jump through his loft hatch. Just as the police entered his house, she heard him gurgling, and then the chilling sound of the officers shouting to each other for a knife.

Amy looked at her watch. 5.45. Not halfway through her twelve-hour shift yet, but time to grab a cuppa, and see how many others in the department fancied ordering in a curry tonight from a local, rather good balti house, which was fast turning into their latest canteen. But before she could remove her headset and stand up, her phone rang.

'Sussex Police emergency, how can I help?' she answered, and immediately looked at the number and approximate location that showed on the screen. It was in the Crawley area, close to Gatwick Airport. She guessed from the traffic noise the caller was on a motorway. An RTC, she anticipated – most calls from motorways were either reporting debris lying in one of the lanes, or else road traffic collisions.

As was so often the case, at first the young man seemed to have problems getting his words out. From her long experience, Amy knew that for most people the mere act of phoning 999 was nerve-wracking, let alone the effect that the emergency they were phoning to report was having on them. Half the people who called were in some kind of 'red mist' of nerves and confusion.

She could barely hear the man's voice above the roar of the traffic. 'I just phoned her you see – look – the thing is – I'm really worried about my fiancée,' he stuttered, finally.

'May I have your name and number, caller?' she asked, although she could see his number already.

He blurted them out. 'I think my fiancée is in trouble. I was just on the phone to her as she was driving into the underground car park beneath our flat. She said there was a man lurking in there, he scared her, then I heard her scream and the phone went dead.'

'Have you tried calling her again, sir?'

'Yes, yes, I have. Please send someone over there, I'm really worried.'

All Amy's experience and instincts told her this was real and potentially serious. 'What is your name, please?'

'Jamie – Jamie Ball.'

Despite the background roar he now spoke more clearly. Once again she was typing as she spoke. 'Can you give me the address, her name, and a brief description of your fiancée.'

He gave them to her, then added, 'Please, please can you get someone there quickly, something's not right.'

She looked at her screen then at the map, searching for the pink car symbol, then spotted it. 'Officers are being dispatched now, sir.'

'Thank you. Thank you so much.'

She could hear his voice cracking. 'Please stay on the line for a moment, sir. Sir. Mr Ball? Jamie. My name is Amy.'

'I'm sorry,' he said, sounding more composed.

'Can you please give me your fiancée's mobile and home phone numbers and car registration number?'

Ball gave the details, but suddenly could not remember the entire registration number. 'It begins GU10,' he said. 'Please ask them to hurry.'

'Do you have any idea who the person in the car park might be?

Have you or your fiancée seen anyone suspicious in the car park before?'

'No. No. But it's dark down there and there's no security. Some vehicles were vandalized there a few months ago. I'm on my way home now, but I'm a good half an hour away.'

'Officers will be there in minutes, sir.'

'Please make sure she's OK. Please. I love her. Please make sure she's all right. Please.'

'I'm giving the officers attending your mobile number, sir. They'll contact you.'

'I heard her scream,' he said. 'Oh God, I heard her scream. It was terrible. They've got to help her.'

She typed the details out and sent them by FLUM – a flash unsolicited message – to Andy Kille.

He immediately alerted the Duty Force Gold commander, Chief Superintendent Nev Kemp, and the duty Critical Incident Manager, formerly known as the Silver Commander, Chief Inspector Jason Tingley, that they had a potential abduction.

7

Thursday 11 December

'PC Rain', officers called this kind of weather, only partially in jest. Scrotes didn't like getting wet, and accordingly the crime levels almost always went down in the city of Brighton and Hove whenever there was heavy rain.

Six o'clock on a dark, chilly Thursday evening in December. PC Susi Holliday, with her crew mate, the older and more experienced PC Richard Kyrke, known as RVK, and famed within the police for his photographic memory, were heading west along Hove seafront in their Ford Mondeo estate patrol car. They were passing a succession of handsome Regency terraces to their right, and the deserted lawns, with rows of beach huts, to their left. Further away, beyond the throw of the promenade street lighting, the stormy water of the English Channel tossed and foamed.

They were approaching the end of their shift, with just an hour till the 7 p.m. changeover, and it had been a quiet day. So far they'd attended a minor RTC – a rider knocked off his motor scooter by a van, but without any injury – a call to a chemist near the Seven Dials roundabout, where a man had collapsed in the doorway, from a suspected drug overdose; and, as there was almost without fail on every shift, a call to a domestic incident, which they had sorted, and arrested the live-in boyfriend. It was the fourth time the woman had called the police after being assaulted by this man in the past eighteen months. Perhaps now she would throw him out for good, but Susi Holliday doubted it. The true tragedy for many victims of domestic abuse was that they became so demoralized, losing all their confidence, that they rarely had the courage to chuck their partner out or to leave – or the ability to believe they could make a life on their own.

In a few hours, the downtown area around West Street with its

16

bars and nightclubs would, inevitably, turn into a potential war zone as it did every Thursday, Friday and Saturday night, kept mostly under rigid but friendly control through Operation Marble, a massive police presence late into the night. But luckily, on their current shift pattern, they would escape these nights of dealing with constant fights and with drunk, abusive chavs. Although, in truth, some officers enjoyed getting in a good 'bundle', as they called it – it was one of the adrenaline rushes of the job.

Susi Holliday was driving in the stop-start traffic, the wipers struggling to clout away the rain, the brake lights of the car in front flaring against their rain-soaked windscreen. RVK was engrossed in a text he was sending. They were both off for the next two days and Susi was looking forward to a quiet time with her husband James, shopping for stuff for the new flat they had recently moved into in nearby Eastbourne, where the property prices were substantially lower than Brighton.

'What are your plans for your days off, RVK?' she asked her colleague.

'Uh,' he said, and raised a finger, signalling he needed to finish his texting task. After a moment he said, 'Taking Joey to the football.' Joey was his twelve-year-old son, whom he doted on. 'Then we're going to the outlaws after. You?'

Their radios crackled. Then they heard the female voice of a Resource Room supervisor.

'Charlie Romeo Four?'

RVK answered. 'Charlie Romeo Four.'

'Charlie Romeo Four, we have a report of an incident in the underground car park of the Chesham Gate flats, at the corner of Stanley Rise and Briars Avenue. A woman may have been attacked by an intruder. Can you attend? Grade One.'

'Chesham Gate?' Kyrke replied. 'Yes, yes. We're on our way.' Then he turned to Susi. 'Spin her round.'

Susi Holliday switched on the blue lights and siren and, adrenaline pumping, made a U-turn straight out into the opposite lane and accelerated. Like most of her colleagues, she always got a massive buzz out of responding to a Grade One 'shout'. Along with getting in a 'bundle', driving on blues and twos was one of the great kicks – and perks – of the job. And a big responsibility. The lights and siren were, in law, a request to be allowed through, not an automatic right. And with what seemed like half of all drivers on the road either deaf, blind or just plain stupid, all blue-light runs were fraught with hazards and heart-in-the-mouth moments.

She had one now as a Nissan Micra in front, with apparently no rear-view mirrors or indicators, suddenly switched lanes right into her path as she bore down on it at over 60 mph. 'Asshole!' she hissed, missing its rear bumper by inches and undertaking it.

As she drove, Constable Kyrke was taking down details from the supervisor, who read out the make and partial index of the woman's car and a description of her.

Ninety seconds later they tore over the roundabout by Brighton Pier, thanks to an intelligent bus driver stopping for them, and on up Marine Parade. They made a left, blazing up past the bed-and-breakfast hotels of Lower Rock Gardens. Less than two minutes later, driving up the steep hill before the hospital, they saw the apartment block, Chesham Gate, ahead to their left.

They pulled up beside the closed entrance to the underground car park, climbed out and walked up to the full-height gates. They peered through the bars of the grille into the darkness below. Susi Holliday took out her torch, switched it on and shone the beam through, but could see little other than a row of parked cars, some beneath fitted covers.

'Any idea how we get in?' she asked her colleague.

'I'll see if there's a caretaker's flat,' he said, and sprinted off towards the main entrance. Suddenly she heard a clank, and the gates began to open. Moments later, she was lit up by the glare of headlights, and heard the roar of an engine behind her. She turned to see a small BMW convertible, driven by a young woman. Raising her arm, she walked towards it and told the driver she wouldn't be able to enter the car park at this time because of a police incident.

She hurried down the ramp, triggering the automatic lights, and could now see much of the interior, switching her torch off to conserve the battery. She was looking for a white Fiat 500, index beginning GU10, and a slim woman in her mid-twenties with long brown hair.

There were about sixty or so parking spaces, most of them occupied, as well as several motorcycles and a cycle rack.

But there was no sign of life. She began working her way along the rows of parked cars, breathing in the smells of dust and engine oil, and all the time keeping a wary eye out for anyone else who might be down there.

She reached the end of the row and turned left, towards a darker section. One light above her flickered intermittently, emitting a loud buzz, and she switched her torch back on. She passed a bike rack, with several heavily padlocked bicycles, and a beautiful old convertible Mercedes, caked in dust and sitting on four flat tyres. Then she saw, neatly parked, a white Fiat 500. The first digits of its index were GU10. The car looked wet, as if it had only recently been driven in here.

She stopped and radioed her colleague. 'I think I've found the car,' she said.

'I'm on my way down with the caretaker,' he responded.

She approached the car cautiously, then shone her torch beam in through the side window. The interior was empty. A discarded chewing-gum wrapper lay on the passenger seat, and there was a ticket sitting on the dash. She looked at it closely and saw it was a pay and display from a car park in nearby Lewes. She checked both driver and passenger doors but they were locked. The car bonnet was warm.

Just then, PC Kyrke appeared, accompanied by a short man in his fifties wearing chinos and a fabric bomber jacket and holding a mobile phone.

'This is Mark Schulz, the caretaker for this block,' he said.

'So what exactly is the problem?' the caretaker asked.

'We need to ensure the owner of this car, Ms Logan Somerville, is safe,' she said. 'Have you seen her since she arrived back?'

He shook his head. 'No, I finish at half past five.'

'Do you have CCTV here?'

He raised his hands with a gesture of despair. 'It's not been working for six weeks. I told the management company, but nothing happens.' He shrugged. 'What can you do, eh?' Then he hesitated as they walked towards the stairs. 'Shall I phone her?'

'Yes, please.'

'Very nice lady,' he said. 'Nice boyfriend. Nice people.' He held his phone up, scrolled through the display, then dialled. After some moments he looked at the two officers and shook his head. 'No answer.'

'Do you have a key to her flat?'

'Yes, give me a few moments to find it.'

'I'll stay down here and have a look around, and stop anyone else from entering or leaving,' Kyrke said. 'You go up to the flat.'

Susi Holliday went up the internal staircase to the ground floor, then waited in the corridor while Schulz went into his flat. He came back out holding a bunch of keys, like a gaoler, and led her into the lift.

At the ninth floor they stepped out into a gloomy corridor with a badly worn carpet and a musty smell. Somewhere, music was pounding out insanely loudly. Susi Holliday recognized it as 'Patient Love' by Passenger. She followed the caretaker along the corridor, till he stopped outside a door and pressed the bell.

After some moments he rang again. Then he knocked hard. He waited several seconds then looked quizzically at the police officer. 'No answer.'

'Could you open it so I can check if she is there?'

'I don't really like to go in, you know?'

'We're very concerned for her safety – we need to know if she is all right.'

He shrugged. 'OK, sure, no problem.'

He opened the door and called out, 'Hello! Miss Somerville! Hello, it's the caretaker! I have the police with me.'

They were greeted with silence. The place had a deadened, empty feeling.

'Do you mind if we go in?' PC Holliday asked.

He rolled his mouth pensively, then gestured with his hand. 'No, do go in.'

They entered a small hallway, with two mountain bikes leaning against the wall and a cluster of coats and anoraks hung above them, and then walked through into a bright, airy but untidy living/dining room. It had a modern feel, with a cream carpet, beige sofas, and a breakfast bar dividing the room from the small kitchen, on which lay a copy of the *Independent* newspaper and *The Week* magazine. At the rear of the bar was a tropical fish tank, immaculately clean and brightly illuminated, with several tiny fish swimming around.

There were a number of framed photographs, which Susi Holliday looked at with interest. One showed a good-looking young couple, both in cycling gear, posing with muddy bikes against a rugged, mountainous landscape. Another was of the same couple lying on a beach, looking up and grinning at the photographer. Another showed them in ski gear. There were several large, colourful abstract prints depicting deckchairs on the beach, the skeletal remains of the old West Pier and a row of beach huts, and a spaniel which looked like it was by an artist she really liked, a Lewes-based painter called Tom Homewood.

They checked the bedroom, which contained a double bed with a neatly folded duvet and plumped pillows, a television and a table with a lamp either side of the bed. A stack of books lay on one table and a woman's magazine and a partially empty water glass on the other. Susi Holliday noted a boot lying on the floor, and then saw what looked like a small bloodstain at the bottom of the en-suite bathroom door, and some tiny drops on the floor.

The bathroom was tidy and dry, with a wicker laundry basket, on top of which lay Lycra cycling shorts and a vest. The shelves were lined with shower gel, shampoo, body cream and other unguents, male and female razors and several bottles of perfume, cologne and aftershave. It seemed as though no one had been here for a few hours, at the very least.

Susi Holliday radioed in her report, and stated that whilst there was no sign of a struggle, she had seen a small amount of blood.

The controller told them that the woman's fiancé was now just minutes away and to wait at the scene.

8

Jamie Ball, normally a careful driver, tore like a man possessed along Edward Street, peering through the windscreen blurred by the pelting rain, weaving in and out of the heavy rush-hour traffic, flashing his lights and hooting, and ignoring the angry horns and waved fists that came back at him. His entire body was pulsing with fear.

A speed camera flashed him and he didn't care. He was oblivious to everything but the desperate need to get home, to make sure Logan was OK. He turned sharp left, the car skidding on the wet surface, the tyres juddering for traction as he accelerated up the hill, then made a right into their street. Ahead he saw a police patrol car parked close to the entrance to their apartment block.

He pressed the clicker, waited impatiently for the electronic gates to swing open, then started to drive down the ramp. Almost straight away he was stopped by a uniformed police officer who ran up out of the car park. He identified himself and was directed into an empty bay.

Immediately he jumped out of the car, leaving the door open, and to his immense relief saw her little white Fiat neatly parked in its usual space. She was OK! Thank God, thank God! Then he turned to the police officer and asked, 'Where's Logan, my fiancée, what's happened? Is she OK?'

'I think it would be best if you go and speak to my colleague who's gone up with the caretaker.'

He felt a sudden chill of fear. 'Why? What's happened?'

'They'll be able to update you upstairs, sir.'

Jamie raced along to the lift, and rode it up to the ninth floor. As the doors opened he stepped out, and saw a uniformed police officer, accompanied by Mark, the caretaker, emerging from their flat.

'Hi!' he called out. 'Is everything OK?'

'Hello Jamie!' the caretaker greeted him.

'Logan? Is she OK, Mark? She phoned me – she said she saw an intruder in the car park.'

'I haven't seen her,' Mark said. 'She's not home yet, Jamie.'

'Yes she is, her car's downstairs!' He looked at the police officer, ignored her quizzical stare and eased his way past her and into the flat. He strode down the hallway, past their mountain bikes leaning against the wall, turned left into the small anteroom which they had lined floor-to-ceiling with bookshelves, housing his entire collection of Lee Child novels and many of their other favourite crime, horror and sci-fi writers, and into the large, untidy, square living/dining room. No sign of her.

'Logan!' he called, hurrying back into the hallway. He checked their bedroom, the boot Logan had tripped over earlier still lying by the bed, the en-suite bathroom, the tiny guest bedroom, the kitchen, the guest loo and shower room. He went back into the living/dining room and opened the door to the small balcony. Sometimes she went out there for a cigarette, despite his attempts at getting her to quit. But the two plastic chairs and little white table sat there, forlornly drenched in the rain, the soggy stub of a cigarette lying in the ashtray in a pool of water.

He stepped back into the living room and closed the door against the elements. The police officer had returned, with the caretaker standing behind her. 'I'm PC Holliday,' she said. 'My colleague and I attended at the underground car park of this building following your call, earlier. So far we haven't found anything suspicious – Logan's Fiat is parked and locked in its allocated space downstairs, and there's no sign of any disturbance in your flat.'

'She phoned me from the car park as she drove in. Then she screamed, and her phone went dead.'

'Have you tried her again, sir?'

'Yes, I've been calling her constantly all my way here.' He tugged his phone out of his trouser pocket and dialled her number again. Six rings and it went to voicemail. 'Darling,' he said. 'Call me, please, as soon as you pick this up, I'm really worried.' He ended the call and looked back at Susi Holliday. 'She always calls me back within minutes. It doesn't matter what she's doing – she always calls me back – and I always call her back.'

'She definitely drove to work herself, sir? She didn't get a lift from a colleague, which could explain why her car is here?'

'No, for God's sake! She called me from her car, down in the car park. She said she'd seen a man down there and screamed. It was a terrible sound. It wasn't like her. Can we go back down to the car park and take a look?' Jamie pleaded.

The officer's radio crackled. Jamie heard a disembodied female voice say something he couldn't discern.

'Charlie Romeo Four,' Susi Holliday answered. 'We're still attending at Chesham Gate.'

'Thank you, Charlie Romeo Four. Let me know when you stand down.'

'Yes, yes,' she replied. Then she turned to Jamie Ball.

'Did you and your fiancée have any kind of an argument today, sir?' Susi Holliday asked.

'Argument? No, why?'

'I noticed blood on the bottom of your bathroom door, earlier.'

'Oh, that. She tripped getting out of bed and gashed her toe on it. She was going to go to the hospital this morning to get it looked at.'

'The hospital would be able to verify that, would they, sir?'

'Yes, of course.' Then Jamie Ball hesitated and stared at the officer. 'Oh God, you think I did something to her? For Christ's sake!'

'I'm afraid we have to ask these questions, sir.'

Jamie grabbed the spare keys to Logan's car and then they took the lift back down to the car park to join Kyrke, and the three of them headed over to the Fiat.

'One thing I should add,' Ball said, 'is that Logan's diabetic. She's Type-2 – needs to keep her sugar levels up, otherwise she can risk a hypo.'

The officer nodded. 'Where do you work, Mr Ball?'

'In Croydon, Condor pet foods.'

'We've got two Rhodesian Ridgebacks,' PC Kyrke said, walking over and joining them. 'The wife swears by Condor – *Condor Vitalife*.'

'Good to hear that,' Jamie said, without enthusiasm. 'It's an excellent product.'

'Better than raw meat?'

He shrugged. 'From what I know it's more of a balanced diet than raw meat.'

They reached the Fiat.

'She was down here when she called you?' PC Holliday asked. She held up her iPhone. 'It's a very poor signal.'

Jamie nodded. He pulled out his phone again. The signal veered from one dot, to zero, to two. He dialled Logan's number again, and moments later heard it ringing. Very faintly.

They all could.

For an instant, the caretaker and two officers looked at him. Frowning, he fumbled with the key then opened the car door. Instantly the ringing was louder.

Her phone was lying in the footwell almost under the passenger seat.

He started to lean across to pick it up, but was held back by PC Holliday, who reached past him with a gloved hand. The ringing stopped. Holliday knew that recovered phones were normally re-tained for forensic digital evidence, but as a life was potentially at risk she decided to check the phone immediately. She held it up and asked him for the code, which he gave her. She tapped it in and stared at the display, and saw nine missed calls from 'Jamie Mob'. She asked if it was him and he confirmed it was.

He looked at the two police officers. 'She'd never – she'd never leave her phone. She wouldn't go anywhere without it.'

But although he could see sympathy in their expressions, he could also see they were a tad sceptical.

'I'm afraid all of us leave our phones behind sometimes,' PC Holliday said. 'Done it myself.'

'Me too,' the caretaker chipped in. 'I couldn't find the thing for two days.'

'Something's happened to her. Please believe me. Something's happened. I heard her scream, for God's sake!'

Their radios crackled again and once more he heard a female voice.

'Charlie Romeo Four,' PC Kyrke said, tilting his head and speaking down into the radio clipped to the left of his chest.

'Serious RTC at the A23–A27 junction. RPU need some assistance. Can you advise me when you're free to attend, Charlie Romeo Four?'

'Yes, yes,' Kyrke said. 'But I think we're going to be a while.' Then he turned to Jamie Ball. 'Excuse me being personal, sir, but was everything all right between you and your fiancée? No arguments or anything like that?'

'Nothing. We've bickered like every couple, but we've never had a real argument in all the time we've been together. We love each other so much.'

Susi Holliday stepped away from the others, feeling increasingly concerned about what she had heard. She radioed Control and requested that the Duty Inspector attend urgently.

9

Roy Grace arrived home shortly after 6.45 p.m. on Thursday night. The Detective Superintendent had three and a half more days to go as the on-call Senior Investigating Officer for Surrey and Sussex Major Crime Team, before the buck got passed to another senior detective at 7 a.m. on Monday for the following seven days.

The county of Sussex averaged twelve homicides a year, and it was around ten in Surrey. In the whole of the UK there were about six hundred and fifty a year. Every homicide detective hoped to get a challenging murder. Not that they were bloodthirsty people, but it was what they trained for, and what challenged them the best. And it had to be said that a high-profile homicide raised your own profile, and promotion prospects.

Not that Roy Grace ever wished anyone dead.

Over the past few years, weekends had been jinxed for him. On each occasion that he had hoped for a quiet one, because of a social engagement, or more recently wanting to spend time with his wife, Cleo, and their five-month-old son, at the last minute he had been called to a homicide investigation. He was really hoping for a peaceful weekend so that he could focus his energies on helping Cleo to sort her possessions, in preparation for the move next week from Cleo's house, which they were sharing, to the cottage they had bought together, near the village of Henfield, eight miles north of Brighton.

Cleo stood up, carefully removing a large book of fabric swatches from her lap and placing it on the coffee table, on top of a pile of other fabric and wallpaper sample books.

Grace turned to his eleven-year-old goldfish, Marlon. 'You're going to be moving to the country next week. How do you feel about that? We're going to have hens. You've never seen a hen, have you?

27

Other than on television. But you're not that big on watching television, are you?'

Cleo slipped an arm around his waist and kissed him on the neck. 'If someone had told me, a few years ago, that one day I would be jealous of a goldfish, I wouldn't have believed them. But I am. Sometimes I think you care more about Marlon than me!'

Marlon opened and shut his mouth, looking as ever like a grumpy, toothless old man, on his never-ending circumnavigation of his round tank, passing through the fronds of green weed and over the submerged remains of a miniature Greek temple, which Roy had bought some years ago after reading an article in a magazine on the importance of giving goldfish things to interest them in their bowls. But nothing Roy had ever bought seemed to interest this lonesome creature. Over the years he had attempted on several occasions to provide Marlon with a mate. But every companion he had bought had ended up either gulped down by this mini-monster or floating dead on the surface, while Marlon continued, day in, day out, his eternal circular motion.

He had won the fish at a fairground stall all those years back with his long-missing first wife, Sandy, who after ten years' absence had recently been declared legally dead, allowing him and Cleo to marry. He'd carried the fish home in a water-filled plastic bag, and according to Sandy's research, the life expectancy of fairground goldfish was less than a year.

Now eleven years on, Marlon was still going strong. In the *Guinness World Records*, which Roy had recently consulted, the longest-lived goldfish in the world achieved forty-three years. Still some way to go, but for sure Marlon showed no signs of pegging out anytime soon. And secretly, Roy was glad about that. In a strange way – one he would never tell Cleo about – Marlon provided a link back to Sandy. He knew that he would be sad when he eventually died. And indeed, every morning when Roy came downstairs, the first thing he did was to look at the bowl, hoping that Marlon would not be floating lifelessly on the surface.

'As we're moving, darling, I think Marlon should move too. I've just read, on the internet, that goldfish need a bigger tank than people realize.'

'Oh? How big? Like an Olympic-size pool?' Cleo said.

He grinned. 'No, but big enough to stretch their legs – or rather, fins.'

'Just so long as it's not bigger than our new house – or I would be getting extremely jealous. And in which case, sushi, my love?'

He looked at her, quizzically. 'Don't even go there!'

'Love me, love my fish, right?'

He put his arms around her. 'God, I adore you.'

She stared into his eyes. 'And I adore you. I love you more than anything I could ever have imagined, Detective Superintendent Grace.'

She kissed him.

Then his work phone rang.

It was Andy Anakin, the Golf 99 – the term for the divisional duty uniformed inspector at Brighton's John Street police station – which had the somewhat unwelcome reputation as the second busiest police station in England. Unlike most of his colleagues, who had the ability to remain calm in any situation, this particular inspector had acquired the nickname of 'Panicking Anakin'. He sounded like he was panicking now.

'Sir,' he said, seemingly out of breath. 'The DI's dealing with another urgent situation, and asked me to call you to give you the heads-up that we have a possible kidnap or abduction. A young woman has gone missing after screaming down the phone to her fiancé that there was an intruder in an underground car park in Kemp Town.'

'What information do you have on it?' Roy asked, immediately concerned.

'Very little, sir, you see, that's the thing. Very little so far. I've units doing a house-to-house in the area, and a distraught boyfriend who believes his fiancée has been abducted. We're doing all we can, but it's not looking good, sir. Really it's not. Ops-1 has alerted the duty Gold and Critical Incident Manager.'

Grace's heart sank. It didn't sound or feel good. 'What do you know about the couple?'

'Her name's Logan Somerville. Twenty-four, recently qualified as a chiropractor, works at a practice in Portland Road, Hove. His name's

Jamie Ball. He's a marketing manager for the pet food division of the Condor Food Group – works at their offices near Croydon. We're checking him out further.'

With eighty per cent of victims of violence harmed or killed by an immediate member of their family or someone close to them, Grace was well aware that loved ones were always people who deserved close investigation. He had been called, he knew, not solely because he was the on-call Senior Investigating Officer, but because he was also a trained kidnap and hostage negotiator. But if this did become an active investigation he wouldn't be carrying out both roles.

'I think we need to seal off the county, sir,' Anakin said. 'Roadblocks on all major roads, sir. Put out an all-ports. I've requested NPAS 15 on standby.'

NPAS 15 was the call sign for the helicopter shared between Sussex and Surrey police forces and now based at Redhill.

'Hold on,' Grace said.

'This is bad, Roy. I'm telling you, this is bad!'

'Andy, calm down. Wind your neck in!' Grace retorted. 'What checks have you done to verify she is missing?'

'Local?'

'Presumably there's CCTV in the car park?'

'Yes, but it's not working.'

'Great.' He grimaced. 'Have you got any local officers searching around the immediate scene? Seeing if anyone's seen or heard anything?'

'I have two there.'

'Not enough. Get more there right away. Have you spoken to the boyfriend?'

'Officers are talking to him at the moment. I'm at the scene myself. I've asked for divisional CID to attend, and thought you needed to be aware, Roy. I understand the woman screamed, and mentioned a man lurking in the vicinity who has not been traced.'

Grace frowned. It didn't look good, but equally Anakin seemed to be rushing in before he had all the facts. 'What do we know about the missing woman, Andy? Does she have anything that would make her a potential kidnap target? Is she an heiress, or does she have rich parents?'

'I'll find out all that.'

'Right. Update me in thirty minutes, please – if not before.'

'Yes, sir.'

Roy Grace stared at Marlon's bowl, his brain racing. Mobile phones dropped connections constantly and sometimes made odd noises. A squeal of car tyres or the scrape of a metal gate or just some interference on the line could have been misinterpreted as a scream. But twenty years as a police officer had given him a rich amount of that instinct they called 'copper's nose'. And this one did not smell good. And the grim truth was that in abduction cases the victim was often killed very quickly. With every hour that passed, the chances of finding the victim alive lessened.

He reflected on what he had been told so far. The man who called it in, Jamie Ball, worked at Croydon and was on his way home. That would be easy enough to verify. A combination of the ANPR – number plate recognition cameras – sited strategically along the M23, and triangulation of his mobile phone, would pinpoint his approximate position at the time he claimed to have received the call from his fiancée. Likewise it would be an easy job to verify that she had made the call and where she was at the time. But with luck it wouldn't come to that. Maybe she'd arrive back with a load of grocery bags having gone foraging in the nearby Sainsbury's Local. He hoped.

Noah began to cry. He saw Cleo rush dutifully up the stairs. Life was complicated. So damned complicated. He suddenly envied Marlon the simplicity of his existence. Did the fish have to worry about anything? Did he fret about food being put into his tank daily or did he assume its delivery?

Marlon would never be robbed; conned out of his life savings; abused. He was unlikely to be murdered or mutilated by a terrorist attack.

His mind drifted back to the evening before, when he had travelled to Worthing with Norman Potting to speak to Bella Moy's mother. He had wanted to see her in advance of her daughter's funeral, to discuss with her the details of the service and if there was anything in particular she wanted him to say. Bella, who had been engaged to Norman, and was one of his core team, had tragically died in a fire.

Then his phone rang again.

10

Shortly after 7.15 p.m. Roy Grace and Detective Inspector Glenn Branson hurried, heads bowed against the driving rain, towards the battery of bright lights illuminating the small Crime Scene Investigation tent that been erected a short distance in front of the Big Beach Café at Hove Lagoon. It was surrounded by two cordons of fluttering blue and white crime scene tape. To the right, inside the inner cordon, was a second similar-sized tent.

So much for a quiet weekend, Grace was thinking. First a possible abduction, and now this. If the abduction was real – and he was increasingly certain that was the case – he would have to delegate one case as he couldn't run two simultaneously.

One particular thought had been troubling him since Panicking Anakin's call, thirty minutes earlier. He remembered that a couple of weeks ago, on a different Senior Investigating Officer's watch, another young woman had disappeared in the nearby seaside town of Worthing. Her name was Emma Johnson, and she was twenty-one years old. She had come from a troubled background, with an alcoholic mother, and had disappeared many times before. On one occasion she had surfaced several months later, living with a small-time drug dealer in another coastal town, Hastings.

Her mother had reported her latest disappearance, and this one had been carefully risk-assessed by the police. Emma had been recorded as a misper, and enquiries had been made. The assumption was that she would reappear at some point, so it had not been treated as a major enquiry. But nonetheless a case officer had been assigned.

Grace had checked the serial on her case just before leaving home to see what, if any, developments there had been. As a rule of thumb Grace knew that most missing persons turned up within a few days.

If they were gone for a month, the chances were they were gone for good.

Emma Johnson had now been missing for fifteen days. During this time no calls had been made from her mobile phone and no payments taken from her credit card, and the case officer had reported growing concerns for her safety.

The circumstances regarding Logan Somerville were very different.

Grace and Branson could see the white Major Incident van parked a short distance away, and a miserable-looking PCSO scene guard, and they could hear the sound of a generator. Two marked cars were parked close to the van along with a plain silver Ford estate car.

They were greeted by the tall, friendly figure of the duty CID inspector, Charlie Hepburn, in a blue, hooded oversuit and protective shoes, and the uniformed duty inspector, Roy Apps, with rain dripping off his peaked cap. 'Nice weather for ducks,' Apps said.

'Yeah, well you should know,' quipped Branson. Apps had been a gamekeeper in his former life before joining Sussex Police.

'Haha!'

'Nice to see you, Charlie,' Roy Grace said. 'How are Rachel, Archie and my namesake, Grace?'

'All good, thanks – Archie and Grace are getting very excited for Christmas.'

'I would be, too,' Grace replied, 'if I'd done any of my bloody shopping! Anyhow, what do we have?'

'A pretty good mess,' Hepburn said. 'Why the hell didn't they stop the moment they uncovered the bones, instead of carrying on?'

'Want us to suit up?' Grace asked.

'I suppose you'd better, so Dave doesn't get even more pissed off.' He jerked a finger at the tent over the path, right behind him.

Grace and Branson went into the second tent, out of the rain. Chris Gee, a Crime Scene Investigator – formerly known as a Scenes of Crime Officer – handed them each an oversuit and shoes and offered them tea or coffee, which they both declined.

They struggled into the suits, pulled on the shoes, went back out and signed the scene log. Then they followed Hepburn into the brightly lit tent covering the exposed parts of the skeleton. There was a smell of damp earth and another more unpleasant smell of decay. The Crime Scene Manager, Dave Green, was in there on his hands and knees, studying the exposed remains. He stood up and greeted them. 'I did a bit of checking before we got here. This path was laid twenty years ago when there was some renovation work done on the café, long before Fatboy Slim bought it.'

Grace peered down at the skeletal arm, the partially exposed rib cage and the skull, with fragments of rubble lying on them. He knelt, pulled out his torch and studied them more closely in the beam of bright light, and noticed a small area of desiccated skin attached to the skull bone, and a few small fragments of fabric here and there. From what little he could see of the body, it looked like it had been buried intact.

'Surely whoever laid this path must have seen the body?' Glenn Branson said.

'Not necessarily,' the Crime Scene Manager said. 'We're below the water table here. It could have been buried deeper and covered in earth, and slowly been pushed to the surface, then stopped from rising any higher by the path.'

Grace stared, thoughtfully, trying to remember what he had learned a year or so ago from the local forensic archaeologist, Lucy Sibun, about identifying age and sex from skeletal remains. 'Female?' he ventured.

'That's my opinion, from the shape of the skull, Roy, but I can't be sure.'

'We might be lucky and get DNA from the body. The teeth are intact and look relatively young. Maybe dental records?'

'There's a good chance of dental records, if she's local,' Green said.

But only, Grace knew, if they were reasonably sure who she was.

Grace stared hard at the U-shaped bone at the base of the jaw. 'The hyoid – if I remember correctly,' he said, pointing with a gloved finger. 'It's intact; a break would have indicated strangulation.'

'Reckon we need to call out a police surgeon to certify death?' Glenn Branson said.

Both men looked up at him and returned his grin. But he had a valid point. The Coroner for Brighton and Hove was a doughty lady who was a stickler for protocol. There had been past occasions when the police had received a flea in their ears from her for not having death formally certified, regardless of the state of decomposition of the corpse.

'Call the duty Coroner's Officer,' he instructed Glenn Branson. 'Tell them what we have. We certainly can't remove anything without their consent, and they need to know my plan to call for a forensic archaeologist and a Home Office pathologist.' He glanced at his watch. 'But I don't think we need to worry about any Golden Hour.'

The 'Golden Hour' was the term given to the time immediately following the discovery of a suspected murder victim. But in this instance, where it was with little doubt a crime scene more than twenty years old, and already partially contaminated by the workmen who had drilled it open, time was less urgent than in the case of a fresh body.

He looked at Dave Green and Glenn Branson, who both nodded in agreement.

He stared back down at the bones. *Who were you? What happened to you? Who loved you? Who killed you? And why? Did they think they would get away with this? Are they still alive?*

We're going to find out everything, I promise you.

Glenn pulled out his phone and slipped out of the tent. Grace smelled the sweet whiff of cigarette smoke. Someone outside was having a crafty fag, and he could have done with one himself. Anything to take away the noxious reek inside this flapping, plastic-sided cocoon. It was one of the many things he loved about Cleo, that although a non-smoker herself, she never objected when he smoked the occasional cigarette or cigar.

'There's little wear in the teeth,' Dave Green said. 'That indicates the person died young. Teens or early twenties.'

'How sure are you about that?' Grace asked.

'I'm pretty sure about that. But not much else. We need to get the rest of the body exposed, then let the forensic archaeologist go to work. Lucy Sibun would be my first choice.'

'I suggest we leave the scene secured overnight, and ask her to come first thing in the morning, if she's free.' Grace nodded at the remains. 'I don't think she – if we're right and it is a *she* – is going anywhere in a hurry.'

Dave Green nodded. 'It's my wedding anniversary. I'd be earning myself a pink ticket with Janis by getting home in time to celebrate it.'

'Happy anniversary,' Grace said.

Glenn Branson came back into the tent. 'Yeah,' he said. 'I just spoke to Philip Keay, the on-call Coroner's Officer. He thinks we should get the death certified, just to be safe.'

'For fuck's sake, it is such a ridiculous policy!' Green said exasperatedly. He jerked a finger at the skull. 'How much more sodding dead does she need to be?'

Outside, they heard the yap of a dog. Moments later the tent flap opened and CSI Chris Gee peered in.

'Sir,' he said. 'There's a gentleman walking his dog across the lagoon who saw the police vehicles and asked if he could help – he said he's a doctor.'

Grace and Branson looked at each other. 'A doctor?' Roy Grace said. 'Well, how convenient is that? Yes, ask him if he would be willing to confirm a death.'

A few minutes later, a short, fit-looking man in his mid-fifties, in a protective suit, mask and shoes, entered the tent. 'Hello,' he said cheerily. 'I'm Edward Crisp, I'm a local GP. I was just walking my dog – your colleague at the barrier is kindly looking after him – and saw all the activity. Just wondered if I could be of any help? I used to serve Brighton and Hove Police as one of your on-call police surgeons up until about fifteen years ago.'

Grace nodded. 'Yes, I remember your name. Well, your timing's impeccable.' He pointed down at the exposed remains. 'Some workmen uncovered this earlier today. I know it sounds a little strange, but we need a medical person to confirm life extinct. Would you be able to oblige?'

Dr Crisp peered down, then knelt and stared for some moments at the skull, then at the rest of the exposed bones. 'Well,' he said, 'I really don't think there's much doubt about that. Poor woman.'

'Woman?' Grace said. 'Definitely?'

The doctor hesitated. 'Well, it's a long time since I was a medical student, but from all I can remember I'd say from the shape of the skull it's female. And from the condition of the teeth, late teens or early twenties.'

'Any idea how long she might have been here?' Glenn Branson asked.

He shook his head. 'I couldn't begin to hazard a guess – you'd need a forensic archaeologist to give you that kind of information. But, yes, indeed, there's no question of life here. I would be happy to confirm that I can see it is a skeleton and there is no life. Is that helpful?'

'Extremely,' Roy Grace said.

'Is that all?'

'Leave your details, I'll send someone round to you tomorrow to take a formal statement.'

'Absolutely! No problem at all.' He smiled. 'Bye for now!'

11

Jamie Ball sat perched on a stool at his kitchen breakfast bar, drinking beer after beer, phone in his hand, calling each of their friends in turn, his back to the rainy darkness beyond the window. He focused first on Logan's girlfriends, then her sister, then her brother, then her parents, asking if by chance – slim chance – she had gone over to see them. As he spoke he stared either at the tropical fish in the tank or at the photograph on the bar counter of the two of them in their ski suits taken on top of the Kleine Matterhorn at Zermatt last March, with snow-capped peaks framing the horizon. They were laughing at some joke their mate John, who had taken the picture, had just cracked.

John, who had introduced them a year earlier, had a simple philosophy that they both often joked about: *Get up, have a laugh, go to bed!*

But Jamie wasn't laughing at that now. With tears streaming down his face, he stared at the woman he loved more than he could ever have imagined loving anyone, who he still hoped would become his wife.

She was twenty-four, with long brown hair and an infectious smile that showed her immaculate white teeth. The first time he had seen her she had reminded him of a younger Demi Moore in one of his favourite movies, *Ghost*. She'd told him he reminded her of a younger Matt Damon, in an un-Matt Damon kind of way. Whatever that meant. She was like that, quirky and oblique at times.

God, he loved her.

Please be OK, my darling. Please come home. Please come home.

Every time he heard a sound out in the corridor he turned and waited, expectantly, for Logan to walk in through the door.

He turned to PC Holliday, who was sitting on a sofa making notes, and asked if there was any update.

12

Logan's head was pounding. She was lying on her back, totally disoriented and with no idea where she was, shivering with cold. She was light-headed and giddy, and experiencing a faint swaying sensation, as if she were on a boat. And she badly needed to pee. Desperately. She fought against it. There was a vile smell in her nostrils, of mildew and something much stronger, a smell that reminded her of the time she and Jamie had come back from two weeks on the Greek island of Spetses last summer to find the mains fuse in their flat had tripped, and the fridge and freezer had been off for many days during an August heatwave.

They had opened the freezer door to find two steaks crawling with maggots and a chicken that had turned bright green and almost luminous. The smell of the decaying flesh had made them both gag, and it had taken days of keeping the windows open, burning scented candles and constantly spraying the place with air fresheners to finally get rid of it.

Was she having a nightmare?

But her eyes were open. She could see a faint green glow of light. She was lying in some enclosed container, hemmed in on both sides so tightly she could not move her elbows. Her eyes were blurred, as if they had some kind of drops in them, and her mind was fuzzy. She tried to sit up and something hard dug into her neck, painfully, almost choking her.

She cried out.

What the hell?

Where was she?

It was coming back now. And with it, the terror. She felt a dark feeling of dread deep inside her.

Driving down into the underground car park. Someone in the

shadows. Then, suddenly, the hooded figure looming above her window. Her car door being yanked open.

The hiss of gas.

Her eyes stinging, agonizingly.

Then nothing.

13

'I really like this Farrow and Ball paper for the dining room,' Cleo said. 'What do you think?'

The question took Roy Grace back almost twenty years, to when he and Sandy had bought their house. But the big difference was, he realized, that Sandy had got on and made all the decorating choices herself, without asking him his opinion in the way Cleo was doing.

Roy had just dropped in, on his way to Chesham Gate, to update Cleo and keep his peace with her. He stood over the sofa and peered down at the grey and white zigzag pattern. It looked busy and a complete contrast, he thought, to the kind of paper Sandy would have chosen. She liked minimalistic, plain. 'Yes,' he said, a little abstractly. The coffee table and most of the floor were scattered with fabric swatches and sample books. To their irritation, Humphrey kept moving around restlessly, sitting on different books. It was as if the dog sensed that change was happening, and was unsettled.

Grace would have loved a drink right now. A really stiff vodka martini or a large glass of cold white wine. But being on call and with all that was going on, he did not dare. It was twenty past eight. Panicking Anakin had phoned him earlier to say that Logan was neither an heiress or came from a moneyed family, and he was going off duty. He'd briefed his replacement Golf 99, who was now the Duty Inspector for Brighton and Hove Police for the next twelve hours and who Roy was due to meet shortly at the Chesham Gate car park.

Roy continued to stare at the wallpaper sample. It was rather elegant, he thought. 'It's fun,' he said. 'You don't think it's too busy?'

'I'd like to put in a dado rail and have plain white above it – I think we can bring a lot of colour in with the curtains and—' Cleo was interrupted by his work phone ringing.

Apologetically he retrieved it and brought it to his right ear. 'Roy Grace,' he said, in a formal tone.

It was the replacement Golf 99, Inspector Joseph Webbon. 'Sir,' he said, 'I know we're due to meet soon, but things are not looking good on this misper, Logan Somerville. There has been no communication from her since the last update. We've checked with ANPR and their camera picked up Ball's car in several locations consistent with the journey he claims to have made from his workplace in Croydon and south to Brighton.'

Grace thought hard for some moments, weighing the options. When people disappeared, they had often been abducted or harmed by someone they knew – frequently their partner. Or they had run away from an abusive relationship, gone off with a lover, had an accident or, in some cases, committed suicide. A huge amount of police time got wasted on missing persons, particularly youngsters, who turned out to be in the next-door neighbour's house watching television with a friend. But it didn't appear to be the case on this occasion.

Panicking Anakin had gone almost straight into abduction mode. It might turn out the inspector had made the right call, although Grace hoped not. Was there anything he was overlooking here that could point a finger at the woman's fiancé? It did not seem so. 'So we can eliminate Ball as a suspect, for now at any rate?'

Webbon sounded hesitant. 'The officers attending reported some blood at the scene – a small amount, but reasonably fresh. When questioned about it, Ball said she had stumbled getting out of bed and gashed her toe on the bathroom door – and subsequently had to go to hospital to have it sorted. We've checked with the Royal Sussex County and they have no record of her having been seen in Accident and Emergency this morning.'

'Domestic violence?'

'Yes, CID here feel that's a possibility, sir. But we have a development. We've been going to all the flats in the building asking if anyone was in the car park around the time she made a call. We've found one lady who was driving in and had to brake hard to avoid an estate car with darkened windows that came out at high speed, and drove off.'

'Did she get the registration? Or see the driver's face?'

'Unfortunately not a good look. She says she was too startled and she thinks he was wearing a hat pulled down low over his face. All she can say is that he was white, middle-aged, clean shaven, with a round face and glasses. She's not very good on car makes, but she says it was a medium-size car in a dark colour. Possibly an old Volvo, navy blue or charcoal.'

'Have you given that to CCTV in the Control Room?'

'Yes, sir, they're on it.'

'What's the woman's name?'

'Sharon Pavoni.'

'Doesn't necessarily mean anything, but we should get a cognitive interview as soon as possible, to see what else she can remember.' Cognitive Witness Interviews were a highly specialized field of their own, involving trained interviewers who could obtain recall from witnesses of things they had seen or heard that they were unaware they had remembered. He looked at his watch. Realistically it would be too late tonight by the time it could be set up. 'We'll arrange it for first thing in the morning – assuming Logan Somerville hasn't turned up. Let me have the witness's contact details, and the boyfriend – fiancé's. I want them both interviewed.'

Webbon gave them to him, and Grace noted them down. Then Grace said, 'Have the whole underground car park sealed off – nothing to go in or out, which I believe has already been put in place. I want Somerville's Fiat removed for forensic examination, but first get a Police Search Advisor and team down there as fast as possible to do a fingertip search. I'm treating this as a crime in action.'

Trained members of the Specialist Search Unit would work on their hands and knees; if there was any evidence – such as a speck of blood or a discarded cigarette butt – they would find it.

As soon as he had ended the call, Roy Grace phoned both the force Gold and the Critical Incident Manager, before he made another call to his new boss, and former adversary, Assistant Chief Constable Cassian Pewe. It was protocol to notify the chiefs of any impending major enquiry, so they didn't hear it first from a journalist and find themselves in the embarrassing situation of sounding uninformed.

Pewe answered almost immediately, his voice smarmily pleasant.

'Roy, very good to hear from you. How are things?' Grace could hear heavy opera music playing loudly in the background. A deep sonorous dirge.

A year and a half earlier, on a temporary posting from London's Metropolitan Police, Pewe had made Roy Grace's life hell for some weeks, when he had taken it upon himself to order the garden of the home Grace had shared with Sandy to be scanned and dug up in a search for her remains. It had started a bitter feud between the two senior detectives which had culminated first in Grace saving the man's life – reluctantly – after a clifftop car chase, and then in Grace accusing him of tampering with evidence. Pewe, with his tail between his legs, had applied successfully for a transfer back to the Met.

What Roy Grace hadn't known then – and still did not know – was that many years back, Cassian Pewe had had a brief affair with Sandy.

Now, to Grace's utter horror and disgust, Pewe had returned to Sussex Police as the Assistant Chief Constable to whom he had to report. The soon-to-be retiring Chief Constable, Tom Martinson, had done his best to assure him that Pewe had no animosity towards him. And, to be fair, so far so good. But Grace felt that lurking behind the phoney bonhomie, Pewe was itching for revenge, and subtly biding his time. Grace had to make damned sure he did not screw up.

He informed Pewe of the missing woman and what they knew so far, and the actions they were taking and, separately, told him about the body at the Lagoon.

As he hung up, he heard Noah crying upstairs. Cleo signalled for him to carry on, and hurried across the room.

He stood still, thinking for a moment. Two totally different cases slung his way in the space of a few hours. The skeletal remains at Hove Lagoon, and this potential abduction. He could not deal with them both, he needed to delegate one to another detective. The remains had been there since before the path had been laid, some twenty years ago, so there was less urgency. Right now the absolute priority was to find Logan Somerville.

His next call was to DI Glenn Branson, updating him and appointing him Senior Investigating Officer for the remains at the lagoon. The police computerized operations naming system, working through famous paintings, had allocated the case the name Operation Mona Lisa. Branson would ensure the remains were recovered by the forensic archaeologist to the mortuary tomorrow. Then he made a call to DS Guy Batchelor, asking him to assemble a Major Enquiry Team for the newly named Operation Haywain, the investigation into the disappearance of Logan Somerville.

Not an entirely stupid name. Looking for a missing person was akin to searching for a needle in a haystack, with one proviso. First you had to find your haystack.

14

Plock . . . plock . . . plock . . . The steady drip of water, from somewhere near. Where was she? Was it raining outside and was water leaking in?

Plock . . . plock . . . plock . . . Each drip echoing as loudly as if the ground it struck was a drum skin. For something to do, something to concentrate on, Logan counted in her head the gaps between each drip, shivering constantly from cold and terror. One hundred and one . . . one hundred and two . . . one hundred and three . . .

Plock.

Fifteen seconds.

She was parched, desperate for water, and she felt clammy and jittery, the deep, destabilizing sense of unease that always spread out through her stomach and up through her body when she was low on sugar. She was very low now. And she was still very badly in need of a pee.

Her eyes felt swollen and all she could see was a green haze. It was as if she was wearing someone else's glasses, someone who had very poor vision; but she wasn't wearing any glasses, so far as she could tell. Her nose was itching like hell, and she was desperate to scratch it, but her hands were pinned either side of her, there was nothing she could do. She was close to passing out, she knew. It was her anger that was keeping her going.

Her anger and her terrible fear.

'Hello?' she called out.

Her voice sounded deadened, as if absorbed straight into cotton wool. 'Hello?' she called again, louder. She must be asleep. Having a nightmare, a lucid dream? Yes, a lucid dream. She'd read stuff about lucid dreaming. Where you could become aware, in a dream, that you were dreaming.

She willed herself to wake up.

But nothing changed.

Then suddenly the light brightened. The green flared into brilliant white, hurting, burning, as searing as a blowtorch. 'Hello?' she said. 'Jamie? Is that you, Jamie? Please let's talk this through. Please. I know you're upset with me for breaking it off – but please, this is enough. Please. Please.'

There was a long silence. She heard a sliding sound. Felt cold air on her face.

Someone was standing over her. Her skin was pricked with goosebumps.

'Jamie?' she cried out. 'What do you want? What the hell are you doing? Let me go! For God's sake get me some sugar, chocolate, I'm going into a hypo. Jamie. Jamie. Jamie. Is it you, Jamie? You know what happens if I get too low. Get me some sugar, urgently, please. Please! Jamiiiieeeeeeeeeeee!'

The sliding sound again. The cool breeze stopped.

Could it possibly be Jamie? Angry at her for calling off the wedding? Had she missed something in his character? Had he set this up?

The bright light moved away, accompanied by the faint shuffle of footsteps. She heard a door close. Then a click nearby. Moments later she heard the sudden, tortured cry of a female voice.

'Help me!'

A slick of terror slid through every cell in Logan's body.

'Help me!' she heard again. Then an even deeper cry of anguish. 'No! No, please noooo! Noooooooo!'

It was followed by the most pitiful scream.

And suddenly she could not contain her need to pee any longer. Embarrassed, she let go, fully expecting to feel the warm stream between her legs. But as she emptied her bladder, something seemed to be absorbing the urine.

Now she knew for sure this wasn't a dream.

15

At twenty past ten, Jamie Ball's entryphone buzzer rang. He ran over to the front door, realizing he was a little drunk, and saw on the fuzzy black and white screen a man's face above a turned-up collar.

'Hello?' he said.

'Mr Ball?'

'Yes,' he blurted, anxiously.

'Detective Superintendent Grace. May I have a word with you?'

'Please come up. Ninth floor.'

Two minutes later Jamie opened the front door to see a pleasant-looking man of about forty, with a rugged face beneath short, gelled fair hair, a nose that looked like it had been busted, possibly more than once, and sharp, alert, blue eyes. He held up a police warrant card.

'Detective Superintendent Roy Grace, Surrey and Sussex Major Crime Team. Have you heard from your fiancée?'

'No – not – not anything, not a word. Please come in – thank you for coming. Can I offer you a glass of wine?'

'No, thank you, I'm fine.' Grace could smell alcohol on the man's breath and he looked a little unsteady. He was a burly, bearded man with a rugby player's build, and with a stacked-up modern hairstyle, dressed in jeans and a V-neck cardigan over a white T-shirt, shoeless in red socks.

He led the detective through into a living room, with a kitchen area partitioned off by a bar, on which stood a beer glass and several empty cans of lager. He ushered him to one of two small sofas either side of a glass coffee table, where copies of *Sussex Life* and *Latest* magazine lay.

Susi Holliday, on the other sofa, stood up and greeted Grace with a respectful, 'Good evening, sir.'

Roy Grace removed his coat, folded it and laid it beside him. Then he studied the man carefully. 'Can you give me your full name, Mr Ball?'

'Yes, Jamie Gordon Ball.'

Still watching the man intently, he asked, 'When did you last see Logan?'

'This morning, about seven o'clock. She tripped getting out of bed and gashed her toe open on the bathroom door. I would have driven her to the hospital on any other day, but I had a very important early meeting at work.'

Grace noted his reply but made no comment. 'She gave you no indication that she was going anywhere tonight?'

'No, none. We'd made plans to have a Chinese tonight – there's a place nearby that delivers – we have it regularly – and we were going to watch a couple of episodes of *Breaking Bad* – we're working our way through it.'

'Great show,' Grace said.

'It is, we're totally hooked.'

'Where does Logan work?'

'In Hove, she's a chiropractor – she works in a clinic on Portland Road.'

So far, the man's body language indicated he was telling the truth. 'How would you describe your relationship?'

Ball was quiet for a moment, then he said, 'We love each other.'

For the first time the man's demeanour indicated that he might be lying.

'Have you set a date for your wedding?' Grace pressed.

He looked even more uncomfortable now. 'Yes – well, not exactly.'

'Not exactly?'

'We're sort of – discussing it.'

'Sort of?'

'Yes.' He shrugged, awkwardly.

Grace looked at him even more intently. 'Has Logan ever done this before – not come home?'

'Never. Look – I heard her scream. I don't know if you've been down there, but the car park here is really creepy. There's been a raft of car break-ins and thefts. The management of this place don't give a toss. She phoned me to say she had seen someone as she drove in. Then she screamed. Then I – '

He covered his face with his hands.

Grace watched him. His distress seemed genuine. Yet at the same time, he was uncomfortable about the way Ball was describing his relationship with his fiancée – something was not ringing true.

'Something's happened to her, Detective – Superintendent – something's happened to her. This is just not like her. Something's happened. She's a strong person, I've never heard her sound afraid before. The fear – the fear in her voice.'

'Tell me what you think has happened to her?'

Jamie Ball shook his head, wildly. 'I don't know. But I think she's been abducted. Kidnapped. Taken.'

'You're watching *Breaking Bad*?'

'Yes.'

'Do you watch a lot of cop programmes? Crime series?'

'Quite a lot, yes.'

'Are you sure you are not being influenced here? Are you one hundred per cent convinced that Logan has been abducted – and not gone somewhere of her own free will?'

'Yes.' He fixed his eyes on Roy Grace's.

Roy Grace left, ten minutes later, unsure about everything except for one certainty. Logan Somerville was missing.

The ANPR evidence seemed to eliminate Jamie Ball. But his body language made him appear guilty. Of something.

What was he lying about?

As Grace drove away he made a mental note that he needed to appoint a Family Liaison Officer first thing in the morning, someone who might be able to shed more light on the relationship.

16

I keep my projects in their own private cubicles in what I like to call my *correction chamber*. Tanks all plumbed in, my projects kitted out with adult disposable nappies. Cleanliness is so important for morale. I keep them healthy, plenty of vitamins, nutrients, electrolytes. I want them to live as long as possible. So that I can make the choices about when to say goodbye. It's all about power. Power is hugely exciting.

I don't like to call them my victims. I prefer the term *projects*.

I'm not a violent person, really I'm not. Once, when I was a kid, I hit a sparrow with a pebble I fired from my catapult. I can still remember that bird spinning round and round like a helicopter, plummeting to the ground. I'd never really expected to hit it – I'd just fired at it for fun. I picked it up, its feathers all soft and its body so warm, and I was crying, trying to breathe life back into it through its little beak.

I dug a grave for it, laid it in the bottom, apologized, covered it with earth and said a prayer.

I felt like shit for days after. But at the same time it wakened something inside me. Every time I looked at a bird, for the rest of my childhood, I would think to myself about the power I had.

The power of death.

Killing things makes me feel strong. Some people will say that's evil.

Here's the thing: does *evil* exist? Surely only if you believe in God. Otherwise you believe in the survival of the fittest. Which means I survive and others I choose to kill don't.

Today I've chosen to kill. I've been looking forward to this moment for days – well, actually, for weeks!

But, of course, you are not capable of ever knowing the pleasure this is going to give me.

17

Water had been steadily filling the tank for the past hour. Restraints across her neck, wrists, stomach, thighs and ankles kept her secured to the bottom of the tank, unable to move. The water was now brimming over her chin. In a few minutes it would be covering her mouth. Then her nose.

He stared down at his project through his night-vision goggles, and saw the terror in her face in the monochrome green light. He liked to keep the correction chamber in darkness, so that his projects could not see one another. He kept them in the dark, so to speak. That term was his little private joke.

Her brown hair floated all around her face. It was a very beautiful sight and he took an infrared photograph of her. She was staring up at him, looking as if she was ready to scream again at any moment. Some of his projects had beautiful screams that sent a surge of longing deep through him. But not this one. She had a really ugly scream. Strange, that such a beautiful woman, with quite delicious-looking lips, could produce such a hideous sound.

He raised a finger to his lips, then leaned down and kissed her, pressing his own lips hard against hers, forming a seal. At the same time he pinched her nostrils tightly closed with his surgically gloved hand. He kept his lips to hers as she struggled, sucking, sucking, sucking the very last breath from her, feeling the water rising up against his face, still sucking. Then he released her nostrils, let go of her lips and stood up. He watched the bubbles rising. Not many at all.

He'd taken that very last breath from her.

Now he possessed her. Forever.

Soon, while she was still warm, he would make love to her.

She could never reject him!

18

Logan Somerville was still missing in the morning, and that knowledge weighed heavily on Roy Grace, who had come straight from a briefing of his team in the Incident Room at Sussex House.

The rain had stopped during the night and the patches of sky in the gaps between the swift-moving clouds above Hove Lagoon were a stark, cold blue. There was an inner and outer cordon marked off by blue and white crime scene tape, each cordon protected by a PCSO scene guard. A knot of onlookers stood just beyond the outer cordon, several of them taking photos with their phones. Inside the inner cordon, there were now four blue CSI tents rippling and crackling in the strong, salty wind coming in straight off the Channel, the guy ropes tugging at their pegs.

It looked like an entire army of people had moved in since he and Branson had been here last night, Grace thought. The Surrey and Sussex Police helicopter, NPAS 15, hovered overhead, taking photographs to map the scene, and added to the feel of a military operation. A cluster of cars and vans and a small mechanical digger were parked nearby. There was a marked police car, the Major Incident van, another van belonging to the construction company and several private cars. One of these, a yellow Saab convertible, Roy Grace recognized to his relief as belonging to Home Office pathologist Nadiuska De Sancha.

Out of the two specialist pathologists covering this area, who could be called in to investigate suspected homicides, all the SIOs in Surrey and Sussex much preferred the pleasant, easy-going Nadiuska to the pedantic and arrogant Dr Frazer Theobald. De Sancha was popular because not only was she good at her job, she was a fast worker and good-natured with it.

A CSI scene sketcher was making a detailed plan of the entire site, and another CSI, like all the others wearing a disposable scene suit, gloves, face mask, hairnet and over-shoe protectors, was scanning the area immediately around the scene with ground-penetrating radar, searching for any other bodies that might also be here.

Several workmen in hi-viz jackets were hanging around close to the construction company van, some drinking tea or coffee and one struggling with the flapping pages of the *Sun* newspaper. A Crime Scene Photographer, James Gartrell, whom Grace had worked with many times, was busy taking photographs of the whole scene, and making a digital recording of the events.

Grace glanced at his watch as he strode with Glenn Branson through the onlookers beyond the outer cordon, towards the uniformed PCSO scene guard who was rubbing her hands against the cold. Several gulls bobbed like marker buoys on the near lagoon, and on the far pond a windsurfer in a wetsuit, under tuition, wobbled on his board, bent over, struggling to bring the sail up out of the water. As they reached the PCSO and signed in, Grace heard a female voice call out behind him. 'Detective Superintendent!'

The two detectives turned to see a young, attractive fair-haired woman, in a bright red mackintosh, hurrying towards them. Siobhan Sheldrake, a recent addition to the *Argus* newspaper reporting team, and a replacement for their previous Crime Reporter, Kevin Spinella, who had been the bane of Grace's life.

The relationship with the press was a vital one for the police to manage well. The press needed sensational stories, which often entailed having a go at the police from many angles. But equally in major crime investigations, the press could be crucial in public appeals for witnesses to come forward. He was hoping for a better relationship with this new reporter.

'Good morning!' he said pleasantly, raising his voice against the loud *thwock-thwock-thwock* of the helicopter. 'You've met my colleague, DI Branson?'

'Yes,' she shouted back, grinning at Glenn almost mischievously. 'Nice to see you again, Detective Inspector.'

'And you too, Siobhan, how are you?' Glenn said.

'Well, a little bird told me you two gentlemen haven't come to a children's playground to have a go on the swings, nor the slide or roundabout – and you don't look like you're dressed for a windsurfing lesson!'

Glenn cocked his head sideways, and Grace noticed the chemistry between them. 'Very astute,' Branson said. 'You could be a detective.'

She laughed. 'So do I have to wait for a press conference to find out what's going on here, or can I get a scoop on the dead body unearthed by workmen last night?'

'Well, at this point,' Roy Grace said, 'you appear to know as much as we do.'

'Is it male or female? Do you know the age? How long has he or she been here?' She pointed. 'You have a fairly big CSI presence and a Home Office Pathologist, and I understand you have a forensic archaeologist in there, too. So, I would say, you are spending serious money at a time of major budget cuts for the police, which means you have a crime scene you consider worth investigating. We're not talking historical relics, are we?'

She was smart, Grace had to concede, and he had to stop himself grinning back at her. Not only was she attractive, she had an infectious smile.

Glenn Branson jerked a thumb at his colleague and best friend. 'I hope that comment isn't referring to this old relic here?' He grinned at Grace. 'Sorry, old-timer.'

'Very witty,' Grace retorted.

The reporter smiled. 'I won't print that,' she said.

There was something about the reporter that Roy Grace warmed to. She seemed a lot more sincere than many journalists he had encountered. And hell, she had made the effort to get here early and was well-informed. She deserved at least a titbit.

'DI Branson will be holding a press conference, Siobhan, as soon as we have sufficient information. What I can tell you so far is that workmen digging up this path yesterday exposed human remains, which have been tentatively identified as female. We don't know the age and we don't know how long they have been here – other than that they pre-date this path, which was laid approximately twenty years ago by the Council. I hope to have more information as the day progresses.'

'Any chance I could have a quick peek inside the tent?'

Glenn Branson gave Roy a quizzical look.

'I'm afraid not at this stage,' Grace replied.

'Is there a Coroner's Officer attending?'

'You mean there's something you don't know?' Glenn teased her.

She grinned back. 'Yes. I am just a rookie, sir.'

'Philip Keay is on his way. But I don't think he'll have anything for you. I think you're going to have to wait for the press conference.'

She shrugged. 'OK. I'll just hang around for a while, if it's OK with you guys?'

'It's a public park,' Glenn said. 'Feel free. But I tell you what, if I wanted a good story, I'd go and doorstep Norman Cook. Ask Fatboy Slim how our local rock star feels having a crime scene outside his café.'

Her face lit up. 'You're right! That's exactly what I'll do. Thank you!'

'Let me know if you need an agent,' Glenn replied. 'My terms are very reasonable.'

She turned back to Roy Grace. 'Separately, is there any news on the misper from last night, Logan Somerville? Operation Haywain?'

Grace stared at her, momentarily thrown by her knowledge. Her predecessor had been fired from the *Argus* for illegal phone tapping, after constantly coming up with information the police had not yet released. Was she doing the same now? Or did she have a source within the police? He had just come from the first briefing, and was due to head over to the car park where Logan Somerville had apparently disappeared, as soon as he had checked out the situation here. He was guarded in his reply.

'What information do you have?' he asked her.

'I heard she had broken off her engagement with her boyfriend recently. Does that make her disappearance suspicious? I understand there is a manhunt underway.'

Grace clocked that piece of information about the engagement to his memory bank. 'We are in the process of gathering information at this point,' he said. 'The Press Office will be able to update you later this morning. But so you know, we have every available officer and PCSO out looking for Ms Somerville, and they've been looking through the night.'

'Thank you, Detective Superintendent.'

'I have your mobile number,' Glenn Branson said. 'I'll call you if there are any developments.'

She thanked him and headed off across the Lagoon.

As they ducked under the tape, they were greeted by Dave Green, also fully suited in protective clothing.

'How's it going?' Grace asked.

'We've found a cigarette butt with the remains,' he said. 'I'm sending it off for analysis. But that's all I'm sending so far.'

As they sat down inside the changing-room tent, and pulled on their protective oversuits, Grace said to Branson, 'Are you a bit sweet on that *Argus* reporter?'

'Just trying to cultivate the local press – like you always taught me.' He gave him a mischievous grin.

'There's a big difference between *cultivate* and *shag*, mate, OK?'

'Yeah, there's a lot more vowels in *cultivate.*'

'Just don't go there,' Grace said. 'I'm serious. If you're ambitious, keep the press at arm's length – not at dick's length. Also think about your kids. It's not that long since their mother died.'

'Yeah, but plenty long enough since she kicked me out and brought in a new bloke as their substitute dad,' Branson said grimly. The DI, struggling to pull his suit over his hips, gave his friend a sideways glance. 'You've recently married one of the most beautiful women on the planet. I never put you down for someone with penis envy.'

'Sod you!'

'You've got to admit Siobhan's well tasty.'

'So was the apple on the tree in Genesis.'

19

Dr Edward Crisp was a short, toned man, with a bald dome and neat, greying hair at his temples. He wore fashionably modern glasses that were too big for his face, giving him a quizzical expression, as if he were peering out at the world through goggles.

A fastidious dresser, he was attired today in a hand-made charcoal suit from Brighton society tailor Gresham Blake, a pale blue shirt and a pink silk tie, both from Jermyn Street, and shiny black Chelsea boots from Crockett and Jones in London's Burlington Arcade. His scruffy black and white dog, Smut, which most of his patients were fond of, slept beside his desk on a cushion inside a wire-framed basket.

Although the modern trend for family doctors was to work with a group in a medical centre, he preferred to work alone, in the same office he had occupied for over twenty-five years. It was a spacious, imposing consulting room on the ground floor of a rather ugly Victorian terrace, close to Church Road in Hove, with a tiny adjoining room for his secretary, Jenni Acton. She was fifty-seven, unmarried, and had worked for him with slavish devotion for twenty years.

The room, as did his immaculate outfit, reflected his particular passion for neatness and order. His qualifications hung in a row, uniformly framed and uniformly impressive. In addition to being a general practitioner, he held qualifications in immunology from the Pasteur Institute in Paris, homeopathy, Chinese medicine and acupuncture, as well as being a Fellow of the Royal College of Surgeons. He had in fact qualified as a surgeon before deciding that working as a family doctor with an exclusive private practice suited him better. And his legion of private patients were glad about that, because he was widely liked and popular, to the extent that his list had been closed for many years, and he would only take on new patients by very special criteria.

One such new patient, Freya Northrop, perched nervously on the edge of one of the two oak and leather chairs in front of his tidy, leather-topped desk, while he talked very charmingly and calmly to someone called Maxine on the other end of the phone. She was clearly distressed about her mother, who sounded, from what Freya could glean, terminally ill and in her last weeks.

The only clue about the doctor's private life was a silver frame on his desk, containing a posed studio photograph of an attractive brunette in her mid-forties with mirror-image beautiful teenage daughters on either side against a sky-blue background. All of them were laughing at some joke cracked, presumably, by the professional photographer.

While he continued talking, making a promise to try to get the woman's mother admitted into the Martlets Hospice, Freya Northrop stared around the room. Most doctors' offices she had been in before were pretty nondescript. But this one was really rather grand, and it had more the feel of museum than a workplace. The wall just to her left displayed photographs and portraits of great medical pioneers; one she recognized as Alexander Fleming, the discoverer of penicillin, and another, the pioneer of X-rays, Marie Curie, with all their names and brief bios in small frames at their bases. Further along was a row of framed copies of Leonardo Da Vinci's anatomical drawings.

There was a display case full of model human skulls. Next to them, and standing tall and proud as if presiding over the room, was a human skeleton on a plinth. It partially blocked the view from the office's one window, with Venetian blinds that were open, looking out onto a parking area at the rear of the building.

The doctor made a note on a pad on his desk with a black Montegrappa pen, then typed something on his computer, all the time continuing to try to reassure the woman called Maxine on the other end.

There were several busts on plinths around the room, adding to the museum-like feel. Freya gazed at one, a man with a curiously elliptical-shaped bald dome and a beard that looked like flames.

'First do no harm!' The doctor's tone had changed.

Startled, Freya looked around and saw he had his hand cupped over the mouthpiece of the phone and was addressing her, with an almost childlike twinkle of humour.

'Do no harm?' she replied.

'Hippocrates! The fellow you're looking at. Bit of a wise old owl. The Hippocratic Oath all medics around the world take, swearing to practise medicine honestly, and all sorts of related stuff. Actually, it wasn't Hippocrates who said "Do No Harm", it was a nineteenth-century surgeon, Thomas Inman.'

'Ah!'

'Won't keep you a second.' He pointed at the phone. 'I have a very worried and upset lady, just need to wait for her to speak to her mother. Yes, Hippocrates!'

The doctor, while he continued with his phone call, was studying this new young patient in front of him. Conservatively dressed, in her twenties, she had a classically beautiful face, with deep brown eyes framed by long hair parted down the centre. She reminded him of the actress Julie Christie, whom he'd had the hots for when he had been a teenager. She reminded him of someone else, too, but that was painful and he pushed the memory aside.

Finally ending the call, he gave her a broad smile. 'So, I haven't seen you before, have I?' He glanced at her name on the computer screen, having to make a real effort to focus. 'Freya?'

'No, I've not come to you before,' Freya Northrop said.

'Interesting name, Northrop. Hmmn. Northrop Frye. Ever read him?'

She shook her head blankly.

'Wonderful literary critic! Wrote some brilliant essays on T. S. Eliot. Really helped raise his profile. Milton's too – especially *Paradise Lost*.'

'Ah,' she said, equally blankly.

'His first name was Herman.'

'Ah,' she said again, a little disconcerted by the curious conversation.

Her best friend, Olivia Harper, had said that Crisp was a wonderful doctor, and so jolly. But he seemed more odd than jolly, to her. She felt as if she was irritating him with her ignorance. 'T. S. Eliot, I've heard of him.'

'*The Waste Land*?'

'OK, right.'

'You know the poem?'

'I don't, no.'

Edward Crisp's mind went back to last night. Walking Smut across Hove Lagoon. You could walk dogs along Brighton and Hove seafront in winter without them having to be on a lead. And sometimes in the evening, when it was dark enough, he could let Smut, his white mongrel with a black spot either side of her tummy, who he'd acquired as a rescue dog ten years ago, shit anywhere she liked without having to stoop and pick up the mess with a plastic bag or, like some cretinous dog people, with a *pooper scooper*.

He was thinking about that terrible image of the skeleton, lying exposed in the ragged hole in the path. He could not get her out of his mind.

'*The Waste Land*?'

The young patient's words jolted him back to reality. '*I grow old*,' he said. '*I shall wear the bottoms of my trousers rolled*.'

Freya Northrop frowned.

'"The Love Song of J. Alfred Prufrock",' he said, and beamed. 'But enough of that. I'm sorry if I'm not totally with it today, I saw a terrible thing last night, and I'm a bit upset. I'm a doctor, I try to make people better. I couldn't help that poor woman. But that's enough about me, let's talk about you. Tell me why you are here?'

'Olivia Harper recommended you. I've just moved to Brighton from London.'

'Ah yes, indeed, what a lovely lady Olivia is. Quite a delight. Yes, of course. Forgive me, I'm very discombobulated this morning. But of course you don't want to hear that. Tell me what brings you here?' He smiled, his eyes suddenly alive and twinkling with humour. He held his elegant, black pen up in front of him and stared at her, as if through it.

'Well,' she said. 'I don't feel ill or anything.'

'Of course not – why would you want to see a doctor if you were feeling ill, eh?' He grinned and it was infectious. She grinned back, relaxing a tad.

'Totally,' she replied. 'Why would anyone?'

'Exactly! I only like to see patients who are feeling well! Who needs sick patients? They take up far too much time – and they reflect badly on me.' He tapped his chest. 'Always come and see me anytime you are feeling well, yes?'

She laughed. 'It's a deal!'

'Right, well, nice to meet you, Freya!' He feigned standing up to say goodbye, then sat down again, chuckling. 'So, tell me?'

Now she got him! 'Well,' she said, 'I've met this guy – that's why I've moved down here – I've been off the pill for a while – but I'd like to go back on it again.'

There was a long silence. He peered at her and his demeanour seemed to have stiffened, and suddenly she felt a chill of unease. Had she touched some kind of nerve in him?

Then he smiled, a big, warm, friendly beam that lit up his entire countenance. 'The pill? That's all?'

'Yes,' she said.

'You're planning to have sex with this – *guy*?'

'Well, we are already having sex. But—'

He raised his hands in the air. 'Beware! Too much information! You want the pill, I'm your dealer! No problem. You are a very delightful young lady. Anything you want, just come and see me. So, OK, let me take some details about you, then I'll give you a check-up. Tell me first some of your medical history?'

She recounted, as best she could recall, her appendectomy at the age of thirteen, her broken shoulder from snowboarding at sixteen, her chlamydia at eighteen, and, blushing, her recurring thrush more recently.

He tapped it all into his computer, seeming to take a particular delight, unless she was mistaken, in her venereal disease history. He then directed her behind the screen to remove her clothes.

While Freya Northrop was undressing, he tapped notes into his computer. Then he stared across the room at the green screen. He twisted the barrel of his pen so that the rollerball tip appeared, then retracted again.

That body in the Lagoon was really playing on his mind.

'I'm ready,' Freya said.

He continued to stare at the tip of his pen.

'Freya Northrop,' he said, almost silently, to himself. He liked her name. Nice lady! He liked her. 'Bye for now!' he said a little while later, as she left. He liked everyone to leave him with a smile.

20

The forensic archaeologist, Lucy Sibun, was a professional-looking woman in her early forties, with neat brown hair and square, modern glasses; she was accompanied by two juniors, here to learn from this rare scene. At this moment she was on her knees, studying the remains intently. Most of her face was hidden behind a gauze mask secured by tapes, and the rest of her slim figure was parcelled, unflatteringly, in a baggy white crime scene oversuit and clumsy-looking overshoes. It was just past 10 a.m. Under the watchful eyes of the similarly suited-up forensic pathologist Nadiuska De Sancha, the Coroner's Officer Philip Keay, and crime scene photographer James Gartrell, the whole skeleton had now been exposed.

It lay, facing up at the bright, jury-rigged overhead lights from its jagged-edged shallow grave. There were fragments of fabric, and mouldy dark stiletto-heeled shoes lying by the foot bones, which would appear to confirm the assertion by the doctor, who had appeared out of the blue last night walking his dog, that it was female.

The most immediate question Roy Grace had for Lucy Sibun was the age of the remains. A key factor in a discovery like this would always be how long the remains had been here. Was this sufficiently recent that the offender or immediate relatives might still be alive, or were these the bones of someone who had died so long ago that anyone connected would now be long dead? In which case a homicide enquiry would be much more challenging.

He turned for guidance to the archaeologist. She was shaking her head, looking angry. 'Why didn't the workmen stop last night the moment they saw the bones, Roy? By carrying on, they could have destroyed crucial evidence for us.'

'So you think this might be relatively recent?'

'No. The path was laid around twenty years ago. I'm speculating that whoever killed this woman was aware the path was going to be laid, and buried her a short while before, knowing she would be covered. The remains must pre-date the laying of this path. Just like the Mafia reputedly bury bodies beneath motorways under construction. Maybe it was even one of the workmen who laid the path. One thing I am pretty sure about, this is the deposition site, but I don't think it was the murder scene. The body has been dug up and reburied.'

'Why do you think that?'

The archaeologist pointed at several barely visible marks on the bones. 'I think these were made by a tool like a spade. She was buried somewhere else, in a temporary grave. Then she was dug up, clumsily, probably by someone nervous and in a hurry, who nicked her bones in several places during the process.'

Grace had a lot of respect for this woman's expertise, which had been proven to him on several previous occasions. 'Anything else that makes you think that, Lucy?'

'Yes. Although this path was laid twenty years ago, I think she's been dead for closer to thirty years. For starters, the shoes are a good indicator. I had a pair like these in my teens. But let's ignore them for the moment and focus on the human remains.' She pointed at a small bone fragment suspended from a tiny strip of desiccated skin. 'See that U-shaped bone – it's the one that keeps the tongue in place. It's often an indicator of the cause of death – the hyoid often gets broken during strangulation. But it's intact here. There are a number of indicators that this was a woman aged about twenty. There is little wear on the teeth, but wisdom teeth present. The pelvis shows auricular surface phase one, and pubic symphysis phase one.'

Grace tried to follow where she was pointing. 'See the wide sciatic notch? Triangular-shaped obturator foramen? The long pubic bone and the wide subpubic angle? The subpubic concavity?'

He nodded, although he did not fully understand.

Then she pointed at the skull, which was partially on its side. 'Less prominent supraorbital ridges. Sharp superior orbit. More upright frontal bone. Small mastoid process. Small rounded nuchal crest. It's definitely female. There's a lot of water under here. If she had been buried ten years before the surface was laid, I think she would have risen towards the surface and it would have been noticed by the original workmen.'

'I've already tasked an officer with finding out who laid the path – and to see if any of the council workmen are still around. It's quite possible they are. Do you have anything that might tell us who she is – was?' Glenn Branson asked.

Lucy Sibun pointed at the jaw. 'There's a deciduous tooth and several fillings that could give us dental identification – if she was local,' she said. 'DNA's a possibility.' She looked up at Nadiuska De Sancha. 'There might be more you could get from a full post-mortem.'

As the strong wind shook the tenting above them, the pathologist nodded, and turned to Roy Grace, then to the Coroner's Officer. 'Yes, I think that would be best. Can we recover the remains to the mortuary, please.'

'I have to go,' Grace said. 'I'll leave DI Branson here.'

He went back to the CSI tent and pulled off his protective clothing, then hurried towards his car. Before driving off, he sat and made more notes. Dental records were a possible method of identification, with a big *but*. There were thousands of dentists throughout the UK, but unlike fingerprints or DNA there was not, as yet, a central dental records database. You needed to have an idea who someone might be – and know who that person's dentist was. And if she was from overseas, there was no chance at all.

DNA wasn't a great prospect either. Going back twenty or so years, it was highly unlikely, even if she had been arrested for an offence, that her DNA would have been taken and logged. If it was thirty years ago that she had died, there was no chance of DNA. Their best hope, he decided, would be the lengthy process of a trawl through all the female missing persons within the time frame that Lucy Sibun estimated. To be on the safe side that would entail checking all female mispers, aged fifteen to thirty, from fifteen to thirty-five years ago.

There were many thousands of people on the current missing persons register of people who had been gone for over thirty days. It would be a massive task and the only way would be to start local.

Assuming the remains were of a local person.

He started the car and headed off towards Kemp Town, to the apartment building underground car park from where Logan Somerville had disappeared.

21

Friday 12 December

'How long? How long are you going to keep me here? How long, whoever the hell you are? Let me go!' Logan shouted out into the green-tinged darkness. 'I need sugar, I need water! Please.'

The sheer terror of her situation had made her forget about her toe, until now. It was throbbing painfully. The restraints across her stomach, wrists, thighs and legs felt as if they were cutting into her flesh. Her right leg was cramping and she desperately needed to stretch it, but she could not move. She tried again to lift her head, but immediately something cut into her neck, choking her.

Her mouth was dry and her lips were sticking together, but her body was clammy. She recognized the signals that she was desperately low on sugar. Soon, she would have a hypo and pass out.

Who had screamed earlier? Was there someone else in this place with her?

Anger had momentarily replaced the deep, sick sensation of fear inside her. How long had she been here? Wherever *here* was? Was it Jamie doing this? What was he going to do? Keep her here until she agreed to marry him after all? That sure as hell would be a great start to a life together.

Yeah, she broke it off, so I drugged her and locked her in a cellar and starved her and refused to give her any sugar or let her pee until she agreed to marry me.

Two weeks till Christmas. Two crucial weeks for her, for Chrissake. She was really starting to contribute to the clinic's profits, and being able to put aside a little money to top up her savings would allow her to buy a small property for herself after she and Jamie parted.

But every day counted. She had no idea of the time, nor how long she had been here. It was her mother's birthday today – if today was

Friday – and she had planned to call her, in advance of driving this weekend to see her parents.

Compared to her previous boyfriend, who was serially unfaithful, Logan had found Jamie, initially, a breath of fresh air. He was kind and gentle, a good cook and she liked his humour.

It had only been as she got to know him better that she began to understand quite how limited Jamie was. In the first few months of dating, they did everything together. Drinks, meals, walks, movies, watching stuff on television. It was very gradually and subtly that she began to realize he really didn't have many interests of his own, beyond watching sport on television and occasionally going to the AmEx stadium to watch Brighton and Hove Albion home games. He was like a chameleon, fitting into her life by adopting everything that she liked to do.

Last year, when she had begun training for the Brighton Marathon, he took up running for a short time, to train with her. She loved road cycling, so he bought a fancy road bike himself, to accompany her. In those early days she'd been all for it, it was nice to have companionship – not many of her friends were that sporty. But gradually she had started to miss her solitude. A big irritation had been three months ago, when she had joined a book group, and immediately, although he rarely read books, except genre thrillers, he asked to join too. After the first meeting at which he'd insulted everyone present by calling them pretentious nobs, he'd abandoned the idea.

He had taken it hard and been tearful when she'd told him she had decided she did not want to marry him, and they should go their separate ways. But never in her wildest dreams did she imagine he would do this to her, kidnap her and keep her prisoner.

If it was him.

It had to be him, surely?

Jamie was not a violent or cruel person. It didn't make any sense. Was there something deeper in his character she had missed? Was he going to keep her down here until she agreed to marry him?

She saw a light moving. A faint green glow. Coming closer.

'Jamie?' she said. 'Jamie, please, let's talk.'

She heard something sliding above her head.

Then a beam shone directly in her eyes, momentarily dazzling her. The beam moved away for a moment.

Someone was standing right above her. Their face obscured by what looked like a gimp mask.

Then she felt something pressed against her lips. Something sweet. She tasted honey and gulped it down. Then two capsules were placed in her mouth, followed by water from a plastic cup.

She heard the sliding sound again above her. Then muffled footsteps receding.

As the sound faded she had a ghastly thought and a terrible slick of fear slid through her.

Was she being illogical in her thinking? What if it was not Jamie? Where did the man in the car park fit in? Were they working together?

What if this was a total random stranger?

22

Jacob Van Dam, seated behind his desk in his Harley Street consulting room, peered like a wise owl through small, round tortoiseshell spectacles. A diminutive figure, with large patches of liver spots across the top of his head and on the backs of his bony hands, the psychiatrist was dressed in a grey pin-striped suit that seemed a size too big for him, as if he had shrunk in the years since having it made, and his collar, knotted with a club tie of some kind, hung around the loose wrinkled flanges of his turkey-like neck.

During many years of practising forensic psychiatry, dealing with a wide range of violent criminals, he had been assaulted on a number of occasions, and these days preferred to keep the barrier of his desk in front of him, for safety.

At seventy-seven he was long past the age at which he could have retired, but he loved his work far too much to ever consider that. Besides, what the hell would he do if he did retire? He had no hobbies, his work had always been his life. He held an endless fascination with human nature – which he saw daily with his patients.

The walls around him were lined with books on medicine and on human behaviour, quite a few of them bearing his name on the spine. His published works, lined along one shelf, included a book on why the public had adored Princess Diana, and another which was considered the definitive analysis of the Yorkshire Ripper, Peter Sutcliffe, who had been convicted of murdering thirteen women. Further along were the three volumes of which he was most proud, which came out of his time working as a psychiatrist within the high-security psychiatric hospital Broadmoor, where one of the criteria to be an inmate was to be diagnosed criminally insane.

What had always intrigued him, from his earliest student days,

71

was the whole notion of evil. Were some human beings born evil, or did something happen to turn them evil? And first, of course, you had to define *evil*. That was the topic he had explored in these three volumes, without coming to a conclusion.

In forty-seven years in psychiatry he had not yet found, definitively, any of these answers. He was still looking for them. Which was why he still came here every weekday morning and saw patients until the early evening, thanks in part to the understanding of his beloved wife, Rachel.

He was writing up his notes on the patient who had just departed from his office, an actor almost as old as himself who was unable to cope with the fact that women no longer threw themselves at him, when his secretary buzzed to announce that his next patient had arrived. Dr Harrison Hunter.

Hastily, he looked up the man's name and the referral letter from his family GP, a Dr Edward Crisp in Brighton. The letter was short and terse and the first referral he'd ever had from this doctor. Harrison Hunter was suffering from anxiety, with frequent panic attacks, and Dr Crisp believed him to be delusional. Van Dam pressed his intercom button and asked his secretary to show him in.

Instantly, for reasons the psychiatrist could not immediately define, this new patient simultaneously both excited and intrigued him – but also sent a wintry chill through his bones.

Van Dam stood up to shake his hand then ushered him to sit on one of the two hard, leather-cushioned antique chairs in front of his desk. For a moment they were forced into silence as an emergency vehicle siren screeched by outside. As the siren faded the only sound for some moments was the hiss of the gas fire in the grate.

Harrison Hunter's body language was extremely awkward. Fifty-five years old, according to the referral note, he looked pleasant enough, conservatively dressed in an off-the-peg business suit, dull shirt and clumsily knotted tie, tinted aviator glasses and sporting a mop of floppy blond hair rather like the style of the politician, Boris Johnson. The hair did not match the man's eyebrows and he wondered if perhaps it was a wig.

His new patient moved his hands from his thighs to his knees, scratched both of his cheeks, then the tips of his ears, then patted his thighs and shrugged.

'So, how are you hoping I can help you, Dr Hunter – may I call you Harrison?' the psychiatrist asked. It was his customary opening line for his first consultation with any new patient. He glanced briefly down at his notes, then placing his elbows on his desk, he steepled his hands, rested his chin on them and leaned forward.

'Harrison is fine.'

'Good. Are you a doctor of medicine?'

'I'm an anaesthetist. But a rather unusual one.' Hunter smiled. He had a dry, slightly high-pitched voice that sounded distinctly neurotic.

They were both forced into silence as another siren screamed past, followed by a third. When it faded the psychiatrist asked, 'Would you like to tell me in what way you consider yourself to be unusual?'

'I like to kill people.'

Van Dam stared at him with an expressionless poker face. Anaesthetists could occasionally be quite spiky, believing their role was as important as the surgeon's, yet they were getting paid less. He'd had one tell him that it was the anaesthetist who held the power of life over death in the operating theatre and who described surgeons dismissively as nothing more than butchers, plumbers and seamstresses. He had heard most things during his career, and patients often said things calculated to shock him. He remained silent, studying the man's face and body language, then looked straight into the man's eyes. Dead eyes that gave nothing away. He held his silence. Silence was always one of his strongest tactics for encouraging people to talk. It worked.

'The thing is, you see,' Harrison said, 'I work in a busy teaching hospital, and I'm expected to lose an average of eight to nine patients a year through adverse reactions to the surgery or anaesthetics – from syndromes such as Malignant Hyperthermia. I'm sure you are well aware of the dangers of anaesthesia?'

Van Dam continued to fixate on him. 'Yes, very aware.'

The anaesthetist finally cast his eyes down for some moments. 'Every now and then I kill an extra one, and sometimes two, each year, for fun.'

'For fun?'

'Yes.'

'How does this make you feel?'

'Happy. Satisfied. Fulfilled. And it is fun.'

'Would you like to tell me about the kind of *fun* you experience when you kill someone?'

Harrison Hunter balled his fists and raised them in the air. 'Power, Dr Van Dam! It's my power over them. It's an incredible feeling. There isn't any greater power a human being can have than taking the life of another, is there?'

'Not such *fun* for your patients, though.'

'People get what they deserve, don't they? Karma?'

'Some of your patients deserve to be killed?'

'This is what I need to talk to you about – it's why I'm here. Are you a religious man, Dr Van Dam, or a Darwinian?'

The psychiatrist stared back at him in silence for some moments, blinking. Another emergency service siren dopplered past. Heading to a crime scene? One of this strange man's victims? He picked up his pen and held it with the forefinger and thumb of each hand, focusing on the black barrel and silver cap for some moments. 'This consultation is about you, Harrison, not about me and the views I hold. I'm here for you. And before we go any further, I must remind you that I am bound by the requirements of the General Medical Council. I'm not bound to protect a patient's confidentiality if I believe him or her to be a danger to society, these days. The reverse is in fact the case, I am duty bound to report that person. So from what you are telling me, I am duty bound to inform the police about you.'

'But first, Dr Van Dam, you would have to get out of your office alive, yes?'

Van Dam smiled back at him. He tried not to show his discomfort, but there was something intensely creepy about this man – although at the same time, fascinating. He exuded a deeply troubled darkness. On occasions in his past, working at Broadmoor, he had encountered similarly disturbing people. But he could not remember the last time he had felt himself in the presence of such feral evil. Dr Crisp had written that his patient was delusional. Was this one of his delusions?

'True, Harrison,' he replied, with a half-hearted laugh. 'Oh yes. Yes, of course.'

'You are not going to go to the police, Dr Van Dam. Firstly, I think you would hate to lose me as a patient. And secondly, I sense that although the law has changed, you don't agree with the change. You're a pretty old-fashioned guy, with old-fashioned views about the sacrosanct right of confidentiality between a doctor and patient. I read a paper you published in the *Lancet* over a decade ago. You put forward a very cogent argument for maintaining it.'

'I wrote that a doctor should not be under a legal obligation, only a moral one. But let's talk more about you. Why are you here, what are you expecting from me? How are you hoping I might be able to help you?'

His patient looked at him with a curious expression. It felt to the psychiatrist that the man was staring right through his soul. 'I need to cope with my guilt.'

A number of thoughts went through the psychiatrist's mind. People did die every year from allergic reactions to anaesthetics – a tiny percentage of all those who had operations. It was a tragic fact that every anaesthetist would lose a few patients over the course of his career. Was this simply Harrison Hunter's way of coping with his guilt, to confess to killing them deliberately? Or was Hunter a fantasist?

Or was he, as he said, really a killer?

The psychiatrist decided to humour him. 'I'm not sure I believe what you told me about you killing people deliberately,' Van Dam said. 'When you qualified as a doctor of medicine, surely you agreed to be bound by the basic ethics of medicine, *Do no harm*. So tell me why you are really here?'

'I've just told you.' He was silent for some moments, then he said, 'There's a local newspaper published in the Brighton area called the *Argus*. Take a look online, later. You'll see a story about skeletal remains of a woman discovered yesterday in a small park close to the seafront, called Hove Lagoon.'

'Why do you want me to look at this story?'

'Because I know who killed her, and why.'

The psychiatrist studied him for some moments, watching his chaotic body language. Then he said, 'Have you told the police?'

'No, I haven't.'

'Why not?'

'Because, Dr Van Dam, you and I need each other.'

'Do we? Can you explain that to me?'

'There's another story in the *Argus* today. It didn't make the printed edition this morning, but you'll be able to read it online. You have a niece, Logan Somerville?'

Van Dam stiffened, visibly. 'What about her?'

'Are you very fond of her?'

'I don't discuss my private life with my patients. What does my niece have to do with this?'

'You haven't heard, have you?'

'Heard what?'

'About Logan. She disappeared last night.'

Van Dam blanched. 'Disappeared?'

'There's a manhunt going on all over Brighton for her. For your niece. Logan Somerville. You need me very badly.'

'Why is that?'

'Because I'm the only person who may be able to save her life.'

23

Roy Grace pulled up outside the Chesham Gate apartment building, behind a white Crime Scene Investigation van, a marked police car and two unmarked police vehicles. A short way along, the silver Specialist Search Unit van was straddling the kerb in order not to block the narrow street. A small knot of curious onlookers were standing around watching, and a youth was taking pictures with his phone.

On his way here, from the Lagoon, he'd had an idea for the brief, but very emotional speech he had to make on Monday, at Bella's funeral. He jotted it down, then he climbed out into the cold, blustery wind.

Fluttering crime scene tape sealed off the entrance to the car park. The gates were open and a PCSO scene guard stood in front with a clipboard. She directed Roy Grace to the van to suit up. He entered and shared some banter with two search officers, the highly experienced POLSA Sergeant Lorna Dennison-Wilkins and a recent recruit to her team, Scott, he had not met before, who were having a coffee break.

As he wormed his way into a protective oversuit for the second time this morning, he asked Lorna what was happening and where the Crime Scene Manager, John Morgan, was.

'Lots of pissed-off residents who can't get their cars out, sir. And another bunch who can't get their cars in. You might like to have a word with some of them. John Morgan's in a stroppy mood this morning and not being at his most diplomatic.'

Morgan was good at his job, but not always known for his tact. Protection of a crime scene was vital to prevent contamination, but when it inconvenienced the public, as was often the case, it required a delicate hand to explain the reasons. Mostly the public were understanding and helpful, but some were anything but – those who hated the police, and those who were just plain selfish or bloody-minded.

He signed the scene log and walked down the ramp into the underground car park in his clumsy, ungainly protective blue oversuit and shoes. A wide variety of cars were parked in the bays, including several sleek shapes beneath covers. There was a sharp, dry smell of engine oil, paintwork and dust. Several search officers, similarly clad, were on their hands and knees, shoulder to shoulder inside a taped-off area. Further along he saw another officer from the unit, on top of the SSU's portable scaffolding tower, checking behind a roof-light fitting.

The stocky figure of John Morgan appeared from around a corner and greeted him with a surly but polite, 'Morning, boss!'

'What do you have, John?'

The Crime Scene Manager shook his head. 'Something that might be of interest – a footprint in a patch of engine oil.' He led Grace over to an empty parking bay next to where the Fiat had been parked, where there was a small pool of black sludge on the ground. 'Looks like a male, because of the size. There are several weaker prints heading across towards the far end of the car park, but that's it.' Then he pointed up at a CCTV camera. 'If that had been working, we might have got a lot more that could be useful.'

Accompanied by Morgan, Grace walked around the entire car park, noting the fire escapes, the lift and the main steps up beside it. Plenty of ways in which someone could enter pretty much unnoticed except by cameras. Then the caretaker took them to the couple's flat, where Grace had met the boyfriend last night. Morgan told Grace that Logan Somerville's laptop and mobile phone had been taken across to the High Tech Crime Unit for a high-priority examination. In particular they'd be looking at recent calls, her emails and social networking sites to see if there were any clues to her disappearance there.

The boyfriend was lined up for a 1 p.m. appeal on the local news, with Grace. Meanwhile the police CCTV camera footage around the city was being examined for any sightings of Logan Somerville, or the estate car that had been seen in the area.

The good news was that most of the mispers reported annually in the UK turned up within a few days, and there was always a raft of different explanations for their absence.

Was Logan Somerville going to turn up within a few days, with a perfectly plausible explanation for her absence? He had a bad feeling about this particular young woman. The report by her fiancé of her screaming. The vehicle coming out of the underground car park at high speed around the same time. Despite Jamie Ball's alibi that would appear to eliminate him from suspicion, Roy Grace was not happy about this man. No one at this stage would be eliminated entirely. He'd be in a better position to decide on the young man after he had been interviewed, and in particular, after his performance at the televised appeal, later. Would he be shedding real or crocodile tears?

He looked at a photograph of the pair in cycling outfits; then at another of them lying on a beach. A young, attractive, happy-looking couple, like a thousand other young lovers, seemingly without a care in the world. Except, in his jaded cynicism, he didn't believe there were many people who genuinely could say they didn't have a care in the world. Everyone had some kind of a problem they had to deal with.

His phone rang. He answered it, looking down at the signal on the display which showed just one dot. 'Roy Grace.'

It was Glenn Branson, his voice crackly, sounding excited. 'Hey, boss, are you very tied up for half an hour? We're at the mortuary. There's something I think you should see.'

Grace looked at the time on his phone. 10.55 a.m. At midday he was due to attend a meeting with ACC Cassian Pewe to brief him on Logan Somerville. He needed to prepare for it, and ensure there was no missing persons procedure he had missed out that Pewe could trip him up on. And he wanted to be in time for the 1 p.m. appeal as well as to observe the interview due to be taking place later with Logan's fiancé – but he could watch the recording if he missed it.

'I'll be over as soon as I've finished here.'

24

Friday 12 December

Jacob Van Dam and his patient stared at each other across, what felt to the psychiatrist, a dark void. Just who the hell was this creepy fellow and what was going on inside his head?

'May I take a moment to verify your story about my niece, Dr Hunter?'

'Be my guest. Provided I can see what you are doing.'

The psychiatrist turned his computer screen sideways, so that Harrison Hunter could see it. 'The *Argus* online you said?'

Hunter nodded.

Van Dam opened Google then typed in the words 'Brighton Argus online'.

Moments later the *Argus* homepage appeared, and he saw the headline.

ABDUCTION FEARS OVER MISSING WOMAN

Both men read the story printed below.

> Logan Somerville, 24, of Chesham Gate, Kemp Town, has not been seen since she left the Chiropractic Life Clinic premises in Portland Road, Hove, where she worked, at 5.15 p.m. yesterday afternoon. Her fiancé, Jamie Ball, 28, a marketing manager, reported to police that she had phoned him, concerned about a stranger in the underground car park of the apartment building where they live, at around 5.30 p.m. yesterday, which was the last communication from her. Her car was subsequently found in the car park.
>
> A police spokesperson said that her disappearance is being treated as a possible abduction, and Detective Superintendent Roy Grace of Surrey and Sussex Major

Crime Team is in charge of the investigation, Operation Haywain. A television broadcast by her fiancé is being made at 1 p.m. today, which will be followed by a press conference, at which more details will be given.

Police are appealing for anyone who might have seen anything suspicious in the vicinity, or a dark-coloured estate car, possibly an older model Volvo, being driven erratically or at high speed around that time. The driver is described as male, middle-aged, clean shaven, wearing glasses.

The psychiatrist was visibly shaking as he looked back at his patient. 'You know where she is?' he said.

'I didn't say that. I said I'm the only person who may be able to save her life.'

'What do you need?' the psychiatrist said sternly. 'Money? How much money?'

'This is not about money.'

'Then what is it about?'

Harrison Hunter stood up abruptly. 'I have to go now.'

'Wait!' Van Dam said. 'You can't go now, for God's sake tell me where she is, what's happened to her. Who is she with? Has she been hurt?'

But his patient had already reached the door. As he opened it, Hunter turned and said, 'Don't go to the police, Dr Van Dam. If you do you'll never see her again. I can help you, you'll have to trust me on that.'

'Please, how exactly are you going to help me, Dr Hunter?'

'By you helping me.'

The door closed behind him.

'Wait!' Van Dam shouted, pulling the door open. But the man had gone past his secretary and out of the far door. As Van Dam reached it, he could hear the man's footsteps heading down the stairs. He stumbled down them after him, but long before he reached the front door, calling out, 'Please wait!', he heard it slam.

He returned to his office, out of breath, looked at the phone number on Crisp's referral letter and dialled it. After a few rings it was answered by a cheery, recorded voice.

'Hello, this is Dr Crisp's surgery. Please leave a message and I'll get back to you as quickly as I can. Bye for now!'

25

Deep in thought, Roy Grace drove around the Lewes Road gyratory system. It was coming up to 11.15 a.m., around eighteen hours since Logan Somerville had vanished. If she had been taken, as he feared, rather than simply gone of her own volition, then with each passing hour the chances of finding her alive diminished. That had long been his grim experience. But he was curious about why Glenn Branson wanted him to come over so urgently.

He turned left, in past the wrought-iron gates attached to brick pillars, and the sign in gold letters on a black background which said BRIGHTON AND HOVE CITY MORTUARY. He was confronted with death constantly in his work, and whilst crime scenes and deposition sites often yielded vital clues for enquiries, the mortuary – combined with the associated pathology and DNA labs – had become in many ways the crucible of murder investigations.

Whilst he preferred not to dwell too much on his own mortality, this place always made him think of it. Not many people, other than tragic suicide victims, actually expected to end up here. And he wondered just how many of those, even, had really wanted to be spending the night in a cold refrigerator, rather than in their beds. He'd interviewed a number of survivors from suicide attempts over the years, and a high percentage of them had told him, and colleagues, that they were grateful to have failed and to still be alive.

This was something that had been backed up by a recent conversation he'd had with a police sergeant who was a regular crew member of the police helicopter. Part of her duty was to do a weekly check, while flying along near the bottom of Beachy Head. The beauty spot, a chalk headland a few miles to the east of Brighton, had a dark side to it. With its 531-foot sheer drop onto rocks at the edge of the

English Channel, it was a notorious suicide spot, claiming victims most weeks of the year, and vied with California's Golden Gate Bridge and Japan's Aokigahara Woods for the dubious status of the world's most popular suicide destination. There was a permanently manned chaplaincy post there to help try to talk desperate people around.

The sergeant had told him that a significant number of victims they recovered from the bottom of the cliffs had chalk under their fingernails – indicating, horrifically, that they must have changed their minds on the way down.

Every sudden death that Roy Grace encountered, whether an accident, suicide or murder, affected him. Death was something that everyone liked to believe happened to other people. Other, less fortunate people. Not many people set out to become victims, and this place haunted him with its sadness.

He and Sandy had had no children. If he had died during the time they had been together, Sandy would have coped fine. She was a strong person. Cleo would cope, too, if anything ever happened to him; her family were comfortably off and, additionally, he'd made life assurance provisions for her and for Noah. But the recent birth of his son had made him think about his death in a way that he never had before. Cleo would always be a brilliant mother to Noah, but as a young, very beautiful woman, she would almost certainly marry again one day – and that person would then become Noah's father.

A total stranger.

It was an odd thought to be having, he knew, but now that he was a father, he valued life more than ever before. He wanted to be around for his son. To be a good father to him, the way his own father, Jack Grace, had been there for him, to try to help prepare him for the world out there. A world that was rich and beautiful, but constantly lay in the shadow of evil.

Even though he had some good associations with the mortuary – it was where he had met Cleo, after all – the place still made him deeply uneasy, as it did most people who came here, and that included police officers. The gates here were always open, 24/7. Always ready to receive the newly dead and, like the skeletal remains of the as yet unknown woman at the Lagoon, sometimes the long-term dead.

Roy Grace always felt that the blandness of the exterior of the building, which looked like a suburban bungalow, added a curiously stark contrast to the grim tasks that were performed inside it. It was a long, single-storey structure with grey pebbledash rendering on the walls, overlooked by a row of houses, and with a covered drive-in on one side deep enough to accommodate an ambulance or a large van. On the other side was a huge opaque window, and a small, very domestic-looking front door.

He drove past a line of cars parked against a flint wall at the rear, and halted in the visitors' parking area. Then he walked around to the front door and rang the bell. It was answered by Darren Wallace, in Cleo's absence, the Acting Senior Anatomical Pathology Technician. He was in his early twenties, with fashionably spiky dark hair, and dressed in blue scrubs, with a green plastic apron and white boots. He greeted the Detective Superintendent and led him through into the changing room.

As he gowned up, Roy wrinkled his nose, trying not to breathe in the all-too-familiar smell of the place, a combination of Jeyes Fluid, Trigene disinfectant and decaying human bodies. A smell that stayed with you long after you left. As did the feeling of cold from the chilled air. Then he went through into the post-mortem room itself, and all the smells became stronger – and the air even colder.

The room was divided into two working areas separated by an open archway, the walls lined with grey tiles and with stark overhead lighting. There was a wide, tall fridge, with a row of numbered doors accessing it; behind each of them, four bodies could be stacked one above the other. The spaces that were occupied were indicated by a buff handwritten tag jammed in the metal frame holder on the door. Accommodation here was stark and functional, Grace thought, it didn't matter whether you were a billionaire or a homeless person, you'd be rubbing shoulders – or at least body bags – in the void behind these doors for however long it took for the Coroner to release you. He shuddered, trying not to think about it. It didn't matter, did it, if you were dead? You'd vacated your body, it was just an empty shell, a husk.

Wasn't it?

That was how he'd felt seeing his dad's body, years back, laid out in a funeral parlour.

There were six stainless-steel post-mortem tables in the two areas, and scales with whiteboard charts on the walls above them, labelled NAME, BRAIN, LUNGS, HEART, LIVER, KIDNEYS, SPLEEN. The weights of each of the organs would be marked up here during a post-mortem – except in the rare cases, such as the one now, where there was nothing left of them.

Three of the steel tables were bare and gleaming. On another two, bodies were laid out beneath white plastic sheeting, the foot of one visible, a buff tag hanging off the big toe. Out of curiosity, as he walked past, Grace read the name, 'Bob Tanner', and wondered *What was his story?*

Then he nodded a greeting at the others in the room, similarly gowned, who were gathered around a table on which lay a grubby-looking skeleton, some parts of it held together by desiccated sinewy tissue, the remainder laid out separately like a painstakingly partially completed puzzle.

It was the skull that drew his eyes. Small, with a full set of immaculately shaped teeth – if badly in need of some whitening. A white ruler had been placed across the left cheekbone by James Gartrell, who was standing by the skull, taking a set of photographs. Near him stood the tall figure of Philip Keay, talking into a hand-held dictating machine, and beside him was Glenn Branson, having a conversation with Deborah Morrison, the Assistant Technician. Lucy Sibun was studying one of the leg bones, and making notes.

Nadiuska De Sancha was bending over the skeleton, carefully probing with a thin steel instrument. A striking-looking woman in her early fifties, the pathologist had high cheekbones and clear green eyes that could be deadly serious one moment and sparkling with humour the next, beneath fiery red hair, which at this moment was pinned up, neatly. She had an aristocratic bearing, befitting someone who was, reputedly, the daughter of a Russian duke, and always wore a pair of small, heavy-rimmed glasses that gave her a distinctly studious appearance. She turned and greeted Roy Grace with a friendly smile.

'Thanks for coming over, Roy, there are a couple of things that Glenn felt you ought to see.' She replaced her tool with a pair of tweezers from a tray of instruments, walked over to the skull and studied it for some moments. Then she pinched something that was almost invisible, at first, and raised the tweezers above the skull.

Grace followed her over, and saw for himself: it was a single strand of brown hair, about eighteen inches long.

'This might be helpful in establishing her identity,' she said. 'It's one of the few remaining strands of hair left on her scalp, but from its length it would indicate that at the time of her death she had a full head of brown hair this length.'

Grace stared at it. His thoughts went to the photographs he had seen of Logan Somerville, who had similarly long brown hair. So, he remembered, had Emma Johnson, who had disappeared from her home in Worthing, turned up in Hastings some while later, then had recently been reported as having disappeared again. Could there be a connection? It seemed unlikely. But possible, even allowing for the gap of decades. He always kept an open mind in any enquiry. It was easy to dismiss something as coincidence – and in doing so potentially overlook a vital clue that might one day come back to bite you.

He turned to the forensic archaeologist. 'Lucy, you said you estimated the woman's age to be around twenty at the time of death?'

She turned to look at him. 'Yes, everything points to that. And I would estimate that she died around thirty years ago. I'd like to get soil analysis done on a number of spores I've found, so far, on part of the remains, because to me they don't look like they come from the sandy soil in the Lagoon vicinity. They appear to be clay deposits, more likely found some distance inland – quite a lot of the interior of Sussex farm and woodland is on clay. This makes me even more certain that the Lagoon wasn't the original crime scene, but merely the deposition site. It'll take me some days – possibly a week or two – to get this confirmed.'

Grace frowned. 'Why would someone move her to the Lagoon from an inland burial site – to such a public place?'

'Possibly because they knew the path was being laid, boss,' said Glenn Branson. 'And that then her remains would never be discovered.'

Grace stared down at the remains, pensively.

'What about,' Branson went on, 'the possibility that the offender was part of the crew laying that path?'

Grace nodded. 'Yes, it's a possibility. You're on to that, aren't you?'

'Yes.'

Grace looked at his watch, conscious of the need not to be late for Pewe. 'Anything else that you have for me?'

Branson nodded with a wry smile. 'Yeah, there is something else.' He exchanged an almost conspiratorial glance with Nadiuska De Sancha. Then he jerked a finger towards the front of the skull.

The pathologist went over to the work surface by the large, opaque window, picked up a magnifying glass and brought it over. 'Take a close look, Roy.'

Peering hard with his naked eye on the front of the skull, where he estimated the top of the forehead would have been, he could just see what looked like a mark, about two inches wide by half an inch high. Then he raised the glass and looked through that. He could make out, very faintly, letters:

U R DEAD

He turned back to Nadiuska De Sancha. 'Strange tattoo to have. Might she have been a Goth, or whatever it was back then?'

'It's not a tattoo, Roy.' She shook her head.

'It's not? So what is it?'

'I think it burned through the skin. It must have been done with a branding iron.'

26

Logan grew up on a small farm near Ripe in East Sussex. Her parents were third-generation tenant farmers, and as the EEC regulations gradually bit deeper, their income dropped progressively. They needed to make savings, and the only real ones they could make were staff. They had to let two of their farmhands go, and a few months later their herdsman, who had been working for their family for thirty years. From the age of eleven, Logan had to take turns with the rest of her family to get up at 5 a.m. and milk the cows. It was a daily routine, seven days a week, every day of the year. Cows didn't understand things like Christmas Day. They just wanted to be milked.

Her father was a committed Green environmentalist who did not believe in mod cons. The only heating in the house was supplied by a coke-fired Esse oven in the kitchen that was kept going all year round, and a wood-burning stove in the hall, that was unlit during the summer months. Years later, although she now lived in a centrally-heated flat in Brighton, she still woke up some nights with the smell of burning coke in her nostrils.

She could smell it now. Sharp, acrid. Was she hallucinating?

Then she opened her eyes and realized she was not, she could smell it clearly. Burning coke. Tickling her nostrils. She saw a blurry, diffused red glow above her. And pinpricks of green light beyond.

Then the familiar sliding sound, and musty-smelling air on her face. Now she could see the red glow much more clearly, directly above her.

Someone was standing over her. Someone holding something that was glowing bright red.

'Who are you?' she said, trembling with fear, her voice quavering. 'Who are you?'

Suddenly she felt a gloved hand clamp her throat, forcing it down against the hard surface she was lying on. Then the red glow descended towards her midriff. An instant later she felt an agonizing burning sensation on her right thigh. She howled, crushing her eyes shut against the pain, writhing, trying to move away, but she was pinioned down. She screamed. Heard the hiss of burning flesh.

Her flesh.

'Noooooooooooooooooo!'

It was like being stung by a swarm of hornets. She screamed again.

'Ssshhhh!' a muffled voice said. 'Ssshhhh! It's OK, babe!'

She writhed in agony, as far as she could move. It was burning, stinging, hurting like hell. She tried to bite into the glove holding her down. The pain was getting worse.

More intense.

'Owwwwwwwww. Owwwwwwww.' It was burning right through her as if her entire leg was on fire.

'Owwwwwwwwwwwwwww.'

Then she felt something cold and soothing on her thigh, for a brief instant. But rapidly the excruciating pain returned.

She saw the red glow rising above her. The hand released her. She gasped. The pain was unbearable.

She vomited.

Moments later a cloth, wet and reeking of some vile disinfectant, was wiping her mouth. The pain in her thigh felt as if it was burning right through to her bone, like corrosive acid.

Then the muffled voice again. 'You'll be OK. The pain will go. No harm done. You'll be fine.'

'What have you done, you bastard? Is this how you get your kicks?'

The sliding sound above her. Then silence. Through her tears of pain she shook in terror.

27

At four o'clock in the afternoon Roy Grace sat in his office on the first floor of the CID HQ, with its view out across the road. The glistening wet grey slab of the Hollingbury Asda superstore sat in the foreground, in the fading light, with the rainy landscape of the city beyond. He slipped the DVD of the interview with Jamie Ball, which he had just been handed, into his desktop computer.

The burly figure of the young man, in a grey suit, shirt and tie and black shoes, was seated, looking awkward, in one of the three red chairs in the tiny Witness Interview Room. Two detectives, DS Guy Batchelor in a sports jacket and black trousers, and DC Liz Seward, a petite woman with short, spiky blonde hair, dressed in a white shirt and dark trousers, sat with him. Above their heads the lens of a wall-mounted camera stared down at them.

Grace watched the formalities of today's date and time being announced, and Ball acknowledging he was aware that the interview was being recorded. Batchelor asked Ball to outline the circumstances of his fiancée, Logan Somerville's, disappearance.

Ball related the events in a precisely identical manner as he had to Roy Grace the previous evening, and that struck Grace as a little strange. Was it rehearsed, he wondered?

'How would you describe your relationship with Ms Somerville?' DC Seward asked.

Grace watched the man carefully. He was replying in a calm voice, but he looked anything but calm. 'We were deeply in love and planning our wedding. I thought everything was great.'

'Are you sure about that?' Guy Batchelor pressed. 'And that she felt the same way?'

'I thought so.'

Ball looked even more uncomfortable. He stared up for some moments at the camera, then scratched his right ear, before checking the knot of his tie.

'Do you know a lady by the name of Louise Brice?' DC Seward asked.

'Yes, very well.'

'How would you describe her relationship to Logan?' the DC asked.

'She's Logan's best friend. They go back to nursery school days. They're very close.'

'How close would you say?'

'They spoke or texted each other all the time. Several times a day, most days.'

'So Louise Brice would be likely to know quite a lot about her?'

He hesitated. Grace noted his expression change. 'Yes.'

'The thing is, Jamie, one of my colleagues spoke to Louise Brice earlier today. I have the transcript of the conversation in front of me.' She looked down for some moments at a sheet of printout. 'Louise Brice told her the same thing that she told a reporter on the *Argus* newspaper who contacted her. That Logan had broken off your engagement. Can you comment on that?'

Again Ball looked uncomfortable for some moments. 'We were very deeply in love,' he said, with a tinge of defiance in his voice. 'But recently there's been some friction – as Logan was suddenly unsure.'

'Why do you think her best friend would have said that to a newspaper reporter?' Liz Seward asked him.

Ball shrugged. 'I don't know. Louise Brice and I never got on that well, if you want to know the truth. She runs Brices estate agency. She told Logan she thinks I'm a bit of a loser, and that she could do better.'

'Better than what?' Guy Batchelor asked.

'Me.'

'How did Logan react to her friend's view?' he asked.

Ball was silent for some moments. 'She told me what Louise had said.'

'And how did you feel when you heard that?' Batchelor stared at him intently.

Ball touched his beard, then his stacked hair. 'I told her that was very hurtful.'

'I spoke to Louise Brice earlier today,' DC Seward said. 'She told me that Logan had a number of concerns about the relationship. Do you want to comment on that?'

Ball's temper visibly flared. 'That's just bullshit! Louise's a snotty bitch, she never liked me, she was always trying to undermine me. Logan and I had disagreements like any couple.'

'What about?'

'Logan can be a loner at times. I felt we should develop interests that we could do together.'

'Did Louise Brice succeed in any way?' the DC asked.

'Logan told me she loved me.'

'So, is there any truth that she broke off your engagement?'

Again Jamie Ball fell silent for several moments. Then he said, 'Yes. Well, the thing is – we were going through a bit of a bad patch. But it was all starting to come good again. I mean – what I mean is – you know – we talked through it. All couples go through rough patches, don't they?'

'I also spoke to Mrs Tina Somerville today,' Liz Seward said. 'That's Logan's mother, correct?'

'Yes.'

'She told me that Logan spent last weekend with her and her husband, alone. Without you. That she had spent much of the time in a state of some distress, telling them that you would not accept that the relationship was over. Would you like to comment on that?'

Again he shrugged. 'I'm surprised – but not surprised. She always told me there was friction with her parents. They're tenant farmers – I don't know if you understand how that system works?'

'Would you like to tell us?' the female detective said.

'Much of farming in England works on a strange – quite feudal system. The aristocratic landowners own most of the land in this country – with their vast estates. Historically they've given farming families three-generation tenancies on fairly low rents. The deal is, in return the farmers look after the land – and make their money out of what they earn off the land. So in one way it's a good deal for the farmers – they get substantial acreages of arable or dairy or sheep-farming land. But the downside is they don't own their farms or their land. At the end of the third generation they have to renew their tenancies. It only works if that generation is happy to take on the same deal – as I understand it. Her parents were not happy that I had no interest in farming, they'd hoped Logan would marry someone who was.'

'So their tenancy was under threat?'

'Yes. They're in their sixties and have never bought a property of their own. So they're faced with the possibility of losing their home. They're angry at her for not finding a potential husband willing to carry on. But the truth is that Logan is not interested herself. Farming is a tough life.'

Grace continued watching the recording, but there was nothing further that Jamie Ball said of any significance. He'd said enough already.

Logan Somerville had broken off the engagement and Jamie Ball had not accepted it. His position was they were on the verge of getting back together again. Not a view shared either by her best friend or by her parents.

Was he behind her disappearance?

Grace did not have enough information to make a decision either way. Yet.

28

Friday 12 December

Edward Crisp said goodbye to his last patient of the week, Rob Lowe, an elderly property developer who was convinced, just as he had been on a regular basis for the past twenty-five years, that he was terminally ill.

Lowe had been one of the patients he had taken on when he had first set up this practice. Referred to him by his then GP who was retiring, the man had initially come into his office complaining of a recurrent sharp pain in his neck, which had convinced him he was suffering from cancer of the throat. Crisp had been able to calm him down by establishing that it was neck strain from tennis. Since then, there had seldom been two consecutive months when Lowe, sometimes accompanied by his wife, Julie, had not turned up in his office with a fresh imagined terminal illness manifested through some other pain in his body. Chest pains. Lumbar pains. Groin pains. Loss of appetite. Weight loss.

One day, of course, if a heart attack, a stroke, an accident or pneumonia didn't carry him off first, Rob Lowe would be right. Almost everyone who lived long enough would eventually be diagnosed with some form of cancer. But at eighty-three, Lowe was still going strong, and his latest imaginary terminal illness, a brain tumour, causing him blurred vision, had turned out to be no more serious than a need for a cataract operation.

Crisp's secretary, Jenni, popped her head in through the door to say goodnight, then stood in the doorway, lingering, giving him the same curious, almost expectant stare she always gave him.

'What are you up to this weekend?' he asked, out of politeness rather than interest.

'Taking my niece and nephew, Star and Ashton, to Thorpe Park tomorrow,' she said. 'Otherwise I don't have any plans.' Her stare was irritating him intensely tonight. Although, at the moment, everything was irritating him. Why was the bloody woman staring at him? Was she expecting him to suddenly leap out of his chair and declare his love for her?

A handsome woman, with a classic English rose face framed by short, elegantly cut brown hair, she was a sad and slightly tragic figure. He knew all about her private life, because she had confessed to him some years ago, when he had taken her out for their traditional pre-Christmas lunch, that she had been having an affair with a married man with three children, a prominent solicitor in Brighton, who had been stringing her along for years. One day, he had promised, when his kids were old enough to understand, he would leave his wife. But Crisp had always sensed that was never going to happen.

He'd tried on more than one occasion to tell her to dump him, to join a dating agency while she was still young enough. She'd ignored his advice. But he had been right. The man's children had long left home and the spark had faded in their relationship. All Jenni had now were her teenage niece and nephew, and she probably would not have them for much longer, once they started to date.

'What are your plans?' she asked.

'Taking Smut for a long walk tomorrow. Then I've been invited to a dinner party in the evening with a bunch of medics. A proctologist, an oncologist, a dermatologist and an anaesthetist, with their other halves. They're trying to fix me up with a woman.'

'Sounds like fun!' she said, brightly, but with a disappointed look in her eyes.

'Huh,' he responded, dismissively.

'Well, call me if you need me.'

He smiled, thinly. She said the same thing every Friday evening. 'Thanks, will do.' In twenty years he never had. She closed the door behind her, and he sat still, alone with his troubled thoughts.

High on the list of these was his bitch wife, Sandra. She was screwing a smug, smooth plastic surgeon, Rick Maranello. A medic friend had told him the news as if doing him a favour, some months ago. It wasn't a big surprise to him – she had gone off sex around that time – and probably longer ago, if he cared to think about it. She'd pretty well gone off it after the second of their two children had been born. But he had bigger problems on his mind than thinking about his wife in bed with a creepily narcissistic plastic surgeon.

His whole livelihood was under threat at the moment, thanks to new government regulations coming in.

Until recently, working as a sole practitioner had been an option for all family doctors in the UK. But ever since another sole practitioner, Harold Shipman, had been sentenced to life imprisonment for killing fifteen of his patients – and his true death toll, though never established, was estimated to be several hundred – regulations for GPs had been changed. For National Health family doctors *revalidation* had been brought in. Their practices had to be scrutinized. They had to have annual appraisals by both professionals – peers or associates – able to monitor their work – and by patients. Half had to be medics, half non-medics. As a result, almost all National Health doctors now worked in medical centres, with a number of other doctors.

Private general practitioners, like himself, were so far exempt from this, so he had been able to carry on, unhindered. But now he'd read that was about to change. All private GPs were soon to come under the same regulations.

Why?

Who were these moronic civil servants and elected creeps, who had decided, because of one bad egg a decade ago, that family doctors were no long able to be trusted? In short, he was going to have to produce printouts from large numbers of patients and from medics testifying to his abilities. How demeaning was that?

How sodding bureaucratic?

The only option would be to join a bloody medical centre of some kind. And risk his patients, whom he cared about deeply, seeing some possibly incompetent doctor when he wasn't available, instead of the reliable locum of his choice. It was bloody ludicrous! All his patients loved him, and he loved them back. The ones at the start of their lives, the pregnant ones full of hope and joy, and the terminally ill ones who he helped through their prognosis, and cared for all the way to their final days – and then attended their funerals.

Medicine was an inexact science. No one knew this better than he did. It was an established fact that one of the most effective of all drugs was a placebo. There were many occasions when he had cured patients of a range of ailments from depression to more serious illnesses by telling them to take some long walks in the countryside or along the seafront.

Now these so-called *health experts* were making ludicrous demands. Calling his ethics – and every doctor's like him – into question.

Well, fuck them. Fuck them all. Fuck his wife – who was already being well fucked by Rick Maranello. Fuck his kids, arrogant, un-grateful little bastards both of them.

Fuck the world.

Because it sure as hell was fucking him.

29

Jacob Van Dam's last patient of the week sat in front of him now. Neil Fisher, an army captain who had been given an honourable discharge after suffering a nervous breakdown after his third tour of Afghanistan, a year ago.

During an assault on an enemy position, the officer's best friend, running alongside him, had been hit in the midriff by shrapnel from a shell. Fisher had carried the screaming, newly-wed man on his shoulders, with half his intestines uncoiled around his face, into the safety of a shell hole, where he had died, sobbing for the arms of his bride. Captain Fisher was now suffering severe post-traumatic stress disorder.

But the elderly psychiatrist was unable to focus on what the former soldier was saying, just as he had been unable to concentrate on any of his patients since his encounter with the strange anaesthetist, Dr Harrison Hunter. His mind was a turmoil of conflicting thoughts.

After phoning his distraught sister Tina to verify that Logan was still missing, he had spent his lunch hour on the internet, frantically searching first the medical register, then googling the doctor's name. The only Harrison Hunter he had been able to find was the Chief Executive of the Canadian Pacific Railway. And that man's photograph didn't bear any resemblance to his new patient.

Dr Crisp had phoned him back, but wasn't able to provide any real insights into Harrison Hunter beyond his views that the man was delusional and needed psychiatric help. He suggested that Van Dam contact the police.

After Fisher departed, clutching a new prescription for antidepressants that the psychiatrist had written out for him, Van Dam sat in silence, thinking hard. Should he phone the police? But to do that he had to be sure he believed Hunter – whoever he really was. And he had a strong feeling the man might be delusional. He'd had patients in the past who had confessed to imaginary crimes they had committed. On one occasion he had called the police, after a confession to murder, only to discover that no such crime had been reported. And in a subsequent session, this patient had admitted to making it all up.

Was Hunter, as Dr Crisp believed, really delusional? If he were to phone the police, giving them false information supplied by Hunter, might it actually harm or slow down the investigation?

Logan was a lovely girl. Bright, warm and natural. His desperate sister had told him what he had already read, about the manhunt that was taking place to find her. He noticed the winking light on his phone. An incoming call. His secretary had left a couple of hours ago. He lifted the receiver and pressed the button to answer it.

'Dr Van Dam?'

'Yes?' He recognized the man's voice. 'Dr Hunter?'

'It's not looking good for Logan Somerville, is it?'

The psychiatrist had prepared himself for a further conversation with the man. He'd lined up a number of questions to test him. 'How well do you know my niece?' he asked.

'I don't know her at all, Dr Van Dam. I only know the man who has taken her.'

'Is that so?'

'He's very deeply disturbed. We are going to have to tread very carefully if we want her to be safe.'

'Tell me why I should believe you?'

'Well, it's because I can tell you something about her that the police don't know.'

'What's her middle name, Dr Hunter?'

'I wouldn't know that.'

'Perhaps you can tell me her birthday?'

'What are we doing – playing some kind of Trivial Pursuit, Dr Van Dam?'

'I wouldn't say there was anything trivial about a young lady who might have been abducted.'

Hunter's voice sounded almost gleeful. 'You see? You don't even know for sure she has been abducted. She might have just run away to safety, to get away from her boyfriend. Sorry, her *fiancé*.'

Van Dam was jolted by this. It was what his sister had told him earlier when he had called her to ask if it was true that Logan had disappeared. What was his connection? 'Can you shed some light on how you know that, for me?'

'It's on her Facebook page!'

'I'm afraid I'm not up to speed on social media.'

'Well, Logan has put a couple of recent posts up on her Facebook page. The first says that she had broken off her engagement to Jamie Ball. The second, a few days ago, says, "Quoting Henry 2nd. Will no one rid me?"'

'Will no one rid me of this turbulent priest?' Van Dam said.

'You're on the money!'

Van Dam frowned. 'Are you saying the reason for her disappearance is to get away from her fiancé?'

'You're meant to be the expert on the human psyche, Dr Van Dam. The lady changes her mind and her fellow doesn't accept it. Perhaps the smart thing is to disappear. Lie low for a bit. Let him calm down.'

Jacob Van Dam suddenly found his entire thought process in a tangle of confusion. Was this true, had Logan engineered her disappearance to get away from her fiancé? But before going down this route, he needed to be sure this man was real, and not, as he had originally feared, delusional or a fantasist. 'How well do you know this man who you claim has taken my niece, Dr Hunter?'

'Well, there's a difficult question. How well do you know any of your patients, I wonder? You will only ever know what they let you know. How well do we really know ourselves? Do you know yourself? I doubt I know myself. Remove my face and my name, and I doubt I would recognize myself if people were talking about me. How about you?'

'I don't think this is an appropriate time for philosophical discussions, Dr Hunter. My niece is missing, and there are people who believe her life is in danger. If you have information to the contrary, I would really appreciate you sharing that with me.'

'You sound very sceptical, Doctor.'

'I don't like people who play games with me. It's six o'clock on a Friday evening. I'm tired and I want to go home.'

'I expect Logan would like to go home, too.'

'You've just told me she might have run away.'

'And I told you earlier today that I'm the only person who may be able to save her life.'

The psychiatrist took his time before answering. All his years in medical practice had not prepared him for someone as odd as this character. Was Hunter the man who had taken Logan? Was he actually a friend or associate of the man who had taken her? Or was the real reason for Logan's disappearance, as he had suggested, altogether less sinister than everyone thought?

'All right,' he said. 'If Logan has run away to get away from her fiancé, what does she do next?'

'I wouldn't want to speculate on that. This is what I'm saying.'

There was something in the man's voice that deeply perturbed Van Dam. It was as if he was gloating about something. Some superior knowledge that he held. He decided to push him.

'Would you say that you know my niece quite well, Dr Hunter?'

'I wouldn't say so.'

'But you know her?'

There was a long silence. Van Dam sensed the dynamics had changed. He needed to get to a conclusion – and he was still far from one at this moment. He decided to push further. 'There is very little you have told me, Dr Hunter, that gives me any indication that you know Logan or anyone associated with her. It's my view that you are a very disturbed man, trying to fulfil some deep inadequacy. So I'd appreciate it if you would either tell me something significant about Logan Somerville, or else crawl back into your hole and go pick on someone more gullible.'

'You really want to blow the opportunity to save your niece's life?'

'Not at all. But I don't believe you are the man who can save her. Answer the question I just put to you. Tell me something significant about Logan that will enable me to believe you.'

'OK, Dr Van Dam. Listen up. I'm going to tell you something. If you go to the police about me, I'll never speak to you again and no one will ever see her alive again. So just keep this to yourself. Your niece has a mark on her right thigh.'

'Does she? What kind of a mark?'

'Three words, two of them abbreviated.'

'What do they say?'

'They say, "U R DEAD".'

30

At 6.15 p.m., carrying a mug of coffee, Roy Grace left his office, and made his way through the security door and along the labyrinth of corridors, past the Major Incident suite – MIR-1 – which his Operation Haywain was sharing with Glenn Branson's Operation Mona Lisa, the body from the Lagoon. As was the Sussex CID tradition, still maintained although they were now merged with Surrey, some wag on each team had stuck pictures up on the inside of the door. His operation was denoted by a photograph, torn from a magazine, of a reproduction of Constable's *Haywain* painting as might have been interpreted by Banksy, with a supermarket trolley sticking out of the stream, and Glenn Branson's by a cartoon of a smiling Mona Lisa holding an iPad.

Suddenly he heard a familiar voice behind him, sounding distraught. 'Chief, can I have a quick word?'

He stopped and turned to see the forlorn figure of Norman Potting, the fifty-five-year-old Detective Sergeant's comb-over looking even more ragged than usual, dressed in a shabby tweed jacket, crumpled shirt, tie askew, and badly creased grey trousers.

'Sure, Norman,' he said with a kindly voice. 'How are you bearing up?'

'It's hard, especially when I'm here in Sussex House.'

'Are you sure you're up to it?'

'I've got to keep busy, chief. I can't just sit at home.'

On Monday was the funeral of Potting's fiancée, Bella Moy, who had died bravely rescuing a child, then a dog, in a house fire in Brighton several weeks earlier. 'I understand, Norman.'

'There's something else – I need your opinion.'

'Yes?'

Three members of his team filed past them, nodding at Grace respectfully, and one of them patted Norman on the shoulder. When they were gone, Potting said, 'It's about my prostate cancer. I have to make some decisions – now – you know – now that keeping my winky action's not so important any more. I've got all the options from the medics – I'd appreciate the chance to sit down with you and go through them – I don't have anyone else I can talk to whose opinion I would respect.'

'Do you want to do it next week, sometime after the funeral, Norman? Or is it more urgent?'

'Next week would be fine, Roy, thank you.'

Tears welled in Potting's eyes, and he walked on, hastily.

Grace stood for some moments, watching him with deep sadness. God, people got dealt shitty hands at times. Norman Potting's private life had been a never-ending disaster. He had been through three – or was it four – failed marriages, but just recently had finally found what really seemed to be true love. Only to have it snatched away. And on top of that the poor sod had recently been diagnosed with cancer.

And that cancer was really worrying Grace now. He'd read that trauma could seriously affect people's immune systems. He had heard of several people who had suffered severe traumas in their lives and who, a short while after, had developed aggressive cancers. He hoped so much that Bella's death wouldn't do the same to Norman. Quite apart from the fact that he was a very fine detective, over the years he had known him he had developed a soft spot for the man.

He switched his mind back to the immediate and seriously pressing task of finding Logan Somerville. As he walked along the corridor towards the conference room of the Major Crime suite, following Potting, he glanced at one of the flow charts that were pinned on the row of red noticeboards lining the walls. The charts were there to serve as a reminder to Senior Investigating Officers, and their team members, of the procedures and protocols of major crime investigations.

Most of the time everyone strode past them, barely noticing them. But, every now and then, Grace liked to stop and reread them. It was all too easy to get complacent and that's when you made mistakes.

He stared up now at the 'Murder Investigation Model' with all its flow charts. Then up at the 'Fast Track Menu'. He was looking for one that related to mispers. He didn't find a specific one but cast his eye down 'Standard Analytics':

1. *Victim Association*
2. *Sequence of events*
3. *Timelines on suspects*
4. *Case comparison*

He stopped at that, and thought hard for some moments. *Case Comparison.* Then he read on.

5. *Mapping*
6. *Scene assessment*
7. *House-to-house*

When he had finished the entire list, he made his way through to the conference room. He had decided to hold the briefing here, partly to contain the large number of team members he had assembled, and partly not to disturb Glenn Branson and his team. Although he had a feeling – which he could not explain or rationalize at the moment – that the two enquiries might not be as disconnected as the three-decade span between them suggested.

Most of the twenty-five members of his team were already seated around the large rectangular table when he entered the conference room. Several whiteboards, brought along from MIR-1, were up on easels. On one were two photographs of Logan Somerville, one just of her, the other with her fiancé, on a beach.

There were also two CSI photographs of a very dark footprint. The first was of the whole print, the second a close-up showing a distinctive zigzag tread pattern.

On another board was an association chart, with representative male and female figures, labelled *Logan Somerville* and *Jamie Ball*. On the third was a timeline chart.

Grace took his place at the far end of the table, with his back to a row of blue screens bearing the Sussex Police crest, nodded at several of his regular members and welcomed the latest member of his team, a stocky forty-five-year-old DS with whom he had worked before,

Kevin Taylor, who had just served a two-year stint away from Major Crime on Professional Standards.

He stared down at the notes his Management Support Assistant, Tish Hannington, had prepared. He waited until 6.30 p.m., when the rest of the team had arrived and seated themselves, then he began. 'This is the second briefing of Operation Haywain, the investigation into the disappearance of Logan Somerville. According to her fiancé – or as we have subsequently learned, her former fiancé, Jamie Ball – Logan has been missing since around 5.30 p.m. yesterday evening. It is still too early to conclude that she has been abducted – although the evidence points that way. Ball may be an unreliable witness. Both her best friend and her mother have informed us that although Logan broke off their engagement, as we've seen ourselves from her Facebook post, Ball was reluctant to accept this. Whatever the truth, we have grave concerns for her safety, and I am unhappy that over twenty-four hours have now elapsed without any word from her. It is unlikely that she has been kidnapped – her family aren't well off and I would have expected to have received a ransom note or some demand or communication by now. So abduction, quite possibly sexually motivated, is the most likely scenario.'

He paused and sipped his coffee. 'I want to make one observation at this point, which may or may not have any relevance. Logan Somerville is twenty-four years old. As you can see from her photographs, she has long brown hair. Two weeks ago another young woman in West Sussex, Emma Johnson, a regular misper, disappeared again. She is twenty-one years old, and the reason I am mentioning her is that she is of similar age and appearance, with an almost identical hairstyle. This may not take us anywhere, but there is an historic pattern of women being abducted who have similar looks. The victims of American serial rapist and killer Ted Bundy, who was executed in 1989, all looked similar, with identical hairstyles. I was at the post-mortem of the victim found at Hove Lagoon last night, and it seems she also had long brown hair. I'm not jumping to any conclusions here, but I want a search done. Start with Sussex and then the south-east for outstanding mispers with a similar appearance, age and hairstyle to Logan Somerville. Begin with the last twelve months, and then back five years.'

He turned to the researcher, Annalise Vineer. 'I'm giving you that as an action, Annalise.'

It was a huge task. 'Yes, sir.'

Then he turned to DS Batchelor. 'Guy, Glenn Branson is the SIO on the case of the skeletal remains of a young woman found at Hove Lagoon yesterday. I want you to liaise with Glenn and see if we can eliminate this woman from any connection with our current enquiry.'

'What makes you think there might be a connection, boss?'

'Little more than a hunch at the moment, Guy. It would be helpful if you could report back on her identity as soon as it is known.' Then he turned to Potting, mindful of the man's current mental state, but wanting to give him a task he could get his teeth into and his head around as a distraction from his current woes. 'Norman, I want you as an action to get me full details on every reported female misper, once Annalise has given you the names. Start with those in the age group sixteen to forty-five.'

Suddenly the *James Bond* theme played. Norman Potting dug a hand into his pocket and pulled out the phone. He gave Grace an apologetic nod, stood up and stepped away. Moments later he returned. 'Sorry about that, guv. The undertaker – about the music for Monday.'

There was a respectful silence. Then Potting sat back down, seemingly consumed by his inner thoughts.

Grace waited several moments, as Potting settled, before moving on to DC Jane Wellings, who had been allocated the CCTV work. 'Have you come up with any more on the Volvo from CCTV and ANPR, Jane?'

'We're still analysing the footage to see if we can find a match for that time and area.'

The Crime Scene Manager, John Morgan, then pointed at the two photographs of footprints on the whiteboard. 'The two images are the same footprint, one showing it in entirety, the other showing the detail of the tread pattern. I've sent copies to the National Footwear Reference Collection, who should be able to give us the manufacturer.'

'And size?' asked DS Exton.

'We might get that from the manufacturer,' Roy Grace replied. 'That zigzag pattern – there's probably a different number of them on each shoe sole, according to the size.'

'Are you going to bring in the forensic gait analyst again?' DS Batchelor asked. 'Haydn Kelly?'

Grace nodded. 'I've emailed the pictures to Kelly to ask him if he thinks he can get anything from the footprint.'

'Do we have enough to question this Jamie Ball character again, boss?' DS Jon Exton asked.

'We do. And I'm still not happy with him. But I'm not convinced he's the offender. The initial search of Logan's social networking sites hasn't taken us any further. His alibi is that he was driving down the M23, close to Gatwick Airport, when Logan phoned him. We know from the phone company's records that a call to her fiancé's number was made from Logan's phone, and it was made in the vicinity of their apartment building. We also know that Ball's phone was answered in the geographic location where he claims to have been. But we cannot be sure at this point that it was Logan Somerville who made the call – we only have Ball's word on that. And we only have his word that it was he who answered it and spoke to her.' As he looked around the faces of his enquiry team, he felt a sudden deep pang of sadness at the absence of DS Bella Moy. And the absence of the familiar rattle of the box of Maltesers which always sat in front of her, and which she ate constantly.

'You're speculating that Ball may have orchestrated this whole thing?' Guy Batchelor asked. 'That whoever took Logan Somerville made the call – let's for a moment say it was Jamie Ball – and it was an accomplice who answered at the other end, driving Ball's car down the exact route Ball would have driven home from work himself?'

'It's one hypothesis,' Grace said. 'It's most unlikely but still needs to be checked out. I'm going to speak to one of our source handlers to see if there is any word out on the street about Ball. People who are jilted can get very angry. Let's see if he's been out shopping around for a hitman. Ideally, we want to eliminate him from the enquiry if he is not involved.'

The youngest member of the team, DC Jack Alexander, raised a hand. 'Sir, what about getting a warrant and searching the couple's flat again? If we found a shoe with a matching tread pattern, that would put Jamie Ball at the scene, wouldn't it?'

Grace smiled back at him. He'd made similarly naive deductions in his early days. 'Not quite sure what that would tell us, Jack, since he lives there.'

There was a titter of laughter, and the young Detective Constable's face turned the colour of beetroot. But he persevered, and said, 'Yes, but it would still be interesting if we find one of Ball's shoes in the flat had made the fresh mark in the sludge.'

Grace nodded. 'Well recovered, Jack – and also to make sure it doesn't belong to any of our officers!'

DS Tanja Cale, a glamorous new addition to his regulars, who had been brought in to temporarily replace Bella Moy, raised her hand. Cale had been tasked with running the outside enquiry team. 'Sir,' she said, 'we have something that may be of interest. A PCSO tipped us off that an elderly lady in Chesham Avenue – five houses along from the entrance to the Chesham Gate underground car park – has a police CCTV camera installed, looking down at the street. She's been having trouble with kids in the area – I gather she shouted at them a few months ago for throwing litter in the street. Since then they've been making her life a misery by daubing her car with graffiti, as well as on one occasion leaving a dead cat in her front garden with a threatening note attached.'

'Was the camera on last night?'

'Yes,' she said. 'It's aimed low, principally at her little front garden and the pavement beyond. But it picked up the bottom half of a car just after 5.30 p.m. yesterday, travelling at high speed. The image is in black and white, so we're not able to get the colour, but it's a dark colour and two Traffic officers have identified it as an old model Volvo estate, about ten years old.'

'Any view of the licence plate?'

'No,' she said, 'unfortunately not.'

Grace felt a beat of excitement at this development, confirmation of a car seen leaving at speed. 'Good work. OK, I'm giving you an action – get a list of every Volvo estate between five and fifteen years old that's owned by a Brighton resident. And see what similar cars CCTV might have picked up in the Brighton area an hour either side of this time.'

'Yes, sir,' she said.

During the course of the next twenty minutes, Grace ran through the lines of enquiry. When he had finished it was 7.05 p.m. Just over twenty-five hours since Logan had disappeared.

Statistics would have her already dead by now. But for Grace, that thought wasn't an option. He had to believe she was still alive, and he had to find her whilst she still was alive. Quite apart from his own determination, he had pressure from the ACC, and from the Police and Crime Commissioner, Nicola Roigard. And soon, after the impending retirement of the Chief Constable, Tom Martinson, which was an open secret, he would be having a new Chief putting pressure on him, as well.

Not to mention all the people with vested interests in this city, such as the head of Visit Brighton, the tourist board, who would be wanting a quick and conclusive result – and not to see this beautiful seaside resort yet again splashed across the national newspapers and television screens for another grim crime. They wanted Logan Somerville back, at all costs.

Alive.

So did he. He'd never in all his life been a defeatist, but the odds of finding her alive, he knew, were not good.

31

Jamie Ball sat on one of the sofas, laptop open, glass of red wine in his hand, alternating between his Facebook page and staring at the constantly changing images on the digital photo frame. There were a few landscapes, a picture of Logan's parents' dog, a happy-looking black labradoodle, and a photograph taken at their engagement party of both sets of parents and siblings, but most of the pictures were of Logan and himself.

He topped the glass up with a shaking hand. His tiredness was really starting to kick in, but instead of calming him, the alcohol seemed to be having the reverse effect, making him increasingly jittery, as if it were strong coffee, shrinking his scalp so tightly around his skull that pains were shooting down it. His eyes were raw and gritty and he could barely focus. Unconsciously he drummed the fingers of his left hand continuously on the coffee table.

His parents had invited him over, but he didn't want to sit in their gloomy house. Logan's parents and her sister and brother had all been very slightly cold and remote to him – not cold enough to sound actively hostile, but enough to hint to him that they were suspicious. A couple of his mates, concerned for him, had invited him out for company to the Coach House in Middle Street for the evening. It was a pub he had been to many times in the past – in happier days – with Logan. But for now he preferred to sit here, alone. He didn't want any company at this moment.

He refreshed the Facebook page, where late last night he had posted the message, 'Please help me find my missing beautiful fiancée, Logan', beneath a row of photographs of her. He saw that another fifteen 'likes' had come in during the past half hour, as well as six new friend requests, in response to his post.

'Good,' he said, suddenly, to no one.

Then his phone rang. He jumped up and grabbed the receiver with his hand shaking so much it dropped and fell to the wooden floor, a piece of the casing breaking off. He knelt and picked it up.

'I wonder if I could please speak to Mr James Ball?' It was the voice of an elderly man, courteous but quite firm.

Few people called him James – he had been Jamie for as long as he could remember.

'Yes, speaking, who is this?' He'd already had several crank calls. One from a medium telling him she'd had a vision of Logan in the hold of a ship loaded with timber. Another from someone claiming to be a private detective, demanding one thousand pounds up front, but guaranteeing to find her. Yep, right.

'I'm Logan's uncle – my name is Jacob Van Dam. She may have mentioned me?'

'Ah, yes,' he replied. 'Yes, she has.' She had indeed mentioned her uncle, the psychiatrist, to him on many occasions, although she'd told Jamie she had not seen him for several years. He was the one famous member of her family.

'I'm going to ask you a rather personal question about Logan, James, but I have a good reason for this, so please bear with me.'

Ball frowned. Was this shrink about to start playing some clever mind games with him? 'OK,' he said, guardedly.

'Does Logan have a mark or words – maybe a tattoo – anywhere on her body?'

He was silent for some moments, wondering where this was going. 'A tattoo?'

'Yes. A mark or tattoo.'

'No, she doesn't.'

'Are you absolutely certain? Perhaps on her right thigh?'

'Yes, I am sure, there's nothing there.'

'What about any writing or script?'

'No, she doesn't have. Why are you asking, Mr Van Dam?'

'I have a reason.'

'No, she has no tattoo. OK?' The man's insistent voice was irritating him, and making him feel even edgier.

'You've been very helpful, I'm sorry to have troubled you. Thank you.'

Ball stared into the receiver as the call ended. Into the tiny holes in the mouthpiece. What was that all about, he wondered?

Jacob Van Dam sat for a long time at his desk, in silence, deep in thought. In his opinion, Ball's reaction had been that of someone distraught because his loved one was missing.

Nevertheless, he had the feeling he was hiding something. But what?

32

After the briefing, Roy Grace went back to his office, deep in thought, needing some quiet time to reflect. On Monday he had to speak at Bella's funeral, which was going to be emotional, he knew. One of the hardest things he'd ever had to do. Then on Tuesday, the removals company were due to be delivering all the packing cases, both to Cleo's house and to his own, in advance of their move the following Friday. Somehow he was going to have to find the time to be at home to help Cleo pack everything up. He was also going to have to supervise the packing of all his belongings in his own house, near the seafront – very close to the Lagoon – which he had shared with Sandy prior to her disappearance.

But all he could think of was Logan Somerville. Her long brown hair. And Emma Johnson, who was missing and had a similar hair-style. Was there a possible link with the body of the woman at the Lagoon – with the strands of long brown hair too?

He tried to dismiss that. He didn't want any links. A solo murder victim was a tragedy, but a one-off nonetheless. The victim of a sexual assault, a revenge attack, a random attack by someone mentally ill, a domestic dispute, a robbery or a jealous lover. These were some of the reasons people killed – and got killed. Single, brutal, final acts.

Linked murders could be game changers. Three or more, in different locations and with time between them, and you had a serial killer by definition. They hadn't had one in this city for a very long time, not in all of his career, to date – at least that the police had heard about.

Earlier he'd told Cleo there was no way he'd be home early tonight, even though she'd tried to tempt him by telling him she'd been planning some of his favourite dishes, a prawn and avocado cocktail, then grilled Dover sole. He was feeling hungry, and would have dearly loved to have headed straight back – to see Noah, have a couple of glasses of wine and a nice meal, and an evening doing what he loved most, spending time with Cleo.

His phone rang.

He answered instantly. It was Glenn Branson. 'All right?' the DI said.

'Not great. You?'

'Well, actually, I've got a bit of a development. Might be nothing – but I wanted to run it by you.'

'Tell me?'

'Fancy a drink? I kind of need one. I'm going off duty.'

'Friday night?' Grace said. 'So you don't have a hot date with that *Argus* reporter – what's her name – Siobhan Sheldrake?'

'Haha, very funny.'

'I need one, too. Have to make it quick and it'll have to be a soft one. Black Lion?'

'Fifteen?'

'Give me three quarters of an hour, I need to swing by my house to pick up some stuff I'm taking to a charity shop.'

'Must be tough for you,' Branson said.

'Yes,' Grace replied. 'Sad, too.'

'But you've moved on now. You're happy, you're in a good place. Life's started all over for you, and I'm happy. I'm really happy.'

'Thanks, mate, so am I.'

Yet as he hung up, Roy Grace had a heavy heart. He went down to the car park and headed into Hove in Cleo's car – she was now driving his Alfa which had been fitted with a baby seat. He had so much to look forward to, he knew, but clearing his old home, bit by bit, was not something he was enjoying.

Ten minutes later he turned off New Church Road, and drove down the street, towards Kingsway and the seafront, where he and Sandy had once been so happy. Christmas lights shone through the windows of the houses on either side of the road, until he reached his own house, a 1930s mock-Tudor semi, on the right, near the bottom, which sat in darkness.

He pulled up onto the drive in front of the garage door. Beyond it sat Sandy's car, coated in dust, where it had been for the past decade awaiting her return. He unlocked the front door of the house. It had been over a week since he was last here, and as he went in he had to push the door hard through the mountain of junk mail and bills and local takeaway menus that had poured through the letter box in his absence.

He switched on the lights, went into the kitchen and pulled out a roll of black bin liners from under the sink, then carried them upstairs into their bedroom, which was still largely unchanged. He opened Sandy's wardrobe, and began to pull out her clothes and stuff them into a bag until it was full. He could smell her scent, faintly, through the mustiness – or could he? Memories flooded back.

He filled one bag, and then a second, all kinds of thoughts of the past being triggered. Empty coat hangers clattered on the rail. He knelt and filled a third bag with her shoes, remembering to go into the downstairs cloakroom and take her coats off the hooks. Then he stood up and looked around the bedroom. There was a chaise longue at the end of the bed, which they had bought years ago, in terrible condition, from an auction room in Lewes, and had re-covered in a modern, black and white pattern which Sandy had selected. On it sat the battered, furry toy stoat she had had since childhood. He put that in the bag, too, then took it out again and placed it back on the chaise longue. He hadn't the heart to give it away. Yet, at the same time, he could hardly take it to their new home.

Shit, this was hard.

What if?

If she ever returned? And wanted it?

And suddenly, he realized, as he had so many times over the past years, he could not even remember her face any more. He walked across to her walnut dressing table, and stared down at the framed photograph which sat between her bottles of perfumes.

It had been taken in the restaurant of a gorgeous hotel near Oxford, the Bear at Woodstock, where they had celebrated their wedding anniversary after he had attended a conference on DNA fingerprinting, a short while before she disappeared. He was in a suit and tie, Sandy, in an evening dress, beaming her constant irrepressible grin at a waiter they had asked to take the picture.

He stared at her crystal-clear blue eyes, the colour of the sky. It shocked him to look at her, realizing just how far she had faded into his past. He couldn't give that away, he knew, nor could he throw it away. He would have to pack it in a suitcase and stick it away, somewhere, up in the loft of his new home.

Then he looked at the stack of books, some on her bedside table and others neatly arranged on the mantelpiece above the fireplace that had been boarded over by previous owners, but which Sandy had opened up again, and occasionally lit, because she thought it was romantic.

He picked up one of the books, Anita Brookner's *Hotel Du Lac*, which she had asked him to buy from her Christmas list. He opened it up and read the inscription.

To my darling Sandy. On our fourth Christmas.

To the love of my life. XXXXX.

Whatever happened to you? God, where are you now? Resting in peace, I hope.

He kissed the book then dropped it, along with all the others, into a fresh bin bag.

33

Stationsschwester Anette Lippert was seventy-five minutes into the night shift in the Intensive Care Unit at the hospital where she had trained and spent most of her career to date. The Klinikum München Schwabing was, in her view deservedly, reputed to have one of the finest neurological departments in Germany with a nurse to every patient in the ICU.

As the senior staff nurse she normally took the morning shift, because that was when most of the transfers and operations took place, but with an epidemic of flu sweeping the city of Munich they were currently several nurses down and she was having to work around the clock some days to help cover.

The night shift was long and tedious, during which little tended to happen. The unit was kept at a carefully regulated twenty-four degrees Celsius, which sometimes felt stiflingly warm – although the patients who occupied the fifteen beds there never complained. Many of them never spoke. One exception was the comatose, unidentified woman in bed 12, who made occasional confused, sporadic utterings.

Stopping to check on each patient in turn, and getting an update from their charge nurse, accompanied by two doctors, Lippert reached bed 12. The occupant was a woman in her mid to late thirties, with short brown hair, her face heavily bandaged. She had been semi-comatose since being hit by a taxi a month ago whilst crossing Widenmayerstrasse, the busy main road that ran through one of the city of Munich's smartest districts, separating it from the river Isar.

She had been admitted here as *Unbekannte Frau*.

An eyewitness to the accident had told the police, with disgust, that as she had lain in the road, some helmeted bastard on a motorcycle had pulled up, snatched her handbag from the road and accelerated off.

For forty-eight hours, no one had any idea who she was. Then a young boy, back from football camp, in tears because his mama had not collected him on his return from his trip, had been brought in here by the police and identified her as his mother, Frau Lohmann. Yet, despite this, she remained something of an enigma.

It seemed, so the police had informed the hospital, that Frau Lohmann had gone to some considerable lengths to erase her past. A search of her apartment, her computer and her mobile phone had revealed no clues as to who she really was. It appeared that she had at least two faked identities, including forged passports and social insurance numbers. Her credit cards were in her assumed names. She had over three million euros on deposit in a Munich bank, under one of these names, and had managed to open that account some nine years earlier by getting through its money-laundering protocols with her false documentation.

Interpol would take several weeks before they had results – if any – of fingerprint and DNA tests. But because of the police interest in her, she was due to be moved into one of the private rooms at the side of the ward as soon as one became vacant.

Lippert stared at her now. Her eyes were closed, as they had been since she had first arrived here. Her breathing was controlled by a ventilator, and she was catheterized. Fluids containing the various nutrients that kept her alive were steadily pumped into her through the dual lumen central line catheter that protruded from her upper chest.

Who are you really? Anette Lippert wondered. *Where were you heading to when you were hit by that taxi? Where had you come from? What have you been running away from?*

The police were doing all they could. She had various aliases, they had told the hospital. At some point in her life, before her son was born, she had changed her name, at least twice. But they could not give any reason why. Perhaps to escape from a nightmare relationship? A criminal past? A terrorist? The police were continuing with their investigations.

Meanwhile, Frau Lohmann continued to sleep. Kept alive by the tubes cannulated into her body.

And Anette Lippert continued to stare down at her, with a feeling of deep sadness. *Someone loved you, once. You have a son. Come back to us. Wake up! Your son needs you.*

Occasionally Frau Lohmann would take a sharp intake of breath. But her eyes would remain closed.

Always closed.

There were no relatives – at least, none that her son, Bruno, knew of. He was now staying with one of his friends, whose parents brought him frequently to visit.

What the hell is locked in your mind? Lippert wondered. *How do we unlock it?*

On the fourth round of her shift, shortly after midnight, when Anette Lippert was once again staring down at her, the woman suddenly, and very briefly, opened her eyes.

'Tell him I forgive him,' she said, then closed them again.

'Tell who?'

But all she got back was the steady *puff-hiss-puff-hiss* of the ventilator, and the *beep-beep-beep-beep* from the monitors.

Locked inside her skull, Sandy heard their voices. She understood what they were saying. But she felt like she was swimming underwater at the deep end of a pool. She could not talk back to them.

'Tell who?' Lippert pressed.

But she was gone again. Gone into some deep, inaccessible recess of her brain.

Lippert lingered for some while, then moved on to the next bed.

34

The Black Lion pub in Patcham had a background, which Roy Grace liked – more than he actually liked the pub itself. In 1976 Barbara Gaul, wife of a shady property developer she was in the middle of divorcing, was shot in the Black Lion's car park, and subsequently died from her wounds. It became one of the most notorious cases in all of Brighton's dark history, with links to the Krays, the famous London gangster family, and to two of the biggest sex scandals of post-war Britain, the Profumo and Lambton affairs.

A shame, Grace thought, that such a colourful but tragic background could not be better reflected in the themed interior of the pub, for a long time now part of the Harvester chain – bright and corporate. But it was convenient for Sussex House.

He sat in a booth in a quiet corner, while Glenn Branson stood at the crowded bar, towering head and shoulders over most of the figures there. Grace was on the phone to Cleo, trying to plan a combined house-warming and New Year's Eve party at their new house. As he spoke to her he glanced down at the thick buff envelope Branson had left on the table.

'I think we should have the same yummy Ridgeview sparkling wine we had at our wedding – and nice to support a local producer.'

'Yes, great thinking! We'd better order fast. How many people are you thinking of?' he asked.

'Oh my God!' Cleo suddenly said, with laughter in her voice.

'What?'

'Noah's just put his hand in Humphrey's bowl and taken some food out! Humphrey's just standing there. Amazing! Hang on, I'd better rescue your son!'

'Great!' he said. 'We can save a fortune if we wean him on dog food!'

'Yes, good idea,' she said, sounding distracted. 'Text me when you're leaving, and I'll get your dinner ready.'

'So long as it's not from the dog's bowl!'

'That, Detective Superintendent Grace, will depend on how late you are.'

He grinned. 'I love you.'

'Love you,' she said but a little more coldly than usual. Again he felt the slight distance in her tone.

'Look, I know I'm not being much help at the moment. I'm sorry.'

'I get it, Roy,' she replied. 'I know it's not easy for either of us.'

Grace looked up to see Glenn holding their drinks. He blushed and said to Cleo, 'Have to go!' He blew her a kiss, but did not get one back.

Branson sat down, shaking his head. 'You'll get over it, mate, one day.' He handed Grace a Diet Coke, then sipped the white, creamy head of his Guinness.

'I don't think so,' Grace replied.

'You will, trust me.'

'You're such a cynic.'

'Yeah,' Branson said. Then gave a sad shrug.

'So you and that *Argus* reporter? Siobhan Sheldrake?'

Branson suddenly looked coy. 'What about her?'

'You fancy her, don't you?'

'Rubbish!'

'I've known you too long.' Grace sipped his drink. 'You play with fire sometimes. I could see you were attracted to that Red Westwood on our last case. Just be careful, mate. I'd love to see you with a nice lady but—'

'But?'

'Police and the press make a dangerous combination.'

Branson shrugged. 'I'm having a drink with her tomorrow evening.' He shrugged again. 'She's cool. She and I go back a while, actually – before she joined the *Argus*. We were just good friends – then after Ari died we became closer, but we've been keeping it low key.'

Grace gave him a quizzical look. 'Just remember that old nautical expression, "Loose lips sink ships".'

'Ever see that fantastic submarine movie, *Das Boot*?'

Grace nodded. 'I seem to remember it sank.'

Branson grinned. 'Yeah? That's your memory? I think your brain's a bit addled these days.'

'Just make sure yours isn't in your dick.' He gave him a cautioning look. 'Be careful with Siobhan Sheldrake.'

'I'll wear protection.'

Grace smiled and shook his head. 'So, you've dragged me away from my investigation because you have a development – tell me?'

'You came to the mortuary earlier – remember that, or is it too long ago for your tired old brain?'

'Very funny!'

'Those words on the dead woman's skull?'

'U R DEAD?'

'Yeah.' The Detective Inspector tapped the bulky envelope on the table. 'Take a look at this.'

'Where's it from?'

'Lucy Sibun dated the age of the dead woman at around twenty years old, and estimated she died approximately thirty years ago. Yeah?'

'So I understand.'

'I had my researchers check the files on all mispers and cold cases five years either side of that date estimate, on females of that approximate age. This is what they found. Fill your boots.' He took a large gulp of his drink.

'I'm impressed, you've been moving fast.'

'On it like a car bonnet, mate.'

'Like a what?' Grace looked at his friend quizzically, then picked up the unsealed envelope, which had a musty smell, and pulled out the contents. It contained a batch of documents, with several photographs at the back, held together by two large elastic bands. Handwritten in black marker pen on the outside was *Operation Yorker*.

The first document was a Home Office pathologist's report, headed CATHERINE (KATY) JANE MARIE WESTERHAM. Aged nineteen, she was an English Literature student at Sussex University, residing in Elm Grove, Brighton. She had been reported missing in December

1984, and the young woman's remains had been found in Ashdown Forest in April 1985 by a man walking his dog.

Roy Grace reflected, ironically, just how big a debt homicide detectives around the globe owed to people walking their dogs. He'd often thought, if he had the time, of one day doing some research on the percentage of bodies discovered in this manner.

He speed-read through the document. The body was decomposed at the time it was found, with some bones missing, presumed taken by animals. Fragments of lung tissue and the findings of the pathologist indicated death had been by asphyxiation. But there was insufficient material remaining to provide a conclusive cause of death.

Grace then removed the photographs from the paperclip holding them. The first one was a portrait photograph of an attractive girl with long brown hair, unrecognizable from the remains. He stared hard at it for some moments. There was a striking resemblance, more in the hair than anything else, but also the face itself, to Emma Johnson. And she was a dead ringer for Logan Somerville, who had disappeared yesterday.

He removed several more photographs, which showed her entire decomposed body, in situ, each with a ruler in the frame. Then various close-ups of her skull, her rib cage, and other bones that remained.

Then he pulled out the last photo and froze.

It was again a close-up, marked 'forehead'. The pathologist's ruler, included in the picture, showed the length, of just over two inches, of what looked like tattooed letters on a fragment of flesh.

They were considerably more distinct than on the remains that had been discovered at Hove Lagoon. But they read the same:

U R DEAD

35

'You're very quiet tonight, darling,' Jacob Van Dam's elegantly dressed wife, Rachel, said. Even when they dined alone they always dressed smartly. It was something they had done all their married life, to make it more of an occasion, and the time in the day when they caught up with each other.

The psychiatrist sat at the far end of the oval mahogany dining table, in the smart dining room of their Regent's Park mansion, cradling his crystal goblet of claret, staring pensively at the light reflecting in its facets from the chandelier above. The grilled lamb cutlets on his bone-china plate lay untouched and growing cold, along with the petits pois and gratin potatoes Rachel had lovingly prepared.

'Yes, well,' he said pensively. 'It's been an interesting day.'

'Would you like to share it with me?' Then after some moments, she said, 'Dreadful, the news about Logan, I just can't believe it. No one has any idea where she might be. The police are doing everything they can, apparently. I spoke to Tina myself, earlier, she's in a terrible mess. She said the police don't think it's kidnap, because there's been no ransom demand – they say it's more likely she's been abducted. Apparently they've said if someone her age is abducted it is likely to be a sex offender – and the chances of her being alive lessen the longer she's not found. I feel helpless.'

He barely heard her words he was so consumed by his thoughts about Dr Harrison Hunter.

Whoever Dr Harrison Hunter really was.

U R DEAD

The man had lied to him. His niece had no such tattoo – no tattoos at all. She had been missing, possibly abducted, since yesterday evening. So what was the connection with this man and Logan?

The proper course of action would be to call the police. But Hunter's threat had felt very real. The only thing that mattered now was finding Logan and making sure she was safe. He needed the man to come back, then he would find a way of ensnaring him. Getting the truth out of him. But how long did he have? The rest of tonight? The weekend?

What if Harrison Hunter was just delusional? Someone who had read the *Argus*, and was imagining his involvement?

And had fallen at the first hurdle. *U R DEAD*. Logan had no tattoos.

He sipped some more wine, then sliced into the first cutlet. It was pink in the centre, just how he liked it. 'Beautifully cooked, my dear,' he said.

She gave him one of her penetrating stares. 'Is it something you can tell me about?' she asked.

'Not really,' he replied. 'No.'

'It is so terrible. I mean, what on earth can have happened to her? She'd broken off her engagement – do you think her boyfriend might be behind this? Or involved in some way?'

He continued to stare at the light dancing off the glass. Then he dipped his fork, with a morsel of cutlet, into the mint jelly on the side of his plate and began to chew. When he had swallowed he said, 'Rachel, have you ever in your life had to make a decision that you don't feel equipped to make?'

'You're talking in riddles again, my love. Like you so often do.'

'I apologize. This is delicious, by the way.'

'Good.'

He dabbed his lips with the linen napkin. 'Patient confidentiality.' He picked up his glass and stared, forlornly, at it. 'That's the decision.'

'What kind of a decision?' she prompted.

'Well, imagine for a moment you are me, in my office. A new patient comes in, who confesses to killing people. My assessment is that he's delusional. But what if I'm wrong and he has killed? I may have to report this to the police. But if it's merely his fantasy, then I would be failing in my duty of care if I report him. He will never again talk openly with confidence to anyone. He won't trust anyone again.'

'Is that what happened to you today?'

'Yes.'

'Does this have anything to do with Logan? Was he telling you he's the man who abducted Logan?'

He sliced another morsel of lamb. 'No, he didn't claim that, he claimed he knew who had taken her.'

'Can you tell me anything about him?'

He chewed slowly, then sipped his wine. 'I can't say too much, but this man told me something that he assured me would be proof of his bona fides. I checked it out after he left – part of the reason I was so late home tonight – and it wasn't correct. Which leads me to believe he is – I'm not sure . . .'

'A fantasist?' his wife prompted.

'That would be the easy conclusion,' Van Dam said. 'I'm foxed.'

'Then you should call the police and tell them your thoughts.'

The psychiatrist sat silently for some moments, then drank another sip of his wine. 'And risk Logan's life?'

'Why would that risk her life?'

'Because this man told me categorically not to go to the police.'

'That's how seriously you take him?'

'Yes.'

'Then somewhere inside that strange brain of yours, that I've never managed to penetrate fully in all the years we've been together, you must believe, deep down, he was telling you the truth.'

Van Dam smiled at his beloved and wise wife. 'Yes, yes I do.'

36

After leaving the pub, Roy Grace returned to Sussex House, sat in his office and began to look again at the file Glenn Branson had brought him. He pulled out a yellowing, black and white A4 printed sheet, headed, 'SUSSEX CRIME INFORMATION – MURDER'.

> At 8.35 a.m., Saturday, 3/4/85 the body of the after-described was found in Ashdown Forest, Sussex. Cause of death undetermined – but believed to be asphyxiation.

He looked again at the photograph of the pretty young woman, with poker-straight long brown hair, freckles and glasses, and wondered where the picture had been taken, because she was staring at the photographer with a warm, almost serene, expression of trust.

He read on down through the sheet.

> The following property is missing from the body.
> 1) Pair of black shoes, size 6, label on sole 'Made in U.K. Real leather. Leather uppers with man-made soles'.
> 2) Bunch of keys with a leather tag bearing the words 'Chandlers of Brighton BMW', containing one BMW key, one Yale-type key and possibly one other key.
> 3) Handbag, contents unknown.

The next sheet of paper looked like a blow-up of an Ordnance Survey map. Up in the top right-hand corner was a circle in red, marking the spot where the body had been found.

He turned to the next item, a faded orange book marked 'MAJOR INCIDENT PROPERTY REGISTER'.

The next was a colour photograph showing a group of men in

gumboots, sweaters and jeans, each holding a long pole, standing in a woodland clearing around a dark shadow. He shook his head.

God, what a difference! Today these same people would have been in oversuits to prevent them from contaminating the crime scene.

The next photograph showed a dark, human-shaped shadow in deep undergrowth.

In the next, he could make out a pair of blue jeans. Then, as he turned to the one after, he took a sharp intake of breath – as he always did when he saw a new dead body.

There was something so terribly sad about murder victims. He couldn't help it, but for a few moments he always felt like a voyeur. As if he had gatecrashed some party that no one, ever, would have invited him to.

And always, he wondered, would he one day be turning up to the bones of his missing wife, Sandy?

The dead had no choice in who turned up at their deposition sites. It fell upon everyone present to be respectful. Even now, seated at his desk, with darkness pressing against the rain-spattered windowpanes, he felt just that, staring at the side-on photograph of the blotchy face, as if stage rouge had been applied, with the eyes missing, pecked away by birds, dark brown hair unkempt and straggly, in what looked like a home-knitted grey pullover.

Who had knitted it, he wondered? Her loving mother? Grand-mother?

The sweater she had been murdered in.

Then another photograph, this time full-face, showing dark, marbled skin, and the empty eye sockets, like she was wearing a balaclava.

God, he thought. *You were at Sussex University. Your dad had lent you his car for the night, because he trusted your driving and didn't want some drunken student driving you home. But you never did come home.*

He phoned a mobile number, thinking it unlikely that Tony Case, the Senior Support Officer, would still be here at this hour on a Friday night, but to his surprise he caught him just as he was leaving. Case said he had been working late, helping to reorganize the Major Incident rooms.

Five minutes later, he followed the stocky figure of Case down into the basement of Sussex House. Case had been a Traffic officer before retiring after thirty years' service, and then rejoining the force as a civilian, as was common among many officers. He was holding a massive bunch of keys in his hand.

They walked along a corridor then stopped outside a steel-barred door. Case riffled through his keys, selected one and opened the door, then switched on the lights. Several dusty, bare bulbs, two of them with spiders' webs, threw a weak light along the length of the vast storeroom, which was racked out on both sides and at the far end with floor-to-ceiling metal shelving, stacked tightly with green plastic crates filled with evidence bags, manila folders and piles of papers.

Roy Grace always felt a strange sensation when he entered this storeroom, as if it were filled with ghosts. He knew it well from the days when he had been put in charge of cold cases – reviewing all the unsolved murders in the county of Sussex, to see if advances in fingerprint technology and DNA could help solve any of them. Sussex Police never closed the file on any unsolved murder. All of these green crates contained material dating back as far as the Second World War, and a few even further back than that. Each of the cases filled as many as twenty or more crates, and he had felt the burden of responsibility for each case that he re-examined, knowing he might well be the last chance the victims had for justice.

He walked along past the hand-written labelled sections. *OPERATION GALBY. OPERATION DULWICH. OPERATION COR-MORANT.* Several of them he knew well. He could even recall the stomach contents of some of the victims, from the last things they had ever eaten or drunk.

Ghosts.

They stopped when they reached the section, with forty-three crates, labelled *OPERATION YORKER*. The unsolved murder of Katy Westerham.

Tony Case looked at him. 'Which ones do you want up in your office, Roy?'

Grace ran his eyes along the crates. Each of them was filled with dusty folders, with a blue and white label, the serial number written in black ink and sealed with a tamper-proof cable tie.

'All of them, please.'

Finally, close to 11.30 p.m., having done all he could that evening on the disappearance of Logan Somerville, Roy Grace went home. Cleo had left a cold platter for him on the table. But she heard him come in and came downstairs to join him.

'Sounds like it's been quite a day,' she said.

Roy Grace smiled thinly across the dining table at her. 'You're right, it has been. One hell of a day. Sorry if I'm not being good company. You're stuck home all day with the baby, and then I arrive and you're looking forward to some conversation, and all I do is sit in silence and brood.'

'So share it with me.'

'I have a very bad feeling about the case I'm on.' He shrugged and reached for the bottle of sparkling water that Cleo had set in the cooler in the middle of the table, and poured some into his glass.

'Operation Haywain?' she prompted.

He nodded.

'Are you worried about Cassian Pewe?'

'Right now he's the least of my problems.' He could have done with a couple of really stiff drinks, but he needed a clear head more than ever at this moment and, of course, he was on call. 'We've had almost every imaginable kind of crime in this city, but so far we've had precious few – if any – of what could be defined as serial killers.'

'What defines one?' Cleo asked.

'Someone who commits three or more murders on separate occasions. We had a young man, back in 1985, who murdered his father, stepmother and stepbrother with a baseball bat, at the Lighthouse Club in Shoreham. But that was all on the same night. It was a multiple homicide but he wasn't a *serial* killer.'

'Do you think you have one now?'

He fell silent, picked up his glass, then set it down. 'I don't know, yet. But it looks like we might have found a murder from thirty years ago. It's too early to tell for sure.'

'Could he still be around?'

He said nothing, thinking.

'Come on, you've got to eat something, darling.'

He looked at his bowl of avocado and prawn, nodded, and picked up his fork. 'Yes, I'm ravenous, thanks.' But he only swallowed one mouthful before lapsing back into his thoughts.

U R DEAD

Thirty years ago. A double killing? More? Was there a third branded victim out there? A fourth? A fifth? Somewhere else in the UK? From all he had studied in the past on serial killers, they tended to operate in big landscape countries, like the US, Australia, Russia, where they could move vast distances without arousing suspicion. But on occasions they didn't follow that pattern.

Time could be a distance, too.

Catherine Westerham, found dead in 1985, was nineteen and had long brown hair with a centre parting. Emma Johnson, who had disappeared two weeks ago, was twenty-one and also had similar features, and long brown hair. Logan Somerville, who was now missing, had long brown hair. Was he just being fanciful?

Unknown Female, whose skeletal remains had been found in Hove Lagoon, and was as yet unidentified, appeared to have had long brown hair.

He realized more and more urgently that he needed to find the Lagoon *Unknown Female*'s identity. Fast.

Thirty years was a long time. But he knew from case histories of serial killers that he had seen presented at the grandly titled International Homicide Investigators Association's Annual Symposium in the US, which he attended most years, that there could be long gaps sometimes. Twenty years was not uncommon. Dennis Rader in Wichita, Kansas, self-styled BTK – Bind, Torture, Kill – had a hiatus of around fifteen years and had been about to strike again when he was finally caught. The end of Rader's first killing spree had started when his first child had been born. Grace had worked on a case in Brighton, a while ago, a serial rapist who took his victims' shoes – he had stopped for many years before starting to offend again. The reason he had stopped was that he had got married.

Thirty years. Was that too long?

37

He called it *hunting*.

The word had a nice ring to it.

The entire city was his hunting ground. In the summer months, dressed in a blazer and wearing his straw hat at a jaunty angle, he would regularly stroll along under the arches, and then along the pier. Next he would ride on the Volks Railway, where in the cramped intimacy of its hard seats he liked to talk to strangers, telling them this was the world's oldest still-running electric train, and boring them with facts about it.

All the time as he hunted, walking along or sitting among the grockles, he was taking surreptitious photographs of those he considered had potential to be a *project*.

Photography had become so much easier these days, thanks to his iPhone camera. His potential *projects* would just see a man making a phone call. They would never know that they would become part of his Hall of Fame. He liked to spend time studying them all. And planning. Pages and pages of notes filling the filing cabinets in his VSP – his Very Secret Place – where he liked to go sometimes to do his planning, because he could think clearly there, away from the distraction of his current projects, and he enjoyed the fact that it was in such a very visible location.

VSP! He liked having a VSP!

The potentials he most studied were those who radiated vulnerability. Everyone was vulnerable at some point in their lives – but some were always vulnerable. These were the people who showed the biggest fear. And he wanted them to be afraid of him. Very seriously afraid. Nothing excited him more than seeing fear. Hearing fear. Touching fear. Feeling fear. Smelling fear. Tasting fear.

He liked to keep his potential *projects* under observation for long periods of time. Months, often. He liked to follow them. Of course, a lot merely went to the station to return to wherever they had come from. Some went to their cars. Those he would lose. But some walked home or took buses. They made his life much easier.

Thursday, Friday and Saturday nights were his favourite times. West Street in Brighton in particular, where it was so easy to be invisible. This gaudy strip of road, which he called 'Chav Central', ran from Brighton's Clock Tower down to the seafront. It was lined with amusement arcades and clubs, and populated with drunken, scantily clad youngsters, and boisterous hen and stag parties often in ridiculous costumes, all under the watchful eye of a massive police presence. In his view it was a sewer of humanity. A cesspit.

He was always ready to rid it of one of its occupants.

Like the one he saw now, wobbling along on her bike, swinging out, with no lights on, into the sparse King's Road traffic.

It was just gone 12.50 a.m.

Her name was Ashleigh Stanford. She was twenty-one years old. He had been keeping an eye on her for six months now. She worked Friday and Saturday nights behind the bar in a pub in the Lanes. When she had finished, she cycled back home to the flat she shared with her boyfriend in a quiet street in Hove, always looking a little bit drunk.

She was studying fashion design at Brighton University.

Ashleigh Stanford was, it turned out from his research, a distant but direct descendant of the dynastic landowning family, whose ancestors dated back to the seventeenth century and had at one time owned huge tracts of land around what was then called Brighthelm-stone. He liked her historic connection to his city.

But there was something that he liked much more about her. Oh yes.

Ashleigh Stanford was perfect!

He started the engine, glanced in his mirrors, and drove the Streamline taxi liveried Skoda estate he had chosen tonight away from the meter bay, very slowly, his lights on dipped beam. He smiled to himself at his cunning. It was important to vary his vehicles. Taxis never looked out of place, anywhere, and this model was one of the most commonly used in Brighton. He'd bought the vehicle secondhand from a rural dealer in Yorkshire, and had a body shop local to them paint it with the distinctive turquoise bonnet. The taxi insignia decals he'd had made to order from a firm on the internet, and the roof light had been easy to come by.

Ashleigh, with a small rucksack on her back, was pedalling hard, wobbling and swerving around, heading west. Heading home? He'd find out soon enough!

There was something very symmetrical about the number three. *Two's company, three's a crowd!*

Felix would be fine with that. Harrison, as ever, would not be so sure. And bloody pedantic Marcus, he would really be against what he was about to do. And that proved he was right. *Two's company, three's a crowd.*

As his old science teacher at school liked to say, QED. *Quod erat demonstrandum!*

He tailed Ashleigh at such a long distance that his dipped headlamps did not even register on her rear reflector. She pedalled on past the Peace Statue, and swung onto the cycle path alongside the Hove Lawns. He checked his mirrors and there was nothing behind him. Just himself and his pretty, young *project*. Heading home to her boyfriend.

Perfect!

She came off the cycle path and onto the road, to avoid a detour, and went over a red light at the junction with Grand Avenue, below the stern gaze of the statue of Queen Victoria. Then a few minutes later she shot the lights at the junction with Hove Street.

My, you're a reckless one! You need to be taught a lesson in road safety. You're not even wearing a helmet!

He was feeling impatient, shaking with excitement! He'd like to have taken her out now, but he was aware that there were cameras along the road here. Then suddenly, without indicating, she swung into the centre of the road and turned right past a block of flats on the corner, into Carlisle Road.

Oh yes, baby, perfect, thank you!

Turning off his lights, he turned right, also, and accelerated. Then as he drew close to her, he changed gear into neutral, feathered the accelerator pedal and coasted silently for some seconds, perspiring with excitement. Coming up close to her, so close he could see her long brown hair, flailing around behind her, in the glow of the street lighting.

They were halfway up the road, heading towards her flat, just short of the junction with New Church Road. He engaged a gear, silently, pressed the accelerator lightly, drew alongside her, saw her face through his side window, tight with exertion.

He swung the steering wheel over to the left. At the same time as hearing the metallic clang, he felt the impact. He braked hard, without squealing the tyres, not wanting to wake the sleeping street. He pulled the hypodermic syringe out of his pocket, then leapt out of the car and ran towards her. 'God,' he said, 'I'm sorry, I'm so . . .'

But there was no need for any apology. She was lying spread-eagled on the pavement, groaning, in shock. He looked over his shoulder, looked around, up at the windows of the houses on both sides of the street that might have had a view. No sign of any movement.

He knelt beside her, as if pretending to check her pulse, then opened her mouth, as if checking her airways, but instead he pressed the needle into her tongue and emptied the entire vial of ketamine. He sheathed and pocketed the syringe, looking carefully around again.

Then he half lifted, half dragged her to the rear of his car, opened the tailgate and hefted her in. He already had the rear seat folded flat. Then he opened her rucksack with his gloved hands, rummaged in it and pulled out her iPhone. Still looking carefully around, he ran back, tossed the phone into a thick laurel hedge beside a garden path and picked up her bike. He threw that in the rear also, on top of her, shut the tailgate, climbed in and drove off.

He was shaking in anticipation.

This felt so good. It really did!

His new *project*!

He felt such a burst of happiness deep inside him that he wanted to sing out loud and share how he felt with the whole world.

'I got you, babe! Oh yeah!'

Over his shoulder he said, calmly, 'You're going to be another great *project*! You really are! Trust me! I'm on a roll!'

38

Logan lay in a cold sweat, in a vortex of fear, trying to focus her mind which lurched uncontrollably from terror to anger, then back to terror.

Hoping, praying that she would wake from this terrible nightmare.

At this moment, terror swirled inside her like cold, heavy darkness. It filled her mind, her heart, her lungs, her stomach. Her mouth was dry, she was shaking and whimpering, blinded by her stinging tears, and desperately trying to think clearly. To figure her way out of this.

Ever since realizing the muffled voice was clearly not Jamie's, her mind had been in a mist. Who the hell was her captor? What was going on? Where was she? How long had she been here?

The pain where she had been burned on her thigh was agonizing, as if acid were eating through her flesh. The pain in her toe was bad too, a steady, insistent throbbing. But she was trying to ignore all the pain, to blot it out. To think. Think.

She *had* to think clearly.

She had an itch on her nose that was driving her crazy. It had been driving her crazy for what felt like an age.

Surely Jamie would have reported her missing? Wouldn't people be out looking for her? Wouldn't there be police combing the streets, fields, woods, dragging lakes, like she had seen in movies?

How long had she been here? How long? No matter how hard she writhed and twisted her head, she couldn't see the face of her watch.

She thought back to when she had phoned Jamie. Hours ago? Days ago? Weeks ago? She'd heard the instant concern in his voice. He'd registered that she was frightened in those moments before her car door had been ripped open and she'd seen the masked face above her.

A tsunami of fear crashed through her at the memory.

Jamie must have tried to phone her back. What happened when he didn't get an answer? He'd have gone to the police, surely? He'd have known she wasn't joking. So what had he done, who had he alerted? What was happening out there beyond the walls of her prison?

Prison.

Captor.

Her anger flared again. *Whoever the hell you are, what gives you the right to imprison me? How dare you do this to me?* She writhed and pulled and pushed out against her increasingly painful bonds. Shit, this was ridiculous. She had so much to do. Patients who needed her. A big party on Saturday night that she had really been looking forward to, a reunion of all the girls from their year in school, and their partners, at the Exeter Street church hall they had all helped save from developers. There was going to be a load of people there she hadn't seen in over five years.

With a sudden flash of panic she realized she didn't know how far away Saturday night was. Or had it already passed?

Her mind kept veering to horror movies she'd seen. Crazies who kidnapped people and tortured and then killed them. *Hostel. The Bone Collector. The Silence of the Lambs.* Was this what had happened to her? Not here, not in Brighton, not in this city she loved and where she always felt so safe, surely not?

Then she thought of the screams of the woman she had heard. Followed by the terrible gurgling; the rasping sound, like a death rattle, then the silence. How long ago was that? Who else was in here? Was she going to be next?

She was bloody well not going to let that happen. Somehow she had to keep clear-headed. How did people get out of situations like this?

She tried again to move her arms, but they were strapped down too tightly. There was some kind of restraint across her midriff, across her neck, her thighs and her ankles. With all her strength she tried to raise her head again, until the strap cut into her throat too much.

What the hell was she in?

The burning sensation on the inside of her right leg suddenly became even more acute, as if it had caught fire. But she couldn't even move her arms to touch the area.

She lay back in the pitch darkness, her mouth parched again. Her sugar levels were going down again, too, she realized, the all too familiar jittery feeling starting to return. Then she heard a noise that chilled her. Despite the sound being muffled, the words were clear.

A woman's voice. Screaming. 'Let me go, you bastard!'

Then the man's voice, shouting out in anger and pain. 'Owww!' Then again, 'Owww!'

Hope rose inside her.

'Owww, you bitch.'

There was a crashing sound. She heard a woman's voice yelling, 'Get your hands off me, you bastard perv!'

Go! Logan urged. *Go!*

Then she heard a dull thud, followed by the woman screaming out in pain. Then another thud, like a hammer against a sack. Then another. Then the man's voice, in a chilling rage.

'Look what you've made me do, you bitch! You've spoiled my fun. You realize that? You've spoiled my fun.'

Then Logan heard the scream again. It was a terrible sound, deep, powerful, fuelled by absolute terror. 'Help me, oh my God, help me!'

Then another thud.

Then silence.

Logan lay there, shaking. Waiting. Then the man's voice again.

It was followed by another thud. Then another. Then another.

Then silence.

Logan lay, listening, trembling. But all she could hear was the silence.

She was sinking low, she realized. Heading into a hypo.

Suddenly she heard the sliding sound above her and, an instant later, was blinded by a brilliant beam of light. A lump of chocolate was rammed into her mouth. Then the muffled voice again.

'Eat that. I don't want to lose you, too. We're not ready for that yet.'

'Please – please tell me who you are?' she spluttered through her mouthful of sweetness. 'Tell me what you want? Please tell me?'

'I have what I want,' he replied.

The lid slid shut above her.

39

Roy Grace woke at 5 a.m., twenty minutes before the alarm set on the clock and the back-up alarm on his iPhone. Cleo was sound asleep, breathing heavily, facing away from him, spooned against him, his right arm beneath her pillow. He could hear rain pelting down outside, and listened, as he did every time he woke during the night, for the sounds of Noah breathing through the baby monitor. His son sounded fine.

He felt leadenly tired, and could easily have lapsed back into sleep, but he needed to energize himself for what he anticipated to be a long and hard day ahead. Trying not to wake Cleo – Noah had already done that twice during the night – he gently, slowly, wormed his arm free. As he did so, she stirred.

'You off, darling?' she murmured, half asleep still.

'I'll take Humphrey for a quick run.'

'Love you.'

He kissed her shoulder. 'Love you so much,' he said.

Then he slipped naked out of bed and stood, shivering in the chilly darkness. 'Mind if I put on the light for a moment?'

'I'm awake,' she said.

He switched on his bedside light, shuffled through into the bathroom, closed the door then put on the bright light in there and, yawning, switched on his electric toothbrush.

Five minutes later, dressed in his tracksuit and a baseball cap, and trying to shush an excited Humphrey who was jumping up at him and barking, he let himself and the dog out of the front door, holding the lead in one hand and a plastic bag in the other in case, as was likely, Humphrey decided to have a dump en route.

He ran across the cobbled courtyard to the front gates, attached

Humphrey's lead, then ran out into the street and threaded his way past the silent houses and closed shops and cafés down towards the seafront. He loved the city at this hour, when it was still mostly sleeping. Loved the feeling of being up ahead of the rest of the world. He had always been able to cope on relatively little sleep, which stood him in good stead in this job, where snatching just a few hours was often the norm – and he had even more sleep deprivation now that he had a restless baby.

The rain pattering against his face and the salty tang of the air felt and smelled good. He crossed a deserted King's Road in the misty glare of the street lighting, then freed Humphrey, who bounded off ahead, and ran down the ramp by the arches, with the long, dark silhouette of Brighton Pier – or Palace Pier as he still preferred to call it – over to his left, and headed west, towards the sad, rusted skeletal remains of the West Pier, which had been gutted by a fire over a decade ago, and day by day was steadily crumbling into the sea.

As he ran, wide awake and increasingly clear-headed, his thoughts on the day ahead were crystallizing. Just before going to bed at midnight, he'd checked his emails and seen that the Sussex Police rugby team, of which he was the president, was a man short, due to illness, for an important fixture this afternoon. Could he play or find a last-minute substitute? It was a mundane task in the middle of such a critical operation, but he needed to deal with it. So far there had been no replies from the two possible players he had emailed – hardly surprising given the early hour.

His thoughts focused back on Logan Somerville who had now been missing since around 5.30 p.m. Thursday. Thirty-six hours. Both the new ACC and the Police and Crime Commissioner had phoned him late last night for updates, telling him how important it was to find her. Neither of them needed to do that. He was motivated enough as it was. Ever since Sandy had vanished over a decade ago, he knew the anguish the disappearance of a loved one caused. He had lived it every single day, and despite his deep love for Cleo, the pain of Sandy's disappearance was still there in his heart and in his soul.

He had not yet told either Pewe or Roigard of his bigger concerns.

Humphrey looked a tad miffed when he stopped opposite the

remains of the West Pier and turned around. The dog barked, as if saying to him that normally they would run much longer – towards Hove Lagoon at least.

'Sorry, boy, I have to get to work. Have to find someone very urgently. OK?'

Humphrey suddenly bounded ahead and ran onto the beach, crunching across the pebbles, on a mission.

'What is it, boy?' he called.

Then, in the faint glow from the promenade lighting, he saw Humphrey stop, lie on his back and begin rolling vigorously backwards and forwards.

Grace realized to his dismay what was happening. 'Humphrey!' he shouted. 'No! No, boy! No!'

He unzipped his pocket, tugged out his phone, found the torch app and switched it on, then ran, stumbling and unsteadily, over the pebbles, shouting for the dog to stop. 'HUMPHREYYYYYY!'

He stood over the rolling hound and bellowed again.

Contritely, Humphrey scrambled to his feet and stared up at him. Moments later the sickening, putrid smell hit him. In the bright beam of light he saw the splayed legs and claws and white belly of the long-dead, busted-open crab.

He toyed for a moment with dragging the dog into the sea to try to clean him, but the waves were pounding hard and he thought it too risky. So, instead, the stench accompanied him all the way home, as Humphrey ran alongside him, pleased as punch with himself and mightily proud of the new cologne he was wearing.

'This is all I sodding need!' Roy Grace whispered to the dog, holding him tightly by the collar and gagging, as he let himself back into the house. He dragged him, resisting every inch of the way, paws scraping across the floor and up the stairs, into the bathroom, shut the door behind them, then lifted him into the bathtub, turned on the taps, picked up the hand-shower and washed away, as best he could, the worst of the fetid, putrid mess on the dog's back.

Thirty minutes later, having showered, shaved and gulped down a microwaved bowl of instant porridge and a few sips of tea, he kissed Cleo, fast asleep again, goodbye, then slipped out of the house. Humphrey, lying in his basket down in the living room, did not even raise his head. He opened one eye, dismissively, as if some alien dog turd had just departed from his home.

40

Saturday 13 December

Jacob Van Dam had a sleepless night in the spare bedroom across the corridor from his wife's room, where he had spent most nights for the past decade, with a mask over his face delivering compressed air. He'd suffered sleep apnoea for years, snoring heavily and turning restlessly, constantly waking his wife, until she couldn't take it any longer.

He'd actually been sleeping pretty well recently, he thought. But the emotional turmoil in his mind since the strange Dr Harrison Hunter – if indeed he was any kind of medical doctor – had entered his life – and his head – was now keeping him awake.

The man was worrying him like hell.

Who are you, Dr Hunter?

What sick game are you trying to play with me?

He was trying to think clearly through his tiredness.

U R DEAD

What was that about? He'd had plenty of experience, in his career, of people with sick fantasies. They would read of a crime in the media and immediately phone the police and confess to it. Fortunately most clever Senior Investigating Officers kept back certain bits of information that would be known only to the offender and to no one else – which helped them to eliminate time-wasters.

Yet there was something about Dr Hunter that prevented him from dismissing him completely. His confidence, his body language, his whole behaviour, erratic though it was, made him feel deeply uncomfortable.

Would he be helping to find his niece by calling the police and telling them what he knew? Or would he be condemning Logan to death? He felt, and he had been dwelling on this all through the day and night, that Hunter did know something of value. The man had paid his secretary the five-hundred-pound consultancy fee in cash, before the appointment. Would someone who was just a fantasist really have done that?

He looked at the luminous digital figures of his clock radio. 6:05 a.m. Logan was beautiful, smart and kind. She had always had a child-like innocence about her. She was not the kind of person to suddenly disappear.

What did Harrison Hunter know?

Where did his idea that she had a tattoo come from?

He drifted into an uneasy sleep. When he awoke a short while later, to Rachel standing over him with a cup of tea in her hand, wishing him a good morning and reminding him they had to go to the christening of their granddaughter, Hannah, today down in Chichester, his mind was no clearer as to what he ought to do.

41

Logan stood on a white sandy beach, with the flat blue ocean stretching out beyond. She was in a silky, slinky white dress, and Jamie in a white suit stood by her side, in front of the chaplain. Everyone she loved and cared about stood all around her in the glorious, warm Phuket sunshine.

Jamie kissed her on her cheek. 'We've had our differences but we got through them, didn't we, my angel?'

She kissed him back and whispered, 'We have, my darling. You're the one I want, the only one I've ever wanted. I love you so much. You just make me feel so happy, all of the time, forever.'

Then the sky clouded over. Her father looked up and said, 'It's about to rain.'

The light was fading. 'No!' she said. 'Please don't let it! Please stop it!'

Then darkness enveloped her. She woke. Total darkness. She was drenched in perspiration, remembering. Remembering. And began shivering.

The sounds she had heard some while ago. Screams. Terrible screams. She squirmed in terror at the memory. 'Help me!' she cried out. 'Someone please help me!'

She became aware again of the painful burning sensation on her right thigh. Again she tried to move her arms. Then her painfully cramped legs and her throbbing toe.

She hadn't prayed since her early teens, maybe even before then. But she began praying now, closing her eyes even though it was dark. 'Please God, help me, please, please, help me.'

Then she lay thinking. What the hell was happening? The man in the car park. Who the hell was he and why was he doing this? She remembered reading about the Stockholm Syndrome. People who bonded with their captors. She had to stifle her fury and bond with this man. Somehow. 'Hello!' she called out. 'Hello!' She took a deep breath and then, with all her strength, shouted out again.

'HELLO!'

A few feet away from her, in the darkness, out of her line of vision, not that she could have seen anything, he looked down at his project and smiled. *Oh yes, just how I like you. Shout again. Shout as much as you like.*

As if obliging him, she did.

Again he smiled. *No one will hear you. No one can possibly hear you. No one even knows that where we are exists!*

42

Saturday 13 December

Roy Grace called the Saturday briefing, in the conference room of Sussex House, for an hour earlier than usual, 7.30 a.m. He had a lot to get through, and in addition somehow he had to find the time to finish writing his eulogy for the funeral.

He informed his team that although it was too early at this stage to be certain, there were disturbing parallels between Operation Mona Lisa and Operation Haywain. But, he made it absolutely clear, no one was to mention this to anyone outside of either operation.

Norman Potting raised his arm. He was looking pale and his eyes bloodshot – whether from tiredness or crying over Bella, Grace could not tell. He was aware that the DS hadn't been sleeping. 'Yes, Norman?'

'Boss, I may have a significant development. I've been in contact with some very helpful people at the DVLA. One was on the phone with me for hours last night, going through Volvo estate cars with registered keepers in the Brighton and Hove area. He's just come up with a vehicle registered to a Martin Horner, at an address over in the west of the city in Portslade. A residential house. Sixty-two Blenheim Street.'

Looking close to collapsing from exhaustion, Potting covered a yawn with his hand then continued. 'I went over to the CCTV room at John Street, first checking the records back on the ANPR cameras – they've plotted this same suspect vehicle on a direct path from Chesham Gate, where the victim was last recorded, along Dyke Road, at corresponding times.' He yawned again. 'We then checked the CCTV cameras in the relevant areas and we found the Volvo, and were able to read the rear licence plate. It's the same vehicle.'

'Brilliant, Norman!' Grace said. 'You should go home and get some rest.'

Potting shook his head. 'I want to see this one through, chief.'

'You haven't had much sleep.'

'I'll sleep next week after—' He leaned forward and buried his face in his hands.

After Bella's funeral, Grace knew he meant. He let it ride. Even though he knew the time, he checked his watch. 7.35 a.m. Dawn raids were the best for catching villains at home. But on a weekend, hopefully the offender would be having a cosy lie-in. He weighed it up for some moments. His prime concern was to ensure Logan Somerville's safety. An unsuccessful or botched raid could greatly endanger an abduction victim's life. But statistics were already long against them. It was over thirty-six hours since her reported disappearance. He turned to DC Alec Davies. 'Alec, we need a search warrant application, fast. Go to the on-call magistrate and get it signed. I'll get a Local Support Team unit on standby. Good work, Norman.'

DS Cale raised her arm. 'Sir,' she said to Roy Grace. 'As you know, and for the benefit of everyone else here, I had a call just before the start of this briefing from the duty DI at John Street. There's been another possible overnight abduction of a young woman in the city.'

Grace's sense of foreboding was growing by the minute. Was his worst nightmare coming true? 'Tanja, please tell everyone what we know,' he prompted.

Tanja Cale looked down at her notes. 'Her name's Ashleigh Stanford, twenty-one, a fashion design student at Brighton University. She shares a flat with her boyfriend in Carlisle Road. Her boyfriend phoned in at 3 a.m., concerned that she hadn't arrived home – she works Friday and Saturday nights in the Druids Head pub in the Lanes. Apparently she's always home by 1 a.m. She hadn't phoned him and when he tried to call her, it went to voicemail.'

'Maybe she went off with one of the customers?' Guy Batchelor quizzed.

'It's possible,' Cale said. 'The boyfriend was concerned because she always cycles home. He'd phoned the Sussex County Hospital to see if she'd been admitted following an accident. When that came back negative he then phoned us to report his concerns.'

Grace thought for some moments. Another woman heading

home to her boyfriend? Was there something in that? 'Do we have a picture of her?' he asked.

'No, sir.'

'Get me a recent one, please. Urgently.'

43

An hour later, Roy Grace, with Tanja Cale beside him in the passenger seat, turned the unmarked grey Ford Mondeo left off the Old Shoreham Road into Blenheim Street, a narrow street of small, semi-detached 1950s houses that ran south down towards Shoreham Port.

Cars, vans and a couple of taxis as well as an old, converted ambulance were parked along both sides. Without stopping, they clocked No. 62, a tired-looking house, with flaking paintwork and an unloved front strip of garden. But there was only one Volvo in the whole street – a small recent model with a completely different licence plate. He felt the same butterflies he got in his stomach on every raid he ever attended. What dangers did his team face going through the door? What would they find?

'The car's probably garaged somewhere nearby,' Tanja Cale said. 'He's unlikely to be stupid enough to have left it outside.'

Grace nodded. His mind was on the abducted girl from last night. Ashleigh Stanford. He checked his iPhone to see if a picture of her had come through yet. Then it rang. It was the Critical Incident Manager, Superintendent Steve Curry. 'All in position, Charlie One. Are you ready?'

Grace looked at Cale. She nodded.

'Yes, yes,' he replied. 'Let's go.'

Adrenaline kicking in now, he turned the car around as fast as he could. Two white vans appeared at the top of the street and accelerated down towards him, both of them halting, double-parked outside No. 62 and its immediate neighbours. He pulled up nose-on to the first, a small van, out of which clambered two dog handlers, in black jackets and trousers, with black baseball caps marked POLICE. They opened the rear doors, and led two German Shepherds down the path along the side of the house to cover the side and rear of the property.

Out of the second, much larger Transit van, poured eight Local Support Team officers, wearing blue combat suits with body armour and helmets with visors down. The two front-runners carried the battering and hydraulic rams. They were followed by the rest of their colleagues.

Grace and Cale climbed out of the car but stayed back as the protocols required until the property was declared safe by the LST's Inspector, Anthony Martin.

Six of the eight armoured officers grouped outside the front door, waiting for the command, while the other two followed the dog handlers around to the rear of the house.

The inspector gave the signal. All six LST officers yelled in unison, in classic shock and awe procedure, 'POLICE! POLICE! POLICE!'

The first team member fired up the ram, pushing the two sides of the doorframe wide apart. The second pounded the door with the battering ram, and it splintered open almost instantly. All of them barged through, yelling at the tops of their voices, 'POLICE! DON'T MOVE! POLICE! POLICE!'

The two detectives waited on the pavement. After less than two minutes the tall, thin figure of Inspector Anthony Martin appeared in the front doorway, his visor up and with a perplexed expression. He signalled them to come in.

As they walked up to him, he said, 'Not very convinced about what we have here, Roy – are you sure about your intel?'

'What do you have?'

'Come and see.'

Inside had a smell of musty furniture and cats. He entered a living and dining area, with an elderly three-piece suite and a small dining table, on which lay the remains of a meal and a copy of today's *Daily Express*, and an old fashioned kitchen beyond that reminded Grace of his childhood. Two officers were opening cupboards and removing cushions from the sofa and chairs. Accompanied by Tanja Cale, he followed Martin up the narrow stair treads. As they reached the landing at the top, two fat tabby cats shot past them and downstairs.

'Is the ambulance coming? I thought you was the ambulance,'

said an elderly, whining, female voice. 'I called them – I have to get to Worthing hospital – I have an appointment, you see. I thought you was the ambulance.'

Grace looked down at a carpet discoloured with stains and what looked like cat faeces littering it, and wrinkled his nose. There was a smell of urine and body odour. It was the kind of place officers used to joke, in his early days when he had been a beat copper, where you had to wipe your feet on the way out. Above him was an open loft hatch, with an extended loft ladder down to the floor.

Following the inspector, and trying to step in the patches of carpet between the droppings of cat shit, he entered a bedroom. Lying on the bed was an elderly woman in her late seventies or even mid-eighties, patches of pink skull showing through her threadbare white hair, who was so fat it took him some moments to figure out where her multiple chins ended and her face began. Her face reminded him of one of the three-dimensional maps in geography lessons at school, showing hills in relief.

'They said the ambulance would be here by nine o'clock. I can't get up, you see. I'm ill.'

Grace had to struggle to stop himself telling her what he thought was actually wrong with her, as he stared at the box of doughnuts, and another, almost empty giant-size box of Cadbury's Dairy Milk chocolates on her bedside table. On the ancient television on a table just beyond the end of the bed was a fuzzy image of James Martin cooking in his kitchen.

Instead, he flashed his warrant card at her, holding his breath, trying not to breathe in any more of her stinking vapour than he needed. 'Detective Superintendent Grace, Surrey and Sussex Major Crime Team,' he said. 'I'm afraid we're not your taxi service. I'm looking for Martin Horner.'

'Who d'you say?' She wrinkled her face.

'Martin Horner. His Volvo car is registered at this address.'

'Never heard that name, and he didn't have no car here. Is the ambulance on its way? I'm going to be late for my appointment. I can't get out of bed on me own, you see. I'm very ill.'

'What's your name, madam?' Tanja Cale asked.

'Anne – Anne Hill.'

'Do you have a carer who comes in, Mrs Hill?' Grace asked.

'No. I'm all on me own. I had one for a short time, but not any more. He stopped coming.'

Probably because he'd seen through her, Grace thought, and stared at her eyes. 'What's your full name, Mrs Hill?'

'Hill. Anne. Just Anne Hill.'

Still staring at her eyes, he asked, 'Someone had breakfast downstairs, Mrs Hill – and bought a copy of today's *Daily Express*. Can you explain that?'

'No,' she said. 'No, I dunno nothing about that. I can't get up, you see.'

Grace pressed. 'If you can't get out of bed, then who else is here or was here?'

The old woman was silent for some moments. Her eyes were racing around from right to left, as if searching for a convincing answer. 'Just me, dear.'

Behind him, he heard a voice call out, 'The loft's empty.' He turned to see an officer from the LST, torch in his hand, clambering down the ladder.

'So who had breakfast here this morning, Mrs Hill?' Tanja Cale asked. 'Martin Horner?'

She screwed up her face, looking puzzled. 'Martin Horner – who's he?'

The two detectives looked at each other.

'As you are bedridden and unable to get up, I'm assuming Martin Horner is the man who bought today's *Express* and ate his breakfast downstairs. Unless you have a better suggestion?'

The old woman's face reddened. She looked fearful, her eyes like two marbles, rolling round as if disconnected from any nerves or tendons. 'No – no – I – no, I can't explain that.'

'Anne Hill, I'm arresting you on suspicion of obstructing the police. You do not have to say anything, but it may harm your defence if you do not mention when questioned something which you later rely on in court. Anything you do say may be given in evidence. Is that clear?'

With even greater agility than her two overweight cats, the elderly woman suddenly sprang out of bed, her layers of fat wobbling beneath her translucent nightie, and stood, unsteadily for some moments, then unhooked a filthy-looking dressing gown from behind the door and pulled it around her. 'It's all right,' she said. 'It was me – I went out and got me paper and had me breakfast.'

'Why did you lie to us?' Tanja Cale said, sternly.

To his dismay, because he knew what was coming, Grace realized the woman was telling the truth. Paramedics were always complaining about people like this woman who abused the Ambulance Service. They would feign immobility to get a free ride to hospital, instead of having to fork out for a taxi. It was a standing, sour joke among the paramedics that for many hours each day their ambulances were nothing other than big yellow taxis.

'Shall I call and cancel the ambulance, Mrs Hill?' he asked. 'Or would you like me to arrest you for defrauding the National Health Service instead of a charge of obstructing the police?'

She nodded vigorously. 'Yes,' she said. 'Yes, dear, cancel, I'll call a taxi.'

She scurried, with surprising speed, down the stairs. Grace and Cale looked at each other and shook their heads.

'So where is Martin Horner?' the DI asked him.

'Not here,' Grace replied, gloomily. 'And never has been. We've been led on a sodding wild goose chase.'

As he stepped outside and walked back to the car, his iPhone pinged with an incoming text, with a photograph. It was from the duty inspector at John Street police station.

Roy, was told you needed this urgently. Photograph of misper Ashleigh Stanford.

He tapped on the postage-stamp-sized image on his screen, to enlargen it.

And stopped in his tracks.

44

Logan cried with terror and frustration. The salty tears stung her eyes, and she was desperate to wipe them. She struggled against her bonds, but still she could not move her arms. She lay in the pitch darkness, shaking, alternating with flashes of fury, her thoughts a constant jumble.

Was anyone looking for her?

Was she in Hell?

Her maternal grandmother was devout, a member of a strict chapel. She had warned Logan on every occasion they had met of Hell and Damnation. To beware of sinning and the consequences of being a sinner.

Had the old woman been right?

What the hell was going on? Who was this weirdo who was keeping her here? What was going on in the outside world beyond this hell hole?

Hell.

She was beginning to realize what Hell really was. Hell wasn't some Biblical dungeon of fire and brimstone. Hell was darkness. Hell was listening to people she could not see and did not know crying out in terror and pain. Listening to people being hurt and dying.

Hell was eternal darkness and eternal fear.

Praying had not worked. It had changed nothing.

Her mouth was parched. She had to find a way of communicating with her captor. Had to bond with him, somehow. Whoever he was.

Wherever she was.

Sometime ago, she wasn't sure if it was minutes or hours, she had heard what sounded like birdsong. Very faint. The dawn chorus? Sparrows, thrushes, starlings, blackbirds?

156

Was she in the city or in the countryside?

Suddenly, very faintly, she heard a siren wailing. Her hopes rose. The police? On their way? Still faint, as if in the distance, the siren grew louder. Louder still. *Please, God! Please! Please!*

Then it faded again.

Please come back. Please. Please. Come back.

Her thigh still burned like hell. Agonizing cramp had returned to her right leg and she couldn't stretch it away. She wanted to scream out for help, but she was scared of the man. So scared.

She had to be smart. Strong. But how?

Her thoughts went back to the terrified voice she'd heard some while back.

Help me, oh my God, help me!

The thudding sounds. The cries. More thudding sounds.

And then silence.

Whoever had brought her here – the man in the shadows in the underground car park – must want something.

What?

What could she offer him? Her body? Money? Jamie had always been fascinated by television documentaries on serial killers.

She twisted in terror at the thought.

Maniacs who got pleasure out of torturing and killing women.

Please don't let any of this be happening to me.

She heard a scraping sound above her. The lid was being moved back. She saw a green glow, then blinding light in her face.

Moments later she tasted honey. She sucked it gratefully. Then more. She swallowed. It was followed by deliciously cold water. She gulped it down. Then she said, 'Can we talk? Please? Please can we talk?'

She heard another scraping sound. The lid was closing again.

Then silence.

45

We're having a bloody emergency early meeting this morning. That stupid bitch Ashleigh Stanford should not have hit me, she should not have resisted. My *projects* are meant to be passive. I dictate what happens to them. It's *my* agenda, not theirs. Everything's going pear-shaped. That's how it feels. And it feels that I'm surrounded by flakes. Ashleigh Stanford died before I had any fun with her, the bitch.

Felix is telling me to calm down, that it's fine, that sometimes shit happens. He's really the one I can trust the most. I don't think Harrison's helped matters with his idea about that sodding London shrink. What was he thinking? He has a dangerous sadistic streak. He's a loose cannon. He's suggesting another visit, but I don't think that's a good idea. He says he likes to push the envelope, that it gives him pleasure to present people with conundrums. Although I have to admit what the shrink said made me smile. It's the only thing that has made me smile for a long time.

I've now got two dead *projects*. Two that I need to dispose of. Marcus is angry with me, he thinks I should have controlled myself last night, taught Ashleigh Stanford a lesson, but not killed her. Now I'm all out of sequence. Logan Somerville should have been next. I need to find a new one this week, then I can move Logan up the chain.

The good news is there are plenty of potential new *projects* lining up. The four of us are taking a look at their photos right now, the front-runners in my Hall of Fame!

On the big screen on the wall, copies of each of the thirty-five photographs of the young women who might make suitable *projects*, whom he had spotted and followed during the past months, appeared in sequence, their names and addresses beneath them. Two of them he had first seen on the Volks Railway; another had arrived grinning, with her boyfriend, at the end of the ghost train ride on Brighton Pier; another he had snapped sitting outside Lovefit café in Queen's Road; another he had first seen lying on the grass, with two girlfriends, on the Pavilion lawns; another on the Hove Lawns; another outside the Big Beach Café. Another, one that really excited him for reasons he couldn't totally explain, except that she looked like a younger version of his bitch wife, was eating prawns outside the Brighton Shellfish and Oyster Bar – a cream-painted stall, famed for its seafood, down by the arches.

Eating standing up.

That was a sin in his book. He despised people who ate standing up. Food wasn't just fuel, it should be savoured, enjoyed, shared with friends. Eaten seated. It was like those vile women who smoked while walking along. Smoking sitting down was fine, sometimes elegant. But women who walked with a fag in their mouth were slags.

Flotsam.

They should be eliminated.

But he could hardly be expected to clean up the entire city single-handed. On that point, Felix, Marcus and Harrison were all agreed. Nice to have consensus.

And now, as he froze one particular image, they all agreed again.

'That one!' Felix said.

Harrison studied it for some moments, and then said, 'Yes, that one.'

Even bolshy Marcus, who always took some time convincing, had no issues here. 'I'm with you. That one!'

'All happy, guys?'

They agreed. They were all happy. Unanimous. That was rare! Although she was fairly new, she was so perfect, it had to be her!

Her name was Freya Northrop. He knew a lot about her. He would enjoy taking her.

She'd be a great *project.*

His mood changed. He felt happy again. Happy all over. *We're strong*, he thought. *The four of us – we're like the Four Horsemen of the Apocalypse. Conquest. War. Famine. Death.* He smiled, he liked that a lot. *The Four Horsemen!*

46

Roy Grace dropped Tanja Cale back at Sussex House, then drove as fast as he dared downtown, heading for John Street police station – better known to all the local officers as 'Brighton nick'.

He drove almost on autopilot. He was stressed about their impending move, desperately wishing they could delay it – but it wasn't possible, the new owners were moving into Cleo's house next weekend. Though he had planned to be there to help Cleo with packing everything up, with the way this enquiry was going, that was not going to be an option.

Sure, he was excited about the new house and the prospect of living in the countryside, but he barely had room for that in his thoughts at this moment. His absolute priority, for however long it took, was Logan Somerville, as well as the new potential abductee, Ashleigh Stanford. His concerns for her were deepening and darkening every second.

Martin Horner.

The HOLMES – Home Office Large Major Enquiry System – analyst team on Operation Haywain had so far identified hundreds of Martin Horners in the UK and was working throught the list. One was ninety-three years old, suffering from Alzheimer's, in a care home in Bradford. One was seventeen, at school in Newark, Lincolnshire, and the third was a sixty-three-year-old vicar in Oldham, Lancashire, with a solid alibi.

He was increasingly certain that *Martin Horner* was a cleverly constructed false identity. Clever enough to have been able to register a vehicle in this name. The one mystery remaining was why whoever Martin Horner was had selected Anne Hill's house for his fake registration address.

Did he know her? Or someone who knew her? Or had he just picked her address at random? The old bag who lived there was strenuously denying knowledge of any Martin Horner, and he had a feeling she was telling the truth. But they would find out for sure.

He drove up the steep hill towards the Whitehawk area of Brighton, then made a right into the open, lower car park of the police station, found an empty bay between a row of marked cars, then climbed out, staring affectionately up at the five-storey slab of a building where he had started his career over twenty years ago.

He hurried past a couple of young uniformed officers having a smoke, up to the rear entrance, and used his pass card to open the door. Here at John Street he always felt the pulse of excitement. Street crime, neighbourhood policing, child protection, public order policing, and many other divisional units were run out of this place, which was soon to have a massive facelift.

He'd recently discussed the possibility of promotion to Head of CID. But that would have tied him to a desk and endless meetings. The buzz in his job came from doing exactly what he was doing right now – fully hands-on on a major crime investigation. There was only one promotion he would ever consider, and that was the top job here at John Street – the Chief Superintendent job, Divisional Commander of Brighton and Hove. The current commander, Nev Kemp, and his predecessor, Graham Barrington, had both come from similar CID backgrounds to himself. It could be some years before Nev Kemp moved on up the career ladder, but when that time came, he might be tempted to put himself forward for the role.

But right now, as he bypassed the lift and sprinted up the two flights of concrete stairs, that thought was a long way from his mind. He turned right along the familiar corridor then almost instantly turned right again. Ahead of him were signs saying SUPERINTEN-DENT AND CHIEF SUPERINTENDENT. But before them he stopped at an open door on his left. Inside the small office sat Wayne Brookes, the slightly camp duty CID inspector, hunched over his desk, phone clamped to his ear, writing down notes on an electronic tablet.

Grace waited, impatiently, for him to finish. Then he stepped into the office.

Brookes, a thin, wiry man in a grey suit and with a shaven head, looked up. 'Roy, darling! Good morning! How are you?'

'I've been better. Congrats on your promotion.'

'Four months ago, but thank you, it's wonderful, I'm loving it. Nice to see you here – anything I can help you on?'

'I hope so. You've a reported misper, from last night. Name of Ashleigh Stanford?'

'Yes – that was her boyfriend I was just on the phone to.'

'What's the latest?'

'Not looking good. No one's heard from her. Not her parents, nor either of her two closest friends. Sounds out of character – she's a pretty stable person, not likely to have run off on a one-night stand – although she's a fashion design student – I'd have thought that world might be a bit flighty – or, you know, flaky.'

'What info do you have on her?'

'Just got a couple of pictures through from her mother, and from the boyfriend – that one that was sent to you. I've sent copies up to CCTV – there won't have been that many solitary women cycling home at around 1 a.m. this morning.'

'Can I see the others?'

'Sure.'

Brookes tapped his keyboard. After some moments, the image of an attractive young woman appeared. She was smiling, looking like she hadn't a care in the world, against a glorious, summery backdrop of Brighton Pier and the crowded beach beside it.

Grace stared again at the pretty face he had seen on the text, earlier.

At her high cheekbones, her full lips, her long brown hair.

Ashleigh Stanford, Logan Somerville and Emma Johnson could have been sisters. And so, if you ignored the thirty-year gap, could Katy Westerham.

'Presumably someone's tried her mobile phone?' Grace asked.

'Yes, her boyfriend's rung it continuously. It's still on. We've put a request in to EE, the service provider, for triangulation, but I don't think we're going to get much back for a while.'

'Has the boyfriend been interviewed yet?' Grace asked.

'Not yet, no.'

He looked at his watch. It was just coming up to midday. 'Shit! Why not?' he said, more angrily than he had intended.

'Because I'm short-handed thanks to all the sodding cuts, darling,' Brookes said. 'If you want the truth.'

Grace nodded. 'Yep. OK, give me his address, I'll get one of my team there right now to interview him.'

'Is there something more to this, Roy, that I don't know about?'

'I hope to hell not. But if you want the truth, I think there is, and it's not good news. You need to start increasing the number of officers you have available for this coming week. I'll give you a heads-up now that we could be looking at cancelling all rest days, imminently, and banning new applications for time off.'

The inspector frowned. 'Something big going on?'

Grace stared down again at Ashleigh Stanford's image. 'It's looking increasingly like it.'

47

Sunday 14 December

'They're on the table, getting cold!' Zak shouted. 'And we have to get going!'

Freya Northrop lay in bed, reading and enjoying 'The Love Song of J. Alfred Prufrock' which her new doctor, the eccentric but rather jolly Edward Crisp, had been talking about when she'd had her appointment with him on Friday.

She'd left his surgery, walked straight down to Church Road, turned left and along to where it morphed into Western Road, entered City Books, and asked if they had any volumes of T. S. Eliot poetry. Then headed home.

She yawned and called out, 'Almost finished. Be one minute!' She could smell the tantalizing aroma of warm toast. The alarm clock beside her read 9.40 a.m.

He shouted back, 'You said you'd be one minute already – that was about five minutes ago! You wanted your eggs soft, they'll be stone cold!'

Wow, you sure found out stuff you didn't know about someone when you started living with them, Freya thought. Like, one of them was goodbye to her Sunday morning lie-ins. Zak hated to waste a minute of the weekend, and had already been up for hours, finally realizing the only way he was going to get her out of bed was by tempting her with her favourite Sunday breakfast, scrambled eggs and smoked salmon. Besides, she thought ruefully, in any case Sundays as a day off were about to become a thing of the past.

Zak Ferguson was an accomplished chef. She'd met him six months ago, when he came into the Notting Hill restaurant where she was waitressing, and where he ate alone. He had returned the next night, alone again, and spent every moment that he could chatting her up. She'd realized, by the time she brought him a double espresso at the end of his meal, that she was a little bit smitten.

Being a totally rubbish cook, she had bought herself a bunch of cookery books, and the one she had found the most comprehensible and which provided really tasty and easy to prepare recipes was called *Don't Sweat the Aubergine* by someone called Nicholas Clee. It lay beside her bed now.

Zak had big plans. Thanks to an inheritance – which had also paid for this small executor-sale Edwardian mock-Tudor house in a leafy close near Hove Park – he'd quit his job at an uber-cool restaurant in London's Hoxton and had bought a bankrupt Brighton restaurant, which he was in the process of revamping. When it opened in two months' time, Freya was going to be the front-of-house manager.

Until then he was full-on, travelling to the best seafood restaurants around the country, seeing what was on offer, what ideas he could glean and recipes he could 'borrow' and improve on. Today they were making the two-hour drive to Whitstable in North Kent at the mouth of the Thames Estuary. Famed for its oysters, in recent years the town had become increasingly fashionable with a number of highly rated restaurants. They were booked to have lunch at two of them. But there were two gastro pubs he wanted to check out on the way, hence the early start.

Zak, who had already done a twenty-mile bike ride at 5.30 this morning, remained thin as a rake, despite the eating marathon they had embarked upon. Freya had put on over a stone. One effect, which had pleased Zak, was that her breasts, never her best feature, had become larger. Another effect, which seriously displeased her, was that her thighs had become larger and dimpled. She should start exercising, too, she knew. Dr Crisp had asked her about that, and had frowned when she'd admitted to smoking ten cigarettes a day, and had frowned even more when she'd confessed to downing the best part of a bottle of white wine a day.

'You should stop smoking – and that's too much for someone your age to be drinking,' he had admonished her.

He was right, she knew. But she enjoyed both. And they were pleasures she shared with Zak. After a year on her own, since she'd been crassly dumped by her previous boyfriend, by text, Zak made her smile. She loved his energy, his humour and his ambition. And she loved just how much he genuinely seemed to enjoy cooking for her, trying out his recipes. Although she'd been less happy last night when he'd knocked over a saucepan and two very bolshy lobsters had skittered across the floor, claws clacking, causing her to shriek and jump onto a chair in fright.

She looked back at the T. S. Eliot poem. God, how prescient Dr Crisp had been. It was all about food! References to sawdust restaurants with oyster shells; tea and toast; a life measured out with coffee spoons; tea and cakes and ices. They were in a seaside city and today they were going to another seaside place. And here in this poem Eliot had written about growing old and wearing the bottoms of his trousers rolled.

Would Zak be like this one day? Would they grow old together? Walk along the seashore, he with his trousers rolled up and barefoot in the lapping water. She could see it. For the first time in her life she had met someone she could truly see having a life with. Growing old with.

She put the poem down, slipped naked out of bed and pulled her dressing gown around her. Then she walked barefoot downstairs into the kitchen where Zak was sitting, showered, shaved and dressed in a T-shirt and jeans, smelling of the aftershave she loved, and studying the food pages of the *Observer*. She put her arms around his neck, and kissed him on the cheek. 'You smell delicious,' she said.

The breakfast was laid out the artistic way it might have been in a top-rated restaurant. The eggs splayed on the plate, with slivers of truffle on top, the smoked salmon in neat curls beside it, interspersed with slices of lemon, and a display of sliced cherry tomatoes. The toast was in a silver rack, butter in a square, modern dish. 'This looks seriously yum.' She nuzzled his ear. 'Almost as yum as you.'

'Your eggs are going to be rock hard!'

She slid her hand down onto his thigh, then around to his crotch. 'Hmmn,' she said. 'They're not the only things hard around here.'

'Eat your bloody breakfast, girl!' he said, stifling a grin, then he turned and kissed her back.

*

An hour later they went downstairs again and walked out of the front door of the house, into the dry, blustery morning. Zak's old MX5 was parked in the short driveway in front of the integral garage, alongside Freya's beat-up Fiesta. The MX5, which hadn't been polished in years, had a rip in the canvas roof patched up with black tape, and was spattered with seagull dropping.

'This dog, how long are we going to be stuck with it?'

'Bobby!' she said. 'He's called Bobby and he's totally adorable. You'll want a puppy after you see him!'

'Koreans eat dogs. They have great recipes for them.'

'Zak, that's horrible.'

'Yeah, OK, sorry. It's just I want you to myself, I don't want to have to share you with a dog.'

'You'll love him, I promise you. And it's only for a week.'

She had agreed to look after her friends', Emily and Steve's, mixed-breed terrier, while they were away on holiday. But she hadn't reckoned on Zak being so negative about the adorable creature.

The man inside the small grey Renault saloon parked a short distance up the road, his face masked by the main section of the *Sunday Times*, watched the MX5 reverse out into the road and drive off.

He was reading the front page article about Logan Somerville with great interest. On the passenger seat beside him was a yellow hi-viz tabard and a clipboard. Like taxis, he knew, people never took any notice of someone in a hi-viz jacket holding a clipboard.

48

'Shit, man, that's the oldest trick in the book,' Glenn Branson said in his tiny office, cradling a can of Diet Coke in his massive hand.

'What do you mean?' Roy Grace asked.

'I've been thinking about Martin Horner. I reckon he's taken a dead man's identity.'

Roy Grace should have gone home this lunchtime, he knew, to work on his eulogy for tomorrow morning. But Bella would have understood. If there was the remotest possibility of saving Logan Somerville – and now possibly Ashleigh Stanford – she would have hated that her death in any way hindered the speed of the investigation.

He sipped a small apple juice and, ravenous, munched on an all-day breakfast sandwich of egg and bacon, complemented by a packet of sour cream and red onion flavoured crisps, both of which he had just bought at the Asda superstore across the road. He was glad Cleo was not around – she would have been furious to see him eat what she would have considered to be such an unhealthy meal. But the apple juice, he felt, was arguably the one healthy option that salved his conscience.

Like those fortunate enough to be in a career where they actually had weekends off, Monday-morning gloom loomed tomorrow for him, too, but for other reasons. 'I've been wondering the same thing,' he replied.

'*Day of the Jackal*. Ever see that movie?'

'James Fox?'

'Nah, his brother, Edward Fox. Plays a hitman hired to shoot President de Gaulle of France. He gets a fake passport after going to a graveyard and finding the name of a dead, small boy who would never have had a passport. He uses the dead boy's name to get a phoney passport. It's a top movie.'

'Never saw it,' Grace said, sipping more of his juice, then munching on his sandwich. He pushed the crisps towards Branson, who shovelled out half the contents in one handful.

Through a mouthful he said, 'You know your problem? You're an uncultured philistine. How the hell did you ever get to make such a top copper?'

'By not associating with dickheads like you.' Roy Grace grinned and gave his best friend a hug. 'Actually, I read the novel, years ago.'

'It was a novel?'

Grace looked at him. 'By Frederick Forsyth.'

'Yeah?'

'Yeah. Way before it was a movie. You didn't know that? You never read it?'

'Nope.'

'Now who's the philistine?'

'You're a tosser.' Glenn Branson shrugged. 'But, you know, so far as tossers go, you're up there among the good ones.'

'Thanks a million.'

To Grace's dismay, seemingly oblivious to the fact this was his lunch, Branson tipped the rest of the packet of crisps out and ate them noisily.

'How are you feeling about the funeral?'

'I'll be glad when it's over.' Grace sipped his juice. 'So update me on Operation Mona Lisa. Are you any closer to identifying *Unknown Female*?'

'Yes, we might be. As you know, Lucy Sibun has estimated her death to have occurred about thirty years ago and she was in her early twenties. I used the parameter you set to look at all the mispers in the county aged between eighteen and twenty-five, who are still missing, from twenty to thirty-five years ago, that fit our description. We've been able to eliminate some from their hair colour. We'll have a computer e-fit face tomorrow and we know she had long brown hair. When we have that we should be able to come up with a probable victim. Then we'll have to hope we can trace family members. If we can, there'll be a chance of checking dental records, or getting DNA.'

Grace nodded, thinking about Sandy's disappearance. 'A lot of families who have a member disappear, particularly a child, keep their bedroom as a kind of shrine. There's a good chance there'll be a hairbrush, or toothbrush, or something else to get DNA from.'

'We have one development that may be significant,' Branson said. 'I showed you the file on Friday on Catherine Westerham, the body from Ashdown Forest?'

'Yes, she was nineteen and had the same U R DEAD branding. As well as similar looks.'

'You've gone very pale,' Glenn Branson said. 'You look like you've seen a ghost.'

Grace nodded. 'That's how I'm feeling. I have a very bad feeling about this, mate. These killings have to be linked. The marks, the hair, the age range, the victim profile – there are so many similarities.'

'It was all a long time ago.'

'A long time ago, in another country, and besides, the wench is dead.'

'What?' Branson frowned.

'Christopher Marlowe.'

'Who is he?'

'He wrote that in 1590 – am I still a philistine?' Grace finished his sandwich and his juice, patted his friend on the back and stood up. 'I have to go, see you on parade in the morning.'

But Glenn Branson did not reply. He was studiously tapping Christopher Marlowe into Google on his iPhone.

Grace thought to himself that as soon as the girl from the Lagoon was identified they might be able to establish what the link between the two young women was. Suddenly, Grace felt his phone vibrating. It was DC Liz Seward in MIR-1.

'Sir,' she said, 'I've just taken a call from someone who wants to speak to the SIO. An elderly-sounding man who says he has some information that might be of interest. I tried to get him to tell me, but he was adamant he would only speak to you. Can I give you his name and number?'

49

'Hey, Mole, how come you're so fat?'

'My name's not Mole,' he said, in his squeaky voice that had not yet broken. He stood, naked, in the bathroom of his new boarding school, The Cloisters, in Surrey. It was the start of the second week of term.

'You are gross, Mole!' Gossage said.

A boy pinched the layers of flab on his stomach so hard he cried out in pain. 'What do you call that?'

'That hurt, you creep!'

'Who's Mole calling a creep?' Gore-Parker said. 'Me? I'm a creep?'

'Are you calling Gore-Parker a creep?' taunted Chaffinch, a piggy-faced boy who definitely was fatter than himself – except no one seemed to notice.

'Leave me alone.' He stepped into the shower and turned on the taps.

'Listen, you arrogant piece of whale blubber,' Gore-Parker said, 'you kept us all awake in the dorm last night wanking.'

'I was bloody not wanking.'

'I'm surprised you can even find your dick under all that blubber,' Gossage said.

The others pealed with laughter.

'Tell you what, Mole, you like tunnels, why don't you dig yourself a nice little tunnel out in the woods where you can go and wank away to your heart's content?' Chaffinch said.

'And preferably not come back,' added Gore-Parker.

'We don't like fat wankers!' Gossage said, secure in having the protection of his mates, who had formed a clan during these past few days.

'Just leave me alone.' He had tears in his eyes.

'The matron said you wet your bed last night,' Gore-Parker said. 'Who's a little homesick diddums then?'

'I'm going to report you all to Mr Hartwell.' Hartwell was the housemaster.

'Oh really, Mole,' Chaffinch said. 'What are you going to report us for?'

'I know you're all reading porn. I've seen the magazines.'

Feigning shock, Gossage turned to Chaffinch and Gore-Parker. 'Oh dear, everyone, are we terrified or what? Mole is going to report us for reading porn. What are you reading, Mole, that makes you need to wank all night? Books on tunnels?'

The others laughed.

'You're the bloody wanker,' he said, sullenly, stepping into the water spray and starting to soap himself. He closed his eyes, spreading soap across his face.

Suddenly, he felt a vice-like grip on each wrist. Then he was being yanked, harshly, out of the shower.

'Hey!' he yelled. 'Hey!' He opened his eyes and was instantly blinded by the stinging soap. His feet slithered across the shower tray and then the linoleum floor as he blinked, his vision a blur. He felt himself being lifted, then dumped down into water.

A bathtub, he realized.

His head was right beneath the tap which was pelting out a lukewarm mix of hot and cold water. Straight onto his face.

'No! Urrrrrrrr!' He tried to shout out, but merely swallowed water. Hands were pinning him down.

'Helpglub! Glubbbme!'

Suddenly he couldn't breathe. He writhed in panic. He was drowning.

Then he was jerked forward. Gulping air, he could hear the roar of the open tap inches from him. Then he was pushed back and the torrent of water covered his mouth and nose.

He writhed, twisted, kicking out, desperately trying to shake free, but firm hands held him down.

'You're a dirty bastard, Mole!' Gossage said. 'Moles burrow in earth. You must be covered in earth. Yech!'

'Maybe we should cut your dick and balls off to stop you wanking!' Gore-Parker said.

He was swallowing water. He shook, violently, choking, trying desperately to break free.

Then suddenly he heard a voice. A familiar voice. Stern. Furious. 'What the Dickens is going on here? Gossage? Gore-Parker? Chaffinch? What do you think you are doing? Get dressed and come to my study right away!'

It was the voice of Ted Hartwell, a man Mole had lived in terror of since he had arrived at The Cloisters, from his fearsome disciplinarian reputation.

But this Sunday evening he felt like he was his saviour.

50

Grace stared at the piece of paper he'd torn off Glenn Branson's desk notepad, on which he had scrawled 'Dr Jacob Van Dam'. The name of the man Liz Seward had spoken to, who insisted on talking only to him.

The man's name rang a faint bell.

He hurried along the corridor, logged on to his computer, and then to Google, and typed in the doctor's name.

And was instantly impressed. Now he knew why the name was familiar. Van Dam had been, at one time, among the leading forensic psychiatrists in the country. But looking at his date of birth, he was knocking on, well past retirement age. Curious, he dialled his number.

A quavering man's voice answered after five rings. 'Dr Van Dam?' Grace asked.

The response was guarded. 'Yes, who is this?'

'Detective Superintendent Roy Grace. I'm the Senior Investigating Officer on the disappearance of Logan Somerville. I understand you wanted to speak to me?'

'Well, yes, thank you for calling. I'm very worried about wasting police time, but the thing is – you see I have something that has been bothering me for the past – nearly – two days.' He fell silent.

'Tell me?' Grace prompted.

'The first thing I should tell you is that I am Logan Somerville's uncle.'

'OK.'

'Well, you see, I had a very peculiar patient on Friday, whose name was Harrison Hunter. Does that mean anything to you?'

'Harrison Hunter?' Grace wrote the name down. 'No, it doesn't.' The man was speaking almost irritatingly slowly.

174

'He told me he is an anaesthetist. But so far I've not been able to verify that.'

Grace made a further note.

'Then he made a rather strange claim. I held off contacting you because, to be frank, I rather dismissed him as a fantasist – I've had plenty of people like him during my career. He claimed to know all about Logan's abduction. Then he told me – as evidence of his bona fides – that Logan had a tattoo or a mark of some kind on her right thigh.'

Suddenly Grace's interest in the man increased dramatically. 'On her right thigh?'

'That's what he told me. So immediately he left, I got the name of Logan's fiancé from her mother – and I telephoned him to ask if Logan had a tattoo. He was absolutely adamant that she doesn't.' The psychiatrist fell silent for some moments. 'I've been discussing it with my wife. But the thing is that Logan's parents – her mother is my sister – are worried out of their wits.'

'Understandably,' Grace replied.

'They are worried about Logan's relationship with her fiancé. Apparently she broke their engagement off and he's had a problem accepting it. So it is possible he lied to me when I asked him the question about the tattoo.'

'Why do you think he would lie about a tattoo?'

'I can't explain that. Unless, of course, as the parents think, he might be behind this.'

'Did this Dr Hunter give you any description of this tattoo?'

'Yes, he did. Well, it said, U R DEAD.'

Roy thanked him for the call and sat in stunned silence for a few minutes, thinking hard. Then he made three phone calls. The first was to Glenn Branson, asking him to send one of their detectives to London right away to interview the psychiatrist. The second was to the Chief, Tom Martinson, and the third Pewe, to alert them and schedule a meeting.

This latest information had just turned a major investigation into potentially one of the biggest that he and Sussex Police were likely to experience. There would no doubt be massive national and international media interest, and it would be important for him to keep control of the investigation. He would also have a duty to work with key opinion formers and community groups to ensure that the public's reaction was managed to prevent panic. He would be telling the Chief and Pewe that in his opinion they needed to form a Gold group.

A Gold group was only formed in extreme circumstances, such as a major crime, critical incident, significant public event or natural disaster. The group would consist of senior police officers, senior representatives from the City Council, Safety Officers, the Police and Crime Commissioner, the local MP, the Divisional Commander, members of the Independent Advisory Group and, importantly, a dedicated senior Public Relations Officer. He would be discussing the details straight after the briefing when he went to headquarters.

This was all he needed: a funeral tomorrow, and with this current investigation perhaps the biggest challenge of his career, in the week he was moving house. He picked up the phone to dial Cleo, taking a deep breath before she picked up.

51

Roy Grace ran a rather stilted Sunday evening briefing of Operation Haywain. He was due to meet Martinson and Pewe straight after, to update them on the potential magnitude of the situation. He was not going to be delivering good news, after his conversation earlier with Van Dam and several more phone calls during the afternoon.

The close-up photograph of Logan Somerville's face that had been distributed had been picked up by almost all of the Sunday papers, with several carrying it on the front page. A search operation had been ongoing since Thursday evening, with police, specials, PCSOs and volunteer members of the public, as well as the police helicopter, despite its huge operating cost. The search operation was intelligence-led, together with responses to specific information received from the public. The immediate search of the area where Logan had gone missing had been completed with a negative result.

Ashleigh Stanford's boyfriend seemed a decent young man. He had spent much of the afternoon in the CCTV room at John Street with operator Jon Pumfrey, watching firstly the cameras covering her normal journey home, down West Street and along the seafront. He'd identified the first image of her, pedalling up the pedestrianized Duke Street at 12.52 a.m., then down West Street, and turning right along King's Road.

Over the next eight minutes, four more cameras had clocked her heading west: one passing the Peace Statue, a second along Hove Lawns, a third where she ran a red light at the bottom of Grand Avenue, and the fourth as she crossed Hove Street. The next camera would have picked her up, if she had continued west, at the start of Shoreham Port. But the fact she hadn't showed up indicated that she had either been abducted from this road, with her bicycle as well, or on one of the streets off, such as Carlisle Road, a quarter of a mile along, where she lived.

She had literally vanished off the face of the earth.

Except for one thing that had turned, during the course of the afternoon, into a serious lead. A Skoda taxi had been clocked by the same cameras, driving slower than the speed limit, keeping a steady and substantial distance back from the cyclist. The taxi had also not showed up on the fifth camera, at the start of Shoreham Port, which meant it, too, had turned off somewhere.

Nor had it appeared anywhere else on any of the other cameras that had been searched around all the possible routes it could have taken. However, the registration number had been picked up by an ANPR along the seafront, and they'd got the driver's name, a Mark Tuckwell.

Tuckwell had been found and interviewed. Whilst it was un-doubtedly his registration number, he had been at a wedding reception in Lewes with about a hundred potential witnesses there to confirm his alibi, and his taxi had been in the dealer's garage over the weekend with its engine out.

Someone had gone to a lot of trouble to clone the vehicle and number plate – and it was not easy to get fake number plates made in the UK these days.

There was a parallel with the Volvo that had been sighted outside Logan Somerville's flat around the time of her suspected abduction, which was also concerning Roy Grace. 'There is one possible link,' he said to his team. 'The offender who took Ashleigh and the one who took Logan were both in estate-type vehicles around the time of the girls' disappearance. Neither of them showed up on any further cameras after the alleged abductions. That to me indicates two things.' He took a sip of water, then went on.

'Firstly, that the offender has a detailed local knowledge of the city, and an awareness of the camera locations – and clearly extensive knowledge of all the backstreets to avoid them. And secondly, probably lives locally within the city. I've studied the camera maps this afternoon, and from each of the two abduction sites, it would have been impossible for either vehicle to have left the city in any direction, other than driving into the sea, without being picked up by a camera – either one of our own CCTV network or ANPR. The area where Ashleigh was last seen has been thoroughly searched, and house-to-house enquiries have also been made, but nothing of significance has been found to date.'

He turned to DS Exton. 'Jon, what do you have to report about your interview with the psychiatrist, Dr Jacob Van Dam, uncle of Logan Somerville, and his patient, Dr Harrison Hunter?'

'Well, to be honest, sir, something of a conundrum. The man claimed he was referred by a Brighton doctor, general practitioner Dr Edward Crisp, and produced a letter. I managed to obtain Dr Crisp's home phone number afterwards and rang him to check and he says he has never heard of a Dr Harrison Hunter. Van Dam said Hunter claimed to be an anaesthetist at a London teaching hospital, but Van Dam subsequently checked up on the man and there is no such person listed. He says he was a strange-looking character, in his mid-fifties, wearing tinted glasses and what he was certain was a blond wig – he said the wig reminded him of Boris Johnson. He said he would have been tempted to dismiss him as a nutter except that he claimed Logan had "U R DEAD" tattooed on her.'

Grace nodded. He had a sick feeling in the pit of his stomach. 'Did Dr Van Dam have any idea why this man came to see him, or what he wanted?'

Exton nodded. 'It was his view that he was seeking help of some kind. Dr Van Dam said he was unsure whether the man wanted someone to tell him that killing people was OK or whether he was a fantasist. Or . . .' The detective sergeant shrugged, then fell silent for some moments as if deep in thought.

'Or what, Jon?' Grace pressed.

Exton looked down at his notes. 'I'm trying to recall exactly how Dr Van Dam expressed it, sir. It was as if it was a kind of confession – but a very complicated one. As if he needed to tell someone, sort of to share it, unburden himself. Kind of a cry for help.'

'We could help him,' Norman Potting said. 'We could lock him up and throw away the bloody key.'

There were a few smiles.

Grace asked Exton to ensure he recovered the referral letter, then turned to DS Cale. 'Tanja, you had an outside enquiry team do a house-to-house along Carlisle Road, where Ashleigh Stanford lived – anything from that?'

'No, sir, not so far. I have four uniform officers still out there. They've checked Carlisle Road and the immediate neighbouring streets, but nobody saw or heard anything during the night around that time. They're expanding the search zone. I've also been with DC Seward checking as much of the surrounding area as possible for any sighting of the bike or the taxi, with no luck. It is a fairly distinctive dark blue bicycle, with a sticker embossed with the bike shop, South Downs Bikes, on the frame.'

'Good work, Tanja. Has anyone heard back from EE about the triangulation of Ashleigh's phone?'

'Not good news on that, boss,' DC Emma-Jane Boutwood said. 'Just before the briefing started a neighbour a couple of houses down from Ashleigh's in Carlisle Road called the main switchboard. She'd found a mobile phone in her garden earlier in the day, and it only just occurred to her that it might be connected with all the police activity in the street.'

'Duh, hello?' exclaimed Jack Alexander.

'What kind of bush did she think it was – a phone plant?' Potting asked.

'Two houses away, EJ?' Grace quizzed the DC, pensively.

'Yes, south of where her flat is.'

'And it was the other side of a hedge, in a front garden?'

'Yes.'

'That sounds to me like she didn't just drop it while cycling along. Phones don't bounce over hedges. Did our offender take her as she slowed to dismount, and throw it there? Logan Somerville's phone was left in her car. Now Ashleigh Stanford's phone is left behind also. I think we are dealing with someone very smart here. Someone who knows phones can be tracked. Who knows this city. Who knows not to use the same vehicle twice. I assume the phone has been collected and is currently being examined.' He turned to DC Alexander.

'Jack, how are you getting on with locating Martin Horner?'

'Well, sir, I've found an address for the right Martin Horner – the date of birth tallies with what the DVLA have on file – but I don't think you're going to be very happy about this.' The young detective constable glanced down at his notes, then with a slight, awkward grin said, 'He's currently residing along the Old Shoreham Road, in Hove Cemetery.'

'What?' Guy Batchelor quizzed. 'What do you mean? He's sleeping rough?'

'Not exactly. His full address is Plot 3472, Hove Cemetery, Old Shoreham Road, Hove.'

It took some moments for this to sink in. Then there was a titter of laughter from several of the team, but not from Batchelor, who was having a total sense of humour failure at that moment.

'What the hell is that supposed to mean?' he said, with a frown. But from the look on several faces around, it seemed that some of the team had got there before him.

Jack Alexander stood up and pointed at a large photograph which was fixed to the whiteboard, below the faces of Logan Somerville, Ashleigh Stanford and Emma Johnson. It was a close-up of a small, modest tombstone. The engraving on it was clear and stark.

MARTIN WILLIAM HORNER
OCTOBER 3RD, 1964 – JUNE 12TH, 1965
DEARLY BELOVED SON OF KEVIN AND BEVERLY

'Looks like some sick bastard's taken this dead boy's identity,' Tanja Cale said.

'And registered the car in his name?' Grace confirmed.

'Yes.'

'What about the address, sixty-two Blenheim Street?' Grace asked. 'Whoever did this must have some connection to it.'

'I've had our outside enquiry team talk to the woman who lives there, Anne Hill,' Cale continued. 'She's now being very cooperative – worried as hell we're going to have her prosecuted over faking her infirmity. She's adamant she knows nothing about this vehicle. But she told us one thing that may be significant. Six weeks ago a man turned up, who said he'd been appointed as her carer. He came for a few days running, then vanished. She called her doctor to ask what had happened and he told her that he had no knowledge of any carer having been appointed to her. The timing is significant, I think.'

'Presumably she's given a description of him?' Guy Batchelor asked.

'Not a very good one,' Cale said. 'Middle-aged, quite long hair and dark glasses. But he seemed to have medical knowledge, she said.'

'We need an e-fit,' Grace said.

'Yes,' Cale said. 'We've got that in hand. Someone from the Imaging department is with her now.' Then she looked at her notes, briefly, and went on. 'It was November 2nd that the Volvo was purchased by this Martin Horner. It's possible the carer had turned up in order to grab the documents when they came through from the DVLA.'

'Do we have a description of this man who bought the Volvo – our imposter Martin Horner?' Grace asked.

'Not much of one, boss,' Guy Batchelor said. 'We've found the previous owner, an antiques dealer called Quentin Moon, but he wasn't much help, he didn't see enough of his face to ever recognize him again. The handover was done at night in a poorly lit multi-storey car park in Worthing. When asked, Moon hadn't kept any of the contact numbers. He remembered Horner was wearing a tweed cap, scarf and dark glasses, and paid in folding – fifteen hundred pounds.'

Jack Alexander asked, 'Is there any chance he might still have any of those banknotes, which would give us the opportunity for fingerprints or DNA?'

'Excellent thinking, Jack. Check it out.'

'Didn't he wonder about Horner's appearance?' DC Davies queried. 'Dark glasses at night in a dark car park?'

'All he would have cared about was getting paid for his car, which he was,' DS Batchelor said. 'He's an antiques dealer – probably gets plenty of customers looking a lot dodgier than that.'

Grace smiled. From his team's recent experience working a major antiques case, he couldn't disagree. 'Do they have CCTV in or near that car park, Guy?'

'Yes, there's both,' Batchelor said. 'But Horner bought the car six weeks ago – very few CCTV systems keep recordings that long.'

Grace nodded. But he felt that with increasing use of digital equipment it was worth checking out. He reflected that everything he had just heard confirmed the conversation he'd had earlier with Glenn Branson about who Martin Horner might be.

Norman Potting, looking as bleak as hell, as might be expected on the eve of his fiancée's funeral, raised a hand. 'I've been to see Anne Hill's doctor – a Simon Elkin, who practises at the Portslade Medical Centre – to ask him about the carer who had been appointed for her. He wasn't too complimentary about Mrs Hill. She'd been demanding a carer, but he'd felt she was quite capable of looking after herself. So I went and spoke to some of her neighbours. None of them seem to like her that much. A young couple next door say they see her out and about regularly, but they avoid her, because if they even so much as nod at her she comes over and tells them how ill she is, and complains that no one cares about her. She sounds like a regular Moaning Minnie. No one seems to have seen this carer, nor the Volvo.'

'You really should go home, Norman. Get some rest,' Grace said.

'I'd prefer to keep working, chief, if it's all right with you.'

Grace smiled at him. 'You're doing a good job. We all need some rest before tomorrow.'

'Go tell that to the missing girls,' Potting said.

52

Sunday 14 December

With the Chief Constable living in Brighton, and Cassian Pewe in temporary rented accommodation in Hove, it was decided the three of them would meet in Roy's office at Sussex House, rather than make the twenty-five-minute drive, each way, to Police Headquarters in Lewes where Pewe and Martinson were based.

It was shortly after 7.30 p.m. that the two men entered Grace's modest office, the Chief Constable in jeans and a baggy, cable-knit sweater, Pewe in cavalry twills, suede brogues, a thin roll-neck, and one of those natty tweed jackets with epaulettes and leather patches on the sleeves that, Grace thought, Pewe imagined gave the impression of a country squire, but which made him look more like a spiv bookmaker.

Grace made coffee, then joined them at his small round conference table. He thanked them both for coming out on a Sunday evening, and then launched straight into his reason for wanting to see them so urgently. 'I'm afraid,' he said, 'that all the evidence indicates we have an active serial killer in our city.'

Martinson's face visibly stiffened. Pewe looked like a man who had just swallowed a wasp.

'You realize the implications of this, Roy?' Martinson said.

'Brighton doesn't have serial killers, Roy,' Pewe said. 'I mean – not since the Trunk Murders of the early 1930s. How sure are you?'

Grace brought them up to date with both his own and Glenn Branson's investigations into Operation Mona Lisa and Operation Haywain. When he had finished both the Chiefs were silent. They agreed that there needed to be a Gold group set up, and that Pewe would take on the responsibility for organizing this.

'In advance of meeting both of you,' Roy continued, 'I spoke to

Jonathan Atkins at the National Crime Agency Operational Support Unit today, telling him my views, and he's given me detailed guidelines on how to proceed with the investigations from this point and how to manage the impact on the community. His advice is to go very public and get the press and media on board from the start. I'm also waiting for a callback from an SIO who's currently instructing at the National Police College, who has had past experience on two serial killers.'

'The impact on the community is going to be enormous, Roy,' the Chief Constable said.

'I know,' Grace replied. 'I'm putting together a Prevention Strategy which will include measures we can take to help lessen the risk of future victims.'

'We've had some experience in the Met,' Pewe added, pensively.

'You need to understand Brighton isn't Metropolitan London,' Grace said. 'You have more than an eight million population there. We have just over a quarter of a million. This is much more of a tight-knit community. People are less used to murder here – our strategy needs to reflect that to avoid panicking the city.'

'We've finally lost the very unwelcome title of Injecting Drug Death Capital of the UK after almost eleven years,' Tom Martinson said. 'Now we have this.'

'I agree, sir. And the impact's going to remain until we've got the offender charged and locked up,' Grace said grimly.

'You realize what the consequences will be if you've got this wrong, Roy?' Cassian Pewe asked, the familiar whine, unpleasantly close to a sneer, returning to his voice, as if the wasp was now confidently digested.

'I can imagine there being a short-term impact on the tourist trade, sir,' Grace said, 'as well as a lot of very nervous citizens. But the consequences of not warning the public could result in another death. Maybe more than one.'

'How much detail have you been advised to release to the public?' Martinson asked.

'Well, I've also spoken at length to Detective Investigator Jordan Finucci at the FBI's homicide bureau at Quantico – I met him on a course I attended four years ago. He's had experience with two of the USA's worst serial killers, Ted Bundy and Dennis Rader – BTK. He's given me some advice based on how they caught BTK.'

'Which was?' Pewe asked.

'Well, it's a pretty established fact that the overwhelming majority of serial killers have massive egos. Some homicide detectives in the US have had results by using that knowledge. The advice I've had is to rattle our offender's cage, and try to flush him out.'

'But if you do that, and the missing women are still alive, might that not provoke him into killing them?' Martinson queried.

'The statistics are against us, sir, on them still being alive. Most victims are killed within an hour of being abducted; very few are still alive twenty-four hours later. We have to be positive, and conduct the enquiry with the full urgency of trying to find them and save their lives, but we need to have an eye beyond these young ladies. We have to prevent another one – or indeed several more – from being taken. What we have established is that he's a meticulous planner, or clearly thinks he is. He got clean away with killing at least two women thirty years ago, it would seem, and now he probably thinks he's invincible.'

'You know, Roy,' Pewe said, 'it seems very strange to me that he should suddenly stop and then start again all these years later.'

'With respect, I recently ran an investigation of a serial rapist – the Shoe Man. He'd stopped for many years – the reason being he got married and had kids. BTK in the USA stopped for a similar period, for similar reasons.'

'Roy's right, Cassian,' Tom Martinson said. 'And we don't know for sure this offender did stop offending. We just believe he stopped in Sussex for a long time. He might have continued elsewhere in the UK or even abroad and then recently returned here.'

'Presumably your Intel cell is checking throughout the UK, back thirty years, Roy, for matching offences?' said Pewe.

'Yes, they are working on it, but with no results so far. One other thing I've done today is contact a forensic psychologist, Tony Balazs. He worked on two high-profile serial cases – the M25 rapist, Antoni Imiela, and the Ipswich prostitute killer, Steve Wright. His advice concurs with Jordan Finucci's – flush him out through the media.'

'Roy,' Cassian Pewe said, 'there's an SIO in the Met I've worked with, Paul Sweetman, who was seconded to help with the Ipswich case. Without in any way wanting to tread on your toes, would you object to my asking him to come down and offer his support?'

Grace stared at him, warily. The relationship between Sussex Police and London's Metropolitan Police had never been an entirely easy one. Many good officers had been poached by the Met through a better pay scale.

'Roy,' Martinson said, diplomatically. 'I'm sure Cassian has only the best interests of our city at heart – and has no intention of usurping your command of this case.' He looked to the ACC for confirmation.

'Absolutely, Tom.' Pewe turned to Grace with a smarmy smile. 'Roy, I know we've had our differences in the past, but they are firmly in the past. DCI Sweetman is a good guy. I would only suggest he came down – and in a strictly advisory capacity to you – if you were totally comfortable with this. If not, we'll forget it.'

Grace thought for some moments, realizing he had little choice. If he refused and the operation went pear-shaped, Pewe would hang him out to dry.

'I'm sure he'll be of assistance,' he said.

'Good,' Martinson said. 'Roy and Cassian, I want you both to work on this together, keep me in the loop, come up with a plan. I will keep the Police and Crime Commissioner informed – I know she's going to be highly concerned, and the senior members of the community should be joining the Gold group tomorrow. Despite the funeral, you need to keep your focus on this. I suggest we hold a press conference later tomorrow, after the funeral and the first meeting of the Gold group, at which you make the announcement that we have a serial killer. But be under no illusion, it is going to rock the city to the core. It's going to cause panic. And it's going to hurt the whole area commercially.'

'On the basis of what you are saying, Roy,' Cassian Pewe said, 'I think you should subsume Operation Mona Lisa into Operation Haywain.'

'I've already thought about this, sir,' Grace replied. 'I will be in overall command of the total investigation process, and I have asked DCI Iain Maclean to be my deputy. I will then have key officers running individual aspects of the investigation for each of the victims.'

Pewe nodded, then glanced at his phone which had just beeped.

'Another thing I think we should do,' Grace said, 'is come up with a nickname for the offender before the press think up some sensational name of their own. We don't want the *Argus* coming up with something alarmist such as the Brighton Ripper or the Sussex Strangler.'

'Do you have any suggestions, Roy?' Tom Martinson asked.

'Yes. I discussed it with Tony Balazs, and we want something that doesn't glamorize him too much. The one we both like is the Brighton Brander.'

The two senior officers pondered this for some moments. 'I think it's clever,' Martinson said.

'Yes,' Pewe said. 'Let's confirm that with the Gold group to make sure the community's on board.'

For the next ten minutes they talked about resourcing – and costs. With the potential community impact, Martinson told both officers that money, on this rare occasion, could not be a factor. They had to throw all their resources at this, regardless.

Before the meeting, Roy Grace had already realized the enormity of his responsibility. Now he was feeling it even more.

'Plot 3472 in Hove Cemetery,' Pewe said, suddenly, looking down at the notes he had taken.

'Yes,' Grace said.

From the tone of Pewe's voice, that piece of information was having a seriously detrimental effect on his blood pressure. Grace hoped for a few brief moments it might prove terminal. 'That's the oldest trick in the book,' Pewe said.

'Yes, sir,' Grace said. 'DI Branson has already pointed that out.'

53

Freya Northrop felt stuffed to bursting as she turned the MX5 into the driveway of their house, shortly after 10.30 p.m. She stifled a yawn, totally exhausted. Zak, in the passenger seat beside her, had slept most of the way back from their last stop of the day, an evening meal at The Cat in West Hoathley, a pub restaurant he'd heard great things about and which had not disappointed. He had photographed and written down details about his starter of hazelnut-crumbed goat's cheese with honey-roasted figs and Parma ham, and the coffee parfait served in a cappuccino cup complete with froth and sugar cubes of chocolate jelly, both of which he planned to try out with a view to putting them on his menu.

She never ceased to be astonished at the amount of food Zak could pack away. They'd had two lunches at different restaurants in Whitstable – starters, mains and puds, because he'd wanted to try a range of dishes – and whilst she had pecked at hers, he'd wolfed down all of his and finished hers. And now they'd had a three-course dinner at The Cat, and again he had scoffed the lot. Yet he was, she thought enviously, ridiculously thin.

Her dad had once told her never to eat in a restaurant where there was a thin chef, it wasn't a good sign. Yet Zak was a brilliant cook. He'd been born with supersonic metabolism, he joked. But it was true. Honest to God, where did he put all those carbs? She patted his sleepy, brush-cut head affectionately. 'We're home, my sweet.'

He woke with a start and stifled a yawn. Then he took her hand and kissed it. 'Thanks for driving.' He yawned again.

'Want to sleep in the car?' she said with a grin, opening her door.

He unclipped his seat belt, opened his door and climbed slowly out into the cold, damp night air. 'I've eaten too much,' he said and patted his stomach.

'Coming from you, that's quite something!'

'I might just make myself a little snack before we go to bed.'

Freya laughed. 'Want me to see if there's a suckling pig in the freezer we can chuck on the barbie?'

She stepped up to the front door, unlocked it and went inside, fumbling for the light switch. The smell of fresh paint and new carpet and recently sawn timber greeted her.

Zak followed her in and closed the door behind him. They walked through to the ultra-modern kitchen – the first room to have been completed – with today's *Observer* lying on a huge butcher's block that served as the table.

'As I haven't had a drink all day, I think I deserve a glass of wine before bed,' she said, opening the fridge, removing a half-full bottle of Sauvignon Blanc and tugging out the cork. 'Want one?'

He shook his head. 'Thanks but I've drunk far too much already.'

'No comment!' she said with a grin, lifting a glass and an ashtray out of the dishwasher, and setting them down on the table. She poured some wine, then rummaged in her handbag for her tobacco, filters and liquorice roll-up papers.

As she began placing strands of tobacco in the opened-out paper, she noticed Zak frowning at something.

'What?' she said.

'There's a draught. Can you feel it?'

She nodded, she could. A steady, cold draught.

He continued frowning. 'Where's it coming from?'

'I've never noticed it before,' Freya said. 'It's always been so snug in here.' The kitchen was usually cosy, thanks to the underfloor heating Zak had put in. But she could feel the cold air, definitely.

Zak suddenly stood up and walked across to the back door. 'Freya, darling,' he said, his voice sounding strange. 'We locked the back door, surely – we locked up carefully before we left this morning, didn't we?'

'I locked it myself,' she said. 'I remember doing it – why?'

He pointed at the top and bottom bolts, which were open. Then he pointed at the key in the lock. 'I just tried the key, and it's open, unlocked. Are you sure you locked up?'

She shrugged. 'I'm ninety-nine per cent, yes.'

'Oh shit,' he said, suddenly, staring down at the floor.

'What?'

He pointed at the leaded light window next to the back door. One small square pane of glass, six inches by six inches, was missing. Then he jabbed a finger down at the floor. 'Look.'

She stood up and walked over, and saw the pane of glass lying close to the mat.

'How – how – how did that happen?' She was quivering, staring wildly all around her now.

'Panes of glass don't detach themselves,' Zak said. 'And if they do, they don't fall onto a tiled floor without shattering. And locks don't unlock themselves.' He strode over to a drawer, pulled it open and grabbed a carving knife. He walked through into the hall, brandishing the blade.

'We should call the police,' she said, nervously.

'Do it,' he said. 'Dial 999.' He stepped forward.

'Don't go out there, Zak. If there's someone . . .'

She grabbed the phone and almost dropped it, she was shaking so much. Then, panic-stricken, she stabbed out the numbers.

54

A fine mist of rain fell silently and steadily, soaking the gathering mourners, and glossing the grey, stark, neo-Gothic edifice of St Peter's. The imposing building was the largest church in the city, and had been chosen for today because of the number of police officers and support staff who had expressed the wish to attend.

That morning Grace had brought the team briefing forward again to 7.30 a.m. and left a small core of officers continuing with the investigation, under the leadership of his deputy SIO, Iain Maclean. He was planning to return to Sussex House immediately after the service and committal.

Everything about this Monday morning felt grey, he thought. Even the sky was tombstone coloured. He was attired – a little uncomfortably – in the formal dress uniform he had not removed from its dry-cleaning bag in over four years. The last time he had worn it was also for a high-profile funeral – a Sussex Police officer who had died in tragic circumstances.

Shortly after 10.30 a.m. he walked with Cleo, the two of them huddled beneath an umbrella, down from the rear car park of John Street police station, where he had been fortunate to have been given one of the few available parking spaces, towards London Road. Neither of them spoke much, as he rehearsed what he was going to say in his mind. They were entering what had once been one of the scuzziest areas of the city, but was now up and coming. Normally, out of habit, he would have been checking the faces of everyone he passed, but today his thoughts were elsewhere, mostly focused on the funeral that lay ahead, but frequently switching back to the disappearances of Logan Somerville, Ashleigh Stanford and, possibly linked with them, Emma Johnson.

Cleo held his hand tightly and he was comforted and more grateful than he could ever say for her support. He could not remember the last time he had felt so nervous. He was shaking as he walked, butterflies going berserk in his stomach. He'd been in many dangerous situations in the line of duty, in the past, but nothing he could remember had ever made him feel this way. Above all, he was terrified of cracking up when he reached the pulpit.

'You'll be fine, darling.' She kissed him.

He patted his inside pocket for about the seventh time to check that his speech was there, panicking for a moment that he might have left it behind. He tugged it out and checked it, just to make sure, then carefully replaced it, and checked again that it was safely tucked in.

The approach to St Peter's was lined with motorcycle police officers. Beyond them stood the guard of honour of uniformed officers, already in place, as well as a contingent of fire officers, despite there being twenty-five minutes to go. Swarming around them were press photographers, TV camera and radio crews.

As they neared he saw Cassian Pewe, in full dress uniform, engaged in conversation with Tom Martinson, also in dress uniform, and Nicola Roigard, like Cleo and most of the other women, all in black. Rainwater dripped from the edge of her broad-brimmed hat.

The trio greeted Grace and Cleo with respectful nods. Then Cassian Pewe extended his hand and gave him a limp handshake. 'You know how sorry I am, Roy.'

The problem with Pewe's whiny voice was that anything he said, even condolences like this, sounded like he was sneering, Grace thought. 'Thank you, sir,' he said, stiffly. 'I don't think you've met my wife, Cleo.'

Pewe shook her gloved hand and simpered, unctuously. 'What an absolute delight. I'm told you are sorely missed at the mortuary. Are you enjoying life as a mother?'

'Very much,' she said. 'But I plan to be back at work again soon.'

'Not soon enough, so far as I'm concerned.' He smiled, his lips curling to reveal a viperous set of incisors.

Grace remembered that ACC Pewe was outside the burning building where DS Bella Moy had died, remaining there all day until her body was brought out. He did at least respect his old adversary for that.

'A difficult morning for you, Roy,' Nicola Roigard said.

'Yes,' he said, his voice choked. 'This is my wife, Cleo.'

The two women shook hands. As they did so, Pewe stepped out of the line-up and said to Roy Grace, quietly, 'Any developments overnight?'

Grace saw, heading towards them, the *Argus* reporter Siobhan Sheldrake.

'Nothing since my update of yesterday evening, sir.'

'Excuse me, gentlemen!' Siobhan Sheldrake interrupted them, holding out a small microphone. 'Could I get a comment from each of you about the tragic death of Detective Sergeant Bella Moy?'

Roy Grace had to listen, close to vomiting, as Cassian Pewe launched into a sickly, glib list of superlatives about the diligence, dedication and outstanding courage of the fallen officer. Pewe finished with the words, 'Detective Sergeant Bella Moy was quite one of the most remarkable police officers it has ever been my privilege to work with.'

Except, Roy Grace thought, stifling his anger, Pewe had never worked with her. But this was neither the time nor the place for trying to settle scores. He let Pewe finish, said his own piece into the microphone, then led Cleo towards the entrance of the church, where Glenn Branson was standing next to Guy Batchelor, who was accompanied by his blonde, attractive Swedish wife, Lena.

They smiled at each other, politely, but none of them felt like talking. Grace noticed a faint smell of cigarette smoke on Batchelor and could have happily slunk away for a quick smoke himself right now to calm his nerves. Glenn put his arm around him and gave him a hug. Grace sniffed, pulled out a handkerchief and blew his nose.

'Good luck, mate,' Branson said. He balled his fist and touched knuckles with Grace. Grace always wondered what it would feel like for anyone on the receiving end of a punch from his friend's fist; it felt as if it had been hewn out of rock.

The almost ethereal silence across the city was shattered, suddenly, by the Doppler wail of sirens, as an ambulance threaded its way through the clogged-up London Road traffic. Once it faded away into the distance, an even greater silence followed. It was as if the entire city of Brighton and Hove had ground to a halt. Even the seagulls were quiet. The only sound that could be heard, for several minutes, was the *clop-clopping* of horses' hooves.

Then the cortège came into sight. The coffin was clearly visible, draped with the Sussex Police flag and a policewoman's hat, surrounded by flowers, through the glass windows of a carriage drawn by four black horses. It was followed by a black limousine. Both pulled up outside the front of the church.

Roy Grace put his arm around Cleo and led her inside, accepting the two service sheets that were handed to him, and headed down the aisle, nodding in acknowledgement at faces he knew. As they sat down, Bella's mother, a frail lady with a Zimmer frame, and several others of Bella's family members, including three children, sat down on the pew in front of them.

Roy handed a service sheet to Cleo, then stared at the photograph on the front of his. It was an angelic young child with golden curls, the dates of her birth and death beneath. Bella Kathleen Moy. She was just thirty-five when she died. He opened it and ran his eyes through the order of service, noting the hymns that had been chosen, glad to see that one of his own favourites, the rousing 'Jerusalem', was among them.

Cleo had told him she believed in God, although she never went to church to worship. They'd had a number of discussions about faith, particularly in the days following Noah's birth, and whether to have him baptized. Cleo wanted it; she liked traditions, and the idea of godparents. Grace was not really sure how he felt. Part of him would have preferred not to have a christening, and to let Noah decide for himself when he was older. But if it was what Cleo wanted, he was happy to go along with it.

There had been a time, too, when he had believed. Then he'd gone through a period of being almost a militant atheist, partly prompted by the death of both his parents, and Sandy's absolute cynicism about religion, and then had arrived at where he was today, open-minded. He found it hard to believe in the Biblical notion of God, but equally, he was uncomfortable with the modern atheists like Dawkins. If he had to nail his colours to the mast, he would have said that there was a bigger picture, and human beings weren't – as yet, anyhow – smart enough to understand what it was.

But whenever he entered an impressive church like this one, he could understand something of the mystical spell cast over people. He remained seated in the pew, breathing in the smells of wood and musty fabric while Cleo unhooked her kneeler, laid it down and knelt on it, her face buried in her hands in prayer.

He followed suit, opened his hands and pressed them against his face. He tried to remember the words of the Lord's Prayer, which he had said every night throughout his childhood, and into his mid-teens.

'Our Father which art in Heaven, hallowed be thy name,' he murmured, self-consciously, and stopped, as the next line suddenly eluded him.

Then music began playing. John Denver's 'Leaving on a Jet Plane'.

Suddenly, all around him, people were getting to their feet. He and Cleo stood, too.

As the music played on, the pall-bearers carried the pine coffin down the aisle. He turned, along with everyone else, to see four sombre men, one of them Norman Potting, tears streaming down his face, slowly approaching the altar. Then they placed it, carefully, on the catafalque.

The congregation sat again. As the service commenced, officiated by Father Martin, who only a short while ago had officiated at their own wedding, Roy Grace pulled his speech from his pocket and read through it once more. The vicar said a few words of introduction, then they stood again for the first hymn, 'Abide With Me'. As it drew to an end, the vicar gave a reading from 1 Corinthians 12. Then Norman Potting stood up, slowly made his way towards the pulpit and entered it.

His face was wet with tears and there was total silence in the church. It took him some moments to compose himself. 'This is about Bella,' he said. Then his voice faltered. 'The music she loved. The people she loved. No one ever loved her more than I did.' He began to sob. After several moments, dabbing his eyes again, he said, 'Throughout the time I was lucky enough to know Bella, and for her to become my fiancée, there was one Sussex Police officer who knew all along just how damned good she was.' He pointed straight at Roy Grace. 'You, sir. Roy. Please come and say a few words – I – I can't – I can't say any more.'

As he stumbled down from the pulpit, Grace stood and walked towards it. When he reached Norman Potting he stopped, gave him a hug and kissed him on both cheeks. Then he climbed into the pulpit, took out his speech and laid it on the lectern, and waited for Norman to find his front-row seat and settle into it before commencing.

'The police have come in for a lot of criticism in recent years,' he said, catching Cleo's reassuring expression, then scanning the congregation of almost one thousand faces. 'Fair do's to the press for highlighting the idiots in our forces, the *wrong'uns*. There are over one hundred and thirty-five thousand police officers in the UK. In any body of people that big, you are bound to find some bad eggs. Maybe they number about *one per cent*, although I would guess the figure is lower even than that. So what about the other ninety-nine per cent? Bella Moy was one of these. She worked as one of the most valued members of my team on many cases. During all the time I knew her, despite her obligations caring for her mother, she never threw a sickie, never moaned, never went home early, never took a single day off that she wasn't entitled to. Sussex CID was her life. A life that very recently and for far too short a time, in which she found true love with Norman.'

He paused, faltering, as he caught the Detective Sergeant's eye, and had to take a deep breath to compose himself. He stared again at the sea of silent but attentive faces, most of whom were familiar. 'I've been privileged to serve Sussex Police for twenty-one years, and I've met and know many of you here today. There are few officers in our force, or in any other police force around the nation, who have not, at some time, been in a situation where their life has been on the line. Whether it's confronting, single-crewed, a scimitar-waving drunk at three o'clock in the morning in Brighton's Lanes, approaching a car in a dark country lane, with a suspected armed robber inside, entering a brutal pub brawl, or crawling out on a high-rise window ledge to try to talk down a potential suicidal jumper. What I do know is that all of you officers here today would go into that situation with barely a moment's thought for your own safety, to do your duty in serving the public.' He fell silent, to let the words sink in, before continuing.

'Bella Moy died doing just that. What makes her death even more poignant – and heroic – is that she was off duty. There was a burning building, and she could have driven right by. But she didn't, she stopped. And when she learned that there was a small child trapped inside, she went straight in – and saved that child. The fire services had not arrived at this point and it is likely that if Bella had not gone in, that young child would have died. It was an act of bravery that cost her her life. She knew she was taking a very big risk entering that blazing building but she didn't actually have time to make much of a risk assessment. She knew there was a chance of saving a child, whatever the risks to herself.' He paused to take a breath, then went on.

'I think the words of this American author, Jack London, could have been written about Bella Moy:

> '*I would rather be ashes than dust!*
> *I would rather that my spark should burn out in a brilliant blaze*
> *than it should be stifled by dry-rot.*
> *I would rather be a superb meteor, every atom of me in magnificent*
> *glow, than a sleepy and permanent planet.*
> *The function of a human being is to live, not to exist.*
> *I shall not waste my days trying to prolong them.*
> *I shall use my time.*'

His voice just held out. 'Bella used her time, and it ran out on her. We are all the poorer for that. But the richer for having known her.'

He stepped down and, blinded by tears, made his way back to his pew.

Ten minutes later, after the words of the last hymn, 'Jerusalem', faded, everyone kneeled again. The vicar gave his final blessing. And suddenly, very different music started. Feargal Sharkey's 'A Good Heart'.

The pall-bearers and Norman Potting shouldered the coffin and carried it back out, followed by Bella's family.

Slowly, Roy Grace climbed to his feet and held out his arm for Cleo. Then he picked up his umbrella and followed them along the aisle, struggling to keep his composure.

Outside, among the throngs of people standing in the bitter cold, a young woman in black, with a small pillbox hat over a tangle of fair hair, and accompanied by a small, rather sullen child, suddenly came up to Norman Potting. 'Excuse me – Mr – Detective Potting?'

'Yes?' Potting nodded.

'My name's Maggie Durrant. Your fiancée, Bella, I – I just wanted to let you know that she saved Megan, my daughter – and she saved our dog, Rocky, too. I – I don't know what to say – I just – I just wanted you to know how grateful I am and how sorry I am.' She sniffed, tears trickling down her cheeks.

'Thank you,' Norman Potting said, his voice choked with emotion. 'Thank you.' He looked down at the little girl and gave her a tearful smile, and she gave him the faintest trace of a smile back.

55

Monday 15 December

Logan heard a scraping sound, the lid above her being opened. She saw in the faint green glow a head appear, the features entirely obscured by a black gimp mask, with goggles. An instant later a searing white flashlight beam blinded her.

'Everything's a bit shit at the moment,' he said, in a clear, educated voice. 'But look on the bright side – there always is a bright side – you're still alive. But I thought you should know that you are on borrowed time. But then, aren't we all, eh? No one gets out of life alive!'

Hyperventilating with terror, she heard him chuckle. It was a hideous cackle, like a witch.

'I'm thirsty,' she gasped. 'I need more sugar. Please – please tell me why I'm here. What do you want? I'll give you anything you want. If you want to have sex with me, I won't resist. I'll do anything.'

'Yes, you will. You will do anything I want!' He cackled again. Then his voice suddenly softened. 'You want water?'

'Please.'

Suddenly, without giving her any opportunity to draw breath, a stream of icy water began pouring onto her face. She gulped some of it down, but it kept on coming, covering her whole face, pouring down the sides of her face and her neck. She shook her head, swallowing more down but it kept on coming. It shot up her nostrils, agonizingly. She tried to breathe, but choked on the stuff now. She turned her head sideways, trying desperately to break free of it. But it kept on pouring. She began shaking. Suffocating. Drowning.

She tried to scream but only a gurgle came out. She was thrashing, twisting and turning against her bonds. But the water kept on coming, jetting down on her as hard as a fire hose.

Her whole inside was tight. Her lungs bursting.

The water kept on coming.

Then as suddenly as it had started, it ceased.

Spluttering, coughing, choking, gulping air, she closed her eyes against the searing white light again.

'You talk when I tell you to talk. Slut.'

The lid slid shut above her.

She lay, whimpering in terror, closed her eyes and prayed, silently. *Oh please, God, help me, please help me.*

When she opened her eyes again she realized the lid was open once more. The man in the mask and goggles was staring down at her.

'God doesn't like sluts who break off their engagement,' he said.

The lid slid shut again.

Who was it? Was Jamie behind this, she kept wondering? Had he set this up? Where, oh where the hell was she?

She listened constantly for any sounds to give her a clue where she might be. She'd not yet heard the dawn chorus again. No sirens. No aircraft noise. Just the constant unremitting silence, except when her captor came to visit.

She called out. But only silence came back at her.

56

Roy drove in silence, in the slow traffic behind the cortège, with Cleo at his side. The rain was falling harder, the sky as dark as their mood.

'I've never been to a sadder funeral,' she said, suddenly.

He nodded, too choked to speak at the moment.

'Normally,' she said, 'you know – there's something uplifting. Most of the funerals I've been to have been of elderly relatives. Lives lived. I went to one, a couple of years ago, of an old school friend who'd died at twenty-seven of cancer, but even that one, although desperately sad, didn't affect me in the way this one has.'

'I guess in the police we all know the dangers. Glenn was shot during that raid to try to free a kidnapped couple. Had the bullet gone a couple of inches either way, he'd have been killed or paralysed. And then EJ was inches from being crushed to death by a van she was trying to stop.'

'And you, my darling? Honestly, how many risks have you taken, my love?'

'A few,' he said. 'I suppose one of the closest was at Beachy Head last year, when I had to go over the edge of the cliff to save Pewe's life. And I hated the bastard.'

'With good reason. I'll never forgive him for what he did.'

Grace thought back to Pewe's humiliating attempt to prove he had murdered Sandy by having the garden at the home they'd shared scanned and excavated

'He was determined to prove I had killed her. Then I put my life on the bloody line to save his. Now he's my sodding boss. How great is that?'

'Well, maybe he'll now show his gratitude.'

Grace touched her thigh, gently. 'You know, that's one of the ten

202

thousand things I love about you. You're always looking for the good in people.'

'And you're always looking for the bad?'

'That's what twenty years of being a copper does for you.'

'Don't ever stop looking for the good, Roy. There is good in everyone. Sometimes you just have to drill down deep.'

'I'd like to believe you. Especially when you look at someone like Bella, who was devoted to her job and equally devoted to looking after her elderly, sick mother, then you have a truly good person. I've encountered too many people who were totally dedicated to doing evil.'

'How many of those ever had a chance in life? How many got warped in childhood by abusive parents, lack of education and no role models?'

'Most of them. But does that excuse them? *Hey, I'm awfully sorry, I just beat an old lady to death so I could burgle her house, but it's all right because my mum used to get drunk and hit me.*' He drove in silence for some moments, then he said, 'I'm sorry, darling, I don't want to sound cynical. I don't ever want to be a cynic. But Bella died a hero. A true hero. I'm not sure how many of the scrotes we have to deal with every day in this city would ever be capable of heroism. Or of even doing anything good.'

Finally they entered the hilltop cemetery, and saw the cortège a short distance ahead. They wound past the rows of flat tombstones – the only ones permitted here now because of the long history of vandalism – and halted. A short distance away was the freshly opened family grave, where Bella's father had been buried some years earlier. Green AstroTurf covered the mound of earth on one side, as if peeled from inside the grave. Two planks of wood lay across.

Oblivious now to the wind and driving rain, they hurried over to the limousine that had halted behind the horse-drawn hearse, just as Norman Potting, looking utterly lost and bewildered, tears streaming down his face, and clutching a plastic bag, climbed out.

Grace put a supportive arm around the Detective Sergeant, who was crying inconsolably. 'Be strong for her, Norman,' he said quietly to him. 'Just be strong for the next short while.'

'I don't know how I'm going to be able to go on living without her.'

'You're going to have to go on sodding living, because I need you.' He led him towards the chubby, white-haired figure of Father Martin, who stood by the grave, oblivious to the weather in his black cassock and purple stole, as Bella's family and friends gathered around.

The coffin was carried to the grave and tapes threaded through the handles. For some moments there was total silence, just the sound of the wind and the falling rain, and the deep, intermittent sobs from Norman.

'I am the resurrection and the light, says the Lord,' intoned Father Martin. 'He who believes in me, though he dies, yet shall he live and shall not die eternally.

'Friends, welcome here, to these few moments in the cemetery as we come and bring Bella to this final resting place. We are reminded in the scriptures that we brought nothing into this world and we can take nothing out. The Lord gives and the Lord takes away. Blessed be the name of the Lord. Let's bow our heads for this first prayer.'

Grace listened to the words of the prayer and remembered Father Martin's reading earlier, blinded now by his own tears. He continued to support Norman Potting, who was shaking. He heard the priest's words intermittently.

'But someone may ask, how are the dead raised? With what kind of body do they come?' he heard. 'The body that is sown is perishable. It is raised imperishable . . . Where, oh death, is your sting?'

Potting's sobbing became louder. Grace tried to comfort him.

'We are going to commend Bella to God's keeping,' Father Martin said.

The pall-bearers bowed their heads. Slowly they lowered the coffin, until it was out of sight.

'The Lord is full of compassion and mercy, slow to anger . . . He remembers that we are but dust, our days are like the grass, we flourish like a flower of the field. When the wind goes over it is gone and its place will know it no more, but the merciful goodness of the Lord endures for ever and ever . . . We have entrusted our sister Bella Kathleen Moy to God's mercy, and we now commit her body to the ground, earth to earth, ashes to ashes, dust to dust, in the sure and certain hope of resurrection to eternal life, through our Lord Jesus Christ.'

Then, after the final amen, Bella's mother stepped forward shakily, holding on to the arm of a family member, and threw a handful of earth into the grave.

Moments later, suddenly silent, Norman Potting broke free from Grace's grip, stumbled up to the grave, and knelt. Then from the plastic bag he was holding he pulled a small red box.

Looking around wildly, almost insane with grief, he said, 'Bella will need these. She'll need them. She will.'

He leaned forward, headlong into the grave, and dropped the box of Maltesers on top of the coffin.

Then he staggered back to his feet, helped by Roy who ran forward to support him.

'She will,' Potting said. 'She'll be giving them out in Heaven, to everyone she meets.'

57

'Good morning, boys, it's make-your-mind-up time! *Make-your-mind-up time, chum!*' he said with a giggle. 'Who remembers that line, eh? Felix? Harrison? Marcus?'

'Cilla Black in the TV dating show *Blind Date*?' ventured Felix, always the one to lead.

'No, it was Hughie Green in *Opportunity Knocks* who used it first,' said Marcus.

'What do you think, Harrison?'

'I'm not so sure. But it rings a bell.'

'Ding, ding!' He giggled again.

'It was definitely *Blind Date*,' Felix said.

'I never saw *Blind Date*,' Marcus said.

'Tut tut, what a sheltered life you've led, eh?'

'A better one than this,' Marcus retorted, sullen.

'Tut, tut, tut, what kind of gratitude is that, Marcus?'

'What exactly do any of us have to be grateful about?' he retorted.

'Ooooohhhh, feisty! I like it when you get all feisty, Marcus. It sets all my pheromones racing! You never saw *Blind Date*? Did you spend the 1990s living under a rock? The whole planet saw that show. Except, of course, for you.'

'Myself as well as the one quarter of the earth's population who've not yet made a telephone call, let alone enjoyed the luxury of watching television,' Marcus replied.

'Oh very good, I love your social conscience, Marcus. I like a person with principles. But I suspect that figure you are quoting is lower these days. You're out of date, really you are. I don't know what you spend your time doing, honestly. We'll have to help your cultural enlightenment. I'll see if I can find some recordings of *Blind Date* for you!'

'I think Felix is right,' said Harrison. 'It was Cilla Black in *Blind Date.*'

'Yessss,' he squealed with delight. 'Yesssss, yessssssss, yesssssssssss! So Felix wins today's prize! Let's all hear it for Felix! Let's congratulate him! Felix, you get a Mars bar! I know it's a bit early in the morning, but hey, as my mum used to say, *What's time to the Irish?* Eh?'

He pulled a Mars bar from his pocket, ripped the wrapper off and let it flutter down onto the floor. 'Oh dear, what a litter lout I am!' He held out the chocolate bar. 'Here it is, Felix, enjoy, let the losers salivate over your success! But before you take the first bite, because you're not quite there yet, I want you to tell me what Cilla Black's name was before she changed it. Can you tell me?' He held out the chocolate bar, tantalizing him.

'I don't know,' Felix said. 'I so totally do not know!'

'It was *Priscilla White!*' he said, triumphantly. 'Oh dear, you lose!' He held the bar up. 'All right, while I decide if one of you gets the whole thing, or we all share it, I'd like to know everyone's opinion about my latest *project*, Freya Northrop. Are we all still agreed?' He held up her photograph. 'She ticks all the boxes, yes?'

'She does,' Felix said.

'Harrison, what do you think?'

'Felix is only saying *yes* because he wants the Mars bar,' Harrison replied.

'She's definitely your type,' Marcus said.

'Oh, you are being nice to me now, Marcus. Could it be that you are angling for the chocolate? You are right though, she is my type, isn't she! Oh yes, she's exactly my type all right. She's home early every night to prepare dinner, while her boyfriend – Zak – stays at the restaurant, working away. When he comes home one night this week, big surprise – there'll be no dinner and no Freya!'

'Do you have a thing about couples shacking up together?' Harrison asked.

'Are you going moralistic on me, Harrison?'

'I'm only mentioning it.'

'Purely coincidental, old chap.' He shook his head. 'I'm sensing a lot of attitude this morning.' He put the picture down and looked at his watch. 'Six fifteen. Tut, tut! I've not had my brekkie yet!' He took a large bite out of the Mars bar, and chewed. Through his sticky mouthful of chocolate and toffee, he said, 'Mmmn, not had one of these for a while. It tastes good, really good. Too good to share! And I've got a busy day ahead – need to keep my strength up, sorry everyone!' He pushed the rest of the bar into his mouth.

'Bastard!' Marcus said.

He nodded. 'Yep, I am, you're right about that, Marcus; but then you always have been!'

58

Shortly after 7 a.m. Roy Grace carried a mug of steaming coffee into his office and sat at his desk, reflecting on the events of yesterday, and in particular the first Gold group meeting that had followed the grim funeral and the equally grim wake, before the press conference and the evening briefing. It was dark beyond his rain-spattered window, the Asda superstore complex and the skyline of Brighton barely visible apart from the hazy, misty glow of street lighting.

In between two of the piles of paperwork he needed to tackle sat a foil package containing the egg and tomato sandwich Cleo had made him last night for his breakfast, and six red grapes – she had read in some health column that six red grapes a day were the new big anti-ageing elixir. And the tomato was apparently good for warding off many cancers in later years. Since Noah had been born, he had noticed that she had become more preoccupied than ever with both of them eating healthily. And never ordinarily a nervous person, she had become a tad anxious. No doubt something do with a mother's protective instincts, he thought.

Feeling very flat, he stared up at the photographic print of the words branded on *unknown female, U R DEAD*, pinned to his noticeboard. At least part of the gloom he felt was over the imminent arrival of the Met officer, Detective Chief Inspector Paul Sweetman. Maybe Pewe was acting in his best interests, but from past experience, anything Pewe did needed to be viewed with suspicion.

A lot of people had congratulated him on his eulogy, but he'd barely heard their words. Although he'd had no involvement at all in Bella's decision to enter that burning building, he still felt a strong degree of blame. The fire had been started by the arsonist monster at the centre of the investigation he had been running. If they had caught him sooner, Bryce Laurent would never have started the fire, and Bella would still be alive.

He replayed over and over in his mind the whole scenario of that investigation, Operation Aardvark, from the very first report that a woman, Red Westwood, was in danger from a stalker, to the moment when Detective Sergeant Moy had so bravely – if recklessly – entered that burning building, wondering what he might have done differently to have arrested the man sooner.

It gave him little satisfaction that Bryce Laurent had burned to death in a cell at Lewes Prison, in an apparent suicide. He would like to have seen the man brought to trial, and through that process understood something of what had created such a twisted mind. On the other hand, Laurent's death did mean closure, of a kind, for Red Westwood, the woman whose life he had made such hell. At least she would not have to live with the fear that one day he might be released from prison and come after her again.

As was his morning ritual, he logged on to the serials and checked the tagged summary log. An attempted gay rape of a man in Kemp Town; an escaped prisoner from Ford open prison arrested at an address in Hollingbury; a street robbery; a reported break-in at a house in Hove, nothing apparently stolen, according to the owners, a chef and his partner; and another break-in, at a student house off Elm Grove, where two laptops had been taken.

Next he turned his attention to this morning's briefing on the joint investigation, Operation Haywain. He reached for his sandwich and began to remove the foil wrapper Cleo had put around it, and as he did so, he noticed, among the different piles on his desk, a folder with a yellow Post-it stuck to the top, with Glenn Branson's slanted handwriting on it.

Take a look at this!

He put his breakfast down and opened the folder. And felt a jolt as if a bolt of electricity had shot through him.

He was looking at a copy of one of several CAD – Computer Aided Design – impressions of *unknown female*, the body found at Hove Lagoon, the computer-generated image created from the bone structure of her skull. Each version showed a different hairstyle. She looked an attractive young woman in her early twenties, and in this one, the artist had shown her with long brown hair.

'Shit,' he said to himself, aloud.

'Yeah, that's what I said, too.'

He looked up to see Glenn Branson, sharply dressed and looking a lot fresher than he himself felt, and smelling more strongly than usual of a musky fragrance. He hadn't heard him enter. 'Obviously,' Branson went on, 'the artist has speculated on the hairstyle; a few strands aren't much to go on.'

'Putting the hair aside, their looks are so similar too.' Grace stared down at the blank, expressionless image that was devoid of whatever personality the deceased woman once had. 'Emma Johnson, Logan Somerville, Ashleigh Stanford, Katy Westerham. And now, *unknown female.* Two of them died thirty years ago, three of them have vanished within the past month.'

Time would tell whether these images would be useful or not. But for now it was helpful to have a possible visual focus on the victim.

Branson turned around one of the chairs in front of the desk and sat astride it, his arms folded over the back, staring thoughtfully at his colleague and mentor. 'How did your Gold group meeting go?'

'Good. We formalized the structure, and agreed three main objectives: the safety of the citizens of Brighton and Hove, the direction and progress of the investigation and our press and media communications strategy.'

'Do you want me at the press conference?'

'I did, mate, but Mr Preening Peacock wants to be there himself along with me – so he can take the glory when we get a result, and blame me if we don't.'

Grace looked down at the pictures again, his brain spinning, thinking about the different experienced people he had spoken to for advice. Was he covering all the bases? he wondered repeatedly.

'I have some news which might help us that's come in overnight. We've got the names from the Council records of three of the men who were on the team that laid the path at the Lagoon, who are still alive. Two of them have been located and are being interviewed this morning,' Branson said. 'The total workforce there at the time was seven. Three of the men have since died, and one emigrated to Australia.'

'We'll need to find him and get him interviewed, if he's still alive. It could be that one of them is the killer, and took the opportunity to rebury the remains before the surface went down, thinking the path would be there forever.'

'Norman Potting has a contact in Melbourne Police who he's spoken to and is on it. But the guy emigrated nearly twenty years ago. It might take a few days.'

'We don't have a few days, Glenn.'

'I'll volunteer for the trip!'

'I need you here. If we need to send anyone, and it's a big if, it might be good to send Norman, give him time away for a few days. By the way, what news on that *Argus* reporter you fancy – any developments?'

Glenn Branson raised his hands in the air and swivelled them from side to side.

'What's that meant to mean?'

'I'm being careful with Siobhan.'

'In what sense?'

Branson drew his forefinger across his lip, like a zip.

'Keep it that way.'

'She gets it.'

'She's a journalist. Journalists eat their young. OK?'

'Journalists and Traffic officers.'

'Yep, well the big difference is that I'd trust a Traffic officer. Even if he – or she – booked me.'

'She's cool, I'm telling you. I know her pretty well by now.'

Grace gave his close friend a sideways look. A thought was going through his mind: that it might actually be no bad thing to have a tame journalist at this moment.

Then he stared back at the photograph of the branded words. 'You have someone contacting all blacksmiths in the area, to see who might have forged the branding iron that did this? Someone would remember making this – if he or she's still around – for sure. There can't be many blacksmiths get commissioned to make a branding iron with those words.'

'There aren't that many blacksmiths or forgemasters at all. Yes, there's an outside enquiry team on it, but no luck yet. It could of course be a DIY job.'

Grace nodded, silently, thinking. What would give someone the idea to brand victims? What did branding signify? Power? Ownership? Sheep and cattle were often branded, to show their ownership. Slaves, too. Jews in concentration camps were branded for identification – although they were done with tattoos rather than heated metal. But ultimately the branding was done as a symbol of power. *I own you now, I can do what I want with you. You are nothing more than cattle.*

The idea he had about the *Argus* crime reporter was forming more clearly now in his mind. 'Mate,' he said, 'I need you to ask Siobhan to do something. It's a *you scratch my back and I'll scratch yours* kind of a favour. OK?'

Branson nodded, looking puzzled. 'Yeah, no problem.'

'Keep it work related, OK?'

The DI grinned, and said nothing.

59

Adrienne Macklin enjoyed her job, working in the front office of the Roundstone Caravan Park on the outskirts of Horsham, a prosperous town twenty-five miles north of Brighton, with a modern shopping centre, and surrounded by glorious Sussex countryside. Part of the company's business was the sale of caravans and they had a wide selection on display, from bargain second-hand tourers up to luxurious, top-of-the-range static caravans. The other part was managing the site's two hundred mobile homes.

Some of the owners were permanent residents but many were holidaymakers who came several times a year from not only all over the county of Sussex, but from many other parts of the UK. And then there was the gentleman in Unit R-73.

A widow, Adrienne was always on the lookout for a potential new partner and he ticked a lot of her boxes. This man was good-looking, charming and always cheerful, but so far all her attempts at engaging him in conversation had been – very politely – rebuffed. She knew virtually nothing about him at all.

He had owned a very nice mobile home for many years and kept it in immaculate condition. His visits were sporadic, turning up sometimes during the week, sometimes at weekends, occasionally staying for a few days, but mostly only for a few hours. He always came alone, carrying armfuls of newspapers and magazines, and a Waitrose carrier bag with, usually, the neck of a wine bottle peeping out of the top.

One time she'd asked him what he did for a living. 'Oh,' he had replied, 'I'm in IT, you know, that kind of thing. Very boring.'

'Not to me,' she had responded, trying to keep the chat going.

'It is, dear, trust me.'

Another time she'd tried to find out where he lived, but he had replied, cheery as ever, 'Oh, you know, here and there. I'm planning to retire here. Not long to go!'

So she remained in hope that one day soon he might actually retire here and perhaps she could get to know him better then.

Meanwhile, she attempted a little detective work of her own, snooping around the outside of his mobile home while he was absent. She'd even tried the lock one day, as she kept keys to most of the homes on the park, but without success. There were three separate locks and the door had reinforced steel around it. The windows, with their blinds down, gave her no clue either – it was impossible to see in.

He was clearly a very private man.

Some days she wondered, uncharitably perhaps, if he was a bit of a deviant. Was he some kind of pervert? What did he get up to inside that mobile home with all his papers and magazines?

The only time Adrienne had ever really engaged in any kind of proper conversation with him had been a couple of years back when her daughter, Hayley, had been helping her out as a summer job, to earn some pennies whilst at uni. He'd taken a bit of a shine to Hayley, and had stood in the office for ages, chatting to her about music. It turned out they were both fans of the Kinks, and he told Hayley about a pub in North London which Ray Davies frequented.

It was the first time she had ever been jealous of her daughter. But Hayley soon put her back in her place after he had left for his caravan, clutching his usual armful of papers and magazines.

'What a weirdo!' Hayley said.

'I think he's rather dishy!'

'Get real, Mother!'

60

Following the 11 a.m. Gold group meeting, shortly before midday, Cassian Pewe strutted into the Lounge Assembly Room at Malling House, the Sussex Police Headquarters, wearing a starched white shirt with epaulettes and a black tie.

Roy Grace, in a navy suit, followed him up onto the podium and they stood side by side in front of the microphones facing the largest gathering of press and media Grace had ever seen, amid a dazzling storm of flashlights. He remembered what he had been told many years ago, to take several deep breaths both to calm his nerves and energize him before addressing a crowd.

There were at least fifty people in the room: journalists, television crews from Sky News, Latest TV, BBC South, and radio reporters he recognized from Radio Sussex and Juice FM, as well as half a dozen more he was unfamiliar with. Also on the podium, standing well to their left, was the Police and Crime Commissioner looking smart and elegant in a grey suit and white blouse, and the Chief Executive of Brighton and Hove City Council, Philippa Tomsett, also smartly dressed.

The room fell silent. Pewe began speaking, but no one could hear him.

'Stand a bit closer to the microphone,' Grace whispered to him.

There was a squawk, then a loud crackle, then Pewe's voice rang out. 'Thank you all for coming. I'm Assistant Chief Constable Cassian Pewe, with responsibility for the overall investigation of major crime in Sussex, and on my right is Detective Superintendent Roy Grace of Surrey and Sussex Major Crime Team, who is the Senior Investigating Officer on Operation Haywain. We also have with us on my left the Police and Crime Commissioner for Sussex and the Chief Executive

of Brighton and Hove City Council. I'm asking Detective Superintendent Grace to brief you on the investigation thus far and then we
will take questions.'

As soon as Grace had finished, a sea of hands rose. Siobhan
Sheldrake from the *Argus* called out first. 'Detective Superintendent
Grace, is it true you believe the disappearances of two Brighton women
in the past week, Ms Logan Somerville and Ms Ashleigh Stanford, are
linked with the disappearance two weeks ago of Worthing resident Ms
Emma Johnson?'

Grace took another deep breath and stepped up closer to his
microphone. 'Yes, and we also have reason to suspect that the
offender behind their abductions may be responsible for two murders we believe occurred approximately thirty years ago. One is the
unsolved murder of Catherine Jane Marie Westerham, a nineteen-
year-old student at Sussex University, who failed to return to her
residence in Elm Grove, Brighton, in December, 1984, and whose
remains were found in Ashdown Forest in April 1985. The other is the
remains of a young woman in her late teens or early twenties which
were recovered from Hove Lagoon, who we believe was murdered
around the same time.'

He pointed at the screen behind him, on which photographs of
Emma Johnson, Logan Somerville and Ashleigh Stanford were being
projected. 'The main focus of the investigation at this time is finding
these three young women, and we are appealing to the public for
anyone who has seen them or may know their current whereabouts
to come forward and contact the Incident Room or Crimestoppers,
on the phone numbers behind me.'

'Detective Superintendent,' a slovenly-looking middle-aged
reporter Grace did not recognize called out. 'Are you saying there is a
serial killer who has been dormant for thirty years now active in the
city of Brighton and Hove?'

Grace could feel the sudden silence in the room, and the almost
vulture-like air of anticipation. He chose his words, which he had
rehearsed many times, carefully. 'We are looking for a middle-aged
man with local knowledge and a sadistic streak, who appears to be
targeting young women of a specific appearance. He's already made a
number of mistakes, which I can't go into now. There is evidence we

have found so far where the victims appear to be branded with the same phrase. That phrase is, "You Are Dead".' Immediately the words 'U R DEAD' appeared on the screen behind him. 'I know,' he went on, 'that you out there will want to give him a title, and for this reason we are calling him the Brighton Brander.'

Instantly a barrage of questions was fired at him, each of them desperate to get their questions heard.

'Where were they branded?'

'What was it done with?'

'How big is it?'

'What's the significance?'

Roy raised his hands to try to calm the audience down. 'We don't know the significance of this phrase, but I can tell you it is approximately two inches wide and half an inch high.'

Another question came from the rear of the room. 'How could there be such a long gap, Detective Superintendent?'

'We only know that there was a long gap here in our city,' Grace replied. 'It's possible he may have moved away for a period, offending elsewhere. But there are plenty of examples both here in our country and overseas of patterns of this kind.'

'Are you certain the offender is male?' a sharp-faced woman said from near the front.

'Yes, we are, from forensic evidence.'

'Can you tell us what kind of forensic evidence? Semen?'

'We are not prepared to divulge that at this stage,' Grace replied. 'We would like to hear from anyone who saw an old grey or dark blue K-reg Volvo estate car in Kemp Town or Dyke Road area, in the vicinity of the Chesham Gate apartment building between five and six o'clock last Thursday evening.' They were deliberately holding back the registration number at this stage.

A grey-haired man in a baseball cap, standing by the Latest TV cameraman, called out, 'Do you have any suspects for the Brighton Brander, Detective Superintendent?'

Grace was pleased the man was using the name. 'Not as yet, no. We are working with forensic psychiatrists and a psychologist.' He took a deep breath again, then went on. 'Although we are linking the disappearances of Emma, Logan and Ashleigh, this is a relatively rare occurrence and we don't want to cause unnecessary concern. We will be providing guidance and advice to young women in the city, as well as increasing the police visibility on the streets.'

Pewe suddenly leaned forward and spoke again. 'The important thing is that we don't want to create a situation of panic. We are confident of an imminent arrest.'

Grace gave him a sideways glare, inwardly despairing of the man. He had just said the very word Grace had been so studiously trying to avoid. Panic. Pewe had also promised an imminent arrest, which at this moment, without a live suspect, they had no chance of delivering

'Assistant Chief Constable Pewe, do you think the citizens of Brighton should be taking extra precautions to protect themselves from the Brighton Brander?' said another journalist. It was followed by more questions from all over the room that came too fast for all to be answered.

'Assistant Chief Constable, would you advise all women to stay at home until the Brighton Brander is caught?'

'Detective Superintendent, what advice will you be giving to young women in the city?'

'I'd like to ask the Police and Crime Commissioner if as a result of this she will be providing the budget to restore the number of police officers this city used to have?'

Nicola Roigard outlined the support she would be providing the police for the investigation and to address the community safety issues.

'Detective Superintendent, can you tell us exactly what measures you are taking to find this man you are calling the Brighton Brander?'

'Detective Superintendent, is there any message of reassurance you can give to the people of Sussex?'

Grace leaned towards the microphone and tried to speak, but his voice was lost in the storm of questions now erupting right across the room. Once the hubbub had died down he ran through the rest of the information he wanted to share, and outlined how the public could provide potential information to progress the investigation.

*

An hour after the conference ended, the *Argus* ran a banner headline on its online edition, **POLICE CHIEF WARNS OF SERIAL KILLER PANIC IN CITY**.

On the national news, both the BBC radio and television, and Sky, led with the story that Brighton was in a state of panic following the return of a serial killer after thirty years.

Grace sat, stony-faced, at the 6.30 p.m. briefing of Operation Haywain. On the notepad in front of him he had written the words: *Cassian Pewe. Total wanker.* He had underlined them several times.

But for now he had to keep those feelings to himself.

61

'*Mr Brighton Brander!*' Harrison said and chuckled.

Felix roared with laughter. '*The Brighton Brander!* Oh my God, that is so funny! *Mr Brander!* I so totally love it! You're a *brand* name!'

'*Barker* might have been a better word,' Marcus said. 'Barker as in *barking* mad.'

They were watching the 10 p.m. ITV news feature on the serial killer panic gripping the city of Brighton and Hove.

'How about cutting me a bit of slack all of you?' he snarled.

'You've got to admit it was funny,' Harrison chortled away.

'Go fuck yourself, Harrison.'

'Well, thank you for the offer. I would if I could.'

'Want a pineapple up your rectum?'

'Now now, don't be so spikeful!'

Felix giggled.

'You think that's funny, Felix?'

'Hey ho,' Felix said. 'Listen to me. *Chillax*, dude! Don't you see what that clever-clogs copper, Inspector Grace, is trying to do?'

'*Detective Superintendent*,' he snarled back. 'Yes, he's trying to make me look cruel and sadistic.'

'Well, he wouldn't have to try very hard,' Marcus murmured.

'What was that, Marcus?' He turned and rounded on him. 'What did you just say?'

'You see,' Harrison said, loudly. 'You're all angry and upset, exactly where *Detective Superintendent Grace* wants you. He's poking you with a large stick, trying to make you angry, can't you see that? He's hoping if he gets you riled, you'll make a mistake – and then where are we all going to be?

'We are looking for a middle-aged man with local knowledge and a sadistic streak, who appears to be targeting young women of a specific appearance. He's already made a number of mistakes, which I can't go into now,' said Harrison, repeating the news broadcast. He shook his head. 'Tut, tut, tut. He says you have made a number of mistakes – what are they? I think some serious correction is needed here, don't we all, team? So what are we going to do about it?'

'I know exactly what we are going to do about it. That arrogant shit Detective Superintendent Roy Grace is about to receive the *Order of the Pineapple*. Right up his jacksie. I've not made any mistakes. I've not put a foot wrong. I'm going to sort that copper out.'

'Oh yes, how?'

'Watch this space, guys.'

'Hey, why not?' Felix said. 'We've fuck all else to do!'

'Yes, we'll watch your next mistake!' Harrison said.

He glared at Harrison. Glared at the smug face of Roy Grace on the television. 'You'll be sorry you said that about me, Detective Superintendent, you'll be very sorry.'

'And that's something we all know you are very good at,' Felix said. 'Making people sorry.'

'True,' Harrison replied.

'Yes, very true,' said Marcus.

62

At 10.30 p.m. Roy Grace was feeling mentally and physically exhausted as he pulled up his job car outside the smart Regency front entrance of Limehouse Guesthouse, to drop off Paul Sweetman, the DCI who Cassian Pewe had asked to come down from London to advise him on serial-killer tactics.

So far, so good. Grace liked the calm, curly-haired man, who was soft-spoken and serious, but with a good sense of humour, a pleasant contrast to many of the in-your-face Met officers he had previously encountered. Sweetman had arrived mid-afternoon, reviewed Grace's policy book with him, and then sat in on the 6.30 p.m. briefing. Afterwards Grace had taken him to the traditional Brighton fish restaurant, English's, for a meal, before returning to Sussex House for another two hours.

He had agreed to pick Sweetman up at 7 a.m., to carry on their discussions before the morning briefing, after which they were going to meet with the forensic psychologist Tony Balazs to talk further tactics with him. The media were, as predicted, having a feeding frenzy, and he hadn't yet caught up with Glenn Branson or Iain Maclean, who had been holding the fort in MIR-1. The call-centre facility they'd set up, using support staff, had been handling hundreds of calls, and his team were flat out sifting through the information, identifying and prioritizing possible actions.

He turned right onto Marine Parade, the lights of the seafront, the Brighton Eye and the pier ahead of him, all faintly blurry in the misty rain, a little unsure of the reception he was going to get from Cleo, who'd had to cancel a baby group she was taking Noah to this afternoon because of the removals men arriving earlier than expected with the packing cases. Then his phone rang.

He answered it on hands-free and heard the duty inspector from Brighton police station, Andy Anakin, his voice as ever sounding panicky. 'Roy, thought you should know, a woman's body's just been washed up on the beach in front of the King Alfred Leisure Centre – in case you want to come down and see her before she's recovered to the mortuary. She was found by a young couple.'

Courting on the beach in this foul weather at this hour? Grace thought, his heart sinking at the news. The King Alfred was just a short distance away from Hove Lagoon. His immediate thought was whether this area was going to turn out to be the Brander's deposition site. 'What do you know about her so far, Andy? What age, what condition is she in? Physical appearance?'

'I've got a uniform sergeant attending, along with the on-call Coroner's Officer. Apparently she's pretty badly decomposed. Much of her face has gone – eaten by fish.'

'What about her hair? What colour? Long or short?'

'I didn't ask that information.'

'If you could find that out and let me know, urgently, Andy.'

'Her hair colour – and length? That's significant is it, Roy?'

God, the inspector could be irritating at times, Grace thought. 'Yes, it may be, and her age, please – however rough a guess.'

Anakin said he would get back to him as quickly as he could.

Ten minutes later, Grace parked in the street, then crossed the road and punched in the entry code for the gated townhouse development where he and Cleo would be moving from at the end of the week. The estate agent's 'Sold' board was fixed close by. He walked across the cobbled yard, then heard Humphrey barking inside as he put the key in the front door.

He opened it to be confronted by Humphrey leaping up at him excitedly, and a sea of cardboard boxes. Cleo was lying back on the sofa in a baggy onesie, holding a large glass of red wine in her hand and staring, fixedly, at a scene of devastation in Iraq on the television. Normally she would have leapt up and thrown her arms around him, but to his consternation she didn't even turn her head.

'Hi, darling,' he said. 'I'm sorry I'm so late.'

'I left you some food out'

'I already ate – I told you – I've been stuck all evening with the SIO from London that Pewe foisted on me.'

'No,' she said, coldly, 'you didn't tell me. You said you'd be home by eight, to help me start packing up.'

'I – oh shit.' He suddenly realized in the midst of everything he had completely forgotten to call her. 'God, I'm so sorry.' He strode across, leaned over and kissed her on the cheek. She did not react. 'Darling – I'm really sorry – I've had a nightmare of a day.'

'So it's all right for you to have a nightmare of a day, but not for me, is that it?'

'Of course not. Shit, I need a drink – where's the wine?'

She nodded down at the table. He picked it up and saw to his dismay it was empty. 'You drank the whole bottle?'

'Yes, I drank the whole sodding bottle.'

'I thought – breastfeeding – that wasn't—'

'No, I'm not meant to drink while breastfeeding. So what are you going to do about it?'

'Hey, come on!' He sat on the sofa and put an arm around her, but she pulled away from him.

'I can't cope, Roy. How the hell do you expect me to cope? Noah's been crying all day.' She gestured at the room. 'I can't do it all by myself.'

'We'll have to get help,' Grace said. 'What about your sister, and your parents?'

Her mood softened a fraction as it hadn't occurred to her. 'I'll try Rosie and Caroline, too.' Rosie and Caroline were her two best friends.

'I thought the removals men were going to be packing most of the stuff up?' Grace said.

'They are going to, but someone has to bloody supervise them. God, it's so hard. I know you can't do anything about it on this huge case – but the timing is shit, it's just the worst timing!'

His phone rang again. He stood up, stepped away and answered it. It was Anakin.

'Roy, the details I have back so far is she has short grey hair and is probably in her fifties, or even sixties.'

'Are they sure?'

'Well, I understand she's pretty badly decomposed, as I said. They say she's been in the water for some time, but they're able to give an approximate age from what they can see.'

Grace felt relief wash through him. 'OK, that's good news, Andy.'

'Good news?'

'Relatively speaking.'

'I'm glad you think it's good news.'

'OK, well it sounds like there's not much anyone can do tonight. Let's see what the post-mortem shows in the morning and we'll take a view on the cause of death findings then, if they are suspicious.'

'Let's hope it's still good news, then, sir,' Anakin said, a tad sarcastically.

Grace knew it was not an unusual occurrence for bodies to be washed up along the Brighton and Hove coast. The pattern of tide and currents along the English Channel meant that a high percentage of those who committed suicide by drowning further west, and those who fell overboard from vessels, ended up on the city's beaches. It didn't make anyone's death less tragic, but at this moment, Grace's relief that it was not a young woman with long brown hair was palpable.

He ended the call and turned back to Cleo. She had gone. Her empty glass sat on the coffee table next to the empty bottle.

Wearily, he climbed the stairs, thinking what he could say and what he could suggest to help the situation. As he reached the landing, he heard Noah screaming.

63

At the 8.30 a.m. briefing, Sarah Milligan, the HOLMES analyst, gave the news that *Unknown Female* had been identified, subject to DNA confirmation, and that she had been working through the information that was known. Her name was Denise Patterson, and she had gone missing from her home in Aldwick Bay, Bognor Regis, at the age of nineteen. It seemed possible that, like the other victims, she also had long brown hair.

Roy Grace pointed at the grainy, black and white photograph of the young woman on the whiteboard behind him. As he stared at her face, he wondered what her story was. He had been ten years old, thirty years ago. Sailing his little boats on Hove Lagoon. At the same time as the Brander was killing Denise?

He was feeling bad about the pressure the move – and the baby – was causing Cleo. She was taking it pretty stoically and coping, somehow. Last night's outburst was rare, considering what she'd had to put up with recently. He couldn't help but compare her to Sandy, who regularly got mad at him over his working hours. No one could predict when a murder would take place. Whether it was day or night, or in the middle of a birthday celebration, homicide detectives had to be prepared to drop everything and be gone within minutes, and then virtually live at work for the first days of the investigation, at least. That never went down well with spouses or partners. Because Cleo's own role as Chief Mortician had involved the same instant call-outs, 24/7, she had always understood.

The sight of Norman Potting's drained face didn't help his mood either. The fifty-five-year-old detective sergeant sat at his place at the conference table, smartly dressed in some of the clothes Bella had helped him choose. He caught Grace's eye and gave him a stoic smile.

On the table in front of Grace was a copy of this morning's *Argus* newspaper. It had not really bought into the Brighton Brander damage limitation slant. The dramatic front page splash read: **BRIGHTON BRANDER POISED TO STRIKE AGAIN?**

All of the national tabloid press featured the story prominently, too. *The Mirror* asked whether Brighton was about to regain its former notoriety as the UK's murder capital.

Roy Grace opened his notebook. 'For the benefit of all the team, especially as we have new members, I intend to run through both of the investigations, and the individual investigative leads for each case are here, should there be any further questions.'

He then recapped the circumstances around the disappearance of Emma Johnson. 'We've had very little intelligence or contact from the public in respect of Emma,' he continued. 'She has been missing before but I am sure that on this occasion the circumstances of her disappearance are more mysterious and linked to the man we have labelled the Brighton Brander. We've had no sightings of her since the last time that she was seen leaving her home address, and her whereabouts remain a mystery. Her disappearance has been included as part of the overall operation due to her description and similarities with the other missing girls.'

He turned the page of his notebook and said, 'We will now run through the lines of enquiry and updates on the female remains that were found near Hove Lagoon. She has been provisionally identified as Denise Patterson. She went missing in September 1984. Lucy Sibun is of the opinion that she was probably moved to a new body deposition site at the Lagoon in the mid-1990s.' He went on to outline in more detail the forensic examination, post-mortem and other scientific processes that were being undertaken.

Next, Roy Grace gave a concise summary of the investigation into the undetected murder from 1984 of Catherine Westerham. This case had been the subject of a cold-case review a couple of years earlier but no new leads had been identified. He outlined the actions that various members of the team were carrying out and updates were provided.

Then he said, 'I am now going to talk about the two most recent cases, that of Logan Somerville and Ashleigh Stanford, starting with

Logan. It would seem fairly certain at this stage that her fiancé, Jamie Ball, is not involved. Like Emma, there have been no potential sightings of her and very little information has been forthcoming from the public. It is her appearance that links her to the possible serial killer.'

He sipped some coffee. 'In conclusion I will now deal with the fifth victim, Ashleigh Stanford. There have been no sightings reported since her disappearance in the early hours of Saturday morning in Hove, when it looks like she may have been abducted whilst cycling home from work. Her mobile phone has been found nearby and it is her appearance that again links her to the other young women.' He ran through the details of her particular investigation.

He paused for a moment to let several members of the team finish their notes. 'OK, the next few days are going to be busy and you'll all need to put in long hours. I'm hopeful that our strategy through the media to rile the killer will be successful. There will be the publication of photo-fits and twice-daily press conferences. I'm anticipating the response from the public to be huge, so we'll need to focus on key elements of the investigation in order that we don't get distracted. You should be ready for swift action with house raids, searches, and hopefully interviewing of suspects. You have all been working hard in difficult circumstances and Bella would be proud of you all, as am I.'

Suddenly Grace noticed the conference room door opening, and his new assistant, Tish Hannington, peered in, then signalled to him.

'Excuse me a moment everyone.' He went over to the door.

Tish was a slim, neatly dressed woman in her late thirties, with a seemingly unflappable demeanour. She was holding a small Jiffy bag in her hand. 'Roy,' she said, quietly. 'The editor of the *Argus* has just sent this over, it was waiting for him when he arrived this morning. Someone had pushed it through the letter box during the night.'

'Yep, well I'm not too pleased with the paper after that ridiculous scaremongering headline this morning – just what we don't need. What's in it?'

'I think you'd better take a look, now.'

He slipped his hand inside the envelope. Inside were two plastic sleeves. He looked down at them and read the small writing. He looked back at his assistant.

'Bloody hell.'

64

Twenty minutes later, Roy Grace sat at his office conference table, along with DCI Sweetman and Tony Balazs. All three men were in dark suits, but unlike the two detectives with their short haircuts and sombre ties, the forensic psychologist had a mane of wavy silver hair and was sporting a brightly coloured bow tie. He looked, Grace thought, more like an antiques dealer than a shrink.

All three of them were staring down at the two mottled green paper driving licences, each dating back thirty years. The first bore the name 'Catherine Jane Marie Westerham'. The second, 'Denise Lesley Anne Patterson'. Next to them lay a sheet of white A4 paper with the message printed on it:

Tell Detective Superintendent Grace that he obviously needs help identifying the lady at the Lagoon. Ask him who's the smart one now, after he recieves this. I don't make mistakes.

'He's inverted the "i" and "e" in receive,' Balazs said.
'Is that indicative of anything?' Grace quizzed him.
Balazs nodded. 'Yes, that he's crap at spelling!'
'So he does make mistakes!' Grace said.
All three men laughed, thinly.
'Did the *Argus* have any CCTV footage from last night, Roy?' Sweetman asked. 'Did they catch whoever delivered it on camera?'
'Yes, he looks like that old movie character *The Invisible Man*. Wearing a hat, dark glasses, a scarf around his face covering his – or her – nose. Haydn Kelly and a CSI are there now, seeing if they can get any footprints that match the one in the oil at Chesham Gate underground car park. There wouldn't have been much footfall during the night where the *Argus* is located. We're also having all

CCTV cameras in the area checked to see if they've picked up a slow moving or parked vehicle.'

Grace went over to his desk, picked up a folder, opened it and read it as he brought it over. 'Denise Patterson was on this list of mispers we'd narrowed – which match UNKNOWN FEMALE's age and description. With luck we'll be able to officially confirm with either DNA or dental records that UNKNOWN FEMALE is Denise Patterson,' he said. 'The recovery of these driving licences gives us a definite link to the investigation. Is there anything you can tell from the note?'

Balazs nodded. 'Yes, he clearly has a big but fragile ego. Suggesting he has made mistakes has stung him in the way we had hoped. Also, the fact that he has retained the driving licences indicates he takes souvenirs.' He looked down at them for some moments. 'I wonder if he takes trophies as well.'

Trophies could be locks of a victim's hair, jewellery, pieces of clothing or some of their skin. Grace knew that trophies could be indicative of someone who is a loner, substituting objects for friends.

'He's trying to gain the high ground again with this note,' DCI Sweetman said.

'I agree, the Brander thinks he has the high ground now,' Balazs said. 'In his egotistical mind he's helped you to identify her. I think we need to deflate that.'

'What about playing down the significance of the licences in our midday press conference in the hope he'll send us more trophies? I'd just announce that the *Argus* received them anonymously in the post by someone purporting to be the Brander.'

'If he's as smart as we think he is,' Sweetman said, 'he's going to know we are deliberately winding him up, and I think it'll provoke him into action, to show us.'

'What kind of action, Paul? Killing again?' Grace said.

'Very possibly. But we know he's going to do that anyway, it's just a matter of time. Hopefully by provoking him into going for his next victim sooner than he had planned, and less prepared, he'll make a mistake, and that will be our best chance to stop him.'

*

After the meeting was over, Grace called Cassian Pewe and informed him of the course of action he proposed to take, with DCI Sweetman's full agreement, but he wanted the ACC's sanction too.

Pewe gave him an icy reception. 'Roy, I don't think you made a wise decision going public with this. Just as the Chief and I feared, the whole city is close to meltdown with panic.'

'Sir, you, I and the Chief Constable agreed this strategy on Sunday evening.'

'Have you no idea of the terror your announcement at the press conference yesterday has created?' Pewe's voice was sounding more nasal and high-pitched than ever. 'We're just one week from Christmas; I've had the head of Visit Brighton on the phone this morning. Hotels are getting cancellations pouring in; restaurants are losing Christmas lunch and New Year's Eve bookings. You've scared the hell out of the city.'

'With respect, sir, it's our killer who is scaring the city, not me.'

'Nicola Roigard rang me herself just a short while ago to express her concerns about the public reaction.'

'I would *expect* the Police and Crime Commissioner to be concerned,' Grace said. 'It would be a bit strange if she wasn't.'

'Don't try to be clever with me.'

Grace lifted his phone away from his ear and stared at it for some moments, almost unable to listen to the whiny voice any more. He had broken all the rules in risking his own life to save Pewe's last year. In this job you had to break rules and take risks. But now his boss was running for the hills at the first sound of gunfire. 'Sir, if you would like to give me instructions I will obey them.'

There was a long silence. Then finally in a reluctant tone Pewe said, 'You're running this operation, you have to make the decisions.'

'I'd feel a lot more comfortable if I had your agreement on such a big decision, sir.'

'Tell me exactly what you want me to agree to?'

'My announcing at the midday press conference that the *Argus* received two driving licences, in the names of Katy Westerham and Denise Patterson, the body at Hove Lagoon. They supposedly came from our suspected serial killer. If the Brander wants to communicate with us, we would ask him to give us demonstrable proof that it is him. I intend to play down the significance of the driving licences and announce we had already identified the Lagoon victim before they arrived.'

Grace then outlined his proposal for the conference and when he had finished, very reluctantly, Pewe gave him his sanction, and told him he would inform the Chief Constable and Police and Crime Commissioner.

After he had hung up, Grace made a careful note of the date and time and content of this last telephone conversation in his policy book.

65

The cramps in her legs were getting worse. Sometimes the pain was so acute Logan cried out; particularly her right leg. It was going into spasm again now. It felt at times as if the muscle was a giant elastic band that was about to snap and rip through the flesh. She desperately, so very desperately, wanted to be able to stretch her leg. To stand up.

She fought the pain, gasping, breathing faster and faster until it subsided, leaving her spent, with tears that she could not wipe away stinging her eyes.

How long? God, how long had she been here? She shivered from cold, from fear. Then she remembered something she had been taught, that deep breathing was a way to relax. She took in several deep breaths, filling her lungs, slowly. She had time to fill. So much time. Then she wriggled, as much as she could before the bonds cut into her wrists and ankles, raising her head the small distance the strap around her neck would allow.

She tried to make plans in her head. If she could get the bastard to untie her, even if just for a few moments, she might be able to headbutt him. She had strong hands from her work; if she could momentarily stun him and get a grip on his neck she might be able to choke him.

But if she tried and failed, what then?

She thought about it constantly, turning it over and over. At some point, surely, he was going to have to untie her. Wasn't he?

To pass some of the time, and to try to get back into a positive mood, she played a game of thinking back on different happy moments in her life. The summer holidays when she was a kid going with her parents to the cottage they rented every year in Cornwall. Rowing on the river and picnicking beside it with her parents and her brother and sister. Peeling a hardboiled egg and dunking it in a little mound of salt on her paper plate, then biting into it; followed by a mouthful of buttered crusty bread; then a bite of a tomato picked from the greenhouse that morning.

She was salivating. Craving, suddenly, a hardboiled egg with bread and butter. Anything other than the bland-tasting protein shakes her captor had been giving her. She tried to switch her mind to Jamie. To the happy day she had first met him, at a dismal birthday party in an upstairs room of a pub. It had been an old school friend's birthday, but there had been barely anyone in the room she knew, and the people she had talked to seemed universally dull. She was mooching around a table laden with blocks of Cheddar, pickles and slightly stale baguettes, holding a plastic beaker of warm white wine, about to go outside to have a cigarette and maybe to find some better company, when her mate John Southern suddenly appeared alongside her with Jamie and introduced them, before going off to find another beer.

'You look about as bored as I feel,' he had said.

'You can join my escape committee,' she'd replied.

'Willingly, but I think it might be rude to leave before the speeches.'

'I'm going to nip out for a cigarette – do you smoke?' she had asked.

'No, but I'll come out with you.'

Logan thought, for a fleeting instant, she could smell the sweet aroma of cigarette smoke. But then it was gone. The memory of Jamie faded. Then suddenly she heard a faint sound.

Splashing. A scraping sound of something being dragged. Footsteps. Rustle of clothing. A flashlight beam jigging. Something was happening! Hope rose inside her. Something was happening! Had the police come for her?

Then the light went out. She was surrounded once more by darkness and silence.

'Hello?' she cried. 'Hello? Help. Help me! Please help me, someone, please help me!'

66

Wednesday 17 December

At 3 p.m., one and a half hours after his press conference had ended, Roy Grace checked the online version of the *Argus* newspaper and was pleased with what he saw. True to her word, the reporter Siobhan Sheldrake had given him the headline he had asked for.

BRIGHTON BRANDER PROVIDES VITAL CLUES

The story beneath quoted Grace at the press conference, stating that certain items had been received, purporting to have been sent by the killer of Katy Westerham and the victim from Hove Lagoon, believed to be Denise Patterson.

Grace said this was a major mistake by the killer, providing the police with the potential to identify vital forensic evidence.

The words had been carefully chosen by the psychologist Tony Balazs, and Grace had quoted them. Hopefully they would provoke a response. In the meantime forensic work was taking place on the note that had accompanied the driving licences, and the packaging they had come in.

Having again taken no lunch break, Grace hurried down to the car parking area at the front of Sussex House, deciding to pop home very quickly and see if he could talk with Cleo – and give her at least a little help with the packing. As he drove he munched a very old Twix, with white flecks on the chocolate, which he had found amid a ton of parking receipts in the glove box. It tasted stale but he didn't mind. He was so hungry, he realized suddenly, that almost anything would have tasted good.

When he opened the front door of the house, clutching a large bunch of flowers he had bought on the way, he stopped and stared in amazement. Two of Cleo's friends, her sister, Charlie, and her parents were there, all seemingly frenetically at work, wrapping their very personal items in tissue paper and placing them in boxes. Upstairs he could hear Noah screaming.

'Roy, hi!' Charlie greeted him with a kiss on both cheeks. He had always liked her; she was a younger, chubbier version of Cleo and seemed to be permanently cheerful. She pointed a finger at the stairs. 'Noah's in a total grump – I think he's teething, poor thing.' She looked at the flowers. 'Those from you?'

'Yes.'

'Good plan,' she said. 'It might save your marriage.' She grinned.

He said a hello and thank you to Cleo's parents and her two friends, then hurried up the stairs and into Noah's room. And was shocked by how tired and drawn Cleo looked, sitting on a chair beside the cot, holding Noah in her arms and rocking him sideways, trying to soothe his grizzling. She gave Roy a desultory nod.

'I bought you these, darling,' he said, holding them up.

'Great,' she said flatly. 'One more thing to pack.'

'Hey, come on!' He walked across, gave his son's scrunched up face a fond look, then kissed Cleo on the forehead.

She smiled thinly. 'I'm sorry,' she said. 'It's all too much at the moment. On top of that I'm worrying if we're doing the right thing moving to the country. At least when I'm here going stir-crazy with this little one, I can push him around the streets and see life and colour and people. What am I going to do out in Henfield – talk to cows and sheep?'

'Everyone says villages are much more friendly than cities.'

Noah began bawling again. At the same time Grace's phone rang. He stepped out of the room to answer it. He heard a voice the other end in erratic broken English that sounded vaguely familiar, but for an instant, distracted by both Cleo's mood and Noah's screaming, he did not recognize who it was.

'Roy, hello, Roy Grace am I speaking with?'

'Yes, who is this?'

'Marcel Kullen! You are going senile is it with your old age, forgetting your friend from Germany?'

Grace closed Noah's bedroom door and walked through into the quiet of his and Cleo's bedroom. 'Marcel! Hey, how are you? Great to hear from you – what's up?'

Marcel Kullen was an officer in Munich's Landeskriminalamt, the German equivalent of the British CID. They had originally become friends when the German detective had come to Sussex House on a six-month exchange, about five years back. Subsequently they had met again a year and a half ago when Roy Grace had flown over to Munich after a reported possible sighting of Sandy – which had turned out to be erroneous.

'All is good here.'

'How are the kids?'

'Well, you know, OK. My son Dieter is two years old now and driving us crazy – I am thinking it is what you are calling in England the *terrible twos*.'

'Yep, well I have a son now myself. You can probably hear him crying right now!'

'Yah, you have a son? You are married again?'

'Very happily – I'd love you to meet my wife!'

'Bring her to München. What is her name?'

'Cleo.'

'And your son?'

'Noah.'

'So this is the reason I am calling. About your wife – your former wife, Sandy, yes?'

Grace felt a churning in his stomach. 'Sandy?'

'There's a woman who has been brought into hospital here in München after an accident – she was hit by a taxi as she crossed the street. Whilst she was lying in the street, moments after, a motorcycle stopped, took her handbag and drove off. There are some nice people in the world, yes?'

'Regular charmers,' Grace said. 'We have our share of them here. Are you sure this was an accident and not some kind of professional hit?'

'Yah, sure. There were witnesses – she just stepped out and looked the wrong way. This is the kind of mistake English people make sometimes, because you still drive on the wrong side!'

Grace smiled but his nerves were jangling. Whenever Sandy's

name was mentioned he felt a sudden chill deep in his veins. As if a ghost had suddenly entered the room and walked right through him. 'So, tell me?'

'She is in a coma and so far we don't have any confirmed identification, but believe she could be using the name Lohmann. This is the name her little boy gave us. Alessandra Lohmann.'

'How old is he, Marcel?'

'He's ten.'

'Marcel, we didn't have a child – and she's been gone more than ten years.'

'It is – yes, as you say I think, a long shot. But the woman's age kind of fits. To me there are some facial similarities to the photographs I have – but of course these are more than ten years old – and the colour of her hair is dark, not blonde. But I thought I should send you a photograph for you to eliminate her. Can I do this?'

'Of course,' he said, more enthusiastically than he felt. He shut the door, not wanting Cleo to hear this conversation. Could the nightmare that had haunted him ever since falling in love with Cleo be about to come true?

'OK, Roy, I will email some photographs through in a few minutes.'

'*Danke!*'

'You are welcome! I am sorry to make some trouble for you.'

'No trouble, I really appreciate you calling, Marcel.'

'We will see us soon, yah?'

'I'd love Cleo to see Munich, it's a beautiful city.'

'Bring Cleo and Noah. Our house is your house.'

'We might just do that!'

'Come next year, we go to the Oktoberfest together?'

'I'll iron my lederhosen!'

When he ended the call, Roy Grace sat down on the bed, deep in thought for some moments. All kinds of demons had been reawakened inside him. Every time he thought he had finally laid Sandy's ghost to rest, something happened to revive them.

Some moments later the door opened and Cleo came in. She gave him a wan smile. 'I'm sorry, darling,' she said. 'It's just really hard right now. I don't want to be angry with you.'

He stood up and hugged her.

'I'm being useless at the moment, and I'm sorry,' she said. 'I've always been determined never to stand in the way of your work. I guess I just didn't realize how hard looking after a baby would be. But I wouldn't change it for the world.'

'I didn't either. It'll be easier when we get a nanny sorted out. But we'll get through it.'

'We will.'

As he said the words he felt his phone vibrate, signalling an incoming email. He excused himself, saying he needed the loo, and slipped into the bathroom to open the email in private, feeling guilty at his deception.

It was the JPEG from Marcel Kullen.

He opened it and stared at the woman's face. Stared for a full, silent minute. His hands were trembling. Could this be her? Could this be Sandy?

The face was puffy and bruised, covered in abrasions, and a part of it was bandaged, with a plaster on her nose. There were similarities, yes. He couldn't see the colour of her eyes, which were closed and badly swollen. He could see wrinkles where Sandy had never had them before, but this was ten years on. And the short brown hair, in the boyish cut, made it much harder. He enlarged the picture, but it made little difference. It was possible, but . . . But.

Christ, what would it mean if it was her?

What would it mean to Cleo and Noah? To his life? And there was no way he could take the time out right now to fly over and see for sure, one way or the other.

He emailed the German detective back.

Thanks, Marcel. I can see why you sent this, but I don't think it is her. But please when you find out more about her identity let me know. Meantime Happy Christmas and hope to see you again before too long.

He flushed the toilet, ran the sink tap for a moment, pushed his phone back in his pocket and went back into the bedroom.

Cleo gave him a strange look. 'Are you OK, my darling?'

'Yes, I'm fine, thanks. Why?'

'You look like you've seen a ghost.'

67

Thursday 18 December

The following morning, Roy Grace was checking his notes from the Gold group meeting the previous night, preparing for the 8.30 a.m. briefing. The Gold group had agreed to continue the current media strategy.

On his desk was a note from Glenn Branson, regarding Denise Patterson. Her parents had been located, still in their same family home in Aldwick Bay. Her bedroom had been kept as a shrine and her hairbrush had been sent for DNA testing. They also had the name of the dental practice that the dead woman had attended, and hoped to have identification officially confirmed from her dental records later today.

He was interrupted by a knock on his door and DS Tanja Cale came in, looking flustered, holding a Jiffy bag. 'Sir,' she said, 'sorry to barge in, sir, but this might be important.'

'No problem, tell me?'

'We had a call to the Incident Room half an hour ago from the *Argus*. This package was lying on the *Argus*'s front doorstep this morning, addressed to you, care of the editor. You'd better take a look.' She handed him the padded envelope.

He pulled out a plastic bag, inside which were two sheets of paper, one newsprint, the other plain A4 printed paper. The newsprint item was the front page of yesterday's *Argus* containing the news story stating that certain items had been received, purporting to have been sent by the killer and Detective Superintendent Roy Grace's comment about how this had been a mistake.

The second page, contained the typed words:

HERE'S A PRESENT I THOUGHT YOU MIGHT LIKE TO
RECIEVE, ROY. GO TO THE MONUMENTAL INDIAN FOR A
TAKEAWAY TREAT!

Grace immediately noticed the spelling of *receive*. 'Well, he's
either crap at spelling or he's done this deliberately.'
DS Cale frowned. 'Deliberately?'
'His way of signalling his identity. His message yesterday had the
same mistake. And I have a feeling the killer is not illiterate.' He looked
back at the message. 'Monumental Indian?' he said.
'It sounds very cryptic,' she said. 'Shall I google Indian restaurants
that do takeaways in the city?'
'Yes, I'm thinking the same thing. He's enjoying playing with us,
setting us a little puzzle.'
He then read the second part again, aloud. 'Go to the monumental
Indian for a takeaway treat.'
During her pregnancy, Cleo had begun doing newspaper
crosswords, in particular the big daily one in *The Times*, and he
enjoyed attempting to solve them with her. '*Monumental Indian.*'
He pursed his lips, debating for a moment whether to phone Cleo.
Then, suddenly, he got it.
He pushed his chair back and stood up. 'I think I know exactly
what this means. Let's go.'

68

He was fifteen, home for the Christmas holidays from the boarding school he hated so much, The Cloisters, in Godalming, Surrey. Everyone said it was a beautiful school, in a fantastic location, and if you wanted to be a cricketer there was no better place. Situated on top of a hill, the ground drained fast, leaving a good wicket even after torrential rain. And the school's list of legendary old boy cricketers was a hall of fame in its own right.

Except that he wasn't interested in cricket, or in any ball games. The only sport that interested him was one not on the school curriculum, potholing. He was also interested in caves as well as any kind of tunnel.

Which was why they called him *Mole*.

No one actually liked him, they all found him creepy – and swanky. He boasted about his rich parents, their flash cars, their heart-shaped pool, their enormous yacht. They liked him even less for that. Even the teachers didn't like him. He had no friends. The truth was, he was used to that. He'd never had any real friends, and it didn't bother him a jot. He had his imaginary friends and they were far more fun. And he could trust them implicitly.

But on Valentine's Day he had received a very loving anonymous card from a secret admirer, which he had proudly showed off to everyone at school, although he hadn't figured out who had sent it. *I've got a girl, see?*

It turned out the same group of boys who always taunted him had sent it as a joke. They teased him about it for days, chanting whenever they saw him, *Mole's got a girlfriend, Mole's got a girlfriend, Mole's got a girlfriend.*

But the taunts over the Valentine card weren't as bad as the night, a few days later, when they had crept up on him and pulled back the sheets on his bed, to reveal him wanking with a torch gripped in his mouth and a Playboy centrefold open in his left hand.

That so hurt. So much.

He was determined to show them all. It would be different next year. Now he had a girlfriend for this Christmas holiday – well – sort of. Maybe not quite The Cloisters' – top people's school – standard. But she had big tits. Well, they looked pretty big beneath her blouse. When he peered down at her rack he could almost – almost – see her nipples. He imagined them, red, ripe, luscious. The thought made him hard. He had to put his hand in his pocket as he walked with Mandy White towards the ponds of Hove Lagoon. Had to put his hand there to stop the bulge from showing. Not that he needed to worry, Mandy was up for it, he was sure of that. Her mum was the cleaning lady for his parents. Mandy was just a cheap slut with big tits.

But no one at The Cloisters would know that.

They'd been to Marjorie Bentley's ballroom dancing classes a few days earlier in a room near Hove Station. They'd danced close with his big hard thing pressing against her. She'd whispered into his ear that she would like to give him a blow job. But his mum had been waiting outside to drive him home.

Tonight was different. He'd taken her to a pub near Hove seafront for drinks, which he got away with because he looked older than his age. Then he'd suggested walking her home – she lived in a house opposite Shoreham Harbour. It was a bitterly cold night, the temperature way below freezing as it had been for over a fortnight. He gave her a cigarette and they smoked as they walked, making him feel very grown up. And he was horny as hell. But despite the drink she seemed strangely reticent and distant, not at all like when they had been dancing.

He'd persuaded her, despite her reluctance, to walk down from the promenade into the darkness of the playground that was Hove Lagoon. It was ten o'clock and the whole place was deserted. Just the two frozen lagoons, the faint glow of the street lighting shimmering on the inky black ice. And Mandy's big tits shimmering, bulging out of the top of her low blouse beneath her coat. For him. His hard-on was pressing urgently against the front of his trousers.

As they walked around the perimeter of the larger of the two lagoons, he suddenly stopped, pulled her around to face him and pressed his lips against hers.

Instantly she turned her face to the side and pushed him firmly away. 'No!' she said.

'It's all right, I got some thingies. You know. Protection.' He ducked his face and nuzzled her breasts, voraciously.

She gave him such a hard push he almost fell backwards onto the ice. Then she turned to walk away. 'I want to go home.'

He grabbed her arm. 'You said you wanted to give me a blow job last week, before Christmas, in the dance class!'

'Yeah, well you didn't have spots all over your face then, did you? And you didn't stink of aftershave.' She broke free and strode away.

The acne rash that had broken out on his face in the past few days had acutely embarrassed him. Several of them were big, livid pustules and he'd done his best to mask them with Clearasil ointment. He'd also doused himself for his date tonight with Brut aftershave, which he'd seen in a telly commercial. It showed women going crazy for it.

'You fucking prick-teaser!' He ran after her and grabbed her again.

'Lemme go!' she said, her voice raised.

He tried to kiss her again, and she kneed him in the groin.

'Owwww!' he howled, winded.

She broke into a run and he sprinted after her, grabbed her by her coat belt.

'Lemme go, you fucking spotty perv!'

'Just give me a hand job then.'

'Yech. Let go of me.'

He put his arms around her and tried to pull her tightly to him. As she pulled away, he stumbled, losing his balance. Holding her tightly, they fell together, to the left, shattering the thin ice into the freezing cold water of the Lagoon.

Mandy screamed. 'Help, police, rape, police!'

He pushed her face down under the water, crying out in fear and in anger, 'Shut up, you bitch, you cheap, prick-teasing bitch.'

He felt her struggling under him in the shallow water, thrashing with her arms and legs, but he kept her face submerged with both

245

hands pressed against her forehead. She was writhing like a mad thing, but he just kept on holding her down, weakening with the exertion.

He kept up the pressure, holding her head below the surface, invisible in the inky darkness.

Gradually, her struggling lessened. Then she became still, inert. He continued lying there, shivering, his hands growing numb with the cold, his entire body growing steadily numb, his brain racing.

Then, finally, when he was sure she had been under the water for long enough, he scrambled to his feet, climbed back onto dry land, and ran across the grass and up the steps to the promenade. Then, waving his arms like a mad thing, dripping with water, he ran out into the road, screaming, 'Help me, help me, someone! Oh God, please help me!'

A passing car pulled up and he ran, crying, over to the driver's window. 'Thank you,' he said. 'Thank you. Please help me.'

69

Roy Grace left Iain Maclean in charge of the 8.30 a.m. briefing, then drove with DS Cale the short distance down the A27, over a series of roundabouts and up a hill that climbed steeply, adjacent to the dual carriageway. He pulled up close to a five-barred gate and noticed the padlock chain had been cut through and had fallen to the ground. Then they hurried up a grassy hill, avoiding a line of horse dung. It was a cold, sunny, blustery day and Grace was grateful that the rain of the past few days had stopped.

After ten minutes of hard, uphill climbing, following tyre tracks in the soggy grass, he saw the small, domed temple-like structure over to the right nestling among the hills. The tyre tracks veered towards it. The Chattri was one of the city of Brighton and Hove's most beautiful but less well-known landmarks. It was a round, white temple at the top of several flights of stone steps, in a beautiful location on the South Downs. Open to the elements, it comprised a dome supported by a circle of columns.

During the First World War, many Indian soldiers who had been wounded fighting for the British Empire had been brought to makeshift hospitals in England. One had been sited in Brighton in the Royal Pavilion. The Chattri had been constructed on the site where those who had died had been cremated.

As the two of them approached the fence around the monument, Roy Grace stopped, suddenly.

Ahead were two women with long brown hair, lying motionless, side by side on stone slabs at the foot of the monument steps, in front of a neat row of empty benches, their arms folded behind their heads as if they were asleep. But they were too still. Impossibly still. He raised a cautionary hand to DS Cale, signalling her to follow him.

As he stepped closer to them again he stopped. He'd seen enough bodies in the course of his career to be able to tell the difference, even from a distance, between the dead and the living.

These two women were clearly dead.

Young women. One was in jeans and sneakers, wearing a puffa over a knitted sweater; the other was in jeans, also, and a soiled T-shirt. Both had long, dark brown hair.

In death, human expressions changed. They became inert, like waxworks in a museum. But, he knew sadly, he was not staring at two waxworks. From the photographs he had committed to memory he was looking at the bodies of Emma Johnson and Ashleigh Stanford. Their faces were alabaster white. Both of them had their eyes open, blind to the vapour trail of a plane high in the sky.

He did not need to go any closer and touch either of them. Instead he stayed where he was, not wanting to contaminate this crime scene any more than he already had, and pulled out his phone.

He was as close to despair as he had ever felt in all his career.

Then he noticed something fluttering in the wind, behind the neck of the woman he believed might be Emma Johnson. Signalling DS Cale to stay where she was, he stepped forward and knelt down. There was a note wedged between her fingers. Snapping on gloves, he teased it out and read it.

HERE'S ANOTHER PRESENT, ROY. I'M SURE YOU'D LIKE TO ACKNOWLEDGE RECIEPT. THE DOWNSIDE (NO PUN INTENDED RE THE LOCATION) IS I HAVE TO REPLACE THEM. LIFE'S A BITCH, HEY? THEN A BITCH HAS TO DIE. HAPPY SLEUTHING. NO SHIT, SHERLOCK! CAN YOU GUESS MY NEXT VICTIM? CAN YOU SAVE HER? FEEL FREE TO PUBLISH THIS NOTE IN ANY PAPER YOU LIKE. VERY BEST REGARDS. MR BRANDER.

70

Six hours later, in the mortuary, Roy Grace's worst fears were confirmed. Both young women were branded, on the inside of their right thighs, with the wording, *U R DEAD*.

Pathologist Nadiuska De Sancha was standing over Ashleigh Stanford's naked body, taking fluid samples from her stomach and bladder for testing, but she was already fairly confident of the cause of death for both young women. Both had the tiny, blotchy red spots of petechial haemorrhaging in the whites of their eyes, on their eyelids and at the top of the cheekbones, which was brought on by oxygen starvation through asphyxiation. Neither of them had bruising around their necks, nor damaged hyoids, but their lungs were filled with water. They had drowned. Both women had been sexually assaulted but no DNA was found.

Ashleigh Stanford had bruises to her body and abrasions to her face, consistent with falling off her bike. She also had a large bruise to her forehead, sufficient to have caused concussion. In addition, she had seventeen contusions to her body consistent with being struck with a blunt instrument, as well as bruising on her knuckles indicating she had, perhaps, tried to fight off her attacker.

Emma Johnson had ligature marks on her neck, stomach, thighs, wrists and ankles, indicating she had been kept a prisoner.

There was no evidence of strangulation in the two women from thirty years ago either. But there had not been enough soft tissue left of the victims to establish for sure how they had died. They could have been stabbed – but there were usually nicks on the bones of stabbing victims. Possibly shot, but again bullets often struck bones. They might have been poisoned – toxicology tests were being carried out on samples from both bodies. But one problem with testing for poisons was that the pathologists needed to know what they were testing for – which restricted them only to the most obvious ones.

Had they drowned, also, he wondered?

Had the same sicko branded, raped, then drowned them?

What the hell was going on in the Brander's mind?

Was Logan Somerville being held prisoner? Did that mean she might still be alive?

Photographs of the brandings had been sent to an analyst, and in less than an hour he had confirmed they were, in his opinion, an exact match to the brandings on Katy Westerham and Denise Patterson.

In Grace's view, the idea of a copycat could now be ruled out. The Brander, intelligent, arrogant, whoever the hell he was – and wherever he had been for these past thirty years – had resurfaced. He postponed today's press conference, in the light of the present developments, until tonight at 7 p.m.

Shortly before 4.30 p.m., he had left Glenn Branson at the post-mortem of the two women, which was likely to continue for several more hours, and was now back in his office, seated at the round conference table with DCI Sweetman and the forensic psychologist Tony Balazs.

The three of them were staring at the note recovered from Emma Johnson's fingers this morning. Because of the sensitivity of the location of the deposition site, Grace had already arranged for a representative from the Chattri memorial committee to join the Gold group, to manage any possible community impact.

> HERE'S ANOTHER PRESENT, ROY. I'M SURE YOU'D LIKE TO ACKNOWLEDGE RECIEPT. THE DOWNSIDE (NO PUN INTENDED RE THE LOCATION) IS I HAVE TO REPLACE THEM. LIFE'S A BITCH, HEY? THEN A BITCH HAS TO DIE. HAPPY SLEUTHING. NO SHIT, SHERLOCK! CAN YOU GUESS MY NEXT VICTIM? CAN YOU SAVE HER? FEEL FREE TO PUBLISH THIS NOTE IN ANY PAPER YOU LIKE. VERY BEST REGARDS. MR BRANDER.

'He's angry,' the psychologist said. 'And he's leaving you in no doubt of his intentions.'

'That he's about to kill again?' Grace said.

'Yes,' said Tony Balazs. 'Twice.'

Sweetman nodded in agreement.

'How the hell do we find him before he strikes again?' Grace asked.

'Well,' Balazs said, 'one positive is that we've succeeded in riling him. Calm people don't make mistakes, angry people are the ones who do. The Brander is now *Mr Angry*. He's determined to strike again very soon to make a point. One of our best hopes is, as we've discussed, that he'll make a mistake through being in a hurry.'

Sometimes the psychologist came over as highly self-important and pompous, which irritated Grace. There was something about people who wore bow ties, other than at formal functions, that he had never liked. Balazs, in his loud, striped suit and even louder bow tie, irritated him now.

Irritated him, he knew, because he was telling a truth that Grace did not want to acknowledge.

'Great, Tony, that's helpful. But what we have to do is find this bastard before he does that. The press fallout when we announce the double murder is hardly going to reassure the citizens of Brighton and Hove, or Sussex. We have to find him. They will be asking the question: *Have the police tactics caused the deaths of these two young girls?* And we need to deal with it.'

'I agree with you, Roy,' Balazs said. 'But how are you going to do that?'

Sweetman had Roy Grace's policy book open in front of him. 'You're doing this investigation correctly, Roy. I've checked everything, in the light of the resources you have deployed, and I can't find any windows of opportunity you've missed. I think Tony's right.'

'You're saying we have to wait for the offender to screw up?' Grace said, his temper flaring. 'Is that how all serial killer investigations work? Because that doesn't work for me.'

'What do you want to do, Roy?' Sweetman said. 'Put 24/7 surveillance on every woman in Brighton aged between eighteen to thirty who has long brown hair? You have the resources to do that?'

251

'The motto of Sussex Police is "To Serve and Protect",' Grace replied.

'So do you want to put out a statement telling every woman in that category to stay indoors until the Brander is behind bars? Put your whole city into a state of even bigger panic?'

Grace shook his head. 'No, of course we can't do that. I will use the press conference to tell the media that this huge investigation continues, with many lines of enquiry being followed. The tactic of using the media to help identify and flush out the killer is only one aspect of this complex and fast-moving enquiry. We will never know whether the fate of these two young ladies has been hastened by current events, but we do know for sure that their abductor has killed at least twice before.'

The DCI and the psychologist both nodded.

'God, what the hell are we missing? There's something staring us in the face that we're not getting. Where the hell has this bastard been for the past thirty years?' He rested his face in his hands for some moments. 'The HOLMES team has covered every murder in every county in the UK in the past thirty years and there is no potential suspect who matches his profile. Every offender who has killed a woman of similar age and appearance is either behind bars, confirmed as being in a different part of the country, or dead. Interpol has not produced anyone in Europe or further afield and nor has the FBI. Our man is smart.'

'There are parallels with the BTK case,' Sweetman said.

'From what I've researched, he enjoyed taunting the police, the way the Brander seems to be enjoying taunting us, from this note,' Roy Grace said. 'We know he has different vehicles – and somewhere to store them – which suggests to me he's a man of means.'

'The universal profiles of serial killers,' Balazs said, 'is they are aged between fifteen to forty-five at the time of their first murder and between eighteen to sixty at the time of their last.'

'Which fits exactly with our offender,' Grace said. 'If his first murders, that we are aware of, were committed in his late teens or early twenties, being approximately thirty years ago, that would put him somewhere between fifty and sixty now.'

'I would agree with that, Roy,' Sweetman said.

'Have you considered using a decoy, Roy?' the psychologist asked.

'This is not a case for using a decoy,' Grace said. 'It's too dangerous.'

'I agree, Roy,' Sweetman said. 'But I think from the tone of this note that he's already selected his next victim. Our best hope is that he screws up because of his anger. I think he may strike again – within hours, possibly.'

'Within hours?' Grace said.

'I'd bet the ranch on it.'

71

At 5.30 Roy Grace attended the next Gold group meeting. As soon as it ended he sat down with the senior press officer, Sue Fleet, to go through the details for the press conference that was being held at 7 p.m.

'Our number-one priority is to protect the public, Sue. We've got to ensure people are made aware there is now a critical risk to young women on the streets of Brighton. Meantime I'm going to liaise with Nev Kemp and ask him to get every available police resource on the streets of the city, in hi-viz jackets.'

He liked working with Sue Fleet. She was a sensible, pragmatic and totally unflappable person, who always thought at least one step ahead. And frequently more.

'You need to prepare a very concise message for the conference, Roy. I suggest something along these lines: *There is a credible and immediate threat to the safety of women on the streets of Sussex, particularly Brighton and Hove. Women should avoid, where possible, being alone on the streets at any time. They should let people know where they are. Any members of the public who see anything suspicious or who think they know who the killer is should contact the police immediately, using 999.*'

Grace scrawled the words down as she spoke.

'I also suggest you come to the conference having considered the potential questions you are likely to be asked. We can't afford for you to be stumped on any answer – nor to hesitate. We've got to give the impression that you are on top of it, and confident. That's what the public are going to want to hear.'

'Yes,' he replied. And wished he was.

'We agreed at the Gold group that the Chief Constable will be on the podium with you. That will demonstrate to the press and the public the level of police commitment to this. Also, if you are able to, I think you should pay a visit to the families of Emma Johnson and Ashleigh Stanford. I think it would help comfort them and it would send a good message across. Presumably they've got FLOs with them?'

'Yes, I've arranged Family Liaison Officers for each of them, and I was planning to go and visit both families later tonight.'

As soon as Sue Fleet had left he called Cleo, apologetically, to tell her he had no idea when he would get home.

72

Thursday 18 December

Shortly after 8 p.m., feeling dusty and in need of a shower after a day of helping to unpack and move furniture around in Zak's new restaurant, Freya Northrop drove her Ford Fiesta onto the drive of their house close to Hove Park, switched off the engine and climbed out.

Bobby, a mixed breed terrier, which she had just collected from her friends, Emily and Steve, jumped up excitedly on the passenger seat and put his paws on the dashboard. She opened the boot, took out two Waitrose bags of groceries, and the large carrier containing a bag of dried dog food, mince to be cooked, food bowls, Bobby's favourite toys, and two boxes of treats for him that Emily had given her. Then she tucked the little round bed that he always slept on under her arm, and picked up the bags.

The house was in darkness, her path to the front door dimly illuminated by the glow from a nearby street lamp. She frowned, certain that they'd deliberately left some lights on when they had gone out this morning.

Zak had stayed behind at the restaurant talking with the engineers who had turned up to install the sound system. As was usual at the moment, he would get a taxi home later that evening.

She wanted to cook him dinner, but she was filled with angst. How could she prepare a professional chef a meal he would approve of? She had the same anxiety every time she cooked for him, especially as he disliked the whole idea of ready-made meals, whether fresh or frozen. On her own, she had lived on supermarket meals for some years, and he had been trying to wean her off them.

Tonight she planned to surprise Zak. She had been studying the recipes in *Don't Sweat the Aubergine*, and she had one all worked out in her head. Undercooking the aubergine. Grating garlic and ginger. Adding some soy and Teriyaki sauce. Making sure she did not overcook the scallops or the prawns. She planned to accompany it with a salad of beets, goat's cheese, peas and tomatoes. She'd bought all the ingredients from Waitrose.

All the way to the front door, Bobby tugged on the lead, sniffing the path excitedly. Before going in she put the bags down on the step and led him onto the small strip of front lawn, where he cocked his leg. She unlocked the door and went in, followed by the dog. She turned on the hall light, lugged in the bags, closed the door, then unclipped Bobby from his lead.

As she gathered up the bags and Bobby's bed, the memories of the broken kitchen window and the subsequent visit by a detective and the fingerprint team were almost forgotten, Bobby went temporarily bonkers, racing around the hall, his nose buried in the new, thickly tufted carpet.

'Are your new lodgings to your liking, Lord Bobby?' she grinned, carrying everything through into the kitchen. Dumping it all on the floor, she took out Bobby's water bowl, ran the tap until the water was cold, filled it, and set it down.

Bobby trotted over to it and began lapping. She knelt and stroked him. 'Just going to nip upstairs and have a shower, then I'll get you your supper! Are you hungry?' She rummaged in the bag Emily had given her, pulled out a box of marrow-bone roll biscuits, broke it open and placed one down beside him.

He grabbed it in his mouth and raced around the kitchen with it, then jumped on his bed and began crunching on the biscuit.

She went back into the hall and stared for a moment, approvingly, at the colour scheme they had chosen. The walls were a pale, warm cream, the woodwork, including the banister rails, a gleaming, glossy grey. Several photographs and paintings of London scenes, which she had brought down from her previous flat, hung on the walls.

She climbed the stairs up towards the pitch-dark landing, stretching her arm around the corner when she reached the top, wondering why the idiot electrician hadn't thought to put a switch at the bottom of the stairs. She found the switch and pressed it and the lights came on. All three doors to the bedrooms were closed. As she opened their bedroom door and fumbled for the light switch, she heard a faint sound, a tiny ping.

She stood still for a moment, wondering if she had imagined it; or whether it had come from downstairs, Bobby's name tag pinging against his metal bowl while he drank?

He stood inside the wardrobe in the master bedroom, masked and gloved, and wearing a body stocking. He pressed hard back against the wall, invisible behind the racks of dresses, being careful not to move and set any more of the hangers pinging.

He was very aroused, almost unable to contain himself with excitement, and worrying that he might ejaculate too soon. So he calmed himself down with deep breathing.

Oh my God, the anticipation! How beautiful was it when your plans came together?

He listened to her footsteps. Saw the light come on through the cracks in the wardrobe door.

Yes, my baby, yes! Yes, you bitch!

Freya entered their all-white bedroom, grinning at her two tatty childhood bears, each with one eye missing, which lay back against the pillows, arms entwined as she had left them this morning. She walked across to the window and drew the curtains – the neighbours had a view directly in – then stripped off her clothes, pulled the en-suite door open and went into the bathroom, switching on the light. She turned on the power shower, checked the temperature adjustment was where she liked it – Zak preferred his about thirty per cent cooler – tested the water with her hand, then stepped in, closing the door behind her.

She squeezed the plastic shampoo bottle and lathered her hair, then she picked up the shower gel and soaped her body.

A moment later, the bathroom light went off.

73

Roy Grace drove away from the police HQ in his official unmarked Ford and headed back to Brighton, feeling relieved that the press conference was over. Although he'd had some difficult questions, he felt he had managed to field them well, with the support of the Chief and the ACC. But it was not an experience he was looking to repeat any time soon.

Nor was he looking forward to his next task, as he turned off the A27 into the dark streets of Patcham. It was 8.20 p.m. The words of Paul Sweetman were ringing, deafeningly, in his ears.

I think he may strike again, within hours, possibly . . . I'd bet the ranch on it.

He looked at the houses he passed, many of them with Christmas lights in the windows, and some with outside displays as well. Sometimes he saw the flicker of televisions. There were people hurrying along the streets, no doubt to pubs, or to meet friends, or on their way home from work, huddled against the pelting rain.

Was the Brander lurking outside one of these houses now?

Was he already inside one?

Had he already taken his next victim?

He slowed each time he saw a male walking alone, and watched him. The forensic podiatrist, Haydn Kelly, who had helped him brilliantly in the past, had generated a profile from the footprint in the oil sludge in Logan Somerville's garage. Kelly had showed the team a video representation of a man who walked almost exaggeratedly upright, with his feet splayed out widely. The image had been circulated to the Sussex Police CCTV team who monitored the city's 350 cameras. But none of the bedraggled figures he saw, so far, matched that peculiar gait, if indeed the footprint actually belonged to the offender.

He turned into Mackie Avenue, and began peering through the misted side window at the house numbers. His first call was going to be to Emma Johnson's mother, to see how she was, and to give her what reassurance he could that his team were doing everything possible to find her daughter's killer. His next call would be to Ashleigh Stanford's parents. He'd been informed that her boyfriend was currently with them.

Liaising with the family of a murder victim was one of the toughest parts of his job, yet at the same time, the most important. As the father of a child himself, he shuddered to think how he would feel to learn his son, however far in the future, had been murdered. He knew that it would destroy him, that his life could never be the same again. That's what he understood, all too grimly, as he approached Emma Johnson's mother's front door, almost oblivious to the rain. He composed himself on the doorstep, took a deep breath, then rang the bell.

74

Thursday 18 December

Sodding bloody electrician! Freya cursed. In the pitch darkness she rinsed out her hair, then turned her face up into the shower jet.

Then she heard the shower door open.

'Zak?' she said.

A hand grabbed her arm and she felt herself yanked harshly out of the cubicle and onto the bath mat.

'Zak – what the hell are you—?'

'Shut it, bitch, I'm not Zak.'

She knew the voice, she'd heard it before, somewhere. Where? A deep, cold, shudder ripped through her belly. Her brain raced, spinning, trying to make sense. She saw a faint green glow. She lashed out and felt rubber, like a scuba or spandex suit.

'NO!' she screamed. 'HELP ME!'

She felt a hand around her throat.

Something – she didn't know where it came from – some memory, something she had seen on television or in a movie – kicked in. She lowered her head and rammed forward with all her strength, trying to headbutt him, making contact with something hard, but soft at the same time, with an almost satisfying crunching sound.

She heard a howl of pain and the hand released its grip.

She pushed past her assailant, shoving him as hard as she could, hearing the crash of the bathroom door, the sound of someone falling and then a curse.

She raced, in the almost total darkness, across the bedroom, missed the door and crashed into the wall. Scrabbling with her hands, her heart thrashing crazily inside her, she found the door handle, flung it open and launched herself onto the landing, screaming, 'Help, help, HELP ME!'

She stumbled down the stairs, hearing footsteps behind her, then

261

the dog barking below her, excitedly, like they were playing a game. She ran naked across the hall, the dog jumping up. Then an arm was around her throat again, pulling her backwards.

This time, Bobby snarled.

'Fuck you!' the voice said.

Bobby growled. Then she heard a ferocious snarling, followed by, 'Ouch! Get the hell off me, ouch, you fucking – you bloody—'

The arm slipped away from her throat. She collided with the wall, close to the front door. So close. So close.

She heard a yelp from the dog. Then a snarl.

Then a human cry. 'Owwwwww.'

She yanked open the front door and stumbled out into the dull glow of the street lighting, screaming as hard as she could, 'HELP ME! SOMEONE HELP ME! HELP ME!'

Behind her, Bobby snarled, growled, snarled.

She heard the assailant's voice shouting. 'Get off me, lemme go, you sodding bloody thing!'

She sprinted, oblivious to the pain and cold in her feet, along the lane, and out onto deserted Hove Park Road. Behind her she could hear footsteps, gaining.

She made a snap decision, turned left, and ran as fast as she could down towards the busy thoroughfare of Goldstone Crescent, with the darkness of Hove Park beyond. She could see headlights approaching. Oblivious to any danger of being run over, she tore straight out into the middle of the road, stark naked, blinded by the lights. Heard the squeal of brakes.

The car stopped. A woman jumped out of the driver's side. 'What—?'

Stark naked and sobbing, Freya threw her arms around her. 'Help me, please help me.'

Freya was vaguely aware of more headlights, behind the car. The sound of a horn.

'Someone just tried to kill me,' she gasped. 'Please help me.'

She turned and stared, in terror, at the deserted street behind her.

Somewhere, not far away, a car engine started and tyres squealed as it accelerated away.

75

No one ever gave you training for delivering a death message. You just learned as you went along. As a rookie cop you picked it up from your seniors. Some took a gentle approach but others came straight out with it.

It was the part of the job that, almost without exception, every police officer hated.

The sergeant Roy Grace had learned from told him always to say, straight out and bluntly, that the person was dead. That way it presented no possible ambiguity.

PC Linda Buckley had delivered the sad news earlier and was staying to support the family as the Family Liaison Officer while they came to terms with it. Emma Johnson's mother still refused to believe it. Even though Emma's sister had identified her body in the mortuary. She was drunk, angry and bitter. It had been one hell of a twenty minutes in the house and he was relieved to be outside and back in his car.

He was in the process of programming the address of Ashleigh Stanford's parents into his satnav when the call came through, from Panicking Anakin at Brighton police station.

A woman had been attacked in her home near Hove Park.

She had fought off her assailant, helped by a dog. Two officers were with her now.

'Where are they, Andy?'

'In the back of a police car outside her house. She was naked.'

'Don't let them go back inside.'

'I haven't, Roy. I've got a scene guard outside the front of the house.'

Grace reached forward, switched on his blue lights and said, 'I'm on my way.'

76

'Boy, you really screwed up big time!' Felix said. 'You were driven by sheer hubris.'

'You've put us all in danger,' Harrison added, sternly. 'You allowed that detective Roy Grace to rile you into making a mistake. Despite what he said, you've not put a foot wrong before, in all these years. We're all under threat now.'

'We're doomed,' said Marcus, gloomily. 'We don't want things to change, not at this stage of our lives. Now we all face rotting in jail for being accessories to murder.'

'You're being ridiculous.'

'You're the ridiculous one,' Marcus replied. 'BTK would have got clean away with his murders if he hadn't risen to the bait – the tauntings by the FBI. We warned you to keep calm, lie doggo, do nothing. But no, you and your bloody ego!'

'Surely you knew she had a dog?' Felix quizzed.

'I'm telling you she did not have a sodding dog!'

'Oh,' Harrison said, 'so you were bitten by an imaginary dog?'

'Very funny.'

'Which might give you imaginary rabies,' Marcus said pensively. He said it slowly, as if testing this hypothesis on himself, introspectively. 'Psychosomatic.'

'The way when someone loses a limb they can still feel it for years afterwards,' Harrison said.

Marcus and Felix chortled. 'Oh yes, absolutely!'

'It's not funny, boys. I've been bitten, there's blood on my trousers, which means I might have left blood at the scene.'

'Remember Tony Hancock, the comedian?' Felix said. '*Hancock's Half Hour* on television? One of the best was *The Blood Donor.* He went to give blood and then asked how much they would be taking. When they replied it was a pint, he worked out that a normal male human being has nine to ten pints, so he calculated that one pint equated to an entire armful. "I'm not walking around with an empty arm," he said!'

'I know what he meant! At least we don't have to worry about that, eh?' Harrison said.

Felix and Marcus laughed, sourly. Then Marcus said, 'Well, look on the bright side!'

Felix began singing the song from Monty Python's *Life of Brian*: 'Always look on the bright side of life!'

'Shuddup all three of you!' he screamed.

'The thing is,' Felix said, 'how could you have missed that there was a dog in the house?'

'I did a bloody recce. There was no dog bowl – neither for water nor food. I'd have bloody seen it, wouldn't I?'

'Well,' Marcus said. 'Obviously not.'

He rounded on Marcus, glaring. 'I'm warning you.'

'Ooooh, I'm so scared! Mummy, help me, I'm scared. Mr Big has been bitten by a rabid dog and is close to foaming at the mouth!'

'I'm warning you! I won't warn you again.'

There was a moment of sullen silence, then he added, 'There was no sodding dog in the house. She must have brought it with her.'

'And now we're doomed,' Felix said. 'DOOMED!'

'Do you want a smack in the mouth, Felix?'

'If it helps dislodge my aching tooth, yes please!'

'You tossers,' he said. 'You trio of tossers! We have a possible crisis and all you can do is make fun of the situation. Get real!'

'Sorry,' Marcus said.

'Really sorry,' Felix said.

'I'm sorry, too,' added Harrison.

He glared at the three of them. 'Like you all really mean it?'

'Temper, temper,' Felix said. 'Take a deep breath and calm down. Remember what Nelson Mandela said. "Holding resentment is like drinking poison and hoping the other person will die."'

'Go to hell!'

'Not possible.'

'Oh, why not?'

'Because that's where all of us are already.'

77

Friday 19 December

Roy Grace finally got home at a few minutes past midnight. Humphrey sat amid a forest of packing boxes, with one eye open, looking very unsettled and, unusually, did not jump up to greet him. Both Noah and Cleo were fast asleep.

Utterly exhausted, he set his alarm for 3 a.m., and backed it up with his phone alarm, brushed his teeth, then stripped and crawled into bed, slipping an arm under Cleo's pillow. She stirred, momentarily, then was still again. He kissed her naked shoulder.

It seemed only moments later that the alarm was buzzing. Following almost instantly was the *ching-ching-ching* of his phone alarm.

He snapped awake, leaden with tiredness – and with guilt. They were moving today and he wasn't going to be around to help.

He sat on the edge of the bed, head bowed, gathering his thoughts. Had the offender struck again last night and failed?

A young woman, with long brown hair, who fitted his target profile exactly, had been attacked in the shower in her house. Several spots of fresh blood had been found at the scene, presumably from the assailant, and with luck they would have DNA results back later today.

Over one hundred people had turned up for the press conference. If there was one small mercy, it was that it was December, well out of the main tourism season. Six months earlier and the financial consequences to the city's tourist industry would have been even more catastrophic. But that didn't cut him any slack. Brighton was turning into the modern equivalent of a leper colony. And all eyes were on him to return it to normality.

Which meant having a credible suspect under arrest as a starting point.

He was back at his desk in Sussex House at 4 a.m., with a steaming mug of coffee beside him and a banana which was going to have to suffice as his breakfast. The floor of his office was piled with documents from Operation Yorker, the original investigation into the death of Catherine Jane Marie Westerham.

Later this morning he would be holding yet another press conference, where he would be going through the details of the attack on Freya Northrop, and again asking for the public's help. He would also need to brief the Gold group with the latest update, and everyone would have to consider the ongoing safety implications for young women in the city. Perhaps the failed attack could be the game-changer he needed – providing a good description of the offender and hopefully DNA.

He reached across the desk and pulled out the summary details of *Unknown Female*, now identified as Denise Patterson. She had come from a less privileged background than Katy Westerham, and had gone straight to work from school in the Cornelia James glove factory in Brighton.

And was just as dead.

He stared at her photograph, then laid one of Katy Westerham's beside it. They could have been sisters. Just as Emma Johnson could have been, and Ashleigh Stanford.

He stood up, walked over to his round table, where he had more space, and laid out the photographs of the faces of all the women.

Then he sat down and stared at them. Thinking. Thinking.

Why these women?

Did they have anything in common beyond being young, attractive, and having long brown hair?

What was he missing?

In all the studies he had made of serial killers, and in his conversations with Tony Balazs, there was invariably a trigger. A bullying father. An abusive, alcoholic mother. Or, like Ted Bundy, rejection by a girlfriend.

What had triggered the offender?

Was that where it had all begun? Were they looking in the wrong place?

He yawned, then gulped down some coffee. His body was telling him he needed sleep badly. No chance.

Then he realized what he needed to do.

Moments later there was a knock on his door and Norman Potting came in and sat down in front of him.

'You're up early, Norman!'

Potting shook his head. 'No, chief, I haven't gone to bed. Can't sleep. Thought I'd come in and make myself useful.'

Grace smiled at him sympathetically. 'Your timing is perfect!' He ushered him to sit at the table with him.

Potting stared down at the photographs. 'Denise Patterson, Katy Westerham, Emma Johnson, Ashleigh Stanford, Logan Somerville and Freya Northrop,' he said.

'And who else?'

'Who else?'

'Who else in these past thirty years? Could it be that there is no one else, that the offender has experienced something recently that's triggered this new spree?'

'There's nothing that's been found so far, boss.'

'Nothing that's been *found*. But there are an awful lot of mispers in this country who've not turned up during these past thirty years. We know the offender is smart. And we've no idea how many others he has killed that we don't know about – and may never know about.'

A sharp gust of wind hurtled rain that sounded like pebbles against the window.

'You look exhausted, boss,' Potting said. 'If you don't mind my saying.'

Grace gave him a thin smile. 'Thanks, but I'm OK. I'll look a lot less exhausted when we have a suspect behind bars. Something's bothering me about one of the people you took a statement from, Norman. I know at the time he asked a lot of questions about the investigation, and he's contacted you a few times since, asking about how it's all going.'

'Who's that, boss?'

Grace grabbed a sheet of paper from his desk, wrote the man's name down and handed it to the Detective Sergeant.

78

Friday 19 December

Shortly before 9 a.m., Red Westwood sat in her Mishon Mackay liveried Mini, at the top of the short, steep driveway that led up to the red-brick neo-Georgian mansion, with its columned portico, waiting for her clients to turn up. A strong wind shook the car, and the sky threatened rain again at any moment. Not a great day for showing a house, she thought.

A slim, attractive, red-headed woman in her thirties, she was feeling more than a slight sense of apprehension about being here. A little over six weeks ago, she had been abducted by a former boyfriend, posing as a client, from outside a house on this very street, just a few hundred yards to the east. Although he was no longer a threat, his presence hung around her like a ghost. She studied the particulars on the clipboard in front of her, which she had written herself.

Moments later she heard a roar, and a black Porsche pulled up just in front of her. A short man in his late forties, she guessed, wearing an expensive leather bomber jacket and a gold Rolex, climbed out of the driver's side, and a much younger-looking, elegant woman, a good six months pregnant, climbed out of the other.

She opened her door and hurried over to greet them, arm outstretched, the wind tearing at her hair. 'Mr and Mrs Middleton? I'm Red Westwood from Mishon Mackay. Very nice to meet you!'

She shook their hands. He introduced himself as Darren and his wife as Isabel.

Both of them stared up at the front facade.

'This is such a beautiful house,' Red said, enthusiastically.

'The windows are all wrong,' Darren said.

'Well, the thing is,' she went on, 'this house is only twenty years old; it is in immaculate condition. And one major benefit is that it's

271

not a listed building, so if you were to buy it you could of course put in whatever windows you liked.'

'You ever put new windows in a house? You know the cost of doing that in a place this size?'

'Of course, cost is a consideration. Shall we start with the inside, then we'll do a tour of the garden!' she said, brightly. 'The garden really is quite spectacular. I love this area – I really do consider this the finest residential road in the whole city. Partly of course because there is so little traffic noise.'

'Apart from the learner drivers crawling around it like snails. We had to wait twice for learners to make U-turns to get here.'

'It's a beautiful view,' his wife said, as if trying to pacify him.

'Oh, it is, Mrs Middleton,' Red said. 'And of course this side of the street, where the houses are elevated, gets the finest views.'

The three of them stared over the rooftops of the houses, right down towards the English Channel.

'On a clear day the views are really magnificent,' the estate agent said.

'How many clear days do we get a year?' Darren Middleton asked.

'Two hundred and seventy-two out of three hundred and sixty-five, Mr Middleton,' Red replied.

'You're having a laugh.'

'No, I assure you, I'm not. Lloyds actuarial statistics show that there are just ninety-three days a year here in Brighton in which there is some precipitation during the twenty-four hours of that day. This is one of the sunniest places in the British Isles!'

He looked up at the threatening sky. 'Could have fooled me.'

Red led the way to the front door.

Fifteen minutes later, Red walked them through the huge conservatory, and unlocked the patio doors. The Middletons followed her around the edge of the infinity pool that abutted the house, with its electric retractable glass roof, and onto the terraced lawns beyond, with their wealth of statues and Romanesque follies.

Whilst his wife gazed around in wonder – imagining the lavish parties she could throw here, Red hoped – Darren Middleton went over to the east wall, mostly masked with plants, pushed aside the branches of a mature fig tree and hauled himself up.

Then he turned in horror. 'Excuse me, what is that monstrosity?'

That was the one problem, Red knew. The derelict house next door, with its untamed jungle of a garden, was an eyesore. But the truth was, unless you jumped up on the wall, like Mr Middleton was now doing, it was invisible. Except, of course, from a few upstairs windows of the house, which she had carefully kept them away from.

'Well,' she responded brightly, again. 'The great thing is that the property has been unoccupied for very many years. The garden is simply wonderful for wildlife. All the nettles provide a haven for butterflies and birds.'

'And urban foxes,' he said, dubiously. 'Who owns it?'

'The house is owned by an overseas company. The one next to it is owned by a doctor.' Then, as if realizing this was a plus factor, she added, 'He's a very respected figure in the local community.'

Middleton jumped down from the wall. 'It's a breeding ground for rats and other vermin!' He shook his head. 'Presumably someone, at some point, is going to buy it and develop it? They might try to build a sodding high-rise there!'

Red, feeling increasingly gloomy about these people as prospects, said defensively, 'I don't think the planning officers would ever allow that in this residential area.'

'I've dealt with planning officers before. They can be somewhat unpredictable.'

'Well, that's true, but I cannot see them ever allowing a high-rise development here. Now, would you both like to see indoors again?'

'We've seen enough, thanks, Ms Westwood. We'll need to have a think.'

79

Edward Crisp liked to get to his office early – he always had. Most people needed seven to eight hours of sleep, but he had always got by on five – and less on occasions, with a little help from his *friends*, as he was fond of calling the vials of drugs in his medicine chest. They'd help him stay up all night if he needed to. He was one of the few doctors who still liked to do house calls.

By the time his first patient of the day was in his waiting room at 9 a.m., he had already worked through his outstanding emails, and read most of the endless mountains of bureaucracy that were heaped on him, and every other family doctor in the UK.

Every new directive made him more and more angry. And it did not take a lot to make him angry this morning. Just after he thought everything was settled with his bitch wife, she had come back with a whole set of new demands. He was beginning to feel all over again as if it was himself versus the world. Or, at least, against *her*.

But he never let his anger show to his patients. To them he was always – in his mind – *Mr Charming, Mr Attentive, Mr Perfect Bedside Manner*. When the regulators finally had their way, and he was forced into becoming part of the litigation culture, all that would change. But for now he continued in the way he always had.

'You really want a gastric sleeve, Rosamund?' he said to the forty-year-old, straggly-haired woman seated in front of him, whose more than ample figure inside a dress the size of a small marquee overflowed either side of the chair. During the fifteen years she had been his patient, she had been growing steadily fatter, and now seated in front of him, she reminded him of a giant jellyfish covered in seaweed he'd seen on the beach recently when walking Smut.

'I can't help myself, I just keep eating. Ever since my husband left me, it's all I do.'

Maybe that's why he left you, he thought, but did not say. It was hard to remember how pretty she had once looked, a mere nine-stone, slender blonde. 'When did you last take any exercise?'

'I can't,' she said. 'It hurts my legs too much.'

'But you walked in here.' *Waddled would have been a better description*, he thought.

'Coz I couldn't get my mobility scooter up the steps to your surgery.'

'Mobility scooter?'

'It helps me get around. To the shops.'

'To buy food?' He shook his head. 'Rosamund, a gastric sleeve will shrink your stomach, which will make you eat less.'

'That's why I want it.'

He gave her a kindly smile. 'There's something else that would achieve the same result for you, but in a much better way.'

'There is? Pills?'

'Not pills, no.' He tapped the side of his head. 'In here. Mission Control.'

'Mission Control?'

'Your brain, my dear! The boss inside your head. Willpower.'

'I don't have any.' She looked down, a little shame-faced. 'I need help, Dr Crisp.'

'Last time I saw you, you wanted a full check-up.' He looked at his computer screen. 'That was three weeks ago. Since then you've had an abdomen, pelvis and virtual colonoscopy CT scan, a CT heart scan and a CT chest scan. Your colon is clear, you have a brilliant coronary artery calcium score of zero. Your liver is normal, as are your pancreas and kidneys. Your lungs are in fine order.'

By some bloody miracle he would have liked to have added. 'I've seen patients, similarly overweight to yourself, who are virtual in-valids. I don't want to see you like that. You are a healthy woman in the process of destroying your health. In another five years you'll have diabetes and cardiovascular disease will follow. Is that what you want?'

'No, that's why I need a gastric sleeve.'

He looked at his screen again. 'You live in Wilbury Villas, about half a mile away, yes?'

'Yes.'

'Forget the gastric sleeve. Drive home in your mobility scooter, stick it in the garage and put it up for sale on eBay. Then take up walking.'

'Walking?' She looked at him as if he was mad.

'Have you planned your funeral?'

'My funeral? What are you saying?'

'Take up walking – your heart can stand it. Take it up or else start planning your funeral.'

'I came here for help, Dr Crisp – I don't like what you're telling me.'

'Bitter medicine, eh? Come back in two years' time and tell me then that you don't like it. Then we'll look at a gastric sleeve.' He glanced at his watch.

'That's all you're going to do for me?'

'Rosamund, the first rule of medicine is *Do no harm*. I'm not sanctioning surgery when the boss inside your head can do a much better job. You just have to let it!'

Midway through his morning list of patients, just as a pregnant young woman had left his office, his secretary phoned through on his intercom. 'Dr Crisp, there's a police officer – a detective – who would like to have a word with you. Shall I tell him to come back at the end of your surgery?'

'Police officer? What about?'

'Apparently you were at Hove Lagoon last Thursday night and gave the police some assistance.'

'Ah – yes – yes of course, Jenni. Send him in now, I doubt it will take long.'

He beamed broadly as the door opened and his secretary ushered in Norman Potting.

The doctor stood, and reached a welcoming hand out across his desk, clasping the detective's rough hand and giving it a firm shake. 'How very nice to see you again, Detective Sergeant.'

'Thank you for seeing me at such short notice.'

'No problem at all – have a seat. We'll have to be brief, I have a long list of patients waiting. So tell me, how is everything going with the investigation?'

Norman Potting lowered himself into one of the two chairs in front of the doctor's desk, and stared, briefly, at a skeleton to the right of it, wondering if it was real or plastic.

'We're making progress, thank you. That's a nasty-looking bruise on your face, Doctor.'

Crisp laughed, dismissively. 'Yes, I fell over in the bloody shower! A friend of mine told me never to fall over in a shower, because that's what old people do!'

The way the detective stared at him made him feel uncomfortable.

'End of,' Crisp said.

Potting nodded. 'Been there, done that, got the T-shirt.' He shrugged. 'I apologize for intruding on your busy working day. Last Thursday night you were kind enough to certify as dead human remains that were found close to the Big Beach Café at Hove Lagoon. Subsequently I took a statement from you.'

'Yes, well, I'm afraid there wasn't much to that. A long time back I was a police surgeon, I often used to get called out at all hours to do the same thing – certify death. Frankly, with that poor woman's remains at the Lagoon it was a bit silly, really. But I understand you need to do everything belt and braces.'

The detective pulled a notebook from his inside jacket pocket and jotted something down. Then he said, 'I have a few more questions. Could you tell me, Dr Crisp, you were walking your dog across Hove Lagoon last Thursday night – is that a regular place for you to do that?'

'In winter, yes. It's too crowded in summer. Bloody kids every-where. She loves the beach.'

Potting smiled, and looked down at the sleeping mongrel. 'You always take her to the office?'

'Since my wife left me.' He jerked a finger at a framed photograph on his desk of an attractive-looking woman with long, dark hair, flanked by two similar-looking teenage girls. 'Not fair to leave her at home all day – and most of my patients like her. It's particularly good to have her here for breaking the ice with my younger patients.'

'I've been there too – wife leaving me,' Potting said. 'A few times.'

'Ah, didn't Oscar Wilde say that to lose one wife was unfortunate, to lose two was carelessness?' quipped Crisp.

'I thought the line was about parents,' Potting retorted. '*The Importance of Being Earnest*?'

'Aha, a cultured man! Quite right!'

'How long ago did your wife leave, Dr Crisp?'

'About six months – she'd been having an affair – but – that's how it goes, eh?'

'Women!' Potting said.

'Indeed.' The doctor shrugged.

Changing the subject back, Norman Potting said, 'Your dog – does she need a lot of exercise?'

'I take her round the garden in the morning – I've got a large garden which she loves. Then at lunchtime I usually walk her down to the beach and have a bite at my club, the Hove Deep Sea Anglers, or else at the Big Beach Café at the Lagoon.'

'The Deep Sea Anglers is close to the Lagoon, isn't it?'

'Very.'

'Where do you live, Dr Crisp?'

'Tongdean Villas.'

'Nice street – it's where I'd choose to live if I won the Lottery. There must be good money in private medicine.'

'In some fields, yes, but not for general practitioners. I have private means, fortunately.' Crisp smiled.

'So at this time of year, you take your dog down to the Lagoon twice a day?'

'Yes, at lunchtime and after I finish work in the evening.'

'Like clockwork?'

'Like clockwork.' He smiled. 'You seem very interested in my dog-walking habits, Detective Sergeant. Is there some reason why?'

Potting shrugged and gave him a baleful smile. 'I recently lost my fiancée, in a fire. I'm thinking of getting a dog as a companion, but I'm wondering if I would have the time to look after it properly.'

'A fire? Was she a police officer?'

'Yes, she was.'

'I read about that – it was very recent? Just a few weeks ago? She was trying to rescue a child – and a dog? I'm so sorry.'

Potting nodded and sniffed.

'Are you all right? Are you being looked after?' Crisp said, with concern. 'Are you sleeping?'

'Not really, no,' Norman Potting said.

'Oh dear, oh dear. Do you have a doctor helping you?'

Potting shook his head.

'I can give you something to help you sleep, if you would like. Sleep when you are suffering grief is very important. I can give you a mild sedative that will help you get back into a natural rhythm.'

'That's very kind of you, but I'm coping. Just about.'

'Is there anything at all I can do for you?'

Potting hesitated. 'Well, there is one thing. I shouldn't be telling you this, it's not very professional of me. But I've recently been diagnosed with prostate cancer, and I'm at a bit of a loss as to what to do. I'm getting a lot of conflicting advice about different treatments.' He fell silent for a moment. 'You see, the thing is, I'm concerned about some of the routes, which would give me a risk of a loss of – you know . . .' He fell silent.

Crisp waited patiently, with a gentle smile. 'Erectile dysfunction?'

Potting nodded. 'Yes, exactly. Winky action.'

'How old are you?'

'Fifty-five.'

'Well, I know some very good specialists I could refer you to. If you'd care to send me all the details of your diagnosis, and who you've seen so far, I'd be happy to try to help you – with absolutely no charge.'

'That's very good of you, doctor. I rather feel I'm imposing on you.'

'Not in the slightest. As I said, I was a police surgeon for a number of years, and I have the greatest respect for police officers. I would be only too happy to help. I have your card which you gave me last time. I'll send you some information on a few organizations that offer help and advice to prostate cancer sufferers.'

'That's very kind of you. If I could have some contact details? Could you let me have your mobile phone number?'

'Of course.' Crisp wrote it down on a Post-it note, licked his finger to separate the note from the pad, tugged it clear and handed it to the detective.

Potting folded it carefully and slipped it into his pocket.

80

Coming up to 1 p.m., Roy Grace turned his car off the A27, halted at the roundabout, then took the second left into Dyke Road Avenue, a street lined on both sides with mansions, some privately owned, many now turned into nursing homes, and halted behind a queue of traffic at a police roadblock.

Chief Superintendent Nev Kemp, Brighton and Hove's Divisional Commander, was doing a fine job of providing police reassurance to the city, he thought. Police vehicles – cars, vans and motorcycles – along with officers and PCSOs in hi-viz jackets were everywhere. It felt similar to what it must be like to enter a war zone.

When it came to his turn, he held up his warrant card and was waved on, past a car with two officers peering into its opened boot. His car radio was tuned to Radio Sussex, monitoring their broadcasts. The presenter, Danny Pike, was at this moment interviewing the Police and Crime Commissioner in his normal courteous but incisive style.

She was standing up to his interrogation well, he thought.

'Tell me, Commissioner,' Pike quizzed, 'don't you think in the light of the latest developments, that you should order a curfew after dark in this city?'

'Danny, we don't as yet have enough evidence to connect the incident in Hove last night with the other offences we are so deeply concerned about. And of course the police do not have the powers to order curfews.'

'Why not? I understand the woman who was attacked in her home fits exactly the profile of the previous victims. Are you getting pressure from commercial interests in Brighton and Hove to sort this out?'

'The only consideration at this stage is for the safety of all citizens of this city, and visitors. The police are doing everything within their powers to find the offender as quickly as possible and put him safely behind bars.'

'Are you sure he's not having a laugh on you? The detective in charge of the case taunted him openly in a press conference, and the offender's response was to deliver two more victims. Do the police actually know what they are doing? Is Detective Superintendent Roy Grace the right man for a case of this magnitude?'

'I have every confidence in the SIO appointed to this case. And you should know, Danny, that he is not operating in a vacuum. We have also drafted in the Metropolitan Police's most experienced officer in dealing with serial killer offenders to provide support to the investigation, as well as a highly experienced forensic psychologist.'

'So are you saying, Commissioner, that you are close to an arrest?'

'No, I am not saying that, but I have every confidence in my police force. Surrey and Sussex Major Crime Team is doing a fine job. There is no need for panic in this city, nor in the rest of the county, but I would like to repeat the warnings given out in last night's press conference, that women should avoid being on the streets of Brighton alone at any time of the day or night wherever possible, not taking unnecessary risks; they should let people know where they are; they should be accompanied at all times. I'd also like to repeat the appeal to any members of the public who see anything suspicious, or who think they know who this person is, to call Sussex Police or, alternatively, if they want to be anonymous, call Sussex Crimestoppers.' She gave out the numbers.

Grace turned right and headed down a leafy street with smart, detached houses on either side, towards Hove Park, one of the city's largest recreation areas. He saw a Radio Sussex outside broadcast van as well as BBC South and Latest TV vans parked along the kerb. He passed them and turned left onto the rough, almost rural surface of Hove Park Lane.

Ahead of him he saw the huge truck of the Specialist Search Unit, the smaller white Scientific Support Unit van, and two marked police cars. A barrier of crime scene tape, fronted by a PCSO scene guard, closed off the far end of the lane near the house where Freya Northrop had been attacked was sited. Several newspaper reporters, photographers and cameramen were milling around.

He halted his car and then dialled Cleo. She answered, sounding harassed.

'How's it all going?' he asked.

'One of the removals men just smashed Marlon's bowl.'

He felt a sudden wrench in his gut. Ridiculous with all else that was going on to feel distressed over a goldfish. But Marlon represented far more than that to him. 'Is he OK?'

'Yes, your sodding goldfish is fine. He's in a bucket at the moment.'

'Thank God!'

She blew him a kiss. 'Go back to saving the world. We're fine. Marlon's going to be travelling in style. He likes the bucket.'

Roy Grace smiled. As he left his car, the press members all turned towards him. Siobhan Sheldrake, from the *Argus*, closely followed by the senior Latest TV reporter, Tim Ridgway, and a cameraman, hurried towards him.

'Detective Superintendent,' Sheldrake said. 'How close are you to arresting Freya Northrop's attacker from last night? The man you call the Brighton Brander?'

'Sorry, I've nothing to say at this moment, we'll be holding another press conference as soon as we have more information.'

He eased his way past them and hurried along to the CSI van, where he gowned up, and snapped on a pair of gloves. Then he approached the scene guard, who recorded his name and the time on the log, as he ducked under the tape and headed to the house. His absolute priority right now was to establish, urgently, whether this attack was linked. In Tony Balazs's view, a failed attack would have a big psychological impact on the offender. It would either send him to ground for a while, or, if they could provoke him sufficiently, they might be able to goad him into another rushed attempt. Neither scenario made Grace happy.

The Crime Scene Manager, David Green, in a similar blue protective oversuit and overshoes to everyone else inside, took him around, and told him that they had found several spots of blood on the hall carpet, from which he was confident of getting a good DNA profile of the offender. But both of them accepted this would only be of value if the offender's DNA was already on record.

As evidence of just how seriously Grace was viewing the attack, the place was crawling with CSIs. They were searching every inch of every room, and fingerprinting every object. Green led him, on the gridded track laid down by the CSIs to prevent contamination of the carpets, upstairs to the master bedroom, and then through into the bathroom and pointed out the shower cubicle where the attack on Freya Northrop had begun. Then back out to the bedroom, where a sliding, mirrored wardrobe door was open, with several dresses fallen to the floor.

'It looks like her attacker may have been hiding in here, Roy,' he said.

'What's happened to the dog?'

'The dog's fine – seems a rare instance of his bite being worse than his bark!'

Grace thanked him, and stood staring at the cupboard, thinking hard. From the information he had so far, Freya Northrop had arrived home alone and entered the house, carrying groceries and accompanied by a dog belonging to friends that she had agreed to look after.

The dog might have saved her life, he contemplated. And might lead them to her attacker.

Was Freya Northrop a bit dim, he wondered? Only a few days ago, on Sunday night, she and her boyfriend had arrived home from a day out to find the place had been broken into. But they hadn't as yet bothered to change the locks. She arrived here last night to find the lights were off, although she was certain they had left some on, deliberately.

Yet she had still gone inside.

He let himself out of the back door and walked out into the unkempt garden. Tall trees provided a lot of privacy and the nearest neighbour's wall, which rose above the far end, was windowless.

A quiet, unmade close, off an almost equally quiet residential road. A rear entrance that was not overlooked by anyone. A woman who matched the offender's target profile exactly.

Putting himself in the offender's shoes, this would have been a perfect choice. Yet, with the help of the dog, she had managed to fight him off and escape – unlike the other victims. How did the offender feel about this?

Grace's phone rang, and he answered it instantly. It was Glenn Branson.

'Boss, the interview with Freya Northrop is going to start in about twenty minutes. You said to let you know.'

'Thanks, I'll be there as soon as I can.'

'Where are you now?'

'At Freya Northrop's house.'

'The Bates Motel.'

'Bates Motel?'

'Yeah, *Psycho*?'

'Psycho?'

'Sometimes I despair. *Psycho*, the movie. Tony Perkins and Janet Leigh. She was slashed to death in the shower.'

'Ah, right,' he said, distractedly, staring at the rear of the house. There were builders' ladders lying on the ground, and several tins of exterior paint stacked up. The intruder could easily have gained access through an upstairs window.

A Crime Scene Investigator was kneeling, photographing an area of the lawn.

'Found anything?' Grace asked her, after ending the call.

'Yes, sir, there are several footprints – they were covered and protected overnight.' She pointed down at one on the earth just below a ground-floor window. 'I'm photographing them before we take impressions.'

'Get them to Haydn Kelly as quickly as possible.'

'He's already been and taken his own photographs, and casts.'

'Good.' He stepped away and stared up again at the small house. It was pretty, in an idyllic location in the city. Freya Northrop had only recently moved down from London. If her attacker had been the Brighton Brander, as he strongly suspected, how had he found and targeted her?

And why on earth, he again wondered, after their break-in last Sunday night, hadn't Freya and her boyfriend, Zak Ferguson, had the locks changed, as they had been advised? God, there was only so much the police could do to protect the citizens of this, or any, city. People had to help themselves, too.

He went back into the house, and upstairs to the master bedroom. Then back into the bathroom.

She had been attacked here in the shower. Reminiscent of *Psycho*, indeed, he realized. But fortunately this time there'd been no dead mother on a swivel chair. Just a very terrified victim who had escaped. No thanks to him or any of his team. But thanks to a dog.

He went back into the bedroom, stared around at the modern, distressed furniture, the neatly made bed with a white satin cover and several white cushions scattered around the base of the silver headboard. On one of the bedside tables was a stack of cookery books and a cube-shaped alarm clock. On the other was a Simon Kernick thriller and a half-empty water tumbler.

He walked over to that side and with his gloved hands pulled open the drawer in the table. Inside was a small book with a photograph on the cover of a woman in a blue shirt kneeling over a naked man. It was titled *Sex: A Lover's Guide*.

He shut the drawer with a wry smile. Cleo had given him the same book for his birthday.

Then he stood, deep in thought. Thirty years ago. Now, again. Five women of similar age and appearance – and with Freya Northrop, possibly six targeted. Was the Brander modelling himself on Ted Bundy?

Before his execution, Bundy had confessed to thirty-nine murders, although the FBI believed that his real tally might have been as many as one hundred and six. All of them, bar one, which appeared to have been a mistake, of similar age and appearance.

Bundy's spree had been triggered by his first girlfriend, who'd had long brown hair with a centre parting and had dumped him. According to all he had read on the serial killer, Bundy had begun killing young women of similar appearance in revenge.

Then, suddenly, he had a thought.

He phoned Branson. 'Glenn, I'm not going to make the interview, I'll watch the recording later. Call me if anything interesting comes out of it.'

'Where will you be?'
'At the Jubilee Library.'
'Library?'
'Yes.'
'This is one hell of a time to try to fill in gaps in your education.'
'Very funny.'

81

Friday 19 December

Half an hour later, Roy Grace was seated in front of a microfiche reader in the Reference section of Brighton's Jubilee Library, a building he had loved ever since it first opened. He had decided to get away for an hour, giving him time to think. He could still be contacted if he was needed urgently.

Up until now they had been looking at the dates between Katy Westerham and Denise Patterson's disappearances and the present. But he had a strong feeling they might have been looking in the wrong direction, at the wrong time period. He needed to go way further into the past, way beyond the dates of those first two murders.

Back-issue after back-issue of the *Argus* newspaper scrolled down the screen in front of him. He had taken as a starting point the date of Katy Westerham's disappearance, December 1984, and was working his way backwards from then. Headlines of monumental events in the city and in the world flashed past his eyes.

A South Korean jetliner which strayed into Soviet airspace was shot down with the loss of 269 people. Sally K. Ride became the first woman astronaut. Nazi Gestapo chief Klaus Barbie was found in America. Should Brighton and Hove be given City status? He went back to 1983. Brighton and Hove Albion football club made the Cup Final and drew 2–2 with Manchester United.

He continued all the way back to 1975. Pol Pot became leader of Cambodia, with the nightmare of the killing fields yet to unfold. Jimmy Carter was elected President of the USA. The Queen made an official visit to Brighton. Bjorn Borg won Wimbledon. A Brighton town councillor was jailed for corruption.

It was half past two. He was hungry and thirsty, his vision was becoming blurred and he was desperate for water and for coffee. He was aware that his concentration had waned and he had perhaps scrolled too fast through the past couple of months. Had he missed something? He went back.

Then suddenly he stopped. And stared. Stared at the photograph beneath the headline.

A young girl, with a pretty face and long brown hair.

The date of the paper was 30 December, 1976.

The *Argus* headline said:

HOVE LAGOON DROWNING TRAGEDY

He read on.

> An ambulance crew was unable to resuscitate teenager Mandy White, 14, who fell through the ice on Hove Lagoon's big pond after a night out. She was rushed to the Royal Sussex County Hospital shortly before midnight, but was pronounced dead on arrival.
>
> The emergency call had been made by her companion for the evening, Edward Denning, 15, who admitted to the police that they had been drinking heavily. According to Denning, Mandy, daughter of an employee of his family, decided to try skating on the ice, despite his warning. He said he tried to restrain her but she shook free of his arms, and moments later fell through the ice. He tried to pull her out, but became overwhelmed by the cold water and decided to go for help instead.
>
> Mandy's family are said to be devastated. Her mother was too distressed to speak to the *Argus* yesterday. Her father, Ronald White, said she was the apple of his eye, and a lovely girl who worked hard at school and with her paper round. Close to tears he said, 'She's my daughter – our only daughter – and I want her back so much.'
>
> Detective Inspector Ron Gilbart of Hove Police said it looked, sadly, as if misguided high jinks by a pair of youngsters had gone tragically wrong, but that a full investigation into the events would take place.

The story dominated the entire front page. Roy Grace read it through twice, making a note of the names, then sat thinking. It had happened close to forty years ago. Some years earlier than Katy Westerham and Denise Patterson. He remembered Tony Balazs's words from yesterday.

The universal profile of serial killers is they are aged between fifteen to forty-five at the time of their first murder and between eighteen to sixty at the time of their last.

Could there be a connection between this incident and his current investigation? The time frame fitted. Could this be where it had begun, he wondered?

He photographed the image on the screen with his iPhone, then took a second photograph as backup.

Detective Inspector Ron Gilbart. Ambitious officers back then would reach that rank in their early thirties to early forties. Was Gilbart still alive now? If he was, he'd be in his seventies or eighties. He knew exactly who to call to ask.

As he hurried out of the library, he phoned Tish and asked her to get him the number of David Rowland, a former Sussex policeman now in his seventies, who coordinated the local Association of Retired Police Officers. Standing on the pavement in the light drizzle, he waited for her to look up the number. She said she'd call him back in a few moments. As he went to call Cleo's number quickly to see how everything was going, his assistant came back on the line and gave him the number.

He dialled it immediately, but it went straight to voicemail. He left a message asking Rowland to call him back urgently. He strode swiftly up to the Church Street car park, paid what he considered to be the rip-off sum of money demanded by the machine, then began to drive out. Just as the barrier rose, his phone rang.

It was David Rowland. The former copper had a voice that was both elderly, but at the same time imbued with an infectious, almost youthful enthusiasm. 'Sorry I missed your call, Roy, I was down in the cells of the Old Police Cells Museum and I'm afraid there's no mobile signal down there. How can I help you?'

'Detective Inspector Ron Gilbart – do you by chance remember him?' Grace drove through the barrier, then stopped and waved a man wheeling a bicycle past, followed by a young couple with a baby in a pushchair.

Rowland sounded surprised. 'Yes, very well indeed. We were both at Hove together for quite a time. Sorry to see that station go, it holds good memories for me. What do you want to know about him?'

'Do you happen to know if he's still alive?' In his mirror he saw another car, a black Range Rover, pull up at the barrier behind him.

'Yes he is, but he's not very well, poor bugger. Had a stroke a couple of years ago and he's pretty much housebound. Got all his marbles, but he struggles with his speech. His wife's pretty good at helping him out. They've got a bungalow in Woodingdean.'

'Have you got his address and number?'

The Range Rover gave him an angry blast on his horn. Ignoring it, Grace tapped the number into his phone. Moments later, a short, bald man banged angrily on his window.

'Get a fucking move on, you tosser!'

Grace pulled out his wallet and flashed it open to show his warrant card to the man as he dialled. The bald man raised both arms in the air in frustration. Ignoring him, Grace listened to the ringing tone, then a moment later a female voice answered. It was Gilbart's wife and yes, Ron was home.

Current regulations restricted the breaking of speed limits to emergencies only. In his view this was an emergency. He bullied his way out into the traffic, and drove as fast as he could towards Gilbart's home.

82

Logan Somerville was hyperventilating. 'Help me, someone! Help me! Help me!' she shouted, her voice becoming increasingly hoarse. She had been shouting since she had woken, some while earlier, in a terrible panic. She'd not heard a sound in hours – or maybe even days. She had totally lost track of time, and was ravenously hungry, and desperate for water. Her sugar levels were dropping and with that sensation came the shakes and paranoia.

What if?

So many bad possibilities sparked in her mind.

What if her captor had died?

Or been arrested?

Or he had just decided to let her rot and die?

She began working again on her bonds. On her arm restraints, on her leg restraints. But with no success, other than to feel the pain where her flesh had rubbed.

She was not going to get out of here unless someone came to free her. And she did not want to die here, all alone.

'Police. POLICE! Hello! HELP ME!'

Oh, God, please someone help me.

She saw a faint green glow.

'Hello?' she said, weakly. 'Please, I need water, sugar. Please.'

Then she heard his muffled voice. 'I nearly had you out of here today! But it went a bit wrong. Don't worry, I have someone else in mind. As soon as I bring her here, you'll be free! Free as a bird.'

'Thank you,' she gasped.

'You're welcome.'

83

Ten minutes after leaving the Church Street car park, Roy Grace turned left up a steep hill opposite the Nuffield Hospital, and drove a short distance looking at the house numbers. It was 3.30 p.m. and already it was starting to get dark. Christmas lights sparkled in most of the downstairs windows, and two adjacent houses had garish light displays in their gardens. He pulled up outside No. 82. A small people carrier with a blue Disabled badge was parked on the driveway.

He stepped up to the porch and rang the bell. Moments later he was ushered inside by Gilbart's wife, Hilary, who was a tiny, sprightly lady nudging eighty, with a twinkling face and neat white hair. 'I'm afraid he has trouble hearing as well as speaking, Detective Superintendent,' she forewarned him.

The house felt like a sauna, and there was a faint smell of roasting meat. Much of the tiny hall was taken up by a trophy cabinet filled with silver cups, and a team photograph of rugby players standing in their midst. 'Ron's rugby and golf trophies!' she said proudly. 'He played for the police rugby and golf teams for years – right up until his stroke, really.'

A male voice called out, slurred and slightly aggressive. The words were just about decipherable. 'Schlooo ish it? Warrer they want? Make shure they show shere identity.'

'It's the police officer, darling, the one who phoned a little while ago. Detective Superintendent Roy Grace. The friend of David Rowland.'

'Urr.'

A few moments later, seated on a sofa in front of a blazing gas fire, feeling himself beginning to perspire, Grace was almost deafened by the television. On the wall behind it hung a framed Sussex Police

Commendation. He watched the former Detective Inspector, in his recliner armchair, Zimmer frame beside it, grapple with the remote, struggling to mute the television which was showing a cricket match somewhere overseas. Gilbart was a large man, with massive shoulders and thinning grey hair on his liver-spotted head. He gave Grace an expression that could have been a smile or a leer. 'Yurknowd-d-d-david-rowla?'

'Yes, I've known David for years,' Grace said. 'I was just admiring your trophies out in the hall – I'm President of the Sussex Police Rugby Team.'

'I carplaynymore,' he said, and looked so sad.

Hilary Gilbart came back into the room with a cup of tea for Grace and a piece of shortbread in the saucer, then she sat on the sofa. 'I'll help translate,' she said.

Grace thanked her, then turned to the retired detective. 'Ron,' he said, 'do the names Mandy White or Edward Denning ring a bell at all? Mandy's body was found in Hove Lagoon in December 1976, when you were the Duty Inspector.'

Staring straight ahead at the silent television, watching a bowler begin his run, Gilbart said, 'Lord Denning. Bloodyyud j-j-judge.'

'I don't think Detective Superintendent Grace was referring to Lord Denning, my love,' Hilary said. 'It was *Edward* Denning he asked you about.' She turned to Grace. 'If you give me a few moments, I will get Ron's scrapbook – I am sure there's some information on that case in it.'

Gilbart again stared at the screen. The ball was returned to the bowler by a fielder, and he walked away from the crease, pacing out his next run. After several moments, Grace was beginning to wonder if the old man had fallen asleep, when suddenly he spoke, quite vehemently, his voice raised.

'Lil shit!'

'Little shit?' Grace prompted. 'Edward Denning?'

'Lil shit.'

'In what way?'

'Couldvsave – couldvsave – her – gl– gl– gl–'

'Could have saved the girl?' his wife checked, coming back into the room. 'Is that what you're trying to say, my love?'

He nodded.

'Why didn't he, Ron? Why didn't he save her?' Grace asked.

Gilbart's mouth dropped open, and he stared again at the cricket match, his head nodding for some moments. 'Becar – becarl – becarl ye lilled her.'

84

Roy Grace arrived back at Sussex House moments before the start of the 6.30 p.m. briefing. It was the day of their house move. Cleo and Noah would be in their new home by now; he so wished he was with them but he had no idea what time he would get there tonight. Not until very late for sure. He took his place in the conference room, made a quick note about his meeting with Ron Gilbart and what he had read in the scrapbook in his policy book, then looked through the minutes that his assistant had prepared.

The door flew open and Norman Potting, looking a lot more animated than he had seen him in a while, rushed in. He stopped for an instant, staring around at the entire assembled team as if assessing whether it was appropriate for him to interrupt or not, then clearly decided it was.

'Chief,' he said. 'I think I have something of interest!'

'Well, we haven't actually started yet, but go ahead, Norman,' he said.

'I went to see Dr Edward Crisp again this morning, as you requested. He's a slippery bastard. Interviewing him is like trying to write on a wet egg. We know he appeared walking his dog at Hove Lagoon on the evening that the body of Denise Patterson was discovered by the workmen. I wasn't happy with the explanation Dr Crisp gave me as to why he was there. He said this was his regular evening constitutional after work. He also told me that his daily routine was to walk his dog in the same area during his break, stopping at the Hove Deep Sea Anglers Club or the Big Beach Café for lunch.'

Potting paused and pulled a crumpled sheet of paper from his inside pocket and glanced at it for some moments. Then he held it up, waving it around. 'This is a triangulation report from his mobile phone company. Dr Crisp is quite correct when he talks about his lunchtime routine, because this backs it up. But he has lied about his evening routine. Every evening, regular as clockwork, he normally walks home from his office in Wilbury Road to Tongdean Villas, via Hove Park, according to this. On the night of Thursday, 11th December – the night Denise's body was discovered – he suddenly varied his routine and went down to Hove Lagoon. I think we need to know why. One of the reasons you asked me to go and talk to him again was that he seemed overly interested in the progress of the investigation. He has contacted me seven times.'

DS Jon Exton raised his hand. 'Could it be that on his lunchtime constitutional he saw the workmen drilling up the path, and returned out of simple curiosity?'

'I don't think any normal person would be curious about workmen digging up an old path, would they?' Potting said. 'But it might be a different matter if they saw their deposition site being excavated.'

'So far we've had no useful information from any of the workmen we've located who laid that original path?' Grace asked.

'Norman spoke to the one who's now living in Perth, Australia,' Guy Batchelor said. 'He was on the original crew and claims he saw nothing.'

'What's his name?' Grace asked.

'Tony Scudder. I had a long chat with him over the phone. I don't think he saw anything suspicious.'

'Do we know anything about Scudder's background?'

'We've checked for any criminal record, but there's nothing.'

Grace stood up. 'OK, now I have something potentially significant to report, myself.' He relayed his findings in the library and his subsequent meeting with Ron Gilbart. 'It wasn't an easy session because the poor bugger struggles to speak. But we managed with the help of his wife. He told me about a case back in December 1976, when he was the duty DI at Hove. A teenage girl was found drowned in the Hove Lagoon. She'd been on a date that evening with the son of her mother's employer, called Edward Denning. Her mother worked as a cleaning lady. According to the newspaper report, she'd fallen through the ice while trying to skate on the lagoon, which was frozen over during a freak cold spell. The Coroner's verdict was accidental death, but Gilbart had not been happy with this, and had done some investigation of his own. He told me the couple, who were both under age, had been drinking heavily for much of the evening – rum and Cokes – at a pub close by, just off the seafront. Gilbart's convinced Denning murdered the young girl. But he was never able to prove it.'

'So Denning walked free?' Jon Exton said.

'He claimed she'd fallen in, and that he'd tried to save her. He'd flagged down a passing motorist yelling for help. There were no witnesses.'

'What makes Gilbart feel that Denning murdered her?' Guy Batchelor asked.

Grace shrugged. 'Copper's nose. But there is something very significant for us.' He smiled. 'I found some cuttings on the case in an old scrapbook of Gilbart's. Two years after the death of this girl, who was called Mandy White, Edward Denning's parents divorced. No prizes for guessing the name of his mother's second husband.'

'Crisp?' ventured Jack Alexander.

'Bingo!' Grace said.

'*Edward* Denning – *Edward* Crisp?' DS Exton said. 'Shit!'

'I'm not making any assumptions. But the more I learn about this doctor, the less comfortable I feel about him,' Grace said. Looking first at Norman Potting then at Jon Exton, he said, 'I'm giving you both an action. I want to know everything about Edward Crisp. His whole background, right back into his childhood. I want to know about all his relationships, his school friends, his teachers, everyone he's ever dated, his wife, his kids and all his relatives, and anyone he's known to associate with, professionally or socially. And, crucially, I want a list of every patient on his current list – and every patient he has ever had. OK?'

Both detectives nodded.

'Oh, and sir, it may be a long shot,' Potting said, 'but I'd like to send the piece of paper on which Crisp wrote down his phone number for fingerprint and DNA analysis.'

'Good idea, Norman, send it off.'

Then Tanja Cale raised her hand. 'I don't know if this is significant or not, sir,' she said. 'But I took part in the witness interview with

Freya Northrop today. It came out that one week ago she registered as a patient with Dr Edward Crisp.'

Grace felt like he'd been hit by a bolt of lightning. 'What?'

'She said she found him charming, but a bit weird.'

There was a long silence, while Grace thought hard.

'That could be highly significant,' Batchelor said.

Grace nodded, still thinking.

Emma-Jane Boutwood raised a hand.

'Yes, EJ?' Grace said.

'Sir, the outside enquiry team interviewed a lady who lives opposite Freya Northrop's home. Apparently she's the Neighbourhood Watch coordinator for her street. She called the Incident Room today after reading about the case in the *Argus*, to say she'd seen a man in a hi-viz jacket, carrying a clipboard, approaching Freya's home around 11 a.m. last Sunday. She hadn't thought much of it at the time, but she realized now, having read about the incident, it might be significant.'

'Was she able to describe him?' Grace asked.

'Not in detail, unfortunately. She said his face was partly covered by a scarf and tweed cap. Then she got distracted by her young grandchild.'

'Did she describe his build?'

'He was quite slim, she said. Middle-aged, she estimated. She said he was white, clean-shaven and wearing glasses.'

Which fitted Dr Crisp, Grace thought. He turned to the forensic podiatrist, Haydn Kelly, who was dressed as usual in a smart suit and flamboyant tie. It was expensive to keep him on the team on a daily basis, but right now costs were not an issue.

'Haydn, have you made any progress with the footprint in the underground car park?'

'Well, I got excited because I found one footprint in the garden of Freya Northrop's house that looked at first to be an exact match, from the same brand of trainer. But without going into technical details, there are sufficient minor differences for me to have to discount it. I understand there have been a number of workmen at the house over the past weeks, so it could be any of a number of different people who left the print there.'

'I don't think we should exclude any footprints found in the garden, Haydn,' Grace said. 'We've no certainty the footprint found in the oil in the underground car park belongs to the offender – it's pure speculation.'

'Understood,' Kelly said.

'The shoe prints will become more interesting when we have a suspect in custody,' Dave Green, the Crime Scene Manager added.

Grace thanked him then turned to Branson. 'Glenn, have you got a list of all the people who have been working there?'

'I have, boss. The outside enquiry team has interviewed them all.' He looked down at his notebook, and turned back a couple of pages. 'Seven in total. Electricians, plumbers, painters, a plasterer and a carpenter. We've eliminated all of them.'

'What about arresting Crisp and bringing him in for questioning, boss?' Guy Batchelor said. 'We've got enough on him, surely?'

'No,' Grace said. 'He's only just become a potential suspect and we need to do a lot more work, urgently, to ascertain whether he might be our killer.' He took a moment to make a note in his policy book, then looked up. 'There is a lot of circumstantial evidence against Crisp, Guy. But that's all it is at the moment. Whoever the offender is, Crisp, Harrison Hunter, who's not been traced, or someone else, he's obviously a clever individual who's evaded capture for many years. We need to be in a stronger position than we are now if and when we do decide to arrest Crisp. I also think we run a risk of moving in on him too quickly, because if we find nothing and have to release him, and he actually is our offender, it might scare him into going to ground – going dormant again – and then we could lose him for years, maybe perhaps forever. I think he's more use to us free at the moment. Don't forget, Logan is out there somewhere, hopefully alive. It needs to remain our top priority to find her.'

Grace sipped his coffee, paused for a moment, then went on, 'My hunch is this person doesn't go in for anything spontaneous. He plans meticulously – Tony Balazs, who is not able to be here tonight, has the same view. I suspect the Brander watches his victims for weeks, if not months, before taking them. Balazs feels he has already chosen his next victim and is going to strike again soon, to make up for being foiled yesterday. He's without question a potential danger to members of the public, and I'm going to request immediate twenty-four-hour surveillance on Crisp, predominantly because of his link to Freya Northrop.'

Suddenly, the advice of the forensic psychologist, Tony Balazs, was ringing in his ears. *Find ways to rile him. Goad him into making mistakes!*

He smiled as a totally unorthodox thought suddenly entered his mind. Could it work?

Could it?

It was dangerous as it could backfire, and he knew he had to clear it with the Crown Prosecution Service to cover his backside. If, as he desperately hoped, Logan Somerville was still alive – they had very little time left to find her. Every single minute was precious.

He turned to the Crime Scene Manager. 'Dave, I urgently need footage of Dr Edward Crisp walking and a close-up photograph of him. Can you position a photographer near his home tomorrow morning? He normally walks the dog between 7 and 8 a.m. Make sure he's not seen by Crisp. And make sure you get the necessary authorizations.'

'Yes, boss.'

Fifteen minutes later, Roy Grace left the meeting and hurried back to his office, feeling a surge of hope for almost the first time since this enquiry had started. He had that tingling sensation he sometimes got when he felt a case turning in his favour, and they were starting to close in on a suspect. Tightening the net.

Crisp.

Dr Edward Crisp.

But he was well aware that he mustn't put all his eggs in one basket and forget Harrison Hunter. It was worrying him a lot that Hunter had still not been traced.

He then thought back to last Thursday night at Hove Lagoon. Most members of the public reacted to dead bodies with shock. Crisp had seemed jolly about it and quite unaffected. But then again, doctors were different, and he had been a police surgeon. They were like coppers in having their coping mechanisms which gave them an indifference to death, and an ability to laugh at it, sometimes.

The escape valve of all those who had to deal with death on a regular basis. Emergency service workers, medics. They all shared a gallows humour. Grace remembered attending a road traffic accident just outside Brighton, where a car had rolled into a field of sheep, and the driver lay dead in the wreckage, impaled by a fence post. A Traffic officer standing beside him had said, 'Poor bugger, his wife only sent him out for a steak.'

Guy Batchelor came back into the office.

'How did the surveillance request go, Guy?' Grace asked him, knowing that these requests often took a while, because of their sensitive nature and complexity. He smiled with relief at Batchelor's reply.

'Granted.'

85

At midday the following day, Roy Grace stood on the podium alongside Cassian Pewe, in the Lounge Assembly Room of Malling House. It was again rammed with press, photographers, TV news cameramen and radio reporters.

The Assistant Chief Constable, as usual for these public appearances, spoke first. 'These are our updates since yesterday. We are taking increased measures, daily, to protect the women of Brighton and Hove. Thanks to the support of our Police and Crime Commissioner, Nicola Roigard, we have been allocated extra budget to enable us to draft in police officers from other divisions. Starting today, additional officers will be out on our streets. And thanks to a bungled attack on Thursday of this week and a very clear-headed witness, we now believe we have a suspect. Detective Superintendent Roy Grace, the Senior Investigating Officer, can tell you more about this.' He stepped back from the microphone.

Staring at Pewe's moist, serpentine lips, Grace felt, for some moments, like a mouse that had been dropped through the lid of a cage containing a hungry snake. He took a deep breath and then addressed the throng.

'We have an e-fit of the person we are seeking urgently to help us with our enquiries, who was seen near Hove Recreation Ground on Thursday night,' he said. He then indicated the first of the two artist's impressions on the screen behind him. 'This refers to the man seen driving away at the time of Logan's abduction.' Then he pointed to the sketch that had only been completed half an hour ago, pinned to a whiteboard behind him, and which was being projected on a large screen over to his right.

Pewe frowned quizzically at him, but Grace pretended not to have noticed.

The sketch had been carefully created by the artist, working with Grace and Potting, from a photograph taken secretly of Dr Crisp earlier this morning. Very deliberately the drawing did not depict Crisp too precisely, it was more a representation of his facial features and hair. This approach had been agreed with the Crown Prosecution Service lawyer appointed to the case.

Grace, blinking against the barrage of flashlights, kept a poker face, but inside he was smiling. They were buying this. It would worry Crisp, but it was not an accurate enough portrait for him to be positively identified, nor was it accurate enough to send him scurrying underground.

'We would like any members of the public, particularly young females, who might have been approached by this man, or anyone who has seen him acting suspiciously to contact us.'

'Are you able to name any suspects?' someone shouted from the back of the room.

'Not at this stage, no,' Grace replied. 'I would appeal to anyone who might recognize either of these to contact us urgently.'

'Detective Superintendent, has there been any ransom demand for Logan Somerville?'

'No, we have received no ransom demand.'

'Roy, do you believe Logan Somerville is still alive?'

'We are hopeful she is alive and we are doing everything that we can to find her.'

'Detective Superintendent Grace, what is your latest advice to the women of this city?'

'We advise all young women to be extra vigilant, and not to go out in the evening alone; to ensure they don't leave doors unlocked or windows open at night and to call us if they are worried by anything they think might be suspicious. Please don't worry about false alarms, we would rather hear from anyone who has concerns than not.'

'Detective Superintendent, is there anything to link this to the disappearance of your own wife ten years ago?'

Although Grace had been prepared for this question, it still pierced his heart. Because, he knew, it was always a possibility. 'There is no evidence to suggest this,' he replied.

'How close to an arrest are you?'

'You've heard how the investigation is progressing. We need the help of the public and we are doing everything we can to find and arrest this killer.'

'Have you conclusively linked the murders of Emma Johnson and Ashleigh Stanford to the ones thirty years ago of Katy Westerham and Denise Patterson?'

'There are certain parallels which we continue to investigate,' Roy Grace said, circumspectly. 'But at the moment we are keeping an open mind.'

'Have you found the branding iron yet or where it was made?' a woman reporter called out.

'No, we haven't,' Roy replied. Several more questions about the Brighton Brander followed.

'Are you able to name any suspects? Is this the Brighton Brander?' a man shouted from the back of the room.

For the next forty minutes Roy continued to field questions, and also took the opportunity to provide more information to the assembled media representatives.

At the end of the conference he left the podium, feeling totally drained, and drove back to his office at Sussex House. So much was going through his head. This morning's surveillance report on Edward Crisp was that he had been at home all last night. Two officers had established that by ringing his front doorbell at the gates, dressed smartly, saying they were Jehovah's Witnesses. He had left the house at 7 a.m. today, taking his dog around Hove Park, and returned an hour later. He had not been out since.

Dr Edward Crisp, Grace thought. A middle-aged family doctor. Could he really be behind all this?

Then he only had to remind himself that Britain's worst-ever serial killer had been a middle-aged family doctor, Harold Shipman. All of his victims had been patients. Surely it would be too coincidental for another doctor to be Brighton's first serial killer?

The danger, he knew, from having a good suspect was always the temptation to focus on that suspect and ignore anything else. What else was he missing?

The only other potential suspect was the strange Dr Harrison Hunter, phoney anaesthetist, who had gone to see Jacob Van Dam. Middle-aged, blond wig, medium build.

Dr Crisp in disguise? An alter ego?

Van Dam had now been interviewed three times. Why the hell had Hunter gone to see him?

Grace knew the answer probably lay in the erratic mind of the offender. Murder was never a rational thing. It was a line that, fortunately, most decent folk never crossed. But equally it was a line that, once crossed, there was no going back from. You could never undo the fact that you had taken a life. Most people gave themselves up at some point after doing that, because they couldn't live with the guilt. The truly dangerous ones were the people who found they could live with the knowledge. People who, in the recesses of their twisted minds, actually enjoyed it.

For them it made no difference whether it was one killing or twenty. Once they crossed the Rubicon of their first murder, and found they were comfortable with it, there was no turning back. Even if they wanted to.

Many murders were committed by schizophrenics – people like Sutcliffe, the Yorkshire Ripper, who heard voices from God telling him to go and kill prostitutes.

Barring those who killed after losing their temper, the majority of murderers were sociopaths – or psychopaths – the same thing in Grace's view – people born without empathy. People capable of killing with little emotion or guilt.

Had Hunter gone to see Jacob Van Dam to boast? To be absolved? To show off? To sadistically torment him as Logan's uncle?

But Van Dam was not particularly close to Logan.

What the hell was that all about? A cry for help of some kind?

It was the only answer, at this moment, that he could come up with: that perhaps the offender was feeling guilt and wanted to be caught to stop him from offending further.

Tony Balazs agreed it was a possibility.

Grace felt certain that the clue to finding the offender lay in that visit. Despite the wig and tinted glasses that Dr Harrison Hunter had been wearing, from Jacob Van Dam's description, his build fitted Dr Crisp.

Feeling almost too exhausted to think straight, he laid his head on his arms on his desk and closed his eyes. Moments later, it seemed, he woke with a start to a dull buzzing sound, like a trapped insect.

His phone, which he had switched to silent for the press conference, was vibrating on the desk.

'Roy Grace,' he answered, confused, only half awake. He looked at the time. Shit. He'd been asleep for almost an hour.

It was Jack Alexander. 'Sir,' he said. 'I've just taken an urgent call from a woman at the Roundstone Caravan Park in Horsham. She's seen the images on the lunchtime news and reckons she might know this man – she thinks he has a mobile home there.'

86

Logan's captor had not been to see her in what felt like more than a day. It could have been longer. She had no sense of time.

What if, she thought with a deep, dark shudder of panic, she had been abandoned?

Left here to die of hunger or thirst?

She pulled hard with her arms, with every ounce of the feeble strength she now had and, suddenly, she felt the bonds on her right wrist slacken, just a fraction. She tried again, then again. It came a fraction looser. She tried again, oblivious to the pain as it cut into her flesh. Then again. Again.

She was sure it was getting looser!

Then she heard a sound. The roof of her prison was sliding back. She saw a haze of green light above her and she froze.

'Won't be long now,' the voice growled at her.

The roof closed.

87

Residents of Horsham had different theories about where the name had first originated. Some said it was from *Horse Ham*, meaning a place where horses were kept. Others claimed it was named after a Saxon warrior, called *Horsa's Ham*, who had been granted land in the area.

Roy Grace knew this from his dad, who had been passionately interested in Sussex's history. He liked the town, but with its modern urban sprawl in all directions, equally it frustrated him, because he always got lost there.

'Where the hell is this place?' he said.

'We should have taken the A24 like I suggested,' Glenn Branson replied.

Grace, trying to read the satnav app on his jigging phone, shook his head. 'This thing should bloody know.'

There were three missed calls from Cleo on his phone. So far he'd only spent a few hours in their new home. He had no idea what time he would get back today or when he would be able to start unpacking any of his things.

Ten minutes later, a vast array of shiny caravans appeared on their right, each with a price tag in the front window, and a large sign which said, ROUNDSTONE CARAVANS, HOLIDAY HOMES, CALOR GAS.

During the drive Grace had started making the initial arrangements to move some extra resources towards their location, as he was confident this sounded like a good lead, and he hoped they would be needed sooner rather than later. He had asked them to meet at an RV point a short distance away.

They turned in through the gates and followed the signs to reception, a modern building attached to an attractive, large

Edwardian house. They pulled up and climbed out. A sign on the office door read, WHEN CLOSED RING HOUSE BELL.

They walked up to the porch of the house and Grace rang the bell. A dog barked and after a few moments a short, well-preserved fair-haired woman in her mid-fifties appeared, dressed in a black roll-neck sweater, jeans and boots.

'Good afternoon,' she said with a friendly, if quizzical, smile.

Grace held up his warrant card. 'Detective Superintendent Grace and Detective Inspector Branson of Surrey and Sussex Major Crime Team. We had a phone call a short while ago from an Adrienne Macklin here in response to an appeal on the lunchtime news.'

'Ah, yes,' she said. 'Adrienne who made the call on my behalf is off this afternoon – I'm the owner – Natalie Morris. I have all the information you need. Would you like to come in?'

She led them through into a large, cosy living room, with a log fire burning in the grate, and ushered them to a sofa, then sat down in an armchair opposite. 'How can I help you? Would you like a drink? Cup of tea?'

Branson was about to say yes, but Grace, in a hurry, cut him short. 'We're fine, thank you, Mrs Morris.' Then he pulled a photograph of Edward Crisp from his pocket and handed it to her. 'Do you recognize this man?'

She studied the photograph for a few moments. 'When I saw him on TV I was pretty sure that's our Mr Hunter, but now I am not so certain.' She looked again. 'It's not a very clear picture.'

Grace leaned forward, adrenaline surging. 'Harrison Hunter?'

'Give me a couple of minutes,' Natalie Morris said.

She hurried out of the room, then reappeared with a large burgundy-covered ledger, and began leafing through it. 'Mr Harrison Hunter!' she said. 'Unit R-73.'

'Unit R-73?' Grace queried.

'Yes, it's quite a substantial mobile home. One of our permanent ones.'

'How long has he lived here?'

'Quite a while. I do hope I'm not wasting your time. The thing is,' she said nervously, 'we don't pry into our customers' lives.'

'Of course not,' Glenn Branson said. 'Why would you?'

'It wouldn't be very nice for them, would it?' she said. 'We always hope that we have respectable people here. We just let them come and go as they please.'

'So long as they pay their rent on time?' Grace said.

'Precisely.' The woman was starting to look increasingly ill at ease.

'How well do you know Hunter, Mrs Morris?' Grace asked.

'To be honest, I don't really know him at all. He pays on the nail, he is always pleasant. But he's not really here much at all. We don't ask questions. Some of our residents use their places for – you know – meeting their ladies. Others as an escape from city life. My attitude is so long as no one is any bother to the other residents, what they do is up to them.'

'Mr Hunter's not here at the moment?'

'I haven't seen him,' she said. 'There's normally a car outside when he is.'

'What car?'

She thought for a moment. 'From memory it's a big dark grey thing.'

'Do you have a contact phone number for him?' Glenn Branson asked.

She looked again at the ledger. 'I'm afraid there's nothing here. But that's not unusual.'

'Could you point out Mr Hunter's unit for me, please?' Grace asked, his excitement surging.

'Certainly.' She stood up and walked across to an aerial photograph of the site on the wall. 'Unit R-73,' she said, indicating with her finger. 'I could take you over, you could see the outside, but if he's not in, I don't have a key.'

'I don't want to approach it obviously at this moment,' Grace said. 'Do you have an old raincoat or anorak, a hat or a cap, and a wheelie bin I could borrow for a few minutes?'

She gave him a strange look. 'Well, yes, I do.'

The light was failing and in less than an hour it would be pitch dark, Grace thought, as he pushed the empty bin across the wet grass, wearing an old tweed cap and an anorak several sizes too big for him, which the proprietor had found. He zigzagged his way past the caravans and mobile homes of different sizes, trying to look nonchalant, as he finally reached Unit R-73, and trundled his bin on past it.

The blinds were down, and there were three keyholes on the door, he noticed, which looked like overkill. There did not appear to be any lights on inside and he could hear no sound. However, just in case he was being watched, he continued past, slowly completed his circuit and returned to the office. Then he stopped before entering, called the Ops-1 Controller and asked if the helicopter was free. Sited at Redhill, it would be a little over five minutes' flying time from here.

To his relief the Controller told him it was.

Grace asked him to get it airborne immediately, while there was still some daylight, and that he would email over a JPEG of the aerial map of the site. He needed the helicopter to use its thermal-imaging camera to tell him whether anyone was in Unit R-73. He re-entered the office and asked Natalie Morris for permission to photograph the plan, which she gave him.

As Grace was doing that, Glenn Branson asked, 'Do you have security issues here, Mrs Morris?'

'No,' she said. 'The whole estate is monitored by CCTV and we have someone on security around the clock. We have very little trouble. I can't remember the last time we had a break-in at any of our units – it was when my husband was alive – over ten years ago, at least.' Then she hesitated, looking nervous, suddenly. 'Surely you don't suspect Mr Hunter of being this Brighton Brander man, do you?' she asked.

'What makes you think we might?' Branson asked.

'Oh, you know, I like cop shows on the telly. Sometimes my imagination runs riot. But Adrienne and I saw the pictures on the news, and we both said, "That could be Mr Hunter!"'

'And what sort of person is Harrison Hunter?' Grace interceded.

She smiled. 'Well, not weird, exactly. No, I wouldn't go so far as to say that. More, just very private.'

'I'm going to request a search warrant, Mrs Morris. It will take about an hour. I don't want to inconvenience you, or cause you any problems with any of your residents. So we'll be as discreet as possible.'

Natalie Morris raised her hands. 'I'm always very happy to

cooperate with the police.'

Grace thanked her.

'Perhaps you'd like a cup of tea, or coffee, or something stronger while you are waiting?'

'Coffee would be good,' Grace said.

Branson nodded. 'Yes please.'

Moments after she left the room, Grace could hear the distant clatter of the approaching helicopter. His phone rang and the Ops-1 Controller told him it would be overhead in one minute.

Grace thanked him then said quietly to Branson, 'I think we're going to need to be prepared to move fast, in case we find something significant in there – and I just have a feeling we will. Once we've put the door in, if this Hunter comes back he'll know we're on to him. We can't risk driving him underground. My sense is either we're going to find something in this caravan that connects us to the killer, or it's completely innocent. But I don't think someone innocent would make their place quite so secure.'

'You're thinking Dr Crisp.'

'If we bring him in, I want it belt and braces. I want a fingerprint or DNA.' He pulled out his phone and called the Critical Incident Manager, Chief Inspector Jason Tingley. He explained the situation and asked if he could have a Local Support Team on standby in position near Edward Crisp's address, to support the Surveillance Team.

Tingley agreed.

The Ops-1 Controller called Grace back to say that the helicopter's camera had not detected any life in Unit R-73.

Grace thanked him, then asked if NPAS 15 could be diverted to Brighton to do an immediate high-altitude photo survey of Dr Edward Crisp's home and the surrounding terrain, while there was still sufficient daylight.

He was assured the helicopter would be over Crisp's house in twelve minutes, flying high enough not to alert anyone.

88

'You've never told us – what exactly was your agenda in going to see the shrink in London, *Dr Harrison Hunter*?' Marcus sneered.

'Was it your ego again, running rampant?' Felix quizzed. 'Or was it because, as we've always known, you are just plain raving mad?'

'Come on, guys, give me some credit!'

'We're all ears!' Marcus said. 'Yes? Talk us through the credit?'

'It was to try to take the heat off us.'

'There was no heat on us,' Felix said. 'Now there's a fucking picture out there of you.'

'It doesn't look that much like me.'

'Yeah, right,' Marcus said, sourly. 'We all recognized you without much trouble.'

'That's because you know me.'

'If I didn't know better,' Marcus said, 'I would say you had some kind of a death wish. That you're bored. You think it's time for game over. You're having one final tilt at Mr Plod. Am I right? You've decided it's time to abandon us. Easy for you to exit. But what about us?'

'Give me one reason why I should give a toss about you?'

'Because we're your life, all you have. Your wife walked out on you. Your children have gone with her. You're just one of life's losers, like you always were.'

'Tch, tch. You never read Sun Tzu's *Art Of War*, did you? You know something he said that might give you some insight into why I went to see Dr Jacob Van Dam? *Stand by the river bank for long enough, and you'll see the bodies of all your enemies float by.*'

'Just what the hell's that meant to mean?' Marcus demanded.

'Oh, you'll find out soon enough. Really quite soon.'

'The suspense is killing me,' Felix said, then broke into giggles. 'I'm so waiting for that day!'

'You don't get it, do you?'

'What's to not get? We've been floating down your river for decades. We've all grown to like it. We even like you!'

'Yep, well, don't like me too much. Because there's another quote I'm favouring at the moment.'

'And that is?'

'*Life's a bitch, and then you die.*'

89

Saturday 20 December

Norman Potting drove the unmarked Ford along the congested high street of the small, rural Surrey town. The pavements were crowded with people, dressed up against the biting cold, and in the falling darkness the shop windows flashed, twinkled and sparkled with Xmas decorations and messages. As he sat waiting for traffic lights to change he could hear a brass band belting out 'Good King Wenceslas'.

A tear trickled down his cheek and he wiped it away with the back of his hand. *Christmas*, he thought. He and Bella had rented a cottage in Cornwall where they had been planning to spend their first Christmas together – taking her elderly mother with them. Now he had no plans. His sister had invited him to spend the holidays with her family in Devon, but although he liked her he wasn't up for the jollity of a family gathering. His preference at the moment was to spend the time immersed in work.

Taking the winding road out of the far side of the town, he reached a picturesque humpback bridge over a river. Ordinarily, in happier times, he would have defaulted to the child inside him and accelerated hard, gleefully, and felt the car lift off over the brow. But he was in no mood for that any more – if he ever would be again, he pondered.

He reached a junction, then turned left and started driving up a long, steep hill, following the signs to The Cloisters, one of the nation's most famous schools. He passed a row of terraced cottages, then smart, detached houses either side of the road. A cluster of large, modern, institutional buildings loomed up on his left. Towards the top of the hill he passed beneath a stone bridge, following the signs to the school, made a sharp right turn, followed by another and drove through a Gothic-revival archway with leaded-light windows above it. He entered the school grounds, with more Gothic-looking buildings all around and a huge chapel in front of playing fields, over to the left. He saw two teenage boys in tweed jackets and grey flannel trousers walking along, one with the middle button of his jacket done up, and halted beside them, lowering his window.

'Can you tell me how I find the Bursar's office?' he asked.

'Oh ya,' one of the boys said, with a cut-glass accent.

Two minutes later, following the instructions he had been given, Potting drove past a cloistered courtyard, and several more boys similarly attired, and pulled up in front of a dull, single-storey building with a modern glass and concrete structure just beyond it. A modest sign on the blue front door read, BURSAR'S OFFICE.

The Detective Sergeant climbed out of the car, paused to look around, walked up to the door and rapped on it. Moments later it was opened by a tall man in his fifties, with a military bearing. He was dressed in a brown corduroy jacket over a checked shirt, knitted tie and beige cavalry twill trousers, and sported a short-back-and-sides haircut. He spoke with a confident, faintly patronizing, public school voice.

'Detective Sergeant Potting?' He gave him an enthusiastic smile.

'Yes,' he said and produced his warrant card. 'Surrey and Sussex Major Crime Team.'

'I'm Neville Andrew, the Bursar.'

'How do you do?' Potting said, then added a deferential 'sir' as the man shook his hand, firmly. 'Bit of a posh establishment, this.'

'Yes, it is rather splendid here!' he said, whilst studying the card more assiduously than most people usually did. He led Potting through into a small office, with a tiny, old-fashioned wooden desk on which sat a computer monitor flanked by a photograph of a conservatively dressed woman in her fifties, and another of three children. Two old and functional wooden chairs with leather seats faced it. The room was crammed with grey metal filing cabinets and on the wall behind him hung a framed crest and the school motto, in Latin, which Potting was unable to decipher. There was a faintly musty smell of old paper and the sterile, weekend scent that many offices had, of polish.

'Founded in 1611, this marvellous establishment,' the Bursar said, brightly. 'Originally in London, then moved out here in 1843 – a bit before both our times! Are you a public schoolboy yourself?'

'Oh no,' Potting replied in his deep rumble of a voice, heavily tinged with his native Devon burr. 'A comprehensive in Tiverton. Don't think my parents could have afforded the fees for a place like this. Bet they run to a pretty penny.'

'About thirty-five to forty thousand a year depending on extras.'

'Pounds?'

'Yes.'

'That's what I earn in a year!' he exclaimed. 'Bloody hell! All that money to watch your spoiled little bastard get bullied!'

'I was a pupil here myself,' the Bursar said. 'I don't recall being a spoiled little bastard, or being bullied. Can I get you a tea or coffee?'

'Er – builder's tea, please,' Potting said. 'With two sugars.' Then he added, 'I appreciate your coming in on a Saturday, and I hope I haven't inconvenienced you.'

'Got me out of a dreaded shopping trip to the supermarket with she-who-must-be-obeyed – so not at all.' He thawed a little. 'We've one or two of our old boys who've joined your finest. One we're particularly proud of is a superintendent in the Sussex Police, who's in regular contact with us, Stephen Rogan. Ever come across him?'

'Superintendent Rogan? Yes indeed. Didn't realize he'd been to a top people's school. Do you keep up with all your old boys – alumni, isn't that the right word?'

'Oh, we like to keep tabs on them all, the good ones and the occasional not-so-good. Part of my role is to try to convince them to support their alma mater – and persuade them to leave bequests to us in their wills. It's not easy to keep a place like this going, financially.'

'Well, I'm here to talk to you about one particular old boy,' Potting said.

'You said on the phone it was in connection with a murder enquiry?' He raised his eyebrows.

'It is actually a murder and an abduction enquiry. We believe the abducted woman may still be alive and this is time critical.'

'Most intriguing – I'll be back in a mo.' Neville Andrew disappeared through a doorway, and Potting took the opportunity to look around. There were several photographs on the walls of football, cricket and hockey teams, as well as an army regimental picture with, presumably, Andrew in one of the rows of officers, he thought, scanning the picture in search of him without success. He glanced back at the photographs of the woman and three smartly dressed and happy-looking children on the desk, and thought wistfully of his own private life. A string of former wives, and numerous children – most of whom he hadn't spoken to in over twenty years. And now his fiancée dead.

The Bursar reappeared after a few minutes with two steaming mugs and a plate of digestive biscuits, handed one mug to Potting then sat down in front of the desk, his tall frame dwarfing it. 'So how can I help you on this enquiry, Detective Sergeant? It's fairly recent your merger of Surrey and Sussex, I believe?'

'Within the last couple of years,' Potting said.

'Working well, is it?'

'Reasonably,' Potting replied. He felt a bit like a fish out of water here in this grand school, as if he was in a different world – almost a different universe – to the one he was familiar with. He pulled out his notebook. 'To come to the point, Mr Andrew—'

'It's Brigadier, actually.'

Potting raised a respectful finger in the air. 'Ah, mea culpa! I beg your pardon, *Brigadier* Andrew.'

The Bursar seemed pleased with his use of Latin, Potting thought. He ploughed on. 'You had a pupil here during the 1970s, by the name of Edward Denning. At some point his parents divorced and he took his mother's new name of *Crisp*. He subsequently became a private family doctor in Brighton and he is currently a person of interest to us in our enquiry. I'm wondering if you could give me any information on his early background?'

Andrew frowned. 'Denning? Then Crisp? Hmmmn. This is actually ringing a bit of a bell. When I came here, three years ago, I introduced a computer program to connect us with all our alumni, and to establish links between them. If you can bear with me?'

'Of course.' Potting helped himself to a biscuit, which he dunked into his tea. To his minor irritation, part of the biscuit detached and floated on the surface of his tea. Embarrassed, he attempted to fish it out with his fingers and then clumsily dropped some onto his trousers.

The Bursar pulled on a pair of half-moon glasses, and tapped his keyboard for some moments, peering intently at the screen. 'Ah yes, here he is.' Then he hesitated. 'You do know I shouldn't really be telling you any of this without something more formal from you, because information I have here falls under the Data Protection Act.' He shrugged. 'Denning came here in the summer quarter, 1974, in Lark House, and left in the summer quarter, 1979. He continued his studies at Sussex University and King's College medical school in London. And you are quite right. During his time here he changed his name to Crisp.' He continued reading. 'Not a particularly distinguished pupil. He became a house monitor in his last year. A rather solitary character, he showed no interest in sport or team games of any kind, but did join the school potholing and caving trip to Wales. Left with respectable A-level grades in physics, chemistry and biology.' Then he frowned again. 'But there is something a bit interesting about this chap.'

'Oh?' Potting said, sipping his tea. He was tempted to try another dunk, but decided against and instead put the piece of dry biscuit into his mouth and chewed.

'Well, yes. I told you we try to keep tabs on all of our alumni, in the hope we can persuade them to support the school. Well, this concerns some of Crisp's contemporaries, whom I've not been able to trace.'

'How many pupils do you have here at any one time?' the DS asked.

'We have seven hundred and ten, currently. Four hundred and eighty boys and the rest girls. It was different back then, of course. Hardly any girls.'

'How many of your past pupils are you unable to trace?' Potting asked.

'Gosh, there's over three hundred on our *missing* list.' He grinned. 'But I'm bloody well determined to track them down. I began my career in the Army in the Intelligence Corps. I'm on a mission to find every damned one of them and wring whatever spondula I can out of them. For the sake of future generations.'

Future generations of toffs, Potting thought, but did not say. Instead he asked, 'What can you tell me, Brigadier, about these contemporaries of Crisp you are unable to trace?'

The Bursar hesitated. 'Well, I'm afraid I really can't give out any information – because, as I said, of the Data Protection Act.'

'This is a murder enquiry, Brigadier. I would appreciate your full cooperation. You might not think that information you have is relevant, but we need to know everything and then we can decide.'

'I appreciate that, Detective Sergeant, but I am bound by the law. I have reluctant permission from the Headmaster to talk to you about Edward Denning, but not anyone else.'

Potting stared at him for a moment. Roy Grace had warned him earlier today about difficulties in dealing with schools like this, and the slightly high-handed attitude of this man was increasingly irking him. The power of the *old boy* network. He sipped some of his tea and swallowed the soggy morsel of biscuit that he hadn't extricated. 'I understand that venerable establishments like this operate under a certain code.'

'Code?' Andrew said.

'You think you're above the law – that you operate under some kind of privilege. You might throw pupils out, but you'll never let them down. Would that be a fair summary?'

'I can assure you that is not the case.'

Potting tapped his own chest. 'Actually, Brigadier, I'm the one to give the assurances that this is not the case.' He looked at his watch. 'I can have a team of officers here with a search warrant within ninety minutes. We'll remove all your computers and all your files, if that's how you want to play it? Wouldn't look too good if the press got to hear about it. Top people's school raided by the police. I think a few of the papers would have a field day.'

Neville Andrew gave a nervous flick of his tongue, wetting his lips. 'Well, I've never heard it put like that.' Then he smiled. 'I'm sure we can sort something out.'

'Good,' Potting said. 'It would be extremely helpful to our enquiry if you did not withhold any information, however irrelevant you feel it might be, or however protected by any Act of Parliament.'

'Regarding Crisp's contemporaries?'

'We need to know everything we can about Crisp and I need to talk to anyone who was in contact with him during his schooldays. To start with, is there anything in Edward Denning – or Crisp's –

past behaviour at this school to suggest an erratic nature of any kind?'

The Bursar peered at his screen. 'Well,' he said. 'I have copies of his leaving reports from his housemaster – the teacher here who would have known him best. It has always been a tradition here at The Cloisters for housemasters to write one report for the pupil – and his or her parents – and another for our records only.'

'And?'

'I'll read the one for his parents to you, first. *Enigmatic and unpredictable as ever, he fits into no known mould, and has clearly taxed his tutors' powers of prophecy. He carries many grudges, as if he feels the whole world is against him. A medical career seems inevitable, although there may be a number of false starts.'*

Potting wrote it down verbatim.

'Now,' said Andrew, peering at the screen. 'This is the one from his housemaster for the school records only. *Edward Crisp is a very strange individual. Impossible to get close to him, or to even know what he is thinking. He keeps to himself, seems to have few friends, and, frankly, I find him deeply disturbed and lacking in empathy. I put some of this down to the split-up of his parents' marriage, and some of it down to a very traumatic incident in his life in the winter of 1976 when he witnessed a young girl drown in a recreational lagoon in Hove. During his early days here, he was bullied by a number of boys. Not to put too fine a point on it, and I have no medical training to substantiate this, but I would say that Edward Crisp displays classic symptoms of a sociopath. I am sure he will ultimately be successful, because those with sociopathic tendencies are able to play the game of getting to the top better than anyone else. But I'm not sure I would ever want to be one of his patients should he pursue a medical career.'*

Potting pursed his lips. 'Well, that doesn't paint too good a picture of him. But it fits. What about his missing contemporaries?'

'Well,' Andrew said, a little hesitantly. 'As it happens, the timing of your visit is rather coincidental. Only this past week I've been preparing a report on his housemates in his particular year. It would seem there are three boys who were all direct contemporaries of Edward Crisp in Lark House who seem, literally, to have vanished off the face of the earth. It's really quite odd.'

'Odd in what sense?' Potting pressed. 'Mispers – as we call missing persons – are very common. Thousands of people are reported missing in the UK every year. A large number are still missing after one year. So three doesn't strike me as being particularly notable.'

The Brigadier frowned. 'Direct contemporaries of Crisp, from the same house? I'd say that was very odd. Old boys die, sadly, or they emigrate overseas. But normally we're able to trace most of them – we are pretty thorough.' He tapped his keyboard and peered at his screen again. 'What flags up these three is that each of them was reported missing to the police, by their families, and to our knowledge they've never been found.'

'How many pupils are there in Lark House?' Potting asked.

'Well, it's one of the smaller houses. There were seventy-eight boys there in Crisp's year. So three missing is quite a high proportion and I would imagine a high proportion compared to the national average – the appalling statistics you've just given me.'

'Missing, presumed dead?' Potting asked, increasingly interested now.

'Well, I can't answer that. But they all came here in 1974. None of them have been heard of for more than twenty years. They were all in their late twenties or early thirties at the time of their disappearance.'

'And each of them friends with Edward Crisp, Brigadier?'

'I can't tell you if they were friends. They were all slightly older – a year or so – and of course when you are thirteen, a year's age difference is a big gap.'

With his pen poised, Potting asked, 'Can you give me their names?'

The Bursar hesitated again, then said, 'Felix Gore-Parker, Marcus Gossage and Harrison Chaffinch.'

Potting wrote them down. Then he gave the Bursar his mobile phone number, in case he thought of anything else, and went back to his car. He sat for some moments looking at his notes before starting the engine. As he drove out of the school grounds he felt distinctly more uneasy about Crisp than when he had arrived.

He pulled over and phoned Roy Grace.

90

At a quarter to six Roy Grace thanked Potting and ended the call, then updated Glenn Branson. The two detectives were seated in the tiny front office of the Roundstone Caravan Park, watching the bank of CCTV monitors that covered the entrance and much of the floodlit grounds for any sign of movement. Watching for a man whom Haydn Kelly had predicted might be walking almost exaggeratedly upright, with his feet splayed out widely.

'*Classic symptoms of a sociopath?*' Branson said. 'Aged eighteen?'

'Sociopaths present from the age of four,' Grace said. 'A lot of them are cunning at hiding it.'

'Sounds like a smart teacher.'

Grace shrugged. 'Perhaps. Three contemporaries of Crisp missing without trace. What's all that about? Coincidence?'

'They were all male. Doesn't fit the victim profile of females with long brown hair.'

'No,' Grace replied, pensively. He was thinking back to his conversation with former Inspector Ron Gilbart. Had Crisp killed that girl at Hove Lagoon, as Gilbart had suspected? Had he killed three fellow pupils subsequently? What could have been his motive? Bullying? Surely not. Had the three men planned to disappear together for some reason? To become mercenaries? And had no one at the time connected them?

He phoned the researcher, Annalise Vineer, at the Incident Room, gave her the names of the three missing young men, and asked her to find out everything she could about their case histories.

It was fully dark outside now, and they had not seen a soul in the past hour. As Natalie Morris had told them, apart from a handful of permanent residents, the place was deserted at this time of year.

There would be a few arriving over the Christmas period, perhaps half a dozen at most.

He phoned Cleo's mobile, but the line was crackly and it was hard to hear her.

'Well, we're still here,' she said, sounding tired but cheerful. 'I'm trying to get sorted but we're still in complete chaos – oh, apart from Marlon who is fine in his swish new tank!'

Grace smiled. 'I'll be there as soon as I can, but it'll be late, I'm afraid.'

'How's it going?'

His phone started beeping. 'I'll call you straight back,' he said, then took the incoming call.

It was Haydn Kelly. 'Roy, I've now completed the gait analysis comparison with the footage of Dr Edward Crisp, and the footprint in the oil sludge in Logan Somerville's underground car park. I'm afraid, because of the quality of the print in the oil, I have to allow a fair margin for error. There are enough similarities to establish a likeness but not for a complete match beyond all reasonable doubt. Around a fifty to sixty per cent probability.'

'Which means getting on for a fifty-fifty chance that it's not Dr Crisp, right?'

'Yes,' the forensic podiatrist said, apologetically. 'That's about the size of it.' Kelly paused. 'Or put it another way, getting on for a fifty-fifty chance that it *is* Dr Crisp, as he cannot be excluded on this basis.'

Grace masked the disappointment in his voice that the comparisons were not more certain. 'Well, that's helpful, Haydn. It's not conclusive, as you say, but it's one more pointer in his direction.' As he ended the call, he heard a car pull up outside.

Both detectives went to the front door and outside into the darkness.

A young, enthusiastic uniformed constable, Pete Coppard, ran towards them brandishing a piece of paper, a huge smile on his face. 'I've got it signed, sir, Detective Superintendent Grace! The search warrant. JP Juliet Smith signed it for me – she was so helpful!'

Moments later eight officers from the Local Support Team, in body armour, approached Unit R-73. They were followed by Grace and Branson huddled against the freezing cold in their coats. A frost was already starting to coat the ground. One dog handler had been dispatched to cover the rear of the mobile home and the other the main rear entrance to the park, just in case the helicopter had missed someone inside, who made a run for it.

The first two LST officers climbed the steps at the front, paused for several seconds, then one swung the bosher at the front door. It bounced off it. The officer behind him then placed both arms of the hydraulic ram against the sides of the door frame and fired it up. The frame creaked and groaned, then buckled.

The first officer swung the bosher again, and this time the door budged a fraction, with paint flaking off. He swung the bosher again, then again, the door giving way a fraction more each time. Then he stopped to take a breather. 'What the sodding hell is this?' he said. 'Fort bloody Knox?'

He swung the yellow bosher one more time and the door gave way, violently slamming right back on itself. Instantly two more LST officers scrambled up the steps and entered.

Grace, standing back, saw flashlight beams piercing the interior as the initial assessment was made.

After about thirty seconds, interior lights flickered on. The LST Inspector, John Walton, a tall, lean, highly experienced public order policeman, appeared at the door. 'No one here, sir,' he said to Roy Grace. 'Bit of a weird place though!'

Grace stepped inside, followed by Branson. The interior felt much larger than it had appeared from outside, and felt even colder than outside; it was like an icebox. He wrinkled his nose at a faintly rancid smell, like days-old spilt milk that had not been properly mopped up. There was a seating area around a wooden dining table, on which was a tall stack of newspapers, and a tower of box files. Opposite was a built-in sofa that probably converted into an extra bed, Grace thought, on which were more box files stacked up. There was a large, wall-mounted television, with a tidy galley kitchen area just beyond it. Through an open concertina-door he could see a bed. He clocked it all, but barely took any of it in. It was the walls he could not stop looking at.

'Shit,' Glenn Branson said, peering down at the date of the top newspaper. The headline story was the suspected abduction of Logan

Somerville. 'This is last Saturday's – he's been here recently.' He pulled on gloves and began leafing through the pile.

Grace barely heard him. His eyes scanned the walls. Almost every inch of them, and the windows, with their closed shutters, was covered with photographs, all the same eight-by-ten size. Each was tagged with a typewritten note and date. Headshots of young women, their ages ranging from late teens to mid-twenties, Grace estimated. Some were tight close-ups, some showing part of the upper body as well. Photographs taken mostly outside, in public places – in many were recognizable backdrops of Brighton and Hove. The one common denominator between all of the women was their hairstyles.

Each had long brown hair.

A chill rippled through Grace. He stood still, staring around, and shivered from the cold, and from what he was looking at. In the silence he heard a clicking sound from the fridge, then a low hum as it started up. He peered closely at one photograph, a smiling woman in her early twenties, wearing dark glasses, and read the note that was attached as a strip to the base.

July 23rd 1983. On Volks Railway. Ainsley ? (snk) V.

Further along he saw photographs of two different women from different months in 1984. Between them was a gap, where a photograph had been removed. There was another gap further along the same section. Katy Westerham and Denise Patterson, he wondered?

The photographs were in date order, running right the way around the interior. He looked at another. This one was younger, sixteen or seventeen tops, he estimated. She had a mischievous look and was holding a stick of Brighton rock between her lips in a suggestive pose – but the pose was to someone other than the person who had taken this, Grace suspected. Some of the pictures appeared to have been taken from a distance.

Aug 21st, 2011. Btn Pier. Megan Walters L. Followed. Flat 7, 233 Havelock Street. 3 girls.

'What does that mean?' Branson pointed at the 'snk' and 'V' after Ainsley's name.

Grace frowned. Then looked at the 'V' after Ainsley's again. He checked other photos and all had a tiny 'V' or 'L' after their names. Some had 'snk' as well, others not. Then he realized.

'SNK – *surname not known*,' he said.

Branson nodded. 'You're getting sharper in your old age.'

Ignoring the jape, Grace said, 'V is for *visitor*, L for *local*. He's hunting. This is his hunting room.'

'So we should find Logan Somerville's mugshot here?'

'No.' Grace pointed at other gaps where photos had been stuck with Blu-Tack. 'We won't find Denise Patterson, Emma Johnson, Katy Westerham or Ashleigh Stanford.' Then, as an afterthought, he added, 'Logan Somerville or Freya Northrop, either. All these are the women he hasn't yet taken. He removes their photographs when he's taken them.'

The last photograph showed a pretty, rather aloof-looking girl of around twenty, with a model's poise, seated on an outdoor terrace, smoking a cigarette.

May 17th, 2014. Bohemia. Louise Masters. L. Followed. Flat 1b, Palmeira Villas, Brighton. Solo.

She looked vaguely familiar. He recognized her face but couldn't place it, nor her name. He had definitely seen her somewhere. He always remembered faces.

Louise Masters.

The name was also vaguely familiar, too. From where?

The last photograph on the wall. The Brander's last target here? Before? Before he moved on?

He called Directory Enquiries, gave Masters' name and address and asked for her number. Moments later it was texted through to him. He dialled it. After six rings he got her voicemail. A really friendly, strong, confident voice.

'It's Louise. If you're getting this I must be out. Leave a message or if it's urgent call my mob.' She gave her number.

Grace wrote it down and immediately dialled it. It went straight to voicemail. He left a message. 'Hello, Louise Masters, would you please call Detective Superintendent Grace of Surrey and Sussex CID the moment you get this. The time is 6.50 p.m. Saturday. It is extremely urgent.' Grace left his number, reading it out twice for safety, slowly and clearly.

Another, much deeper shiver rippled through his bones. He called the Critical Incident Manager. The moment Chief Inspector Tingley answered, Roy Grace said, 'Jason, our man could be targeting a Louise Masters, Flat 1b, Palmeira Villas – she fits his profile and I think she could be his next victim. I've tried calling her and she's not picking up. He could even be at the premises now. Can you get a unit there to check on her? She needs to be found as an absolute priority, and I want an officer to be with her around the clock until we've found our man.'

'What if she's not there, Roy?'

'I'm going to keep trying her number. I really do think she could be in immediate danger. She's next on his list after Freya Northrop. If he's watching her, this could be a perfect time for him to take her. Saturday night, maybe she's out on a date, or with friends. I'm going to email you a photograph of her – can you get it circulated to every officer and get them to look for her in every bar and club in the city? Someone has to know her, and where she is. Hopefully she's heeded our advice to be accompanied.'

'I'll put a team on it now, Roy, and get someone over to her home address.'

Grace thanked him and hung up, then immediately took a shot of her photograph on his phone and sent it to Tingley.

God, please don't let her be taken, too, he thought, fervently. *For God's sake please don't.*

Then he tugged a pair of gloves from his pocket, snapped them on and opened the fridge door. He saw on the shelves a half-empty bottle of semi-skimmed milk, several apples, a row of energy bars, a tub of Lurpak butter, and two large plastic bottles of Evian water. On one of the shelves inside the door was a row of unlabelled vials. He made a mental note that these would need to be examined in due course.

He lifted out the milk and looked at the 'use-by' date. It had four days still to go.

He looked down at the copy of the *Argus*. When had Hunter last been here? Presumably from the fact that he hadn't discarded the milk, he was planning to return some time soon, he thought. But how soon? Within four days? What if he was on his way here now, he wondered, with alarm?

If Hunter saw the police activity, he'd run.

He asked the LST inspector, urgently, to move his vehicles out of sight, and to position officers to watch the front entrance from hidden positions. He told the dog handlers to move their vehicle out of sight, too. Then he phoned the Crime Scene Manager, told him he wanted to keep the site under observation for the next two hours, but after that to send in a Search Team and treat the trailer as a crime scene.

He shivered again. From the cold. From tiredness. But most of all, he knew, from the sheer damned creepiness of this place. This was not anyone's holiday home. This was a lair. The Brander's lair.

What did this creep do? Sit in here? Staring at the photographs and touching himself? Choosing his next victim?

He asked the officers to leave, in order to avoid further contamination as a proper crime scene, and followed them. He closed the trailer door as best he could. In the darkness the damage would not be immediately visible to Hunter until he got close. Then he went back to his car and sat in the darkness. It gave him time to think through what he had found and the way the investigation was proceeding, confirming his instincts that Crisp and Hunter were strongly connected in the abductions and deaths of these women.

Forty minutes later his phone rang. 'Roy Grace,' he answered instantly, hoping it might be Louise Masters. But it was Chief Inspector Tingley and he was sounding grim.

'Roy,' the CIM said. 'I've just found out Louise Masters is a young officer here at John Street, recently finished her probation and joined the Neighbourhood Policing Team. She's on lates at the moment and her shift started at 4 p.m. But she hasn't turned up, hasn't called in sick, and no one's been able to reach her. She's not picking up and hasn't returned any calls. Her boyfriend's a PC on Response here, Adrian Gonzales. I've just spoken to him. He last saw her at 11 a.m. – she was going into town to do some Christmas shopping before starting her shift. He's checked her flat and she's not there.'

Grace had a sick feeling in the pit of his stomach. 'Shit,' he said. 'Shit, shit shit.' His mind momentarily became a blur. 'Jason, we should be able to track her movements from mobile phone triangulation. And if she was going shopping we could find out what she spent on her credit card and where – her boyfriend might know what kind of card she has. If we can establish where she was shopping we might be able to locate her on CCTV cameras in that vicinity.'

'I agree, Roy,' Tingley said. 'I assume you'll be tasking your team with this?'

As soon as he had finished the call, Roy Grace radioed the Control Room and asked to be put through to the Surveillance Team at Crisp's house. What the surveillance officer reported back was not what Grace was expecting to hear. The doctor hadn't appeared to have left his house since his early morning walk with his dog.

91

Logan heard noises. A strong female voice shouting. 'Let me go, you bastard! Let me – let me – let me – ouch! Let me—'

Who was it? What was happening?

The voice sounded weaker by the second.

Then silence.

What the hell had happened? What had happened to the other women she'd heard in here?

Moments later she heard the familiar sound of the roof of her prison sliding back and she squirmed in terror. A water tube was pushed into her mouth and she drank, greedily, desperately. She'd lost track of how long it had been since her last drink.

'Good news!' her captor growled. 'You have a companion now! That means you'll be leaving soon. Very soon!'

She gasped, 'What do you mean? Please tell me. Please tell me what's happening? What's happened to the other people here – I heard their voices. Who are you, please tell me? Please let me go, don't kill me, please let me live.'

'I'll bring you your last meal here, before you go.'

'Thank you,' she said, her voice shaky.

'Oh, you are most welcome. As my longest stay guest, and one of my least troublesome ones, you really are most welcome!'

92

'If Dr Crisp's been home all day, does that mean we're back to square one?' Branson asked.

'No. Not necessarily. There could be another explanation for Louise Masters not turning up for her shift.'

Branson gave him a sideways look. 'Ockham's Razor? Remember what you taught me about that?'

'Yes.'

William of Ockham was a thirteenth-century monk who had a profound influence on centuries of intellectual thought after his death. He believed in taking a razor to cut to the core of any conundrum. That the simplest and most obvious explanation was usually the right one. It was a principle that Roy Grace used frequently.

'So,' Glenn Branson said. 'Louise Masters, last on the Brander's hit list, has disappeared. Isn't the simplest explanation that we are looking in the wrong direction with Crisp? Surely now we've found this mobile home belonging to Hunter with all that stuff in?'

Grace nodded. 'While we've been sitting here, I've been thinking. Crisp and Hunter may be far more connected than we'd originally thought – I think they might well be the same person.' He had been wondering if he'd fallen foul of his own rule, earlier, that the danger of having a credible suspect was the temptation to focus on them and ignore everything else. But he felt he had sidestepped that trap.

Was there anything else he had ignored? Something that was staring him in the face?

He pictured in his mind the claustrophobic walls of the mobile home. The photographs of the Brander's possible victims. Was he mistaken about these? About the offender? Now he had a new boss who inherently disliked him. And he knew fine well that Pewe was waiting in the wings of this operation for him to screw up.

Where the hell are you, Louise Masters?

Then his phone rang. 'Roy Grace,' he answered immediately. And heard the instantly recognizable West Country accent of Norman Potting.

'Boss, I have some information for you that I think you're going to like.'

'Tell me?'

'I've just got back to MIR-1 from The Cloisters school and there was an urgent message from the lab. I'd sent them the Post-it note on which I had Dr Crisp write his mobile phone number for fingerprint and DNA analysis.'

'Yes?'

'I called the lab. The DNA is a strong match with the blood found at Freya Northrop's house on Thursday.'

'How strong – close?' Grace felt a surge of adrenaline.

'There's a lot of figures and calculations I need to have explained to me,' Potting said. 'But the summary is pretty conclusive. One billion to one chance of it not being Crisp. That conclusive enough?'

'It'll do!' Roy Grace said, a huge grin breaking out on his face. He thanked Potting then instantly rang the Critical Incident Manager.

93

Two hours later, in the conference room of the CID HQ, Roy Grace barely needed the caffeine hit from the mug of coffee in front of him. He was running on adrenaline now, his thoughts crystal clear, totally focused.

He stood with his back to a row of whiteboards. Seated attentively – and apprehensively – around the table in front of him were Glenn Branson, Tanja Cale, Guy Batchelor, and the team leaders he had selected, whose Saturday-night plans were now in tatters. But no one was complaining. They all sensed the same infectious anticipation that was coursing through his own veins. The thrill of the chase, of closing in on their quarry.

Everyone present was dressed in dark clothing, mostly black except for the Local Support Team, who would be going in first in navy fatigues that would be covered in parts with body armour. Several of the officers in the room had mugs of tea or coffee, and were munching sandwiches, chocolate or energy bars.

The briefing of the team was being managed by the Critical Incident Manager and Roy Grace. Their team leaders included the Duty Inspector of the Local Support Team, Anthony Martin, and an LST sergeant, a Tactical Firearms Unit Sergeant, an Exhibits officer, a senior CSI, the Custody Inspector, a Crime Scenes Manager, a Public Order Team Inspector, a Dog Unit Sergeant, and Grace's friend, Inspector James Biggs, from the Road Policing Unit, who had already moved units into place, ready to create a cordon of roadblocks around Crisp's neighbourhood from the moment Grace's team went in, in case Crisp attempted a runner.

On one whiteboard was a street plan showing Tongdean Villas and the immediate surrounding streets, bounded by Dyke Road

Avenue, Shirley Drive, Tongdean Road and Woodruff Avenue. The area contained within these borders comprised some of the most expensive and exclusive real estate in the city.

On the next whiteboard were wide-shot and close-up photographs of Crisp's house taken from the helicopter a few hours earlier. On the third whiteboard were photographs of Dr Crisp, Logan Somerville and the recently missing PC Louise Masters. On the fourth were street views of the gated entrance to Crisp's mansion, and the similarly gated entrances to his immediate neighbours. The fifth whiteboard had the floor plans of the basement, ground floor and first floors of the house, obtained from the city's planning archives.

Grace checked his watch. It was 9 p.m. He ran his eye down the list of names, checking that everyone was present, then turned first to the Custody Inspector, Tom McDonald. Tom, I want a cell ready for the offender. I need him to be taken straight there after he's booked into custody – I don't want him mixing or having contact with any-one else. He may well have crucial forensic evidence on him from his victims. I want him isolated and immediately put in the cell and his clothing and body swabbed, without any possible cross-contamination. OK?'

'Understood, sir.'

Using a laser pointer pen, Grace then indicated first the gabled Edwardian mansion that was the target location, then the gates, then a photograph of the long, steep driveway up to the front facade of Crisp's house. 'This driveway is the only way in and out of this property,' he announced. 'As you can see from the aerial photographs, there is a high brick wall at the rear – over twelve feet – so it would be extremely hard for anyone to scale this. There is a large property on the far side, again with one driveway in, which we will cover off in the unlikely event of him trying to exit that way.'

'What about the other neighbours either side, Roy?' the Local Support Team Inspector asked.

Grace pointed the red dot on the property immediately to the right, a sprawling, modern, white structure with a strong Spanish influence. 'I doubt he'd be daft enough to try to bolt this way. This place is owned by a person well known to some of us, Jorma Mahlanen, the slippery Finn.'

There were a few grins around the table.

'He's out on licence from a fifteen-year Class-A drugs sentence, and paranoid as hell – he's got a battery of floodlights, four Rottweilers that roam his grounds freely and two goons in permanent residence. I think he's upset a few people in his time and likes now to keep himself to himself. I don't think Crisp would get too far if he nipped over Mahlanen's wall.' Then he moved the red dot to the left. 'This property to the west is the street's one eyesore – or it would be if anyone could see it,' Grace continued. 'It's been derelict for many years – no one knows much about it. A few local property developers have attempted to buy it from time to time, but it's owned by some anonymous property company registered overseas that has never responded. Probably just one insignificant property in the portfolio of some billionaire tax exile. But this could be a possible escape route, as the boundary to it is in poor condition.'

'And we're pretty sure that Crisp is home?' the Tactical Firearms sergeant asked.

The Surveillance Team Inspector replied. 'Yes, he hasn't emerged since early morning to walk his dog.'

'I think it's possible Logan Somerville may still be alive and being held captive in the target's house,' Grace said. 'As may be Louise Masters now. We know that Crisp has no compunction about killing his victims. I want to remind all of you that the principal mission of this operation is to rescue any victims alive. Arresting Crisp is vital, but takes second place to the victim safety. I cannot say for certain Logan is still alive, but that's what we must assume. So speed of entry is going to be critical. I want maximum shock and awe tactics from you on entry, and a full, fast search of the property. OK, our first hurdle is the entry point.'

He moved the laser to the street view of tall, wrought-iron gates, set between high, spiked brick walls. Then he swung the beam to the right. 'This is the doorbell panel, with a camera and floodlight. When we move to open the gates, the camera lens must be obscured. Once the gates are opened, the LST vehicles will drive straight to the front door, enter and secure the premises.' He moved the pointer to the fifth whiteboard, showing the plans of the three floors of the house, from the 1907 archives.

Grace turned to the LST Inspector, who would lead the initial teams into the house. 'Anthony, we don't know what modifications have been made to the interior of the house since these original plans were lodged. But they should give you a reasonable idea.'

The Inspector nodded. 'Yes.'

'Any questions?' Grace asked.

'Do we have any intel on weapons?' the Tactical Firearms Unit sergeant asked.

'Dr Crisp doesn't have a firearms licence – that's been checked. But I'm not taking any chances. I want you in place as possible back-up. And everyone who enters the house, until it is declared safe by Anthony, is to be in body armour. Hopefully one thing we have in our favour is the element of surprise. We've not specifically named Crisp or said that he's under suspicion, so I'm hopeful he won't be expecting this.'

'To play Devil's Advocate, boss, what happens if he's not there?' Guy Batchelor asked.

'Then, Guy, in the vernacular of Cockney rhyming slang, we are all *Donald Ducked*.'

There was a nervous titter of laughter.

Grace looked at his watch. 'Any more questions?'

There were none.

94

Saturday 20 December

Shortly before 10 p.m. Roy Grace, accompanied by Glenn Branson, pulled his unmarked Ford up close to the front gates of Crisp's house, and called the Ops-1 Controller to tell him they were in position.

'NPAS 15 ETA five minutes to overhead, Roy,' Andy Kille replied.

'Five minutes. Thanks, Andy. Tell them to hold their lights until I give the signal.'

'Hold the lights, yes, yes.'

Grace waited with increasing butterflies, going over in his mind the dynamic entrance plans for Crisp's house, and hoping desperately for a result. The exclusive, tree-lined avenue was quiet. This wasn't the kind of neighbourhood where curtains twitched every time a vehicle pulled up. A short distance along, on the other side of the road, several cars were parked either side of swanky gates from which hung a cluster of balloons. Unobtrusive among the cars was a small grey van with *K. T. Electrics Ltd* emblazoned on the side panel.

As he climbed out into the frosty night, he could hear the distant pounding beat of party music. A solitary male some way in the distance stopped beneath a lamp post to let his golden retriever sniff around it. Brighton had a few streets that could lay claim to being millionaires' row, but in Roy Grace's opinion, this was the one that took the crown. It was quiet and secluded, with little traffic, and all of the grand houses, set well back from the road behind fortress walls, tall hedges or fences, had panoramic views to the south, across the entire city and down to the English Channel.

He double-checked that the search warrant was tucked in his inside pocket, along with photocopies of the floor plans of the house then, followed by Glenn Branson, he walked a short distance along the street, as plain and marked police cars and vans moved into their pre-determined positions, and stopped in front of the gates of the derelict neighbouring property to Crisp. He pulled a small torch from his pocket, switched it on and studied the gates for a moment. They were wooden and looked badly in need of varnish. But looking closer he saw they were electrically operated. The mechanism did not look old – or rusty.

'Someone uses these regularly,' Branson said.

'Probably a security firm keeping a regular check.' He shone the beam down the long driveway, which was bounded by unkempt laurel hedges. It was paved, but little of it was visible beneath the weeds and grasses that had pushed through. In the beam he saw some of the vegetation on either side had been flattened, probably by the tyres of a vehicle.

The two detectives hurried across the road to the electrician's van, and immediately the passenger-door window lowered. Inside were two surveillance officers.

'Good evening, sir,' said the blunt northern voice of Pete Darby, whom Grace knew well. He did not recognize the other man in the van.

'Evening, Pete.' Grace pointed at the wooden gates. 'Has anything driven in or out of there recently?'

'Not since we've been here, Roy. We started at 7 p.m. on our shift change. At handover we were told that no person or vehicle had either entered or left the premises. I'll check about next door.'

Across the road he saw the figure of Anthony Martin, now in full body armour and wearing a riot helmet with a full-face visor, towering a good six inches above the next tallest of his team of eight LST officers, all of whom were similarly attired. One officer was putting masking tape over the gate camera on the entryphone panel, another wielded the heavy yellow battering ram, and another the hydraulic. Next to them a dog handler held a German Shepherd on a tight leash. Four officers from the Tactical Firearms Unit were parked a short distance away on standby.

They crossed the road. Several more officers were emerging from vehicles and he directed two of them to stand guard outside the wooden gates of the derelict house. He glanced at his watch again, and moments later heard the faint *thwock-thwock-thwock* of the helicopter. It was growing rapidly louder.

Andy Kille informed the CIM, 'The helicopter will be overhead in one minute, Jason.'

'Remind them to hold the floodlights until I give the signal.'

'Hold the lights, understood.'

Then Tingley, standing beside Roy Grace, instructed Martin to proceed.

The LST officers piled into the van and approached the gates. Moments later the burly officer in front of the gates swung the bosher hard against their centre. It bounced back with a loud, metallic clang. He swung it again, then again, the gates juddering each time, until finally, on the fourth swing, they parted.

Then, keeping well back, Roy Grace and Glenn Branson followed the LST van on foot, along with the dog handler, up the steep, curved driveway. As they rounded the first bend, the mansion came into view, higher still above them, one hundred yards ahead. Within moments, the sound of the helicopter growing louder, the entire property suddenly burst into brilliant white light.

The first two Local Support Team officers, one with the battering ram and the other with the hydraulic ram, closely followed by Inspector Martin, entered the grand porch.

'GO, GO, GO!' screamed Martin.

With all eight LST officers bellowing, 'POLICE! POLICE! POLICE!' one used the hydraulic ram to push apart the door frame, and another slammed the battering ram against the door. On the second swing, the door opened with a splintering crunch and, torch beams streaking the interior, all eight of them piled in, still shouting, 'POLICE! POLICE! POLICE!' at the tops of their voices.

Regulations dictated that Grace and Branson stayed back until the scene was declared safe, but as the rest of the officers dispersed throughout the house, and the main lights came on, Grace could not hold back. Followed by Branson, he stepped inside then stopped, staring around momentarily in awe. It was like entering a small stately home.

They were in a wide, oak-panelled hall, dominated by a large, gilded chandelier. There was fine antique furniture and the walls were hung with ancestral oil paintings. In front of them was an ornately carved, sweeping staircase. To either side and above them they heard the tramping of boots and the continuing shouts, 'POLICE! POLICE! POLICE!' Somewhere nearby in the house a dog was yapping.

Grace and Branson waited in the hall.

'Seems a bloody grand pad for a GP!'

'He's in private practice. And from what I understand had inherited a family fortune.'

'I inherited a family fortune, too, when my dad died,' Glenn Branson said. 'Five thousand, seven hundred quid.'

Grace smiled, looking around him and up the stairs. All the doors to the rooms on the ground floor were open, and the lights on. A couple of minutes later, Anthony Martin came down the stairs, talking into his radio. Then he clocked the two detectives.

'All clear, sir,' he said to Grace. 'No sign of anyone.'

Instantly, Grace's heart sank with an intense feeling of anti-climax. 'Are you certain, Anthony?' His eyes darted all over the place as he wondered, wondered, wondered. Had they missed something? There would be a million hiding places in a property this size. Crisp had to be here. And hopefully – please God – Logan Somerville.

'We've checked all floors, boss. We'll start searching again more thoroughly. But I don't think there's anyone here.'

Grace's mind was whirring. He was thinking about the tyre tracks from the derelict property next door. Had Crisp fled during the surveillance watch changeover? Or had Martin's team – which he doubted – missed something? He called the surveillance officer in the van out on the street.

'Pete, did you get any info from the previous watch on the house to the west?'

'Just in, boss. They didn't see anything enter or leave all day, but it's been raining heavily down here for much of the day and visibility's been poor.'

Grace pulled on a pair of gloves, then, followed by Branson and Martin, walked through an open door into a tidy, sizeable room, furnished with a large antique roll-top desk, the lid closed, a leather sofa and a glass coffee table with several medical journals laid out on it. On the mantelpiece above a grandiose marble fireplace stood a row of cylindrical glass display cases, of varying sizes, each containing a stuffed animal. One was a grey squirrel, its paws around a piece of wood. Next to it was a duck, and next was a gerbil. A frog was in the next one along, in a fluid that he suspected was formalin.

The walls were lined floor-to-ceiling with bookshelves. Grace ran his eye along them. He noted several shelves of books on forensic psychology. Then a whole row of books on the Second World War. One was titled, *Escape From Germany: The Methods of Escape Used by RAF Airmen During the Second World War.* Another was called *Barbed Wire and Bamboo: Stories of Captivity and Escape from the First and Second World Wars.* Further along he saw *The Great Escape.* Then, *Escape From Colditz.*

Grace always believed you could tell a lot about a person by looking at their bookshelves – or lack of them. He got confirmation moments later when he came to the next section. Shelf upon shelf of books on serial killers, many of whose names he recognized. Ian Brady, Myra Hindley, Dennis Nilsen, Dennis Rader, Jeffrey Dahmer, John George Haigh of the Acid Bath Murders, Ed Kemper, Fred and Rose West, Peter Sutcliffe, Richard Ramirez, David Berkowitz – Son of Sam, Kenneth Bianchi and Angelo Buono – the Hillside Stranglers, Peter Manuel, Andrei Chikatilo – the Butcher of Rostov, Gary Ridgway, Harold Shipman, and California's notorious Zodiac Killer, whose identity was, to this day, unknown.

Dr Edward Crisp would one day be added to that vile hall of fame, he thought, grimly. And, with luck, very soon.

Below them were several books on taxidermy.

'*Psycho!*' Glenn Branson said.

'*Psycho?* You said that about Freya Northrop's house,' Grace replied.

Branson nodded. 'Yeah, but this is the real deal. That's what Norman Bates was into, taxidermy. Remember his mother?'

'As I recall, he hadn't done such a great job on her. She was pretty much skeletal.' He could hear the noise of the helicopter above them. Through the leaded-light windows he could see part of the garden brightly illuminated by the NPAS-15 floodlights. Topiaried hedges and a swimming pool with its winter cover secured.

He stared at a silver-framed studio photographic portrait of a happy family. A younger, smiling Crisp, in a cardigan over a blue shirt and grey slacks, his arm around an attractive woman of about forty. Two girls, in their teens, neatly dressed and smiling, stood beside her against a pale blue background. All three had long, shiny brown hair.

The wife who had recently left Crisp, he assumed, from Potting's report. He raised the lid of the desk. Inside was a neat leather-topped surface on which sat a pen-holder and a large, hard-covered note-book. He opened it. The front page listed, in neat handwriting, tradespeople and their phone numbers. Plumber, electrician, cleaning lady, building contractor, pool maintenance company, burglar alarm company, electric gates maintenance, garage door company, television repair man, gardener, lawn-cutting service, vet, Ocado groceries delivery, newsagent.

He turned the next page, which was blank. He turned several more pages, then stopped and stared. There, neatly held in place by photographic corners, was a photograph he recognized instantly. It was Denise Patterson.

On the next page, also neatly held in place, was Katie Westerham. On the following page was Emma Johnson. And on the next, Logan Somerville, then Ashleigh Stanford, then Freya Northrop.

These were the missing photographs, he realized, from the mobile home at the Roundstone Caravan Park.

95

'We're in the right place,' Roy Grace said, tersely, leafing again through the pages and staring at the photographs. 'The bastard's here, some- where, he has to be. Glenn, check upstairs yourself – every closet, every loft hatch, look under every sodding bed.'

He turned to the inspector. 'Anthony, I want your team to tear this house apart. I want the floorboards up, any hollow walls cut open. This is his place. Even if he has other locations we don't know about, we're going to find something here. What about the grounds?'

'They're all out there checking now.'

'Has anyone found the dog yet? It was barking earlier.'

As if in response, there were several deep barks from a police German Shepherd, close by outside, as the dog and handler ran past the window, brightly illuminated by the overhead floods from the helicopter.

'Crisp's dog is called Smut. The dog handler's locked it in a toilet, Roy, for safety.'

In a house this big, and with grounds of well over an acre, there were any number of hiding places possible, Grace knew. 'What about releasing it and seeing if it leads us to its owner?' he said.

'It was just standing in the kitchen when we entered,' Martin said. 'It was looking bewildered – and distressed – as if it's been abandoned, I'd say.'

'OK, how do I get to the basement?'

'I'll show you.'

He followed the inspector along a corridor and through into a vast, modern and well-equipped kitchen, with an island unit, a large American-style fridge, and a refectory table. It looked spotless. Martin

345

pointed to an open door, with a weak light beyond illuminating steps down.

'There, Roy. Want me to come down with you? We have checked it already.'

'No, get a full search team up here to start taking the place apart, get a CSI crew, and meantime join the others in checking the grounds, Anthony. If he's not in the house, he has to be in the garden somewhere – the pool house, a shed, garages, or even up on the roof. He's bloody here! Just make sure he doesn't give us the slip in any direction.' Outside, above the steady *thwock-thwock-thwock* roar of the helicopter, he heard the police dog barking again, louder now. A deep, steady *woof-woof-woof*, and he felt a burst of excitement and hope. Had the dog found something?

On the radio a crackly voice relayed from the team outside, 'Only a sodding fox!'

His thoughts in turmoil, Roy Grace, gripping his small torch in one hand and the handrail in the other, hurried down the steep, bare wooden treads. *The bastard had to be here. Had to be.* At the bottom he entered a cavernous, icy-cold, low-ceilinged junk room that looked as if it had once been the children's playroom. Dusty, bare bulbs hung from the ceiling, only three of them working, throwing a dim light across the whole area. There was a thin, dark green carpet on the floor and some of the paper was peeling off the walls. It smelled musty, with a hint of damp, as if no one ever came down here. A complete contrast to the floor above, Grace thought.

Stacked against the far wall was a trampoline. In front of it was an old ping-pong table and a rocking horse. Grace saw a large, Victorian-looking oil painting of marigolds in a vase, in an ugly, ornate frame, propped against one arm of a busted sofa.

At the other end of the room, past several lumpy shapes beneath dust sheets, was an open door, with a feeble light shining beyond. Grace walked over to the dust sheets and raised one. Beneath were two old armchairs, one with a fringed lampshade perched on the seat, and an old pinball machine with a spider's web crack in its glass top. Then he crossed to the open doorway. Ahead was a narrow passageway with bare brick walls and a concrete floor, lit by another low-wattage bulb. A cluster of very old-looking electrical wires, taped together, ran along the wall just above head height.

He switched on his torch again, for the beam to supplement the light, directing it at the floor. He was looking for any signs of possible recent work, but it did not look as if it had been touched in years. He stood still for some moments listening for any sounds beyond. He could hear the muffled rumble of a boiler, and he detected a faint but distinct reek of sour wine. He continued, warily, along the passage for about ten feet, heading towards the dark space ahead, the vinous smell getting stronger with every step, then stopped in amazement as he reached the end and flashed his beam around.

He was in a brick-walled wine cellar. But not like any cellar he had ever seen in a domestic house before. On either side of him and stretching away thirty or forty feet into the distance were wooden wine racks, floor to ceiling, stacked with dusty bottles. There must be thousands, he guessed. With his gloved hand he carefully gripped the neck of one bottle, at random, and lifted it out. It was covered in decades of dust, and he had to peer closely to read the printing on the label.

In outlined red letters was the word, PETRUS. Above, even more faint, was the date, 1961. Above that was a black and white drawing of a bearded man that looked to Grace like St Peter.

He was no expert on wine, but there were a few famous names that he recognized, because they had been in the news at some point or other, and Petrus was one of them. He had the sense the bottle he was holding was very valuable, and replaced it carefully. He stood still, listening again, then walked on between the racks, shining the torch beam down at the floor, checking it carefully.

Then he stopped and frowned.

The bottles on the fully stacked wine rack to his right looked cleaner than the rest down here – their necks at least. Were they a recent purchase?

He lifted one out, and it was much lighter than he had expected. The label read, GEVREY CHAMBERTIN 2002. It felt too light. He shone the beam of his torch directly on it. The bottle was empty. Puzzled, he pulled out the one directly below it. That was empty, too. He tried more on the same rack, and they were all empty as well. Each had its cork pushed right in and the seal intact. The rack took six bottles lying across. There were forty-eight bottles on the entire rack.

Were they showcase samples? Like in some restaurants where you saw all kinds of different-size bottles upright, on display?

Why the hell would anyone have an entire rack full of dummy bottles? To show off? Were other parts of this cellar filled with dummy bottles, also?

His phone rang. It was Pete Darby. Reception was bad down here, the surveillance officer's voice crackly and breaking up.

'I've double checked with the previous shift, and no one has been in or out of there.'

'You are certain?'

'Yes – we were keeping an eye on the street, but our focus as briefed was on the target's house.' Then the voice became too crackly for Grace to decipher the words. He heard, 'Fair . . . traffic . . . through . . .' Then silence.

He looked down at his phone and saw the words *no service* on the display.

Grace put his phone back in his pocket, staring at the rack again. Something was wrong about it. He studied it carefully, playing the beam of his torch along each row. Then a faint glint caught his eye. It glinted again as he moved his torch. Hastily he removed several bottles from the rack, and then could see what it was. A hinge.

He felt a sudden beat of excitement. Gripping the wine rack firmly with both hands he gave a gentle pull and, taken by surprise, stumbled backwards as the entire section of the rack swung out easily and silently, on well-oiled hinges. Yet all that was behind it was just a continuation of the solid brick wall.

He played the torch beam across it, then noticed that the bricks directly behind the rack seemed newer and more even than those on either side. Frowning, he ran the torch beam up and down the join on the right. And saw the faint, vertical hairline crack. Then a horizontal one, about five feet high. And another vertical crack joining it and running down to the ground. Holding the torch in his mouth he pushed hard, first on one side then the other, and suddenly a whole section swung forward, inwards. He was right, he realized with a chill. It was a concealed wooden door, clad on the outside with brick tiles.

Crisp had gone to a great deal of trouble to keep something hidden, Grace thought, crouching and shining the light through the opening. It was a short, rough-hewn tunnel, with crude wooden uprights and cross-beams every few feet along, holding back the walls and supporting the roof. Hessian matting covered the floor. It was like something out of a World War Two movie about prisoners escaping from German prisoner of war camps, he thought.

Then he remembered the particular section of books on the shelves up in Crisp's library. Had the idea come from those? Or the technique?

He pulled his phone out and tried to call for backup. The display showed no signal. He knew he should get backup but his adrenaline rush was pushing him forward. He jammed it back into his pocket, then shone the torch warily all around the cellar behind him, watching the shadows jumping. His nerves were jangling. What the hell was at the far end of the tunnel?

He shone the beam along it again, and a tiny pair of eyes sparkled like rubies, ten feet or so in the distance. He'd always been claustrophobic, and right back as a child had felt uncomfortable playing hide and seek, when he'd had to conceal himself in a closet, or one time in an old trunk in his parents' loft. He remembered a case when he'd had to crawl along a storm drain to see a body that had been discovered there, and it had taken all his courage.

Gripping the torch in his teeth again, and ignoring his fear, he entered the tunnel, keeping his head as low as he could. Ahead of him the beam fell away into darkness for some moments, then he saw the tiny rubies sparkling again. The rat scurried off as he approached.

He should go back, he knew, get Martin's team down here, but curiosity and determination kept him moving forward. Something that felt like a spider's web brushed his hair and he shuddered, swiping at it with his right hand, and continued. Thoughts were flashing through his mind. They had moved house – home – yesterday. And he was in this sodding tunnel. With what at the end of it?

The air was cold, but intermittently there were strange eddies of warmth. The ground was rough and stony beneath the matting. Each time he tried to raise his head it bashed against the tunnel roof. Part of him wanted to retrace his steps, go back and send in a search team.

But another part, the voice of resolve and determination inside his head that had always driven him, told him to keep going.

Keep going.

Logan Somerville might be at the end of this. Could she still be alive?

And suddenly, the tunnel gave way to a vast, pitch-dark space. He shone the beam of his torch up and saw a high, vaulted brick ceiling. He straightened up, held the torch in his hand and flashed the beam around, striking more bare brick wall in every direction.

Then a voice rang out of the cavernous darkness. It was crystal clear, a posh public school accent, slightly condescending, accompanied by a faint echo.

'Detective Superintendent Grace, I presume? How very nice to see you. We've been expecting you.'

96

It felt for an instant as if all the warmth had been drained from his body. Roy Grace dropped the torch in shock. The beam jigged as it rolled a short distance along the concrete floor, and he ducked down, grabbed it, swinging it in a wide arc. Disorienting reflections from shiny objects glared back at him. There was a dank smell.

Then he saw three glinting pairs of eyes staring straight at him.

For an instant he froze in shock.

Moments later the entire chamber was illuminated by weak, green-hued wall lights. Grace saw what had glinted in his torch beam. Three cylindrical glass tubes hanging from the ceiling by metal chains. Each was filled to the capped top with a liquid that looked faintly murky, like pond water, in the green light.

Inside each cylinder was a pale pink creature, held upright in suspension by a wire around its neck. At first he thought there was an animal inside each one. A pig?

Jesus, was Crisp conducting secret experiments on animals down here?

But as his eyes sprang from one cylinder to the next and then the next he realized, with a chill that rippled deep inside him, that these were not animals. They were human beings. It was their eyes staring at him.

Naked adult males, in their late twenties, or early thirties, their eyes wide open, staring sightlessly. Without arms or legs. One was almost bald, two of them had ragged hair, and each had several days' growth of stubble.

His skin crawled. For an instant, he felt as if he had walked onto the film set of a modern *Alice In Wonderland*. Were these holograms? Some trick of projection? What in God's name was he looking at?

Then, suddenly, a huge screen lit up a short distance to his left. On it was a video of Edward Crisp, seated in a leather chair in front of a desk, in the office Grace recognized from upstairs in the house. He was immaculately dressed in a suit and tie, and wearing a very smug grin. The doctor leaned forward, raising his arms, animatedly. The same posh public school voice boomed out all around Grace. 'Really, Detective Superintendent, it is quite a privilege to welcome you to my little secret abode! I'd like to introduce you to my colleagues who have helped me so much in my planning for my *projects*. These are my dead friends! I don't think you've had the opportunity to meet Marcus, Harrison and Felix? We really have become very dear friends, although it wasn't always that way.'

Grace glanced again, in revulsion, at the limbless bodies, then back at the screen. Crisp's eyes gleamed with pure joy behind his glasses.

'Marcus Gossage, Felix Gore-Parker and Harrison Chaffinch – although I think you might know him as Harrison *Hunter* – a much classier name, I thought. Marcus is the one without much hair!'

Grace looked back at the man in the glass cylinder on the left. He had a prematurely balding dome and wispy hair on either side, piggy eyes and a pouting expression, like a beached trout.

'Next to him,' Crisp continued, 'is Felix Gore-Parker, a rather mean-looking fellow, I think you'd have to agree?'

The body in the middle cylinder had a long, equine face, with lank fair hair and a sour expression. Roy Grace realized he had not noticed before that he was wearing, bizarrely, a pair of round, wire-rimmed spectacles.

'And lastly we have Harrison. He was very overweight, I don't think he would have ever made old bones. But, hey, he doesn't have to worry about that now, does he?'

The hairs on the back of Grace's neck stood up.

'These were the three school bullies who made my life hell, Detective Superintendent. They called me *Mole*, because they didn't like my interest in tunnels and potholing. Well, to be truthful, they didn't like anything about me. But they all loved me in the end. I got each of them to say those words to me before I killed them. Although actually, it had never been my intention to kill them, I'd planned to keep them alive long enough to teach them a lesson they would never forget. And I sure succeeded!'

Grace stared around him, warily. Where was crazy Dr Crisp? Lurking in the shadows while he was distracted by the video?

He swung the torch beam into the darkness behind him, then all around. Was the doctor out there, waiting to pounce? He wished he had brought a more powerful torch. And backup. He stared at his phone, but it still showed there was no signal.

'They say revenge is a dish best served cold, I'm sure you are familiar with that, Detective Superintendent? I waited for a good length of time after leaving The Cloisters school before taking my first project, Marcus Gossage, the one on the left. I sent him a wedding invite. Told him as a special school friend I'd be sending a chauffeured car to pick him up. Of course, he got that, a lovely Mercedes. I was the driver. Knocked him out with a gas spray and brought him down here. Then I had fun amputating his arms and legs, but keeping him alive, and suspending him from the ceiling in a muslin sack, in nappies, and with a drip feed. You really cannot imagine how sweet that was!'

Roy Grace turned back to the three bodies in the glass tanks. Another shudder rippled through him. He was feeling sick. For an instant he wondered if his mind was playing tricks. Could this be real? Could any human being have done this to another human being?

'With Felix Gore-Parker – I invited him to an old school house reunion. Told him I would give him a lift as I wasn't drinking. Harrison was a doddle – told him I wanted to pop round to see him to talk about helping to save the school! Of course, there were police enquiries at the time. But I'm no fool, Detective Superintendent. I left a good couple of years' gap between each of them. Felix had been living in Edinburgh at the time, Marcus in Manchester and Harrison in Bath. The police had no reason to link their disappearances.'

Grace stared at them all in disbelief. Was this possible? Had Crisp really done this – and kept these bodies down here for so long?

'I know what you are thinking, Detective Superintendent, you are wondering where is Logan Somerville. And of course my latest *project*, the policewoman. Don't forget her. I'm particularly proud of sneaking this one in at the very last minute – after my last project went pear-shaped when the bloody dog bit me – and I have to admit she was a bit of a challenge! But I needed to distract you and remain in control. It really is so nice to finally meet you – I'm only sorry it is not in person. But I figured that meeting you in person wouldn't result in a very happy ending. And I'm a bit of a sentimental old fool really, I like happy endings! Don't we all? So I've good news – my three boys are finally free! Have fun, Harrison, Marcus and Felix. Hope you've enjoyed your time down here with me. I wish I could have kept you alive, in the original sacks I had for you – they were rather appropriate containers for you, since you are three bags of shit! Your bullying at school gave me a life sentence, but I'm not a monster. You've done your time. So now, hey, enjoy your release!'

He gave a broad beam.

Transfixed, Grace studied the doctor's body language. His eyes were all over the place. His face was twitching. He crossed and uncrossed his legs. He was giving out all the signals of someone who had totally lost the plot.

'You didn't come here expecting to find these, did you, Detective Grace? This is a little bonus for you. What you want are the girls. But I thought you should know that initially I planned to keep these three alive, hanging here in muslin bags, for the rest of their natural lives, just like Catherine the Great did – I'll tell you more about her anon. But with my family life and my work as a doctor, and all the tunnelling stuff that's my hobby, it all got just a little too inconvenient. They needed too much maintenance, and I'm pretty much a low-maintenance guy. So I found a solution. *Formaldehyde* – or *formalin* as some call it. I wanted them around to remind me of how sweet revenge can be, which it did every day I saw them. They've been hugely helpful in all of my escapades, never disagreeing once with any of my plans! But enough about these, they're history now. You need to find little Logan Somerville and little Louise Masters. Ask the boys, they know everything. They're my accomplices. I could never have done any of this without them!' He raised an arm in the air and wiggled his immaculately manicured hand. 'Bye for now, boys!'

Crisp folded his arms and sat back for some moments. Then he opened his arms again, expansively. 'Oh dear, I forgot, Felix, Marcus and Harrison have very limited conversational skills these days. The ladies you are looking for are in the room next door, behind this screen. Bye for now!'

The screen faded to black.

97

Guided by his torch, and grim determination, Grace strode across the floor towards the screen. It was a drop-down fabric affair, and he lifted it up. Behind was a thick wooden door, which he opened and went through, stabbing the torch beam warily into the darkness. He was greeted with a smell of damp and the sound of dripping water. 'Logan!' he called out. 'Logan Somerville? Louise Masters? This is the police! You are safe, this is the police!' His voice echoed.

'Thank God! Over here!' a female voice screamed, her voice echoing back. 'I'm Louise Masters, thank God you are here!'

He took several steps forward and the beam fell on two rows of four rectangular wooden boxes, the length of coffins but several feet taller, and squared off equally at both ends. What looked like hose pipes were connected to each of them. Each of them, except for one, was covered with an opaque lid.

He reached the open one and shone the torch inside. The interior was lined like a glass tank. A woman in her early twenties, in police-issue trousers and shirt, lay there looking terrified, steel cords fastened over her neck, wrists, thighs and ankles. The ones around her wrists, where he could see congealed blood, were cutting into her flesh.

'Louise?' he said.

She nodded.

'I'm Roy Grace, police, you're safe. Do you know where Logan Somerville is? And is anyone else here?'

She shook her head. 'No. I – I don't. I just got into my car outside my home – I'd gone back to change, ready for my shift, after shopping – and the next thing I knew I was here.' She gave him a weak smile. 'Thank you. Thank you for coming.'

He tried to free one of her wrists, but she winced in pain and cried out.

'I'll get someone to cut you free. I'll leave you for a few moments, but don't worry, we have the place surrounded and secure.' He turned to the box beside her, and slid back the lid. The interior, another glass tank, contained about three feet of water, but nothing else. He moved to the next box.

And stood rigid for an instant.

He stared down at what looked like a corpse. He recognized the young woman instantly, from the photographs. It was Logan Somerville.

Unlike Louise Masters, she was naked. Her face was the alabaster colour of so many corpses he had seen before. Her long brown hair was matted and spread out around her head, like a dark shroud.

He looked in horror at the branding on her right thigh.

U R DEAD

Shit. Was he too late? Too damned late?

'Logan?' he said, softly. 'Logan?'

There was no reaction.

As he looked down at her, he felt the utter despondency of failure. Thinking about her boyfriend, Jamie Ball. Those photographs of her looking so happy, that were spread around her apartment. Thinking about her parents, so desperate for news, clinging to hope.

Dead.

Dead for no other reason than her hairstyle?

Because she had been unlucky enough to be picked up by the radar of a total madman?

Her cheek moved, just a tiny fraction. Or had he imagined it?

He peered closer, kneeling. 'Logan?' he said. 'Logan? Logan?'

She was motionless.

In the silence he heard the steady dripping of water.

Where the hell was Crisp? How had he slipped the net? How many more deaths were on his hands? How many had died, like Logan Somerville, because he hadn't been smart enough to catch Crisp in time?

Then she opened her eyes and whispered, weakly, 'Help me.'

98

Grace sprinted back, through the room with the three limbless cadavers, avoiding the horror of looking at them. He scrambled along the tunnel, and out into the wine cellar. He ran past the racks, then back up the stairs into the kitchen, staring at his phone, willing a signal to appear. As he burst through the door, he almost collided head-on with Glenn Branson.

'Searched the whole upstairs and ground floor again, and some of the team are up in the loft spaces,' Branson said, breathlessly. 'There's no one here. Nothing. You?'

99

Shortly after 2 a.m. Grace went into the tiny kitchenette at the rear of the deserted Detectives' Room at Sussex House, and made himself a coffee. A nationwide manhunt for Dr Edward Crisp was underway and all the authorities had been circulated with Crisp's photograph and the request to arrest him on sight.

He was holding a press briefing, with Cassian Pewe, at 10 a.m. – less than eight hours' time. He had no prospect of going to bed before then – and no inclination for sleep either. He desperately, desperately wanted to find Crisp.

The doctor was out there, somewhere. The derelict house and grounds next door to Crisp's house had also been searched. There were roadblocks on all routes out of the city. Passenger manifests on all outbound flights at every airport in the UK were being checked, along with CCTV footage of all airports in the south of England, all foot passenger and car ferry ports, and the Channel Tunnel. So far the results were negative.

As he carried the steaming mug back to his office, he felt deeply despondent, despite the fact that Logan Somerville and Louise Masters were safe and currently being checked at the Royal Sussex County Hospital. He sat back down at his desk, and once more worked through, in his head, Crisp's timeline.

He'd abducted Louise Masters shortly after 3 p.m. from outside her house. Crisp would have got back to his house by around 3.30 p.m., and it would have taken him time to manhandle and secure the policewoman in her box. Grace allowed an hour. Which left about a six-hour window before his team had arrived at Crisp's house.

The doctor could, conceivably, be almost anywhere in the UK or Europe by now. Or on an intercontinental flight. Judging by the video

359

the doctor had made, he had clearly planned his escape meticulously. The teams of surveillance officers on duty all day were adamant no vehicle had entered or left Crisp's house or the derelict one next door during their entire shifts. But there was no other entrance to the derelict house. Had the officers missed Crisp driving out and in? It was possible.

The even bigger mystery to him was why Crisp would have taken his last victim, policewoman Louise Masters, and then simply abandoned her. He'd said it was a distraction, but was it? From the photographs on the wall of his mobile home at the Roundstone Caravan Park, PC Louise Masters appeared to be Dr Crisp's last planned victim. So he had captured her, imprisoned her, then immediately fled. Why?

He yawned, realizing he must be more tired than he thought – or wanted to admit to himself – and his brain more addled. He wasn't thinking straight. Surely Crisp had abducted Louise Masters with the intention of killing her and, doubtless, Logan? And yet he had suddenly fled. What had alerted him?

Roundstone Caravan Park? Had a concealed camera alerted Crisp to the raid? He must have known after the dog bit him that there was a chance of the police now having his DNA, and been on his guard.

His thoughts were suddenly interrupted by an alert on his computer screen, announcing an incoming email. It was a Hotmail account, from a sender he did not recognize. He opened it and saw a short, unsigned message.

Roy, check this Dropbox link!

He clicked on the link, and saw a Dropbox file download. He went to his Downloads folder and clicked on the most recent, and moments later a video clip appeared.

It was Dr Crisp again. In the same armchair, in the same smart suit he had seen earlier. The same cheery smile.

'Hello, Roy! I couldn't say this in front of them of course, but I'm delighted you've met charming Marcus, Felix and Harrison. They're among my more successful *projects*. They'd all mellowed over the years, under my expert tuition. I turned them into much better people than they would have been, left to their own devices. They were nasty children. They damaged me and other boys at the school.

Being bullied is really not a nice thing. It can destroy you. My life story is one of people not understanding me, you see. I know. *Primum non nocere* – that's the good thing about English public schools. They teach you the classics. Good old Hippocrates! My Latin teacher was a bit of a bully himself, but I did learn from him. *Primum non nocere* – first do no harm. The first rule of medicine. I don't know what drove you to become a policeman, Roy, perhaps because you naively thought you could help people. But that was not the reason I chose medicine. I did not become a doctor to help people, no. I became a doctor in order to get revenge!'

Grace was studying the man's erratic body language as much as he was listening to his words.

Crisp paused, then spread his arms expansively again, with an equally expansive smile. 'I've always found history interesting – in particular Russian history. The Canadian novelist Steven Erickson wrote, "The lesson of history is that no one learns the lesson of history." So very true. So I tried to abide by that. I read that Catherine the Great used to cut off the arms and legs of her enemies, and keep them hanging in sacks down in the dungeon of the Winter Palace. Once a year, she'd have them all brought up and arranged in a semi-circle in front of her. "Hello boys!" she'd say. "Delightful to see you again. All had a good year, have we?" Then she'd dismiss them, and have them all taken back down into the dank darkness again. Years that turned into decades. A true living hell.'

It was the smile on the doctor's face as he told the story that Roy Grace found the most disturbing – the sheer, gloating relish.

'These three chaps – my original *projects* – if I'd let them loose on the world, God knows what havoc they would have wreaked. We've all been better off with them safely contained. Just like I contained that ghastly Mandy White all those years ago. She rejected me, because she wasn't smart enough to understand my true value. Katy Westerham and Denise Patterson were both women I dated, who rejected me. All three of them had one thing in common: long brown hair. Clearly that was a sign of something evil. Evil that needed correction. It made them ideal *projects*.'

Crisp went almost cross-eyed for an instant. His face twitched, and he was rubbing his hands together as if soaping them. He leaned back in his chair for some moments and closed his eyes with a contented smile on his face. Then he opened them again. 'I'm sure you are wondering why the long gap between the first two girls, and Emma and Ashleigh, aren't you? The truth is, Detective Superintendent Grace, that I thought I had found redemption in my wife and children. Then a few months ago I found out the bitch was having an affair. I'd been fooled all along. These women are vermin. Toxic. Fortunately I hadn't stopped my hunting activities and I had a rich cache of fresh projects. I did wonder if the problem was me, and I tried to get help recently, but the shrink didn't want to understand me. No one does. I knew the game was over here when that sodding dog bit me. You're a good cop, Detective Superintendent, but you've had a lot of help on the way. I've never had any help. But I'm philosophical. There comes a time when the hunter has to move on. The prey might be the same but the backdrop will be different.'

Grace watched, intently. The more he looked at the doctor, the crazier the man seemed. One moment so smug, so self-satisfied, so assured; the next, quivering, confused, almost vacant.

'Do please tell the families of Harrison, Marcus and Felix from me, that I would have liked to have said it had been nice knowing them, but I hate to lie. I can tell you that what I did to them for the time I kept them alive changed them for the better. But even so, the world has been a better place without them.'

Crisp leaned forward and smiled. 'Oh, and one more thing. Actually, two. Firstly, give them all a special message at your next press conference, from the Brighton Brander. Tell them the fat lady ain't sung yet. And, secondly, in the words of one American serial killer replying to the judge who sentenced him to death, a few years ago, "Have a good time on earth, sugar." Oh, and thirdly, I'm sure you would like to know how my projects each died? I made love to them, using protection of course – I would never be reckless – after kissing them goodbye by placing my lips tight over theirs, sucking their last breath out of their lungs, and then drowning them. That way I possessed them forever. They were never going to reject me again. It felt so good, so incredibly good. It's a feeling you'll never know. But trust me, it's good! And it's one I'm going to have again. Many times!

A word of warning to you and your clever team, Detective Superintendent. Don't try to find me. Not unless you'd like me to possess you all forever, too! I have nothing to lose, I never had. You have everything – a lovely little son, a beautiful wife and a delightful new home. I'd hate you never to see any of them again. Really I would. Trust me!'

He gave a dinky little wave. 'Bye for now!'

The screen went blank.

100

There was an enormous sense of relief at the second of the day's briefings, in the conference room of Sussex House, that the female police officer, Louise Masters, and Logan Somerville were safe. But with the knowledge of the terrible suffering Dr Crisp had inflicted on his three former school colleagues, before murdering them, and the fact that he was still at large, the atmosphere was subdued and focused.

Earlier that afternoon both Logan Somerville, accompanied by some of her family, and Louise Masters, had visited the Incident Room at Sussex House to meet the team that had been working on the investigation, and to thank them personally for their efforts. Grace was pleased to see that Logan seemed to be coping well with the trauma of her ordeal.

A new whiteboard had been added to the row behind Roy Grace, on which were two photographs. One was of Logan Somerville imprisoned in the box in Crisp's cellar, the other showed a close-up of the branded words on her thigh, about two inches across and half an inch high.

U R DEAD

Several new faces were gathered in the crammed conference room, including the senior surveillance officer, Pete Darby, and the diminutive but extremely tough POLSA Sergeant Lorna Dennison-Wilkins, who was in charge of the search of Crisp's house and the caravan.

'Into tunnelling passages, is he?' Norman Potting said. 'If I get my hands on him first, he's going to find those words branded up his own back passage.'

There was a titter of laughter and even Roy Grace smiled, glad to see Potting had regained some of his former, if terrible, humour. His watch said 6.30 p.m. but out of habit he checked it against the wall clock, and then against the one on his phone. He stifled a yawn. Earlier in the day, after the morning press conference, he had gone into the Chief Superintendent's large, empty office, phoned Cleo to update her, then kicked off his shoes, loosened his shirt and tie and slept for two hours on his boss's sofa.

Although he had showered and freshened up in the Major Incident suite washroom, and used the change of clothing he kept in his locker, he still felt grungy and his eyes were raw, as if they had been rubbed with sandpaper. But he did not care. The adrenaline was pumping again. He felt the scent of the chase – accompanied by a growing darkness of despair.

The Surveillance Team had not seen anyone leave either Crisp's own residence nor the derelict house next door. Yet Crisp had gone into Brighton, abducted Louise Masters and brought her back. How?

And where the hell was he now? No one had seen him leave either premises. Yet every available search officer in Sussex and Surrey had been drafted in, spending the day going through both properties inch by inch. If Crisp was there, wherever he was hiding, they would have found him.

He looked down at his notes. 'As you all know from this morning's briefing, following our rescue of Logan Somerville and PC Louise Masters, we made a number of significant discoveries at the Tong-dean Villas residence of Dr Edward Crisp, and the derelict property next door,' he said. 'Financial work is being done on Crisp, but we are restricted by it being a weekend. However, paperwork found in a filing cabinet indicates that he owned the derelict property via a Liechtenstein company. We don't know at this stage whether that was for tax reasons or to ensure he was never connected to the place. We believe at some point during the early evening of yesterday, 20 December, he fled – possibly leaving the country, although we have no intelligence on any other links Crisp may have had abroad. We have requested all UK forces to do searches for any homicides that match the Crisp profile, and, of course, we've asked Europol to take a special look at Liechtenstein.'

He sipped his coffee. 'Tanja Cale and Guy Batchelor went to see Crisp's wife earlier today, and she is going to be interviewed formally tomorrow. But according to their initial report she had suffered years of bullying abuse at his hands, and had finally left because she couldn't take it any more.' He looked at DS Cale. 'Do you have anything to add at this stage, Tanja?'

'No, sir. What do we currently have on him?' she asked.

'I've done a spreadsheet,' DC Kevin Taylor said, proudly. 'You might find this interesting, chief.'

Grace signalled him to go ahead.

'Well, we know as a teenager that Crisp was present at the death of a young woman who bears a similarity to all his subsequent victims – despite the age difference – and to his estranged wife. The detective on that case was convinced Crisp was responsible for killing her but could never prove it. Denise Patterson, possibly his next victim, worked evenings part-time behind the bar in a pub he frequented whilst a student at Sussex University. Katy Westerham was a Sussex University student. All of them had a similar hairstyle. Then he married a young woman with a similar appearance and hairstyle, and the killings appear to have stopped.'

'Good work, Kevin,' Grace said. 'Do your spreadsheets give us any indication where Crisp might be now?'

'I'm afraid not, no, not so far. I'm working on another, on his credit-card spend. But I can't predict from that where he might be now.'

Grace nodded. 'OK, so far the search of his house has discovered three different false passports and large quantities of cash in five different foreign currencies.'

'So he could be anywhere in the world?' Jon Exton said.

'Yes,' Grace said, despondently.

'Anywhere in the world, under any name,' Exton continued.

'But why would he have left so much money and these passports behind?' Grace asked. Then suddenly he had a thought. Norman Potting's crude quip had jogged something in his tired mind. He'd struggled to take it all in at the time, because it was so surreal. Now some of Crisp's words came back to him.

They called me Mole, because they didn't like my interest in tunnels and potholing.

He turned to the POLSA. 'Lorna, has your team checked every drain and manhole on the two properties and the grounds?'

'Yes, guv. We brought in a sludge sucker. All the drains have been emptied and their contents taken to be analysed. We lowered remote cameras down every manhole, and we checked under the cover of his swimming pool. We also brought in Ground Penetrating Radar and checked both gardens and the cellars of both houses.'

He thanked her and then stood up and turned to the whiteboard on which were pinned the aerial maps taken earlier from the helicopter. The boundaries of both properties had been outlined in thick red marker pen. 'Somehow, Crisp left one or the other of these properties, abducted PC Masters, brought her back whilst she was unconscious, imprisoned her, then left again – and no one saw him. Maybe we should rename him Harry Houdini.' He turned, grimly. 'I can accept that maybe the Surveillance Team missed him exiting or arriving back once – but not three times.'

'There's no way we missed him even once, boss,' Pete Darby assured him.

Grace turned back to the aerial map, and pointed. 'Both of these properties are accessed from Tongdean Villas. There are twenty properties to the east and the immediate neighbour on that side has four guard dogs – there's little likelihood Crisp could have used that as an exit. There are two properties to the west and then Tongdean Road. There are further substantial properties to the north of the two homes, directly beyond the perimeter walls, all protected with CCTV, which we understand has shown nothing. Crisp had to have entered and exited via Tongdean Villas. There is no other—'

Then he hesitated, as he noticed something for the first time, and wondered how he hadn't seen it before. Diagonally north-west of Crisp's house was an isolated building, a large shed or a double garage. The access to it was from Tongdean Road, a steep hill. There was a driveway to it, bounded on both sides by brick walls.

The garage was about a hundred yards from the derelict house.

Was it possible, he wondered?

Anything with Crisp seemed possible. He turned back to his team.

'I'm terminating this briefing early.' He pointed to Glenn Branson, Guy Batchelor, Lorna Dennison-Wilkins, and four others. 'Come to MIR-1 right away.'

101

An hour and a half later, with the search warrant signed, Grace, Branson and Guy Batchelor went through the tall wooden gates that screened the building off from the street, walked swiftly through light drizzle and up the neglected-looking driveway between the brick walls, following a dog handler and Inspector Anthony Martin, plus seven members of the Local Support Team in body armour and riot helmets. A short distance in front of them, lit by the beam of their torches, was a lichen-covered breeze-block garage with two up-and-over doors that looked in newer condition than the rest of the dilapidated construction itself.

One LST officer held the bosher, another a crowbar. Grace signalled everyone to wait, then telling Branson to take the right-hand side, he ran down the left, looking for a window or another way in – or out. They met around the rear, where there was a discarded, rusted bicycle that clearly had not been used in years, and was almost covered in fallen leaves. But there was no door.

Grace hurried back round to the front and gave a nod to Martin. The Inspector issued an instruction. Instantly one LST officer stepped forward and tried the handle of the right-hand door, but it did not budge. He moved aside and his colleague swung the battering ram. There was a loud metallic clang and the door shook but did not give. Then the officer with the crowbar tried to jam it between the side of the door and the wall, without success.

'Shit,' he gasped from the exertion. 'These things are usually as flimsy as hell.' Two others grabbed sections of the crowbar and all three of them tried, grunting. Then with a metallic screech it went in behind the edge. They levered the gap wider, inch by inch, for some moments, the door protesting. Then suddenly something gave, with a sound like a shot, and the door partially detached from its mountings and dropped down.

They trooped in through the gap, with Roy Grace right behind them, then stopped. One of them found the light switch and turned it on. Two vehicles sat there, side by side on the concrete screed. The old Volvo and a Skoda estate in the turquoise and white Brighton Streamline taxi livery. Behind them was a Lambretta motor scooter, with a helmet on the pillion.

And now he knew for sure he was in the right place. The old Volvo estate that had been sighted by witnesses the night that Logan Somerville had been abducted. A Skoda taxi had been seen on CCTV following Ashleigh Stanford's bicycle.

As the LST officers swarmed around the vehicles, opening the doors and boot and bonnet and checking underneath, Grace touched the bonnets of both vehicles. They were stone cold. He gazed around the interior of the building, at the bare walls, looking for any clues. There was a solitary metal shelf on which sat a tyre pump and gauge, a set of jump leads and a trickle charger. Further along the garage was an ancient chest freezer, covered in dust and unplugged.

He knelt down and looked first underneath the Volvo, then the Skoda for himself. Nothing. Then a voice called out, urgently, 'Sir! Take a look here!'

One of the female LST officers stood by the freezer, holding its lid up. He hurried round, along the side of the Volvo and looked inside.

And felt a surge of excitement.

102

The exterior of the freezer was just a shell. All the baskets had been removed, and there was just a sheet of rusty tin covering the base. Roy Grace leaned over into the freezer and eased his fingers under one edge of the rusty tin, then prised it up, instantly feeling a blast of dank, cold air.

It rose from a deep shaft the freezer was concealing.

He switched on his torch and pointed the beam down; but all it revealed, flaring into the darkness, was the raw earth shaft and metal rungs disappearing into the void of darkness. He couldn't see the bottom, or guess how deep it was.

He stood back to enable Glenn Branson and Guy Batchelor to take a look, warning them to be careful. They both stepped forward.

'Bloody hell!' Batchelor said. 'Bloody hell! The man's a total lunatic.'

'Unfortunately a very clever one,' Grace replied.

'What is it?' Branson said.

'Crisp's escape route. No surprise the Surveillance Team missed him.'

'We'll go down and check it, sir,' the LST inspector said.

Grace shook his head and, swallowing his fear of heights, said, 'I'm going first, this is personal.' He gripped his torch between his teeth, climbed into the freezer and lowered his right foot to the first rung.

'Keep three limbs on the rungs at all times, sir,' the inspector cautioned. 'We'll follow you.'

Grace began to descend, followed by an LST officer, Gregory Martis, then Glenn Branson. The others remained at the top, waiting for instructions. He descended as fast as he dared, doing what the inspector advised – which was what he had learned himself some years ago on a training course in working at heights. He kept on going for what seemed an eternity, his arms getting increasingly tired.

'Any sign of the bottom, boss?' Guy Batchelor called down.

'Not yet.'

'Ever see that movie, *Journey to the Centre of the Earth*?' shouted Glenn Branson.

'I think we're going to come out in sodding Australia!' Grace retorted. As he did so his right foot touched something solid. The bottom. He lowered his left foot, checking, warily, with the torch. He was standing on a concrete floor in a confined space. He turned, shining the beam around, and saw that directly behind him was a tunnel, with primitive timber supports the size and thickness of railway sleepers, lower than the one that ran from the wine cellar in Crisp's house to where the three limbless men had been kept. But instead of hessian matting, the floor of this one was concrete.

Grace called up to the others at the top. 'We're on the bottom and entering a small tunnel.'

He knelt and began crawling along it, followed by the other two. After several moments he saw faint streaks of light ahead. They grew slightly brighter the further along he went. He looked dubiously at the railway sleeper struts supporting the tunnel. One on the left had a big split, and another on the right was a good six inches shorter. Some of the cross-beams looked like several wooden planks nailed together. These beams, every few yards, were all that was holding up the roof. The whole damned tunnel, like the last one, did not look professionally made, and it very definitely did not inspire confidence.

This was crazy, he should not be down here, he knew. And he should not have let anyone follow him. But if there was a chance of finding Crisp down here, however remote, that was all he cared about at this moment.

A short distance along the tunnel, he came to a trapdoor in the floor, with light shining faintly around the edges. Perspiring heavily, he turned and signalled the two officers to be quiet. Then he began raising the wooden trapdoor, inch by inch, peering down.

And felt an adrenaline rush.

Just below him, at the bottom of a free-standing steel ladder, was a small, well-lit room, hollowed out of the earth. It looked cosily furnished with cushions, a television, fridge, microwave oven and a sink. Reclining on the cushions, with a glass tumbler in his hand, dressed in a shirt, cardigan, jeans and loafers, and wearing a set of large headphones, was Dr Edward Crisp. He was nodding cheerfully, waving his free hand as if conducting the orchestra, and looking oblivious to all else. He was clearly not expecting visitors.

Grace's nerves were jangling. He could scarcely believe his eyes, or his luck. *Got you!* he thought. *Got you, you bastard, you murdering little shit.* He lowered the door silently, with shaking hands. Was this Crisp's cunning plan, to make them believe he had escaped, but meanwhile to lie doggo, waiting until the heat was over, before quietly slipping away?

Years back, when he had been a probationary uniformed constable before joining the CID, he attended break-ins frequently. He learned it was a common ploy of burglars, who had fled from premises they had just targeted, to then stroll nonchalantly back towards them, thinking that the police would be looking for someone running in the opposite direction. Was that why Crisp was still here, he wondered, thinking the police would never suspect, having searched the properties thoroughly, that he was holed up beneath their very noses?

Was there an entrance to another tunnel he might try to escape along the moment they descended the ladder? Let him try, he thought, he wouldn't have a hope in hell against his trained team.

Talking urgently, as quietly as he could, he informed Glenn Branson and Gregory Martis what he had seen.

'I'll go down first, sir,' Martis said.

Grace shook his head. 'No, I want that pleasure.'

'I've got body armour – he may be armed.'

'Didn't look like it,' Grace said. 'I'll go first, you two stay up here.'

Reluctantly, Martis agreed and asked, 'Do you have any gloves, sir?'

'Only forensic ones.'

Martis handed him his own pair of leather gloves. 'Put these on, you don't want to burn your hands sliding down the ladder.'

'Won't you need them?'

'My hands are like leather.'

Gratefully, Grace donned them. Then looked at each of his colleagues in turn, taking a couple of deep breaths. 'Rock and roll?'

They both nodded.

He hesitated, took another deep breath and flung back the hatch.

Then as his feet touched the first rung Crisp's voice rang out.

'Detective Superintendent Grace, what a very pleasant surprise. Pleasant for me, indeed!'

'Sir!' Martis yelled in warning.

Roy Grace looked down and saw both barrels of an under-and-over shotgun aimed straight at him. A chill ripped through him. *Shit, shit, shit – where the hell had—?*

Suddenly, he felt himself being jerked sharply and painfully upwards, by his armpits. He heard two deafening explosions in quick succession that made his ears pop, and felt an instant, searing pain in his right leg.

As he fell face down on the floor, earth thudded down on top of him.

'Fucking bastard!' he heard Martis shout out.

'Roy, you OK, man? Roy?' Glenn Branson was kneeling beside him.

He nodded, his leg in agony, then heard a splintering crack. He saw the LST officer pulling one of the railways sleepers supporting a beam over the hatch. He realized what the man was doing, he was trying to stop Crisp coming up through the hatch with his gun.

Almost in slow motion the dislodged beam fell down the shaft, accompanied by a shower of earth and, an instant later, by the massive railway sleeper.

Grace heard a cry of disbelief below, followed by a scream of pain.

There was a shower of earth on his face and he had to close his eyes against it. Then he heard another shout – that was more a scream of terror – from Crisp.

'Get me out of here! Please! Get me out of here! Help me! I can't move!'

Grace crawled to the opening and very cautiously looked down. He felt more earth thudding against the back of his head. His right leg felt like it had been stung by a thousand wasps, but he ignored the pain. Below him he saw Crisp flat on his back, pinned to the bed of cushions by the falling debris.

'Help me! I can't move! Help me!'

A solid chunk of earth struck the back of Grace's head, painfully.

'Sir!' Martis's voice sounded anxious. 'Can you hear that rumbling? We need to get out of here.'

Earth was raining down on them now.

'Help me!' Crisp screamed, his face a mask of abject terror as more earth tumbled down onto him.

Someone was tugging at Grace's arm. Martis. 'Sir,' he said. 'We have to get out of here.'

'We can't leave him,' Grace said.

'We don't have a choice, sir. We need to leave NOW!'

He shone the torch up and could see that the entire roof was moving, the remaining timbers vibrating, perilously, more earth falling down.

'Everybody out, back down the tunnel!' Grace ordered.

'Go ahead, sir,' Martis said.

'I'm going last. Go!'

'Please help me, I can't move!' screamed Crisp. 'Don't leave me – please help me, HELP ME, HELP ME!'

Grace peered one last time into the opening. As he looked, a huge object plummeted past him, another railway sleeper, missing Crisp's head by inches then thudding on the floor below.

Suddenly he felt himself being jerked away. He turned to see Glenn Branson pulling him by his good leg.

'Hey!' he shouted.

More earth fell on him.

'He's not worth it, mate. Leave him or we're all going to die!'

Branson pulled him further and further away.

There was a sharp crack above them, followed by a shower of earth. 'Go!' he yelled at Branson. 'Go! Go! Go!'

He heard Crisp scream for help again.

Should he go back for him?

More earth fell on him. He inhaled some of the dust and coughed violently. He thought of Cleo and Noah. Thought of never seeing them again. To try to save a monster? He made his decision and, following his colleagues, he scrambled on his hands and knees, the pain in his leg worsening with every movement and continued, on, on, on. Then his face smacked into the heels of Glenn Branson's shoes. 'Keep going, Glenn, for Chrissake, go!' he shouted.

He shone the torch behind him and saw a wall of dust racing down the tunnel towards them. Gripped with panic, he yelled, 'Go! Go! Go!'

There was a deep rumbling sound behind him.

The message seemed to have got through. Glenn was pulling away from him now. Grace crawled after him as fast as he could, but his right leg was becoming useless. Dank, earthy dust was swirling around him, choking him, filling his lungs. Within moments all he could see was a dark brown fog.

Panic gripped him. He was going to die down here. He would never see Cleo or Noah again. Never live in the new house with them. Never—

Have to think clearly, he told himself. Panic was what killed people. Disaster survivors were the ones who stayed calm, kept their nerve. The shaft was ahead. If he could reach it he would be safe.

He scrambled on. He dropped the torch, but did not stop to look for it, he just carried on. On. On.

Then his face smashed, painfully, into something hard, metallic.

The bottom rung of the shaft.

Relief surged through him.

A torch beam suddenly dazzled him. He blinked, and heard Glenn Branson's voice. 'I'm here, mate, I'm not going up without you, so sodding get on with it! Follow me up.'

He raised his hands, felt the rung above, and hauled himself up. He was spluttering, his mouth arid. Someone was coughing above him, then he coughed again hard himself, a searing pain in his lungs, and almost lost his grip.

Three limbs, he remembered.

But his right leg would barely move.

The rung he was holding was shaking. As if it was about to pull free of the shaft. He moved his right arm up to the next one, hurriedly.

The rumble behind him had turned into a roar, like a volcano.

Everything beneath him was collapsing. He had to keep clambering up. Had to. Had to.

Three limbs at all times.

The rung both his feet were standing on suddenly fell away, and he swung out, hanging from one hand, grimly holding on, but feeling his fingers slipping.

Noah. Cleo. God, I love you so much.

Somehow in the choking darkness he managed to get his other hand onto the rung, then felt it giving way as well. He hauled himself up, just as the rung beneath his feet detached from the side of the shaft and clattered into the swirling brown hell below him, and grabbed the next one. He gripped the rung with both hands, but he could barely hold on.

The roar deepened, deafening now like an earthquake, as both his wrists were seized in a grip like a vice. Feeling like his arms were about to rip out of his body, he was hauled slowly upwards. He looked up to see Branson and Martis's faces.

'It's all right, mate, we've got you, you heavy bastard!'

An instant later he slammed down hard, over the lip of the freezer, his face striking the concrete floor of the garage, panting with exertion.

'All right, Roy? Sorry if I hurt you.'

He turned, looking at Branson. 'I'll get over it,' he gasped. 'Thanks, mate.'

'Bloke like you, at your age, you need one of them Stannah Stairlifts.'

'Up yours!'

Somewhere in the distance he heard the wail of an emergency siren. Then the burning pain in his right leg worsened. 'Shit!' he cried out.

'Can't take the pace any more?' Glenn Branson chided.

Grace shook his head. 'Nah, it's not that. It's your humour. Nothing personal, but every time I hear one of your tired old gags, I lose the will to live.' He grinned, then he turned towards him and hugged him. 'I don't know why, but I do sodding love you.'

'You're not so bad yourself,' Branson replied. 'For an old git.' Then he knelt, looking anxiously at Grace's right leg, and saw the colour draining from his face. 'Shit, Roy, this looks serious.' He turned to Martis. 'We need an ambulance, fast.'

103

'Well, it's not quite home, darling, is it?'

Roy Grace opened his eyes, feeling totally disoriented. The light was too bright, the bed felt unfamiliar, the ceiling looked strange. Fear engulfed him for an instant. Where was he?

What had happened?

Then he saw Cleo's face above him, looking at him strangely, with a quizzical grin.

What was going on? Where—?

She leaned down and kissed him tenderly on his forehead.

Where – where was he?

'You are crazy, my love,' she said.

'Crazy?'

His right leg was throbbing painfully. He saw a woman standing beside Cleo in a pale blue shirt. A name tag was pinned to it, which he couldn't read. She looked like a nurse. Next to her stood a man of about fifty, in dark blue surgical scrubs, and blue and white gauze, like a J-cloth, tied with tapes around his head.

'Welcome back, Detective Superintendent Grace,' the nurse said.

'Back?' Grace said. He was trying to piece together things in his mind. The tunnel. Dr Crisp. The shotgun.

The man in scrubs stepped forward. 'How are you feeling, old chap?'

'My right leg's hurting like hell!'

'I'm not surprised. I've removed eleven shotgun pellets from it. You're lucky, another few inches and you might have lost your leg. We'll keep the pain under control and you'll be back on your pins in a couple of weeks. Although it'll be a bit tender for a few weeks, I'm

378

afraid.' He gave him a lopsided smile. 'Sorry, should have introduced myself. I'm Rupert Verrell, a consultant surgeon here.'

It was all coming back to him now. 'I didn't realize it was that bad. Thank you.'

'Double-barrel shotguns at close range are not good news – thought you as a detective would be the first person to know that.'

'Yep, well I do now,' he said.

'You had a lucky escape – he was clearly a lousy shot.'

'Glenn told me what you did, darling,' Cleo said. 'You are bloody nuts! A few inches in another direction and I might have been a grieving widow.'

'How long have I been here?' Roy Grace asked, feeling sudden panic.

'Two days, darling,' Cleo said.

'What's the date today?' he asked.

Cleo gave him a chiding look. 'December 23rd.'

'What's the time?'

She glanced at her watch. 'Five past ten.'

'Morning?'

'Yes, morning!'

'Shit!' He tried to sit up – and instantly felt as if a red-hot poker was being pressed against his leg. 'Yoowwwww!' He closed his eyes, wincing. 'I've got to go shopping!' he said. 'I've got tons of stuff to get – I have to get your card, your presents!' And, he suddenly remembered, he'd got nothing yet for his godchild, Jaye, either.

'There's no way you're going shopping today, old chap,' the surgeon said. 'Unless you're planning on doing it online.'

'You're not seriously keeping me in here over Christmas? We've just moved into our new house – I – I've got to be at home with my family. I've got to get out and buy presents!'

'I've got my present,' Cleo said. 'It's you. You being OK, being alive, that's the only present I need this Christmas.'

Grace stared up at her, despondently. 'God, darling, I am so sorry.'

'Remember what you told me when I was pregnant with Noah?'

He winced in pain again, then shook his head. 'No, what?'

'That your job was to catch and lock up the bad guys, to make the world a safer place for your unborn child and me. Well, that's what you did. I may be mad as hell at you for putting your life at risk, but I'm proud of you. I don't know many people who are married to real heroes. Noah and I will celebrate Christmas with you here in the hospital. It'll be different from the one we planned. But hey, we'll make it a good one. Right?' She squeezed his hand.

He smiled up at her, blinking away tears, and squeezed her hand back. Then he heard the voice of the nurse, detached and bossy.

'Your husband needs to sleep now.'

'Darling, before you go, what's happened to Crisp?'

'I just know they're still digging.'

104

Grace had had visitors all day, including his sister, and had nodded off watching the television. He was woken what seemed like only moments later by the gruff voice of Glenn Branson.

'Happy Christmas, mate!'

He opened his eyes to see the tall hulk of the detective, in a sharp suit and even more dazzling tie than usual, reeking of alcohol and looking unsteady. He was holding a card in one hand and a massive bottle of champagne, with a blue ribbon around the neck, in the other. Next to him stood an attractive, fair-haired woman in a short black dress, leggings and high-heeled boots. She was holding a basket of fruit wrapped in cellophane with a sprig of holly on the top.

The *Argus* reporter, Siobhan Sheldrake, Grace realized. He looked up at them, wondering what the hell was going on. 'Wassertime?' he asked, still not fully with it.

'One minute to midnight, Christmas Eve. Just call me Santa! Do you know how much rank I had to pull to be let in here?' Branson said.

'How are you feeling, Roy?' the *Argus* reporter said.

'No comment,' he replied.

Was Glenn insane? What the hell was he doing here with this reporter?

'Siobhan's cool,' Branson replied, reading his mate's expression. 'This is a social visit – she's not writing it up. She's already done her piece on you!' He held up the front page of today's *Argus*.

Grace stared at the headline.

HERO COP RISKS LIFE TO CATCH KILLER

Branson staggered sideways, got a grip on himself and put the bottle down on the table beside him. Then he touched Roy Grace's face with his hand. 'You OK?'

'I haven't thanked you properly yet, for getting me out of there,' Grace said.

'Yeah, and you managed to grab the headline!' Branson retorted, sitting down on the side of the bed. 'Hero bloody cop! Huh!'

'You sodding yanked my arms out of their sockets!'

The tall detective grinned. 'Yeah, bummer.'

Grace looked at him, moved his eyes over to the *Argus* reporter, then back to Glenn Branson. 'Want to tell me what's going on?'

'Yeah. Siobhan and I – I know we're a bit pissed. But I thought you ought to be the first to hear the news. We just got engaged.'

105

In the years following Sandy's disappearance, Christmas had been a meaningless time of year for Roy Grace, in which he'd preferred to work rather than try to be jolly with family.

Last year, for the first time, with Cleo, he had actually enjoyed it again. He had been looking forward to it so much this year in their new home in the country. He thought about a roaring open fire, walks in the country with little Noah in a carrier on his back. Instead, he was confined to this small single room, at the Royal Sussex County Hospital.

Every inch of shelf space, and the table beside his bed, was covered in cards – mostly from his work colleagues, along with a mass of flowers and baskets of fruit.

Reluctantly Cleo had left to take Noah home to bed. The television was on, a Christmas special of *Downton Abbey*. He watched Hugh Bonneville raising a toast. Then suddenly the door opened and Cassian Pewe walked in carrying a festive bottle-bag and a card. Yet again he was dressed in one of his loud-checked sports jackets, roll-neck sweater, cavalry twills and distinctly vulgar two-tone brogues.

'Roy! Happy Christmas!' he said in his nasally whine. 'I had planned to come sooner, but you know what Christmas Day is like!'

'Very nice to see you, sir.' Grace did his best to muster a smile, and in truth was pleasantly surprised to see his boss.

'Brought you a little something to cheer you up!' He handed Grace the heavy bag and card.

'Thank you!'

Pewe sat down on the chair beside the bed and Grace smelled the reek of an obnoxiously sweet cologne, perhaps a Christmas gift.

'Nice work, Roy.'

'Thank you.'

'No, thank you. What you've done is over and above anything expected. You've shown the city of Brighton and Hove, the county of Sussex and the entire damned country what good policing really is. We are all proud of you, and indebted to you. You're a hero!'

Grace waited for the negative punchline, but it didn't come.

'Last year you saved my life, Roy. I know we haven't always seen eye to eye, but it's funny how life works out. I don't want to go into the New Year feeling any tension between us – that's why I've come to see you tonight. You're a damned fine copper. You're the best. I'm proud to be working with you, and I'm sorry if I doubted you in the past. OK?' He held out his hand.

Grace shook it. Pewe's handshake was limp and slimy. 'OK!'

'I'm sure you want to know the latest on the recovery of Crisp's body. We've had some problems; the tunnel's flooded from fractured pipes and it's full of water and sewage that we're pumping out but it'll take a few days.

'Now, as I understand it you've just moved home, but Operation Haywain has prevented you from helping out in any way – is that correct?'

'Well, I suppose so. Luckily, I have an understanding wife.'

Pewe tapped his chest. 'And an understanding ACC. I'm told you will be allowed home before the New Year. I understand you'll be on a month's sick leave, Roy. Spend some quality time at home, getting straight, and with your lovely wife and your baby son. And forget all about Major Crime. Come back on Feb 1st fully charged up – we're going to be needing you in the New Year firing on all cylinders. Right?'

'A month?' Grace tried to remember the last time he'd had that amount of time off, and couldn't. Instantly he was suspicious. 'I'm sure I won't need that long.'

'It's not an option, Roy, it's an order. I've seen too many marriages in the police ruined because of the workload of officers.' He grinned, exposing a set of immaculate white teeth, and shiny, rosebud lips.

Five minutes later, to Roy Grace's relief, Pewe left.

106

'I can't believe I have you home for an entire month!' Cleo said, holding the door, then taking his arm to help him out of the car. 'Welcome back!' She handed him his stick, then went around to the rear of the car to get his little suitcase.

Roy Grace grinned, gripping the walking stick, supporting himself on his good leg, and stood in the unseasonably warm sunlight staring excitedly at the cottage, and breathing in the smells of the country air. He could hardly believe he was actually, finally, back. For years he had dreamed of living in the countryside, and whilst they were only eight miles from his beloved Brighton, this was wonderfully rural.

The house was small and rectangular, with whitewashed walls, a white front door and a steeply pitched tiled roof, approached down a bumpy drive that was little more than a cart track. All the tiny windows were a different shape, and one side of the house was covered in unruly ivy. The garden was an overgrown riot of shrubs, bushes and long grass. In a slightly elevated position, it had a view from the rear across miles of open fields. They'd got it for a good price because it was in need of modernization, but he loved it all the more for that. Cleo had great taste and had already begun the redecorating.

As he reached the front door he heard Humphrey barking excitedly inside. Moments later it was opened by Cleo's younger sister, Charlie, in paint-spattered dungarees.

Humphrey came bounding out, almost knocking him over in his excitement, jumping up at him.

Steadying himself on his stick, he hugged the dog. 'Good boy, like your new pad, do you?' Moments later Humphrey spotted something and raced off into the undergrowth, barking furiously.

He went into the hallway, treading carefully across the dust sheets,

385

inhaling the heady smell of fresh paint combined with the sweet smell of an open fire. As he kissed Charlie, wishing her a belated Happy Christmas, he heard Noah gurgling.

'He's been good as gold all morning!' Charlie said. 'He must be excited to have his Daddy home!'

'I'll bring him down!' Cleo said and hurried up the stairs. 'Go through to the living room. I've put a bottle of champagne in the fridge – we've got some overdue celebrating to do!' she called out.

Ten minutes later, on a sofa in front of the crackling, popping fire in the inglenook, with a glass in his hand, and Noah lying on his play mat on the floor, Roy Grace felt almost overwhelmed with happiness. Finally, he felt, his new life was really beginning.

Charlie, whose love life had been a disastrous series of wrong choices, was dating a television commercials director whom the whole family – apart from him – had met and really liked, and she looked happier than he had ever seen her. Humphrey was wrestling to the death with a squeaky rubber toy.

'So,' Charlie said, 'Detective Superintendent Grace is now a country squire. How does that feel?'

He grinned, drained his glass and looked up at Cleo. 'Pretty damned good!'

Charlie refilled their glasses and went to the kitchen to prepare lunch. 'We've got a whole month together, darling,' Roy said to Cleo. 'What are we going to do with it? Have that house-warming for starters?'

'Yes,' she replied. 'And let's have a couple of dinner parties. And we should go to London shopping in the sales – now's the best time to buy stuff for the house. And there's a Bryan Ferry concert coming on at the Dome in three weeks – shall we try to get tickets?'

Later on, when the bottle was almost empty, Cleo scooped Noah into her arms to take him upstairs for a feed.

Charlie excused herself to serve lunch. Grace sat and sipped more of his champagne. Then his phone rang.

It was his German Landeskriminalamt friend, Marcel Kullen.

Instantly his mood changed, as if the sky had clouded over.

'Hey, Roy, Happy New Year. How are you?'

'Happy New Year, Marcel. I'm OK – apart from being shot in the leg just before Christmas.'

'Shot? You have been shot?'

'Eleven pellets removed from my leg.'

'You are serious?'

'Yep, they were an early Christmas present from someone who didn't like me very much.'

'My God, but you are OK?'

'I'm OK, thanks. It hurts a bit to walk, but I'll be fine in another week or so. Alcohol helps! So how are you?'

There was a moment's silence, then Kullen said, 'This lady in the hospital I spoke to you about, yes?'

'Uh huh,' he replied hesitantly.

'I have some more information about this woman. Tell me something, did your Sandy – was she ever taking drugs?'

'Drugs? What do you mean, Marcel? What kind of drugs?'

'Heroin?'

'No way! No.'

'Are you sure?'

'I think I would have known!'

'I do not think always people know, Roy.'

'What are you saying?'

'I have another question. This lady, they are calling Frau Lohmann – she has a son I mentioned who is ten years and six months old. Do you think there is any possibility your Sandy could have had such a son by you?'

He stared at the dancing flames in the grate. 'A son? By me?'

'Could she have been pregnant when she left you?'

'Pregnant? Pregnant, no – no.'

'Are you sure?'

'Yes,' Grace said hesitantly and tried to do the maths. It was just possible, he calculated. Just.

'This son has told the friends he is staying with that his mother has taken him twice to Brighton. The last time he said he went to a wedding with her in November and she seemed very upset. They left the wedding.'

Grace listened, feeling numb. 'Why did you ask about drugs, Marcel?'

'We circulated her three identities and photographs to all police forces and agencies in Germany that might be able to help us. One responded which is in Frankfurt. They have, how do you call it, a drugs consumption room there. It is a place where drug users can go and inject themselves under supervision. They said they knew this woman who came regularly for two years. I think you should come over here, Roy, and make sure this woman is not Sandy. It would be helpful to us if you were able at least to eliminate her.'

'What other details do you have?'

'Well, Roy, with one identity, the one her son gave us, Alessandra Lohmann is the one she seems to be using now. But it is the variation of her first name that she gave to the drugs clinic that might be interesting to you.'

'Which is?'

'Sandy.'

107

Roy Grace stared out of the aeroplane window at the vast expanse of flat land beneath him, as they began their descent into Frankfurt. Was he on a wild goose chase after a ghost?

God, he hoped so.

And yet he could not dismiss that JPEG on his phone. It *could* be Sandy.

Three faked identities?

She was a multimillionaire?

She had a son.

The son's age would have put her just pregnant at the time she vanished. She might not even have known she was pregnant then.

A son who had been twice with his mother to Brighton, last year. Once to a wedding in Brighton on the day he and Cleo had got married?

A son who had said the wedding had upset his mother.

Roy thought again about the nightmare he'd had before the wedding, in which he had dreamed he had seen Sandy in the church. And then, during the wedding itself, when he had turned to watch Cleo walk down the aisle and had seen the strange woman in black with a small boy at the back of the church.

Was it possible? Could Marcel be right?

Was she still alive and had come back to Brighton after all these years? And if so, why? Out of curiosity?

And if it really was her, how the hell would he – could he – deal with that?

His leg had healed to the point where he felt ready to start walking again, although the physio had told him to wait several weeks more before he attempted to start running. He had almost four more weeks at home before returning to work. And whilst he was going to miss work, to some extent, he was looking forward to the time he would spend with Cleo and Noah – and to getting stuck into stripping paint and paper and redecorating.

After the plane touched down he switched on his phone, then waited for a signal. As soon as he had one he texted Cleo to say he had landed. Feeling guilty that for the first time in their relationship, he had lied to her, telling her he had to make this one brief trip because of a witness's vital testimony on a cold case he had been working on.

Immersed in his thoughts in the back of the taxi, he barely noticed the journey into the city. The cab driver, who spoke little English, had given him a dubious look when he had shown him the address. Forty minutes later, at midday, German time, the taxi turned into a seedy, rundown-looking Frankfurt street, with graffiti on the walls, and he could now understand the driver's strange expression.

He saw the street name, Elbestrasse. Amid the strip clubs and sex shops, they passed several construction sites. To his left he saw a row of breeze blocks on the pavement behind a steel cage, and a blue tube running from the top of the building, down past the scaffolding and into a skip. Next to it was a garish-looking club, with the billboard announcing, CABARET. PIK-DAME. On his right they passed the shabby exterior of Hotel Elbe, then Eva's Bistro and Hotel Garni. Then the taxi pulled over to the right and stopped beside several small, beat-up cars partially parked on the pavement, pointed at a drab, four-storey building, outside which several down-and-outs were gathered, some sitting, some standing, and said something to him in German that he did not understand. But he got the message.

They were here.

He paid the driver, went up the steps, lugging his overnight bag, and rang the bell. Moments later he heard a sharp buzz, pushed open the heavy glass door and entered a small, tiled reception area. A young woman sat behind a high counter at the rear, smiling pleasantly.

'Do you speak English?' he asked.

'Ja, a little.'

'My name is Roy Grace – I've come to see Wolfgang Barth – he is expecting me.'

She directed him up the steps past her and along a short corridor towards a door. 'You will find him on the second floor.'

There was a plate-glass window to his left. Through it he could see down into an adjoining room. The drugs consumption room. There were functional plastic chairs against a narrow metal table that ran around three sides of the room. Three of the chairs were occupied, two by young men, one in a baseball cap, and the other by a wizened, bearded man, with long straggly hair, in his late fifties, Grace estimated. All of them were hunched over their part of the table, studiously preparing their drugs. The room was presided over by a young woman, who had a row of metal spoons and hypodermic syringes on paper towels laid out in front of her.

He stopped and stared, driven by curiosity, then moved on through the door. Is this where Sandy had been? Taking drugs?

He climbed the stairs and as he reached the second floor a door opened and a friendly looking man, in his mid-forties, emerged. He was dressed in a blue checked shirt and jeans, and his shoulder-length brown hair and craggy good looks gave him the appearance of a rock musician.

'Detective Superintendent Roy Grace?' he asked in perfect English, with a cultured German accent. 'I am Wolfgang Barth.'

They shook hands and Grace followed him into a bright, airy, cream-painted office, furnished with two desks, an aerial map of the city and several posters on the walls, one prominently worded, CANNABIS.

They sat down at a small conference table and Barth got him a coffee. There was a bowl of assorted chocolate biscuits on the table, which the German pushed towards him. 'Help yourself if you are hungry.'

'I'm good, thanks.'

'So,' Barth said, sitting opposite him, 'you are a detective with Sussex Police. Do you know Graham Barrington?'

'Indeed, very well. He was a Chief Superintendent who recently retired.'

Barth frowned. 'Retired? Such a young man?'

Grace smiled. 'That's the system we have. Most officers retire after thirty years.'

'He was here two years ago, looking at our work – he was keen to introduce what we are doing here into your city of Brighton.'

'He was very forward-thinking. Unfortunately I don't think my country's politicians are as enlightened as yours in dealing with drug problems.'

Barth shrugged. 'In 1992 we had one hundred and forty-seven drug deaths in this city. Now, since we introduced the consumption rooms, like this one, we have thirty. And the number is still reducing.' He shrugged again. 'So tell me, how can I be of help to you?'

Roy Grace unzipped his bag, and pulled out a stiff brown envelope. From it he removed a photograph of Sandy, taken just before she vanished, and handed it to him. 'Do you recognize this woman?'

The German studied it intently.

'About a month ago,' Grace said, 'Munich police circulated a photograph of a woman who was involved in an accident, whose identity was uncertain. They discovered she appeared to have three different names – aliases. One of them was Alessandra Lohmann. You responded that you recognized her, and that she had been a regular at this consumption room a couple of years back, using the first name, *Sandy*.'

Wolfgang Barth put the photograph down and nodded, thoughtfully. Then he went over to a tall metal rack of box files, peered at the covers, pulled one out and opened it up.

'Yes,' he said. 'Sandy Lohmann. She was a recovering drug user who wanted to help by providing counselling services to others. She worked here for free every day from March 2009 until December 2011. But then she stopped coming.'

He replaced the file and sat back down again. Grace leaned forward and pointed at the photograph. 'Is that her? Do you recognize her?'

Barth stared at it again for some moments, then looked at Grace and shrugged. 'You know, this is very difficult. So many faces here. I remember Sandy a little, but she had red hair and wore a lot of, how you call it, make-up. It's possible. She was very thin.' He ran his fingers down his face as if to illustrate. 'Gaunt, you know?'

Grace sat silently for some moments. Then he pulled out the photograph he had been sent by Marcel Kullen, of the woman in the Intensive Care Unit. 'How about this one?'

Barth studied it. 'This is the same woman?'

'Perhaps. This was taken a month ago.'

Barth stared down at it for a long while, before looking up. 'You know, it is possible. But I cannot say yes for sure. She is a person of interest to you?'

'Yes,' he replied. 'She's a person of interest to me.'

108

At 5 p.m. that afternoon, Roy Grace sat in the passenger seat of Marcel Kullen's immaculate fifteen-year-old BMW, heading from the airport into Munich. Ahead of them, out of the falling darkness, blue road signs with white writing loomed up then shot past them. SALZBURG. MÜNCHEN. NÜRNBERG. ECHING.

His old friend had refused to countenance the idea of his spending a night in a hotel, and insisted he stayed with him and his family, which the German detective assured him would give them a good opportunity to sample some fine local beers, some even finer German wines and some even finer still German schnapps.

At 9 a.m. the following morning, with one of the worst hangovers Grace could remember, in a long history of bad hangovers, compounded by his guilt at having lied to Cleo, Kullen drove down a wide, quiet street, through falling sleet, in the smart Schwabing district of Munich. Small, grubby patches of snow here and there lay on the pavement. They turned onto a circular driveway, passing a row of parked bicycles, and pulled up in front of an enormous, handsome beige building, with gabled windows in the roof and a sign over the arched entrance porch that said, KLINIKUM SCHWABING. It looked, to him, as if it might once have been a monastery.

'Would you like me to come in, or wait for you?' Kullen asked.

Grace's mouth was parched, his head was pounding, and the last two paracetamol he had swallowed, an hour ago, had failed to kick in. He felt badly in need of a large glass of water and a multiple espresso. Why the hell had he drunk so much last night?

He knew the answer.

Staring at the facade of the building was scaring the hell out of him.

What?

What if?

What if it was really her, here? How would he feel? How would he react? What on earth would he say?

Part of him was tempted to turn to Marcel Kullen and tell him to drive on, back to the airport, to forget it. But he had come too far now, he knew. He was past the point of no return.

'Whatever you'd prefer, Marcel.'

'I stay. I think this is a journey you are needing to make alone.'

Fighting his reluctance, feeling like he had a dagger sticking into his head, Grace opened the door, and stepped out, limping, into the bitterly cold air. As he did so he heard the *thwock-thwock-thwock* of an approaching helicopter, and looked up. The machine was coming down out of the sky straight towards the building. Moments later it disappeared over the rooftop, and he could hear it descending.

He entered a large foyer, and saw a sign, INFORMATION, above two smartly dressed women at a modern reception desk, backlit in orange. He gave his name, and was directed to a row of chairs to wait. He looked around, in vain, for a water dispenser or a hot drinks machine, then sat down, his nerves shot to hell and back.

After a few minutes, a plump, middle-aged woman with shoulder-length fair hair and glasses, dressed in a black trouser suit and trainers, greeted him very formally. She gave him her name but he didn't catch it.

'Please come with me.'

He followed her down a long corridor, passing beneath an illuminated gantry of signs and direction arrows, then on past a glassed-in café, and stopped at an elevator.

'I understand this lady – she might be your missing wife?'

His stomach was so tied up in knots he found it hard to speak. 'Maybe,' he said. 'Maybe. She has not spoken?'

'Sometimes she has mumbled, but that is all. Mostly she is silent. In her own world. Like she is locked in.'

They rode up a couple of floors, in silence, then emerged in front of a glass door, with the sign on it reading, ANÄSTHESIOLOGISCHE INTENSIVSTATION 16G.

They went through into an orange-painted corridor, with a row of hard chairs on either side, a snacks vending machine, and several picture frames on the wall with portraits of staff doctors and nurses.

A man hurried past them in blue scrubs, with yellow Crocs on his feet, and went into an alcove where Grace saw there was a drinks vending machine.

The woman suggested he sat while she checked it would be all right for him to go in now. As she went through some double doors he walked over to the alcove, poured himself a cup of water, and managed to get himself a black coffee. Then he sat down to wait, wondering whether he should ask Marcel to take him to meet the boy, but decided to delay for now.

He was too nervous to sit, and stood up again, pacing up and down. Wondering. Wondering. Wondering. He was shaking. Had he made a terrible mistake coming here? Was his whole life about to unravel?

Five minutes later the woman returned and said, 'All is fine, it is fine for you to see her now. It is good with comatose patients to touch them. Talk to them. They can recognize smell – perhaps she will recognize your smells, if it is your wife. Also if you have any of her favourite music on your phone, it would be good to play it.'

He followed her in through the doors to the Intensive Care Unit. They passed rows of beds, each with an intubated patient connected to a bank of monitors, and screened off on either side by pale green curtains. A number was fixed to the walls above their heads. They turned a corner and he was ushered into a small room, marked '7', its door already open.

Inside lay a woman with short brown hair, in a blue and white spotted gown, amid a forest of drip lines, surrounded by more banks of monitors, in a bed with its sides up like the bars of a cage.

The woman who had led him there discreetly disappeared, and he was all alone.

He stepped forward, slowly, until he was beside the bed, looking straight down at her face. It was still swollen, and covered in scabs and scars, and partially masked with bandages. One drip line fed into a cannula on her right wrist and another, held in place by a plaster, at the base of her throat. Her eyes were closed and she was breathing rhythmically.

He felt a lump in his throat.

Could this be her?

God.

Was this the woman he had once loved so much?

The truth was he did not know. He really did not. A plaster lay across the bridge of her nose, masking most of it. It was Sandy's mouth.

'Sandy?' he whispered, tentatively. 'Sandy? It's me, Roy.'

There was no reaction.

He held her puffy, bandaged free hand, squeezing it very gently. 'Sandy? My darling? Is this you?'

From what he could remember, her hand felt similar to the way it always had – small, a perfect fit into his. His heart was heaving. One instant he was sure it was her, and the next, he was convinced he was looking at a stranger.

'Sandy?'

She continued her steady breathing.

What the hell was he going to do if she opened her eyes and stared at him in recognition? How could he deal with it? He had been massively devious coming here. How could he begin to explain it to Cleo?

He stared down at her again. Was this the woman he had once loved? Could he ever love her again, if it was her? He felt nothing. Empty of emotion.

She had a son. Was it possible it could be his son? How could he deal with that? This wasn't his life any more. He was looking at a stranger. Even if it was – her.

He felt numb.

Suddenly, he made his decision. He turned and walked back out of the room. The woman who had brought him in was standing just outside, talking to a nurse in a blue tunic and Crocs. She stepped towards him, quizzically.

'Is she your wife?'

He shook his head. 'No.'

109

Three hours later, Roy Grace settled into his seat on the British Airways plane that would take him back to London. His mind was in overdrive. Why the hell had he come here, what had he hoped to achieve? Why hadn't he had the courage to tell Cleo?

If the purpose of this trip had been to lay a ghost to rest, precisely the opposite had happened. He had re-opened the nightmare of the past.

Apart from his injury, which was now healing well, the last year had ended on a high. He had been lauded by his chiefs for saving Logan Somerville, and despite the tragedy of the lost lives, Operation Haywain had succeeded in halting the reign of terror of the Brighton Brander. He'd had several other successes this past year, too, and even with the arrival of Cassian Pewe he had been feeling more positive about the future. During this past year, he felt, more than ever, he had really proved his abilities as a homicide detective.

They had moved into their beautiful new home, and Cleo, despite her exhaustion with Noah and the move, was feeling so happy and positive about the future. She would shortly be going back to work, and they would have to make a decision on a nanny.

They had always been honest and open with each other. Should he tell her the truth when he got home, and lay her mind to rest once and for all? Even if that would mean admitting he had lied to her about this trip?

The past had been a dark place for far too long. He needed to put it back in its box. It had taken him ten long years to finally move forward and find happiness again. He could not let the past destroy him – them.

And yet.

He couldn't shake the image of the woman from his mind.

In room 7, the comatose woman's eyes suddenly opened. Her attending nurse had stepped away for a comfort break and she was, briefly, alone.

'Roy was here,' she said.

Then her eyes closed again.

110

Sunday 4 January

The moment the plane had taxied to a halt at Heathrow Airport, Roy Grace switched his phone from flight mode. It took some moments before it found a signal. As soon as it did, he texted Cleo to say he was back safe.

Then his phone buzzed, indicating he had voicemail.

He checked it. There were two messages from Cassian Pewe, the second sounding more impatient than the first. 'Roy, call me urgently, will you, please.'

A loud *bing-bong* sounded, and people all around him began standing up and removing their belongings from the overhead lockers. Grace joined them, shuffling along and out of the plane. Pewe could wait a few minutes, he decided, and anyway, he was officially on leave.

A little while later, he entered the short-term car park. Then, just as he reached Cleo's Audi, his phone rang again. He looked at the display but the number was withheld.

'Roy Grace,' he answered.

'Where the hell have you been?' said the whiny voice of Cassian Pewe.

'In Germany, sir.'

'Germany?'

'I've just flown back to London.'

'I've been trying desperately to get hold of you. What have you been doing in Germany?'

'Family business, sir,' he said, barely masking his irritation at Pewe's tone.

'Why didn't you tell me where you were going?'

'I'm still on sick leave, sir.'

'I need you back on Operation Haywain right away. We have a very big problem.'

His heart sinking, Grace said, 'What's happened, sir?'

'I'll tell you what's happened. Dr Edward Crisp has happened. The excavation of the collapsed tunnel where you last saw Crisp has been completed. He isn't there.'

'That's not possible, sir. He was buried.'

'Did you see him being buried?'

Grace was silent for a moment. 'No, not *actually* buried.'

'Down in his lair, where he had a cosy little set-up, there was a hatch which dropped down into the main sewer for the area. He must have gone down it. I've spoken to Southern Water who are responsible for the entire Brighton and Hove sewerage network and they say it's very unlikely he could have survived. Apparently after all the rain of the past two months, the sewers have been in flood. He could have been carried several miles along the tunnel but then he would have hit a series of filters designed to stop and break down large objects, before they are carried on to the plant at Peacehaven, and ultimately out to sea.'

Puzzled and dismayed, Grace asked, 'So are you saying Crisp escaped into the sewer system, but would then have drowned, or been ripped to shreds?'

'What I'm saying, Roy,' Pewe's voice sounded on the cusp of a snarl, 'is that we need a damned body, or at least some body parts. Our Specialist Search Unit know how to search sewers. They need to find something urgently. Do you understand?'

'I do, sir, and a Happy New Year to you.'

'Huh.'

111

Sunday 4 January

Instead of heading home from the airport, as he had been intending, Roy Grace carried on down the A23, past the turn-off to Henfield, and then joined the A27 which took him up towards Hollingbury.

A few minutes later he turned off, drove down a steep hill, with the Asda superstore to his right, and entered the front car park of Sussex House, the CID HQ. It was 4.15 p.m.

The Christmas decorations were still up, but there was a subdued atmosphere. A cloud had hung over the future of this entire building ever since the merger of Sussex and Surrey CID departments.

In his casual clothes, he strode along the corridors towards MIR-1, then entered, greeting several members of his team who had remained, until now at any rate, to tidy up all the outstanding elements of Operation Haywain.

Norman Potting stood up from behind his workstation. 'Chief!' he said. 'How are you? You're limping.'

'I'm on the mend, thanks, Norman. Or, at least, I was. Happy New Year! How are you?'

'Happy New Year to you, too. Chief, I think you ought to take a look at this – it just came in.' Potting was pointing at his computer screen.

Grace walked over, behind the row of people seated beside Potting, then leaned over his shoulder and stared at the screen.

On it was an email, sent from a Hotmail account. The sender's name was just a meaningless row of letters and numbers.

'Read the email,' Potting said.

Grace read it.

402

YOU ARE DEAD

Dear Detective Sergeant Potting, it was very remiss of me not to get back to you on your prostate problems that you mentioned when you last came to see me, but I've been busy on an exciting new project. There is an excellent organization that has all the latest information on this vile disease. You can contact them on www.prostatehelp.me.uk.

Good luck, it was nice meeting you.

Bye for now!

Dr Edward Crisp

ACKNOWLEDGEMENTS

As ever with my Roy Grace novels I owe an incalculable debt to so many people in different fields, who have generously given their sanction, advice or time to my research.

Starting with officers, former officers and support staff of Sussex Police, Surrey Police, and other law-enforcement agencies both in the UK and overseas: Chief Constable Giles York, QPM; Police and Crime Commissioner Katy Bourne; Chief Superintendent Nev Kemp; former Chief Superintendent Graham Bartlett; Superintendent Paula Light; Detective Superintendent Paul Furnell; Detective Superintendent Nick May; Chief Inspector Jason Tingley; Detective Inspector Bill Warner; Former Detective Chief Inspector Trevor Bowles; Inspector Andy Kille; Sergeant Phil Taylor; Sergeant Lorna Dennison-Wilkins, PC Martin Light; PC Paul Quinn, PC Scott Kendal and all the team of the Specialist Search Unit. Suzanne Heard; Katie Perkin; Jill Pederson; Ray Packham formerly of the High Tech Crime Unit; Crime Scene Investigators James Gartrell and Chris Gee; Tony Case, Senior Support Officer; Juliet Smith JP, High Sherriff of East Sussex. And last, but also first, my close friend and Roy Grace alter-ego, former Detective Chief Superintendent David Gaylor, the career role model for Roy Grace.

Thank you to those who gave me invaluable medical, scientific or technical help: Dr Wilfrid Assin; Dr Neil Haughton; Iain Maclean; Dr Haydn Kelly; Dr David Veale; Michael Beard; Andrew Davey; Janet Blainey; Martin Pile; Nigel Ostime; Brian Price; Derek Middlehurst; Dr Mark Howard; Dr Nigel Kirkham; Father Martin; Hans Jürgen Stockerl; Wolfgang Barth at the Drogennotdienst, Frankfurt; Anette Lippert; and a particularly special mention to Sigrid Daus and Klinikum Munich, Krankenhaus Schwabing, for their enormous help with this book.

Although writing is a solitary task, there are numerous people in the background working on the editing, sales and marketing, without whom there would, quite simply, be no book. Starting with my computer guru, Chris Webb of MacService; my agent, Carole Blake

ACKNOWLEDGEMENTS

and her team. My editor, Wayne Brookes; Geoff Duffield, Anna Bond. Sara Lloyd and all at Pan Macmillan. My US team – Andy Martin; Marc Resnick; Hector DeJean; Paul Hochman; Elena Stokes; Tanya Farrell and all the rest at Team James USA. My copy-editor Susan Opie; my publicists, Sophie Ransom, Becky Short and Tony Mulliken.

I'm fortunate to have a brilliant support team who help me to hone the manuscript long before it reaches my agent and publishers, and to help with the management of Team James UK; My incredibly hard-working and brilliant PA, Linda Buckley, who is an absolute treasure – as well as a stickler for detail(!) – and my book-keeper Sarah Middle; Helen Shenston; Anna Hancock; Martin and Jane Diplock; Susan Ansell.

A hugely special mention to my beloved Lara, who has put such huge hard work and energy into so many aspects of the research, writing and editing of this book.

And of course no acknowledgements would be complete without a mention of our dogs – who are the first to let me know if they think I've spent too long with my nose in front of my screen, and that I need a walk! – Oscar, and our recent puppy arrival, delightful Labradoodle, Spook.

Finally some sad farewells this year. RIP: Elsie Sweetman, the former Chief Mortician at Brighton and Hove Mortuary and the role model for Cleo Morey. A fantastic and wonderful character. Dr Dennis Friedmann, eminent psychiatrist who gave me so much help on shaping characters – particularly villains – over many books. Phoebe, our beloved German Shepherd who died at 13 – a great age, but she will always be missed with deep affection.

Above all, thank you, my readers! Your emails, Tweets, Facebook and Blog posts give me such constant encouragement. Keep them coming. I love to hear from you!

Bye for now!

Peter James
Sussex, England
scary@pavilion.co.uk
www.peterjames.com
www.facebook.com/peterjames.roygrace
www.twitter.com/peterjamesuk